About the Authors

Maya Blake's writing dream started at thirteen. She eventually realised her dream when she received The Call in 2012. Maya lives in England with her husband, kids and an endless supply of books. Contact Maya: www.mayabauthor.blogspot.com www.twitter.com/mayablake www.facebook.com/maya.blake.94

AlTonya Washington's first contemporary novel, "Remember Love" BET/Arabesque 2003, was nominated by *Romantic Times* as Best 1st Multicultural Romance. Her novel "Finding Love A... *Romantic Times* Reviewer's C... ...cultural Romance 2... ...e" was nominated a... ...tigious EMMA Awa... ...sently resides in No...

Chantelle Sha... ...a happy childhood making up stories in her head. Always an avid reader, Chantelle discovered Mills & Boon as a teenager and during the times when her children refused to sleep, she would pace the floor with a baby in one hand and a book in the other! Twenty years later she decided to write one of her own. Writing takes up most of Chantelle's spare time, but she also enjoys gardening and walking. She doesn't find domestic chores so pleasurable!

Italian Playboys

Italian Playboys: Temptations

MAYA BLAKE

ALTONYA WASHINGTON

CHANTELLE SHAW

MILLS & BOON

First Published in Great Britain 2021
by Mills & Boon, an imprint of HarperCollins*Publishers* Ltd,
1 London Bridge Street, London, SE1 9GF

www.harpercollins.co.uk

HarperCollins*Publishers*
1st Floor, Watermarque Building,
Ringsend Road, Dublin 4, Ireland

ITALIAN PLAYBOYS: TEMPTATIONS
© 2021 Harlequin Books S.A.

A Marriage Fit for a Sinner © 2015 Maya Blake
Provocative Attraction © 2016 AlTonya Washington
To Wear His Ring Again © 2015 Chantelle Shaw

ISBN: 978-0-263-30046-8

MIX
Paper from
responsible sources
FSC® C007454

This book is produced from independently certified FSC™ paper to ensure responsible forest management.

For more information visit: www.harpercollins.co.uk/green

Printed and bound in Spain
by CPI, Barcelona

A MARRIAGE FIT
FOR A SINNER

MAYA BLAKE

CHAPTER ONE

'ONE PLATINUM CHRONOGRAPH WATCH. A pair of diamond-studded cufflinks. Gold signet ring. Six hundred and twenty-five pounds cash, and…Obsidian Privilege Card. Right, I think that's everything, sir. Sign here to confirm return of your property.'

Zaccheo Giordano didn't react to the warden's sneer as he scrawled on the barely legible form. Nor did he react to the resentful envy in the man's eyes when his gaze drifted to where the sleek silver limousine waited beyond three sets of barbed wire.

Romeo Brunetti, Zaccheo's second-in-command and the only person he would consider draping the term *friend* upon, stood beside the car, brooding and unsmiling, totally unruffled by the armed guard at the gate or the bleak South East England surroundings

Had Zaccheo been in an accommodating mood, he'd have cracked a smile.

But he wasn't in an accommodating mood. He hadn't been for a very long time. Fourteen months, two weeks, four days and nine hours to be exact. Zaccheo was positive he could count down to the last second if required.

No one would require it of him, of course. He'd served his time. With three and a half months knocked off his eighteen-month sentence *for good behaviour.*

The rage fused into his DNA bubbled beneath his skin. He showed no outward sign of it as he pocketed his belongings. The three-piece Savile Row suit he'd entered prison in stank of decay and misery, but Zaccheo didn't care.

He'd never been a slave to material comforts. His need for validation went far deeper. The need to elevate himself into a better place had been a soul-deep pursuit from the moment he was old enough to recognise the reality of the life he'd been born into. A life that had been a never-ending whirlpool of humiliation, violence and greed. A life that had seen his father debased and dead at thirty-five.

Memories tumbled like dominoes as he walked down the harshly lit corridor to freedom. He willed the overwhelming sense of injustice that had festered for long, harrowing months not to explode from his pores.

The doors clanged shut behind him.

Zaccheo froze, then took his first lungful of free air with fists clenched and eyes shut. He absorbed the sound of birds chirping in the late-winter morning sun, listened to the distant rumble of the motorway as he'd done many nights from his prison cell.

Opening his eyes, he headed towards the fifteen-foot gate. A minute later, he was outside.

'Zaccheo, it's good to see you again,' Romeo said gravely, his eyes narrowing as he took him in.

Zaccheo knew he looked a sight. He hadn't bothered with a razor blade or a barber's clippers in the last three months and he'd barely eaten once he'd unearthed the truth behind his incarceration. But he'd spent a lot of time in the prison gym. It'd been that or go mad with the clawing hunger for retribution.

He shrugged off his friend's concern and moved to the open door.

'Did you bring what I asked for?' he asked.

Romeo nodded. '*Sì*. All three files are on the laptop.'

Zaccheo slid onto the plush leather seat. Romeo slid in next to him and poured them two glasses of Italian-made cognac.

'*Salute,*' Romeo muttered.

Zaccheo took the drink without responding, threw back the amber liquid and allowed the scent of power and affluence—the tools he'd need for his plan to succeed—to wash over him.

As the low hum of the luxury engine whisked him away from the place he'd been forced to call home for over a year, Zaccheo reached for the laptop.

Icy rage trembled through his fingers as the Giordano Worldwide Inc. logo flickered to life. His life's work, almost decimated through another's greed and lust for power. It was only with Romeo's help that GWI hadn't gone under in the months after Zaccheo had been sent to prison for a crime he didn't commit. He drew quiet satisfaction that not only had GWI survived—thanks to Romeo—it had thrived.

But his personal reputation had not.

He was out now. Free to bring those culpable to justice. He didn't plan on resting until every last person responsible for attempting to destroy his life paid with the destruction of theirs.

Shaking out his hand to rid it of its tremble, he hit the Open key.

The information was thorough although Zaccheo knew most of its contents. For three months he'd checked and double-checked his sources, made sure every detail was nailed down tight.

He exhaled at the first picture that filled his screen.

Oscar Pennington III. Distant relative to the royal family. Etonian. Old, if spent, money. Very much part of the establishment. Greedy. Indiscriminate. His waning property portfolio had received a much-needed injection of capital exactly fourteen months and two weeks ago when he'd become sole owner of London's most talked about building—The Spire.

Zaccheo swallowed the savage growl that rumbled from his soul. Icily calm, he flicked through pages of Pennington celebrating his revived success with galas, lavish dinner parties and polo tournaments thrown about like confetti. One picture showed him laughing with one of his two children.

Sophie Pennington. Private education all the way to finishing school. Classically beautiful. Ball-breaker. She'd proven beyond a doubt that she had every intention of becoming Oscar's carbon copy.

Grimly, he closed her file and moved to the last one.

Eva Pennington.

This time the growl couldn't be contained. Nor could he stem the renewed shaking in his hand as he clicked her file.

Caramel-blonde hair tumbled down her shoulders in thick, wild waves. Dark eyebrows and lashes framed moss-green eyes, accentuated dramatically with black eyeliner. Those eyes had gripped his attention with more force than he'd been comfortable with the first time he'd looked into them. As had the full, bow-shaped lips currently curved in a smouldering smile. His screen displayed a head-and-shoulders shot, but the rest of Eva Pennington's body was imprinted indelibly on Zaccheo's mind. He didn't struggle to recall the petite, curvy shape, or that she forced herself to wear heels even though she hated them, in order to make herself taller.

He certainly didn't struggle to recall her individual atrocity. He'd lain in his prison bed condemning himself for being astounded by her singular betrayal, when the failings of both his parents and his dealings with the *establishment* should've taught him better. He'd prided himself on reading between the lines to spot schemers and gold-diggers ten miles away. Yet he'd been fooled.

The time he'd wasted on useless bitterness was the most excruciating of all; time he would gladly claw back if he could.

Firming his lips, he clicked through the pages, running through her life for the past year and a half. At the final page, he froze.

'How new is this last information?'

'I added that to the file yesterday. I thought you'd want to know,' Romeo replied.

Zaccheo stared at the newspaper clipping, shock waves rolling through him. '*Sì, grazie...*'

'Do you wish to return to the Esher estate or the penthouse?' Romeo asked.

Zaccheo read the announcement again, taking in pertinent details. Pennington Manor. Eight o'clock. Three hundred guests. Followed by an intimate family dinner on Sunday at The Spire.

*The Spire...*the building that should've been Zaccheo's greatest achievement.

'The estate,' he replied. It was closer.

He closed the file as Romeo instructed the driver.

Relaxing against the headrest, Zaccheo tried to let the hum of the engine soothe him. But it was no use. He was far from calm.

He'd have to alter his plan. Not that it mattered too much in the long run.

A chain is only as strong as its weakest link. While all three Penningtons had colluded in his incarceration, this new information demanded he use a different tactic, one he'd first contemplated and abandoned. Either way, Zaccheo didn't plan to rest until all of them were stripped of what they cherished most the their wealth and affluence.

He'd intended to wait a day or two to ensure he had Oscar Pennington where he wanted him before he struck. That plan was no longer viable.

Bringing down the family who'd framed him for criminal negligence couldn't wait till Monday.

His first order of business would be tackled *tonight*.

Starting with the youngest member of the family—Eva Pennington.

His ex-fiancée.

Eva Pennington stared at the dress in her sister's hand. 'Seriously? There's no way I'm wearing that. Why didn't you tell me the clothes I left behind had been given away?'

'Because you said you didn't want them when you moved out. Besides, they were old and out of fashion. I had *this* couriered from New York this morning. It's the latest couture and on loan to us for twenty-four hours,' Sophie replied.

Eva pursed her lips. 'I don't care if it was woven by ten thousand silk worms. I'm not wearing a dress that makes me look like a gold-digger *and* a slut. And considering the state of our finances, I'd have thought you'd be more careful what you splashed money on.' She couldn't stem her bewilderment as to why Sophie and her father blithely ignored the fact that money was extremely tight.

Sophie huffed. 'This is a one-of-a-kind dress, and, unless I'm mistaken, it's the kind of dress your future husband likes his women to wear. Anyway, you'll be out of it in less than four hours, once the right photographs have been taken, and the party's over.'

Eva gritted her teeth. 'Stop trying to manage me, Sophie. You're forgetting who pulled this bailout together. If I hadn't come to an agreement with Harry, we'd have been sunk come next week. As to what he likes his women to wear, if you'd bothered to speak to me first I'd have saved you the trouble of going to unnecessary expense. I dress for myself and no one else.'

'Speak to you first? When you and Father neglected to afford me the same courtesy before you hatched this plan behind my back?' Sophie griped.

Eva's heart twisted at the blatant jealousy in her sister's voice.

As if it weren't enough that the decision she'd spent the past two weeks agonising over still made her insides clench in horror. It didn't matter that the man she'd agreed to marry was her friend and she was helping him as much as he was helping her. Marriage was a step she'd rather not have taken.

It was clear, however, her sister didn't see it that way. Sophie's escalating discontentment at any relationship Eva tried to forge with their father was part of the reason Eva had moved out of Pennington Manor. Not that their father was an easy man to live with.

For as long as she could remember, Sophie had been possessive of their father's attention. While their mother had been alive, it'd been bearable and easier to accept that Sophie was their father's preferred child, while Eva was her mother's, despite wanting to be loved equally by both parents.

After their mother's death, every interaction Eva had tried to have with their father had been met with bristling confrontation from Sophie, and indifference from their father.

But, irrational as it was, it didn't stop Eva from trying to reason with the sister she'd once looked up to.

'We didn't go behind your back. You were away on a business trip—'

'Trying to use the business degree that doesn't seem to mean anything any more. Not when *you* can swoop in after three years of performing tired ballads in seedy pubs to save the day,' Sophie interjected harshly.

Eva hung on to her temper by a thread, but pain stung deep at the blithe dismissal of her passion. 'You know I resigned from Penningtons because Father only hired me so I could attract a suitable husband. And just because my dreams don't coincide with yours—'

'That's just it. You're twenty-four and still *dreaming*. The rest of us don't have that luxury. And we certainly don't land on our feet by clicking our fingers and having a millionaire solve all our problems.'

'Harry is saving *all of us*. And you really think I've *landed on my feet* by getting engaged for the second time in two years?' Eva asked.

Sophie dropped the offensive dress on Eva's bed. 'To everyone who matters, this is your first engagement. The other one barely lasted five minutes. Hardly anyone knows it happened.'

Hurt-laced anger swirled through her veins. '*I* know it happened.'

'If my opinion matters around here any more, then I suggest you don't broadcast it. It's a subject best left in the past, just like the man it involved.'

Pain stung deeper. 'I can't pretend it didn't happen because of what occurred afterwards.'

'The last thing we need right now is any hint of scandal. And I don't know why you're blaming Father for what happened when you should be thanking him for extricating you from that man before it was too late,' Sophie defended heatedly.

That man.

Zaccheo Giordano.

Eva wasn't sure whether the ache lodged beneath her ribs came from thinking about him or from the reminder of how gullible she'd been to think he was any different from every other man who'd crossed her path.

She relaxed her fists when they balled again.

This was why she preferred her life away from their family home deep in the heart of Surrey.

It was why her waitress colleagues knew her as Eva Penn, a hostess at Siren, the London nightclub where she also sang part-time, instead of Lady Eva Pennington, daughter of Lord Pennington.

Her relationship with her father had always been difficult, but she'd never thought she'd lose her sister so completely, too.

She cleared her throat. 'Sophie, this agreement with Harry wasn't supposed to undermine anything you were doing with Father to save Penningtons. There's no need to be upset or jealous. I'm not trying to take your place—'

'Jealous! Don't be ridiculous,' Sophie sneered, although the trace of panic in her voice made Eva's heart break. 'And you could never take my place. I'm Father's right hand, whereas you...you're nothing but—' She stopped herself and, after a few seconds, stuck her nose in the air. 'Our guests are arriving shortly. Please don't be late to your own engagement party.'

Eva swallowed down her sorrow. 'I've no intention of being late. But neither do I have any intention of wearing a dress that has less material than thread holding it together.'

She strode to the giant George III armoire opposite the bed, even though her earlier inspection had shown less than a fraction of the items she'd left behind when she'd moved out on her twenty-first birthday.

These days she was content with her hostess's uniform when she was working or lounging in jeans and sweaters while she wrote her music on her days off. Haute couture, spa days and primping herself beautiful in order to please anyone were part of a past she'd happily left behind.

Unfortunately this time there'd been no escaping. Not when she alone had been able to find the solution to saving her family.

She tried in vain to squash the rising memories being back at Pennington Manor threatened to resurrect.

Zaccheo was in her past, a mistake that should never have happened. A reminder that ignoring a lesson learned only led to further heartache.

She sighed in relief when her hand closed on a silk wrap. The red dress would be far too revealing, a true spectacle for the three hundred guests her father had invited to gawp at. But at least the wrap would provide a little much-needed cover.

Glancing at the dress again, she shuddered.

She'd rather be anywhere but here, participating in this sham. But then hadn't her whole life been a sham? From parents who'd been publicly hailed as the couple to envy, but who'd fought bitterly in private until tragedy had struck in the form of her mother's cancer, to the lavish parties and expensive holidays that her father had secretly been borrowing money for, the Penningtons had been one giant sham for as long as Eva could remember.

Zaccheo's entry into their lives had only escalated her father's behaviour.

No, she refused to think about Zaccheo. He belonged to a chapter of her life that was firmly sealed. Tonight was about Harry Fairfield, her family's saviour, and her soon-to-be fiancé.

It was also about her father's health.

For that reason alone, she tried again with Sophie.

'For Father's sake, I want tonight to go smoothly, so can we try to get along?'

Sophie stiffened. 'If you're talking about Father's hospitalisation two weeks ago, I haven't forgotten.'

Watching her father struggle to breathe with what the doctors had termed a cardiac event had terrified Eva. It'd been the catalyst that had forced her to accept Harry's proposition.

'He's okay today, isn't he?' Despite her bitterness at her family's treatment of her, she couldn't help her concern for her remaining parent. Nor could she erase the secret yearning that the different version of the father she'd connected with very briefly after her mother's death, the one who wasn't an excess-loving megalomaniac who treated her as if she was an irritating inconvenience, hadn't been a figment of her imagination.

'He will be, once we get rid of the creditors threatening us with bankruptcy.'

Eva exhaled. There was no backing out; no secretly hoping that some other solution would present itself and save her from the sacrifice she was making.

All avenues had been thoroughly explored—Eva had demanded to see the Pennington books herself and spent a day with the company's accountants to verify that they were indeed in dire straits. Her father's rash acquisition of The Spire had stretched the company to breaking point. Harry Fairfield was their last hope.

She unzipped the red dress, resisting the urge to crush it into a wrinkled pulp.

'Do you need help?' Sophie asked, although Eva sensed the offer wasn't altruistic.

'No, I can manage.'

The same way she'd managed after her mother's death; through her father's rejection and Sophie's increasingly unreasonable behaviour; through the heartbreak of finding out about Zaccheo's betrayal.

Sophie nodded briskly. 'I'll see you downstairs, then.'

Eva slipped on the dress, avoiding another look in the mirror when the first glimpse showed what she'd feared most. Her every curve was accentuated, with large swathes of flesh exposed. With shaky fingers she applied her lipstick and slipped her feet into matching platform heels.

Slipping the gold and red wrap around her shoulders, she finally glanced at her image.

Chin up, girl. It's show time.

Eva wished the manageress of Siren were uttering the words, as she did every time before Eva stepped onto the stage.

Unfortunately, she wasn't at Siren. She'd promised to marry a man she didn't love, for the sake of saving her precious family name.

No amount of pep talk could stem the roaring agitation flooding her veins.

CHAPTER TWO

THE EVENT PLANNERS had outdone themselves. Potted palms, decorative screens and subdued lighting had been strategically placed around the main halls of Pennington Manor to hide the peeling plaster, chipped wood panelling and torn Aubusson rugs that funds could no longer stretch to rectify.

Eva sipped the champagne she'd been nursing for the last two hours and willed time to move faster. Technically she couldn't throw any guest out, but *Eight to Midnight* was the time the costly invitations had stated the party would last. She needed something to focus on or risk sliding into madness.

Gritting her teeth, she smiled as yet another guest demanded to see her engagement ring. The monstrous pink diamond's sole purpose was to demonstrate the Fairfields' wealth. Its alien weight dragged her hand down, hammering home the irrefutable point that she'd sold herself for her pedigree.

Her father's booming voice interrupted her maudlin thoughts. Surrounded by a group of influential politicians who hung onto his every word, Oscar Pennington was in his element.

Thickset but tall enough to hide the excess weight he carried, her father cut a commanding figure despite his recent spell in hospital. His stint in the army three decades ago had lent him a ruthless edge, cleverly counteracted by his natural charm. The combination made him enigmatic enough to attract attention when he walked into a room.

But not even that charisma had saved him from economic devastation four years ago.

With that coming close on the heels of her mother's illness, their social and economic circles had dwindled to nothing almost overnight, with her father desperately scrambling to hold things together.

End result—his association with Zaccheo Giordano.

Eva frowned, bewildered that her thoughts had circled back to the man she'd pushed to the dark recesses of her mind. A man she'd last seen being led away in handcuffs—

'There you are. I've been looking for you everywhere.'

Eva started, then berated herself for feeling guilty. Guilt belonged to those who'd committed crimes, who lied about their true motives.

Enough!

She smiled at Harry.

Her old university friend—a brilliant tech genius—had gone off the rails when he'd achieved fame and wealth straight out of university. Now a multimillionaire with enough money to bail out Penningtons, he represented her family's last hope.

'Well, you found me,' she said.

He was a few inches taller than her five feet four; she didn't have to look up too far to meet his twinkling soft brown eyes.

'Indeed. Are you okay?' he asked, his gaze reflecting concern.

'I'm fine,' she responded breezily.

He looked unconvinced. Harry was one of the few people who knew about her broken engagement to Zaccheo. He'd seen beneath her false smiles and assurances that she could handle a marriage of convenience and asked her point-blank if her past with Zaccheo Giordano would be a problem. Her swift *no* seemed to have satisfied him.

Now he looked unsure.

'Harry, don't fret. I can do this,' she insisted, despite the hollowness in her stomach.

He studied her solemnly, then called over a waiter and exchanged his empty champagne glass for a full one. 'If you say so, but I need advanced warning if this gets too weird for you, okay? My parents will have a fit if they read about me in the papers this side of Christmas.'

She nodded gratefully, then frowned. 'I thought you were going to take it easy tonight?' She indicated his glass.

'Gosh, you already sound like a wife.' He sniggered. 'Leave off, sweetness, the parents have already given me an earful.'

Having met his parents a week ago, Eva could imagine the exchange.

'Remember why *you're* doing this. Do you want to derail the PR campaign to clean up your image before it's even begun?'

While Harry couldn't care less about his social standing, his parents were voracious in their hunger for prestige and a pedigree to hang their name on. Only the threat to Harry's business dealings had finally forced him to address his reckless playboy image.

He took her arm and tilted his sand-coloured head affably towards hers. 'I promise to be on my best behaviour. Now that the tedious toasts have been made and we're officially engaged, it's time for the best part of the evening. The fireworks!'

Eva set her champagne glass down and stepped out of the dining-room alcove that had been her sanctuary throughout her childhood. 'Isn't that supposed to be a surprise?'

Harry winked. 'It is, but, since we've fooled everyone into thinking we're *madly* in love, faking our surprise should be easy.'

She smiled. 'I won't tell if you don't.'

Harry laid a hand across his heart. 'Thank you, my fair Lady Pennington.'

The reminder of why this whole sham engagement was happening slid like a knife between her ribs. Numbing herself to the pain, she walked out onto the terrace that overlooked the manor's multi-acre garden.

The gardens had once held large koi ponds, a giant summer house and an elaborate maze, but the prohibitive cost of the grounds' upkeep had led to the landscape being levelled and replaced with rolling carpet grass.

A smattering of applause greeted their arrival and Eva's gaze drifted over the guests to where Sophie, her father and Harry's parents stood watching them.

She caught her father's eye, and her stomach knotted.

While part of her was pleased that she'd found a solution to their family problems, she couldn't help but feel that nothing she did would ever bring her closer to her sister or father.

Her father might have accepted her help with the bailout from Harry, but his displeasure at her chosen profession was yet another bone of contention between them. One she'd made clear she wouldn't back down on.

Turning away, she fixed her smile in place and exclaimed appropriately when the first elaborate firework display burst into the sky.

'So…my parents want us to live together,' Harry whispered in her ear.

'What?'

He laughed. 'Don't worry, I convinced them you hate my bachelor pad so we need to find a place that's *ours* rather than mine.'

Relief poured through her. 'Thank you.'

He brushed a hand down her cheek. 'You're welcome. But I deserve a reward for my sacrifice,' he said with a smile. 'How about dinner on Monday?'

'As long as it's not a paparazzi-stalked spectacle of a restaurant, you're on.'

'Great. It's a date.' He kissed her knuckles, much to the delight of the guests, who thought they were witnessing a true love match.

Eva allowed herself to relax. She might find what they were doing distasteful, but she was grateful that Harry's visit to Siren three weeks ago had ended up with him bailing her out, and not a calculating stranger.

'That dress is a knockout on you, by the way.'

She grimaced. 'It wasn't my first choice, but thank you.'

The next series of firework displays should've quieted the guests, yet murmurs around her grew.

'*Omigod*, whoever it is must have a death wish!' someone exclaimed.

Harry's eyes narrowed. 'I think we may have a last-minute guest.'

Eva looked around and saw puzzled gazes fixed at a point in the sky as the faint *thwopping* sound grew louder. Another set of fireworks went off, illuminating the looming object.

She frowned. 'Is that…?'

'A helicopter heading straight for the middle of the fireworks display? Yep. I guess the organisers decided to add another surprise to the party.'

'I don't think that's part of the entertainment,' Eva shouted to be heard over the descending aircraft.

Her heart slammed into her throat as a particularly elaborate firework erupted precariously close to the black-and-red chopper.

'Hell, if this is a stunt, I take my hat off to the pilot. It takes iron balls to fly into danger like that.' Harry chuckled.

The helicopter drew closer. Mesmerised, Eva watched it settle in the middle of the garden, her attention riveted to its single occupant.

The garden lights had been turned off to showcase the fireworks to maximum effect so she couldn't see who their unexpected guest was. Nevertheless, an ominous shiver chased up her spine.

She heard urgent shouts for the pyrotechnician to halt the display, but another rocket fizzed past the rotating blades.

A hush fell over the crowd as the helicopter door opened. A figure stepped out, clad from head to toe in black. As another blaze of colour filled the sky his body was thrown into relief.

Eva tensed as if she'd been shot with a stun gun.

It couldn't be...

He was behind bars, atoning for his ruthless greed. Eva squashed the sting of guilt that accompanied the thought.

Zaccheo Giordano and men of his ilk arrogantly believed they were above the law. They didn't deserve her sympathy, or the disloyal thought that he alone had paid the price when, by association, her father should've borne some of the blame. Justice ensured they went to jail and stayed there for the duration of their term. They weren't released early.

They certainly didn't land in the middle of a firework display at a private party as if they owned the land they walked on.

The spectacle unfolding before her stated differently.

Lights flickered on. Eva tracked the figure striding imperiously across the grass and up the wide steps.

Reaching the terrace, he paused and buttoned his single-breasted tuxedo.

'Oh, God,' she whispered.

'Wait...you know this bloke?' Harry asked, his tone for once serious.

Eva wanted to deny the man who now stood, easily head and shoulders above the nearest guests, his fierce, unwavering gaze pinned on her.

She didn't know whether to attribute the crackling electricity to his appearance or the look in his eyes. Both were viscerally menacing to the point of brutality.

The Zaccheo Giordano she'd had the misfortune of briefly tangling with before his incarceration had kept his hair trimmed short and his face clean-shaven.

This man had a full beard and his hair flowed over his shoulders in an unruly sea of thick jet waves. Eva swallowed at the pronounced difference in him. The sleek, almost gaunt man she'd known was gone. In his place breathed a Neanderthal with broader shoulders, thicker arms and a denser chest moulded by his black silk shirt. Equally dark trousers hugged lean hips and sturdy thighs to fall in a precise inch above expensive handmade shoes. But nothing of his attire disguised the aura he emanated.

Uncivilised. Explosively masculine. Lethal.

Danger vibrated from him like striations on baking asphalt. It flowed over the guests, who jostled each other for a better look at the impromptu visitor.

'Eva?' Harry's puzzled query echoed through her dazed consciousness.

Zaccheo released her from his deadly stare. His eyes flicked to the arm tucked into Harry's before he turned away. The breath exploded from her lungs. Sensing Harry about to ask another question, she nodded.

'Yes. That's Zaccheo.'

Her eyes followed Zaccheo as he turned towards her family.

Oscar's look of anger was laced with a heavy dose of apprehension. Sophie looked plain stunned.

Eva watched the man she'd hoped to never see again cup his hands behind his back and stroll towards her father. Anyone would've been foolish to think that stance indicated supplication. If anything, its severe mockery made Eva want to do the unthinkable and burst out laughing.

She would've, had she not been mired in deep dread at what Zaccheo's presence meant.

'Your ex?' Harry pressed.

She nodded numbly.

'Then we should say hello.'

Harry tugged on her arm and she realised too late what he meant.

'No. Wait!' she whispered fiercely.

But he was either too drunk or genuinely oblivious to the vortex of danger he was headed for to pay attention. The tension surrounding the group swallowed Eva as they approached. Heart pounding, she watched her father's and Zaccheo's gazes lock.

'I don't know what the hell you think you're doing here, Giordano, but I suggest you get back in that monstrosity and leave before I have you arrested for trespass.'

A shock wave went through the crowd.

Zaccheo didn't bat an eyelid.

'By all means do that if you wish, but you know exactly why I'm here, Pennington. We can play coy if you prefer. You'll be made painfully aware when I tire of it.' The words were barely above a murmur, but their venom raised the hairs on Eva's arms, triggering a gasp when she saw Sophie's face.

Her usually unflappable sister was severely agitated, her face distressingly pale.

'*Ciao*, Eva,' Zaccheo drawled without turning around. That deep, resonant voice, reminiscent of a tenor in a soulful opera, washed over her, its powerfully mesmerising quality reminding her how she'd once longed to hear him speak just for the hell of it. 'It's good of you to join us.'

'This is my engagement party. It's my duty to interact with my guests, even unwelcome ones who will be asked to leave immediately.'

'Don't worry, *cara*, I won't be staying long.'

The relief that surged up her spine disappeared when his gaze finally swung her way, then dropped to her left hand. With almost cavalier laziness, he caught her wrist and raised it to the light. He examined the ring for exactly three seconds. 'How predictable.'

He released her with the same carelessness he'd captured her.

Eva clenched her fist to stop the sizzling electricity firing up her arm at the brief contact.

'What's that supposed to mean?' Harry demanded.

Zaccheo levelled steely grey eyes on him, then his parents. 'This is a private discussion. Leave us.'

Peter Fairfield's laugh held incredulity, the last inch of

champagne in his glass sloshing wildly as he raised his arm. 'I think you've got the wrong end of the stick there, mate. You're the one who needs to take a walk.'

Eva caught Harry's pained look at his father's response, but could do nothing but watch, heart in her throat, as Zaccheo faced Peter Fairfield.

Again she was struck by how much his body had changed; how the sleek, layered muscle lent a deeper sense of danger. Whereas before it'd been like walking close to the edge of a cliff, looking into his eyes now was like staring into a deep, bottomless abyss.

'Would you care to repeat that, *il mio amico*?' The almost conversational tone belied the savage tension beneath the words.

'Oscar, who *is* this?' Peter Fairfield demanded of her father, who seemed to have lost the ability to speak after Zaccheo's succinct taunt.

Eva inserted herself between the two men before the situation got out of hand. Behind her, heat from Zaccheo's body burned every exposed inch of skin. Ignoring the sensation, she cleared her throat.

'Mr and Mrs Fairfield, Harry, we'll only be a few minutes. We're just catching up with Mr Giordano.' She glanced at her father. A vein throbbed in his temple and he'd gone a worrying shade of puce. Fear climbed into her heart. 'Father?'

He roused himself and glanced around. A charming smile slid into place, but it was off by a light year. The trickle of ice that had drifted down her spine at Zaccheo's unexpected arrival turned into a steady drip.

'We'll take this in my study. Don't hesitate to let the staff know if you need anything.' He strode away, followed by a disturbingly quiet Sophie.

Zaccheo's gaze swung to Harry, who defiantly withstood the laser gaze for a few seconds before he glanced at her.

'Are you sure?' Harry asked, that touching concern again in his eyes.

Her instinct screamed a terrible foreboding, but she nodded. 'Yes.'

'Okay. Hurry back, sweetness.' Before she could move, he dropped a kiss on her mouth.

A barely audible lethal growl charged through the air.

Eva flinched.

She wanted to face Zaccheo. Demand that he crawl back behind the bars that should've been holding him. But that glimpse of fear in her father's eyes stopped her. She tugged the wrap closer around her.

Something wasn't right here. She was willing to bet the dilapidated ancestral pile beneath her feet that something was seriously, *dangerously* wrong—

'Move, Eva.'

The cool command spoken against her ear sent shivers coursing through her.

She moved, only because the quicker she got to the bottom of why he was here, the quicker he would leave. But with each step his dark gaze probed her back, making the walk to her father's study on the other side of the manor the longest in her life.

Zaccheo shut the door behind him. Her father turned from where he'd been gazing into the unlit fireplace. Again Eva spotted apprehension in his eyes before he masked it.

'Whatever grievance you think you have the right to air, I suggest you rethink it, son. Even if this were the right time or place—'

'I am *not* your son, Pennington.' Zaccheo's response held lethal bite, the first sign of his fury breaking through. 'As for why I'm here, I have five thousand three hundred and twenty-two pieces of documentation that proves you colluded with various other individuals to pin a crime on me that I didn't commit.'

'What?' Eva gasped, then the absurdity of the statement made her shake her head. 'We don't believe you.'

Zaccheo's eyes remained on her father. 'You may not, but your father does.'

Oscar Pennington laughed, but the sound lacked its usual boom and zest. When sweat broke out over his forehead, fear gripped Eva's insides.

She steeled her spine. 'Our lawyers will rip whatever evidence you think you have to shreds, I'm sure. If you're here to seek some sort of closure, you picked the wrong time to do it. Perhaps we can arrange to meet you at some other time?'

Zaccheo didn't move. Didn't blink. Hands once again tucked behind his back, he simply watched her father, his body a coiled predator waiting to strike a fatal blow.

Silence stretched, throbbed with unbearable menace. Eva looked from her father to Sophie and back again, her dread escalating. 'What's going on?' she demanded.

Her father gripped the mantel until his knuckles shone white. 'You chose the wrong enemy. You're sorely mistaken if you think I'll let you blackmail me in my own home.'

Sophie stepped forward. 'Father, don't—'

'Good, you haven't lost your hubris.' Zaccheo's voice slashed across her sister's. 'I was counting on that. Here's what I'm going to do. In ten minutes I'm going to leave here with Eva, right in front of all your guests. You won't lift a finger to stop me. You'll tell them exactly who I am. Then you'll make a formal announcement that I'm the man your daughter will marry two weeks from today and that I have your blessing. I don't want to trust something so important to phone cameras and social media, although your guests will probably do a pretty good job. I noticed a few members of the press out there, so that part of your task should be easy. If the articles are written to my satisfaction, I'll be in touch on Monday to lay out how you can begin to make reparations to me. However, if by the time Eva and I wake up tomorrow morning the news of our engagement isn't in the press, then all bets are off.'

Oscar Pennington's breathing altered alarmingly. His

mouth opened but no words emerged. In the arctic silence that greeted Zaccheo's deadly words, Eva gaped at him.

'You're clearly not in touch with all of your faculties if you think those ridiculous demands are going to be met.' When silence greeted her response, she turned sharply to her father. 'Father? Why aren't you saying something?' she demanded, although the trepidation beating in her chest spelled its own doom.

'Because he can't, Eva. Because he's about to do exactly as I say.'

She rounded on him, and was once again rocked to the core by Zaccheo's visually powerful, utterly captivating transformation. So much so, she couldn't speak for several seconds. 'You're out of your mind!' she finally blurted.

Zaccheo's gaze didn't stray from its laser focus on her father. 'Believe me, *cara mia*, I haven't been saner than I am in this moment.'

CHAPTER THREE

ZACCHEO WATCHED EVA'S head swivel to her father, confusion warring with anger.

'Go on, Oscar. She's waiting for you to tell me to go to hell. Why don't you?'

Pennington staggered towards his desk, his face ashen and his breathing growing increasingly laboured.

'Father!' Eva rushed to his side—ignoring the poisonous look her sister sent her—as he collapsed into his leather armchair.

Zaccheo wanted to rip her away, let her watch her father suffer as his sins came home to roost. Instead he allowed the drama to play out. The outcome would be inevitable and would only go one way.

His way.

He wanted to look into Pennington's eyes and see the defeat and helplessness the other man had expected to see in his eyes the day Zaccheo had been sentenced.

Both sisters now fussed over their father and a swell of satisfaction rose at the fear in their eyes. Eva glanced his way and he experienced a different punch altogether. One he'd thought himself immune to, but had realised otherwise the moment he'd stepped off his helicopter and singled her out in the crowd.

That unsettling feeling, as if he were suffering from vertigo despite standing on terra firma, had intrigued and annoyed him in equal measures from the very first time he'd seen her, her voice silkily hypnotic as she crooned into a mic on a golden-lit stage, her fingers caressing the black microphone stand as if she were touching a lover.

Even knowing exactly who she was, what she represented,

he hadn't been able to walk away. In the weeks after their first meeting, he'd fooled himself into believing she was different, that she wasn't tainted with the same greed to further her pedigree by whatever means necessary; that she wasn't willing to do whatever it took to secure her family's standing, even while secretly scorning his upbringing.

Her very public denouncement of any association between them on the day of his sentencing had been the final blow. Not that Zaccheo hadn't had the scales viciously ripped from his eyes by then.

No, by that fateful day fourteen months ago, he'd known just how thoroughly he'd been suckered.

'What the hell do you think you're doing?' she muttered fiercely, her moss-green eyes firing lasers at him.

Zaccheo forced himself not to smile. The time for gloating would come later. 'Exacting the wages of sin, *dolcezza*. What else?'

'I don't know what you're talking about, but I don't think my father is in a position to have a discussion with you right now, Mr Giordano.'

Her prim and proper tones bit savagely into Zaccheo, wiping away any trace of twisted mirth. That tone said he ought to *know his place*, that he ought to stand there like a good little servant and wait to be addressed instead of upsetting the lord of the manor with his petty concerns.

Rage bubbled beneath his skin, threatening to erupt. Blunt nails bit into his wrist, but the pain wasn't enough to calm his fury. He clenched his jaw for a long moment before he trusted himself to speak.

'I gave you ten minutes, Pennington. You now have five. I suggest you practise whatever sly words you'll be using to address your guests.' Zaccheo shrugged. 'Or not. Either way, things *will* go my way.'

Eva rushed at him, her striking face and flawless skin flushed with a burst of angry colour as she stopped a few feet away.

Out on the terrace, he'd compelled himself not to stare too long at her in case he betrayed his feelings. In case his gaze devoured her as he'd wanted to do since her presence snaked like a live wire inside him.

Now, he took in that wild gypsy-like caramel-blonde hair so out of place in this polished stratosphere her family chose to inhabit. The striking contrast between her bright hair, black eyebrows and dark-rimmed eyes had always fascinated him. But no more than her cupid-bow lips, soft, dark red and sinfully sensual. Or the rest of her body.

'You assume I have no say in whatever despicable spectacle you're planning. That I intend to meekly stand by while you humiliate my family? Well, think again!'

'Eva…' her father started.

'No! I don't know what exactly is going on here, but I intend to play no part in it.'

'You'll play your part, and you'll play it well,' Zaccheo interjected, finally driving his gaze up from the mouth he wanted to feast on more than he wanted his next breath. *That'll come soon enough*, he promised himself.

'Or what? You'll carry through with your empty threats?'

His fury eased a touch and twisted amusement slid back into place. It never ceased to amaze him how the titled rich felt they were above the tenets that governed ordinary human beings. His own stepfather had been the same. He'd believed, foolishly, that his pedigree and connections would insulate him from his reckless business practices, that the Old Boys' Club would provide a safety net despite his poor judgement.

Zaccheo had taken great pleasure in watching his mother's husband squirm before him, cap in hand, when Zaccheo had bought his family business right from underneath his pompous nose. But even then, the older man had continued to treat him like a third-class citizen…

Just as Oscar Pennington had done. Just as Eva Pennington was doing now.

'You think my threats empty?' he enquired softly. 'Then do nothing. It's after all your privilege and your right.'

Something of the lethal edge that rode him must have transmitted itself to her. Apprehension chased across her face before she firmed those impossibly sumptuous lips.

'Do nothing, and watch me bury your family in the deepest, darkest, most demeaning pit you can dream of. Do nothing and watch me unleash a scandal the scale of which you can only imagine on your precious family name.' He bared his teeth in a mirthless smile and her eyes widened in stunned disbelief. 'It would be *my* privilege and pleasure to do so.'

Oscar Pennington inhaled sharply and Zaccheo's gaze zeroed in on his enemy. The older man rose from the chair. Though he looked frail, his eyes reflected icy disdain. But Zaccheo also glimpsed the fear of a cornered man weighing all the options to see how to escape the noose dangling ever closer.

Zaccheo smiled inwardly. He had no intention of letting Pennington escape. Not now, not ever.

The flames of retribution intensifying within him, he unclasped his hands. It was time to bring this meeting to an end.

'Your time's up, Pennington.'

Eva answered instead of her father. 'How do we know you're not bluffing? You say you have something over us, prove it,' she said defiantly.

He could've walked out and let them twist in the wind of uncertainty. Pennington would find out soon enough the length of Zaccheo's ruthless reach. But the thought of leaving Eva here when he departed was suddenly unthinkable. So far he'd allowed himself a brief glimpse of her body wrapped in that obscenely revealing red dress. But that one glimpse had been enough. Quite apart from the rage boiling his blood, the steady hammer of his pulse proved that he still wanted her with a fever that spiked higher with each passing second.

He would take what he'd foolishly and piously denied

himself two years ago. He would *take* and *use*, just as they'd done to him. Only when he'd achieved every goal he'd set himself would he feel avenged.

'You can't, can you?' Oscar taunted with a sly smile, bringing Zaccheo back to the room and the three aristocratic faces staring at him with varying degrees of disdain and fear.

He smiled, almost amused by the older man's growing confidence. 'Harry Fairfield is providing you with a bridging loan of fifteen million pounds because the combined running costs of the Pennington Hotels and The Spire have you stretched so thin the banks won't touch you. While you desperately drum up an adequate advertising budget to rent out all those overpriced but empty floors in The Spire, the interest owed to the Chinese consortium who own seventy-five per cent of the building is escalating. You have a meeting with them on Monday to request more time to pay the interest. In return for Fairfield's investment, you're handing him your daughter.'

Eva glared at him. 'So you've asked a few questions about Penningtons' business practices. That doesn't empower you to make demands of any of us.'

Zaccheo took a moment to admire her newfound grit. During their initial association, she'd been a little more timid, and in her father's shadow, but it looked as if the kitten had grown a few claws. He curbed the thrill at what was to come and answered.

'Yes, it does. Would you be interested to know the Chinese consortium sold their seventy-five per cent of The Spire to me three days ago? So by my calculation you're in excess of three months late on interest payments, correct?'

A rough sound, a cross between a cough and a wheeze, escaped Pennington's throat. There was no class or grace in the way he gaped at Zaccheo. He dropped back into his chair, his face a mask of hatred.

'I knew you were a worthless bet the moment I set eyes on you. I should've listened to my instincts.'

The red haze he'd been trying to hold back surged higher. 'No, what you wanted was a spineless scapegoat, a *capro espiatorio*, who would make you rich and fat and content and even give up his life without question!'

'Mr Giordano, surely we can discuss this like sensible business-minded individuals,' Sophie Pennington advanced, her hands outstretched in benign sensibility. Zaccheo looked from the hands she willed not to tremble to the veiled disdain in her eyes. Then he looked past her to Eva, who'd returned to her father's side, her face pale but her eyes shooting her displeasure at him.

Unexpectedly and very much unwelcome, a tiny hint of compassion tugged at him.

Basta!

He turned abruptly and reached for the door handle. 'You have until I ready my chopper for take-off to come to me, Eva.' He didn't need to expand on that edict. The *or else* hung in the air like the deadly poison he intended it to be.

He walked out and headed for the terrace, despite every nerve in his body straining to return to the room and forcibly drag Eva out.

True, he hadn't bargained for the visceral reaction to seeing her again. And yes, he hadn't quite been able to control his reaction to seeing another man's ring on her finger, that vulgar symbol of ownership hollowing out his stomach. The knowledge that she'd most likely shared that hapless drunk's bed, given the body he'd once believed to be his to another, ate through his blood like acid on metal. But he couldn't afford to let his emotions show.

Every strategic move in this game of deadly retribution hinged on him maintaining his control; on not letting them see how affected he was by all this.

He stepped onto the terrace and all conversation ceased. Curious faces gaped and one or two bolder guests even tried to intercept him. Zaccheo cut through the crowd, his gaze on the chopper a few dozen yards away.

She would come to him. As an outcome of his first salvo, nothing else would be acceptable.

His pulse thudded loud and insistent in his ears as he strolled down the steps towards the aircraft. The fireworks amid which he'd landed had long since gone quiet, but the scent of sulphur lingered in the air, reminding him of the volatility that lingered beneath his own skin, ready to erupt at the smallest trigger.

He wouldn't let it erupt. Not yet.

A murmur rose behind him, the fevered excitement that came with the anticipation of a spectacle. A *scandal*.

Zaccheo compelled himself to keep walking.

He ducked beneath the powerful rotors of his aircraft and reached for the door.

'Wait!'

He stopped. Turned.

Three hundred pairs of eyes watched with unabashed interest as Eva paused several feet from him.

Behind her, her father and sister stood on the steps, wearing similar expressions of dread. Zaccheo wanted them to stew for a while longer, but he found his attention drawn to the woman striding towards him. Her face reflected more defiance than dread. It also held pride and not a small measure of bruised disdain. Zaccheo vowed in that moment to make her regret that latter look, make her take back every single moment she'd thought herself above him.

Swallowing, he looked down at her body.

She held the flimsy wrap around her like armour. As if that would protect her from him. With one ruthless tug, he pulled it away. It fluttered to the ground, revealing her luscious, heart-stopping figure to his gaze. Unable to stem the frantic need crashing through him, he stepped forward and speared his fingers into the wild tumble of her hair.

Another step and she was in his arms.

Where she belonged.

* * *

The small pocket of air Eva had been able to retain in her lungs during her desperate flight after Zaccheo evaporated when he yanked her against him. Her body went from shivering in the crisp January air to furnace-hot within seconds. The fingers in her hair tightened, his other arm sliding around her waist.

Eva wanted to remain unaffected, slam her hands against his chest and remove herself from that dangerous wall of masculinity. But she couldn't move. So she fought with her words.

'You may think you've won, that you own me, but you don't,' she snapped. 'You never will!'

His eyes gleamed. 'Such fire. Such determination. You've changed, *cara mia*, I'll give you that. And yet here you are, barely one minute after I walked out of your father's study. Mere hours after you promised yourself to another man, here you are, Eva Pennington, ready to promise yourself to me. Ready to become whatever I want you to be.'

Her snigger made his eyes narrow, but she didn't care. 'Keep telling yourself that. I look forward to your shock when I prove you wrong.'

That deadly smile she'd first seen in her father's study reappeared, curling fear through her. It reeked with far too much gratification to kill that unshakeable sensation that she was standing on the edge of a precipice, and that, should she fall, there would be no saving her.

She realised the reason for the smile when he lifted her now bare fingers to his eye level. 'You've proved me right already.'

'Are you completely sure about that?' The question was a bold but empty taunt.

The lack of fuss with which Harry had taken back his ring a few minutes ago had been a relief.

She might not have an immediate solution to her family's

problems, but Eva was glad she no longer had to pretend she was half of a sham couple.

Zaccheo brought her fingers to his mouth and kissed her ring finger, stunning her back to reality. Flashes erupted as his actions were recorded, no doubt to be streamed across the fastest mediums available.

Recalling the conversation she'd just had with her father, she tried to pull away. 'This pound-of-flesh taking isn't going to last very long, so I suggest you enjoy it while it lasts. I intend to return to my life before midnight—'

Her words dried up when his face closed in a mask of icy fury, and his hands sealed her body even closer to his.

'Your first lesson is to stop speaking to me as if I'm the hired help. Refraining from doing so will put me in a much calmer frame of mind to deal with you than otherwise,' he said with unmistakeable warning.

Eva doubted that anyone had dared to speak to Zaccheo Giordano in the way she referred, but she wasn't about to debate that point with him with three hundred pairs of eyes watching. She was struggling enough to keep upright what with all the turbulent sensations firing through her at his touch. 'Why, Zaccheo, you sound as if you've a great many lessons you intend to dole out...' She tried to sound bored, but her voice emerged a little too breathless for her liking.

'Patience, *cara mia*. You'll be instructed as and when necessary.' His gaze dropped to her mouth and her breath lodged in her sternum. 'For now, I wish the talking to cease.'

He closed the final inch between them and slanted his mouth over hers. The world tilted and shook beneath her feet. Expertly sensual and demanding, he kissed her as if he owned her mouth, as if he owned her whole body. In all her adult years, Eva had never imagined the brush of a beard would infuse her with such spine-tingling sensations. Yet she shivered with fiery delight as Zaccheo's silky facial hair caressed the corners of her mouth.

She groaned at the forceful breach of his tongue. Her arms drifted over his taut biceps as she became lost in the potent magic of his kiss. At the first touch of his tongue against hers, she shuddered. He made a rough sound and his sharp inhalation vibrated against her. His fingers convulsed in her hair and his other hand drifted to her bottom, moulding her as he stepped back against the aircraft and widened his stance to bring her closer.

Eva wasn't sure how long she stood there, adrift in a swirl of sensation as he ravaged her mouth. It wasn't until her lungs screamed and her heart jackhammered against her ribs did she recall where she was…what was happening.

And still she wanted to continue.

So much so she almost moaned in protest when firm hands set her back and she found herself staring into molten eyes dark with savage hunger.

'I think we've given our audience enough to feed on. Get in.'

The calm words, spoken in direct counteraction to the frenzied look in his eyes, doused Eva with cold reality. That she'd made even more of a spectacle of herself hit home as wolf whistles ripped through the air.

'This was all for *show*?' she whispered numbly, shivering in the frigid air.

One sleek eyebrow lifted. 'Of course. Did you think I wanted to kiss you because I was so desperate for you I just couldn't help myself? You'll find that I have more self-restraint than that. Get in,' he repeated, holding the steel and glass door to the aircraft open.

Eva brushed cold hands over her arms, unable to move. She stared at him, perhaps hoping to find some humanity in the suddenly grim-faced block of stone in front of her. Or did she want a hint of the man who'd once framed her face in his hands and called her the most beautiful thing in his life?

Of course, that had been a lie. Everything about Zaccheo

had been a lie. Still she probed for some softness beneath that formidable exterior.

His implacable stare told her she was grasping at straws, as she had from the very beginning, when she'd woven stupid dreams around him.

A gust of icy wind blew across the grass, straight into her exposed back. A flash of red caught her eye and she blindly stumbled towards the terrace. She'd barely taken two steps when he seized her arm.

'What the hell do you think you're doing?' Zaccheo enquired frostily.

'I'm cold,' she replied through chattering teeth. 'My wrap...' She pointed to where the material had drifted.

'Leave it. This will keep you warm.' With one smooth move, he unbuttoned, shrugged off his tuxedo and draped it around her shoulders. The sudden infusion of warmth was overwhelming. Eva didn't want to drown in the distinctively heady scent of the man who was wrecking her world, didn't welcome her body's traitorous urge to burrow into the warm silk lining. And most of all, she didn't want to be beholden to him in any way, or accept any hint of kindness from him.

Zaccheo Giordano had demonstrated a ruthless thirst to annihilate those he deemed enemies in her father's study.

But she was no longer the naive and trusting girl she'd been a year and a half ago. Zaccheo's betrayal and her continued fraught relationship with her father and sister had hardened her heart. The pain was still there—would probably always be there—but so were the new fortifications against further hurt. She had no intention of laying her heart and soul bare to further damage from the people she'd once blithely believed would return the same love and devotion she offered freely.

She started to shrug off the jacket. 'No, thanks. I'd prefer not to be stamped as your possession.'

He stopped her by placing both hands on her arms.

Dark grey eyes pinned her to the spot, the sharper, icier

burst of wind whipping around them casting him in a deadlier, more dangerous light.

'You're already my possession. You became mine the moment you made the choice to follow me out here, Eva. You can kid yourself all you want, but this is your reality from here on in.'

CHAPTER FOUR

@Ladystclare OMG! Bragging rights=mine! Beheld fireworks w/in fireworks @P/Manor last night when LadyP eloped w/convict lover! #amazeballs

@Aristokitten Bet it was all a publicity stunt, but boy that kiss? Sign me up! #Ineedlatinlovelikethat

@Countrypile That wasn't love. That was an obscene and shameless money-grabbing gambit at its worst! #Donotencouragerancidbehaviour

EVA FLINCHED, her stomach churning at each new message that flooded her social-media stream.

The hours had passed in a haze after Zaccheo flew them from Pennington Manor. In solid command of the helicopter, he'd soared over the City of London and landed on the vertiginous rooftop of The Spire.

The stunning split-level penthouse's interior had barely registered in the early hours when Zaccheo's enigmatic aide, Romeo, had directed the butler to show her to her room.

Zaccheo had stalked away without a word, leaving her in the middle of his marble-tiled hallway, clutching his jacket.

Sleep had been non-existent in the bleak hours that had followed. At five a.m., she'd given up and taken a quick shower before putting on that skin-baring dress again.

Wishing she'd asked for a blanket to cover the acres of flesh on display, she cringed as another salacious offering popped into her inbox displayed on Zaccheo's tablet.

Like a spectator frozen on the fringes of an unfolding train wreck, she read the latest post.

@Uberwoman Hey ConvictLover, that flighty poor little rich girl is wasted on you. Real women exist. Let ME rock your world!

Eva curled her fist, refusing to entertain the image of any woman rocking Zaccheo's world. She didn't care one way or the other. If she had a choice, she would be ten thousand miles away from this place.

'If you're thinking of responding to any of that, consider yourself warned against doing so.'

She jumped at the deep voice a whisper from her ear. She'd thought she would be alone in the living room for at least another couple of hours before dealing with Zaccheo. Now she wished she'd stayed in her room.

She stood and faced him, the long black suede sofa between them no barrier to Zaccheo's towering presence.

'I've no intention of responding. And you really shouldn't sneak up on people like that,' she tagged on when the leisurely drift of those incisive eyes over her body made her feel like a specimen under a microscope.

'I don't sneak. Had you been less self-absorbed in your notoriety, you would've heard me enter the room.'

Anger welled up. 'You accuse *me* of being notorious? All this is happening because *you* insisted on gatecrashing a private event and turning it into a public spectacle.'

'And, of course, you were so eager to find out whether you're trending that you woke up at dawn to follow the news.'

She wanted to ask how he'd known what time she'd left her room, but Eva suspected she wouldn't like the answer. 'You assume I slept at all when sleep was the last thing on my mind, having been blackmailed into coming here. And, FYI, I don't read the gutter press. Not unless I want the worst kind of indigestion.'

He rounded the sofa and stopped within arm's length. She stood her ground, but she couldn't help herself ogling the breathtaking body filling her vision.

It was barely six o'clock and yet he looked as vitally masculine as if he'd been up and ready for hours. A film of sweat covered the hair-dusted arms beneath the pulled-up sleeves, and his damp white T-shirt moulded his chiselled torso. His black drawstring sweatpants did nothing to hide thick thighs and Eva struggled to avert her gaze from the virile outline of his manhood against the soft material. Dragging her gaze up, she stared in fascination at the hands and fingers wrapped in stained boxing gauze.

'Do you intend to spend the rest of the morning ogling me, Eva?' he asked mockingly.

She looked into his eyes and that potent, electric tug yanked hard at her. Reminding herself that she was immune from whatever spell he'd once cast on her, she raised her chin.

'I intend to attempt a reasonable conversation with you in the cold light of day regarding last night's events.'

'That suggests you believe our previous interactions have been unreasonable?'

'I did a quick search online. You were released yesterday morning. It stands to reason that you're still a little affected by your incarceration—'

His harsh, embittered laugh bounced like bullets around the room. Eva folded her arms, refusing to cower at the sound.

He stepped towards her, the tension in his body barely leashed. 'You think I'm a *"little affected"* by my incarceration? Tell me, *bella*,' he invited softly, 'do you know what it feels like to be locked in a six-by-ten, damp and rancid cage for over a year?'

A brief wave of torment overcame his features, and a different tug, one of sympathy, pulled at her. Then she reminded herself just who she was dealing with. 'Of course not. I just don't want you to do anything that you'll regret.'

'Your touching concern for my welfare is duly noted. But I suggest you save it for yourself. Last night was merely you and your family being herded into the eye of the storm. The real devastation is just getting started.'

As nightmarish promises went, Zaccheo's chilled her to the bone. Before she could reply, several pings blared from the tablet. She glanced down and saw more lurid posts about what *real women* wanted to do to Zaccheo.

She shut the tablet and straightened to find him slowly unwinding the gauze from his right hand, his gaze pinned on her. Silence stretched as he freed both hands and tossed the balled cloth onto the glass-topped coffee table.

'So, do I get any sort of itinerary for this impending apocalypse?' she asked when it became clear he was content to let the silence linger.

One corner of his mouth lifted. 'We'll have breakfast in half an hour. After that, we'll see whether your father has done what I demanded of him. If he has, we'll take it from there.'

Recalling her father's overly belligerent denial once Zaccheo had left the study last night, anxiety skewered her. 'And if he hasn't?'

'Then his annihilation will come sooner rather than later.'

Half an hour later, Eva struggled to swallow a mouthful of buttered toast and quickly chased it down with a sip of tea before she choked.

A few minutes ago, a brooding Romeo had entered with the butler who'd delivered a stack of broadsheets. The other man had conversed in Italian with a freshly showered and even more visually devastating Zaccheo.

Zaccheo's smile after the short exchange had incited her first panic-induced emotion. He'd said nothing after Romeo left. Instead he'd devoured a hearty plate of scrambled eggs, grilled mushrooms and smoked pancetta served on Italian bread with unsettling gusto.

But as the silence spread thick and cloying across the room she finally set her cup down and glanced to where he stood now at the end of the cherrywood dining table, his hands braced on his hips, an inscrutable expression on his face.

Again, Eva was struck by the change in him. Even now he was dressed more formally in dark grey trousers and a navy shirt with the sleeves rolled up, her eyes were drawn to the gladiator-like ruggedness of his physique.

'Eva.' Her name was a deep command. One she desperately wanted to ignore. It held a quiet triumph she didn't want to acknowledge. The implications were more than she could stomach. She wasn't one for burying her head in the sand, but if her father had done what Zaccheo had demanded, then—

'Eva,' he repeated. Sharper. Controlled but demanding.

Heart hammering, she glanced at him. 'What?'

He stared back without blinking, his body deathly still. 'Come here.'

Refusing to show how rattled she was, she stood, teetered on the heels she'd had no choice but to wear again, and strode towards him.

He tracked her with chilling precision, his eyes dropping to her hips for a charged second before he looked back up. Eva hated her body for reacting to that look, even as her breasts tingled and a blaze lit between her thighs.

Silently she cursed herself. She had no business reacting to that look, or to any man on any plane of emotion whatsoever. She had proof that path only ended in eviscerating heartache.

She stopped a few feet from him, made sure to place a dining chair between them. But the solid wood couldn't stop her senses from reacting to his scent, or her nipples from furling into tight, needy buds when her gaze fell on the golden gleam of his throat revealed by the gap in his shirt. Quickly crossing her arms, she looked down at the newspapers.

That they'd made headlines was unmistakeable. Bold black letters and exclamation marks proclaimed Zaccheo's antics. And as for *that* picture of them locked together...

'I can't believe you landed a helicopter in the middle of a fireworks display,' she threw out, simply because it was easier than acknowledging the other words written on the page binding her to Zaccheo, insinuating they were something they would never be.

He looked from her face to the front-page picture showing him landing his helicopter during a particularly violent explosion. 'Were you concerned for me?' he mocked.

'Of course not. You obviously don't care about your own safety so why should I?'

A simmering silence followed, then he stalked closer. 'I hope you intend to act a little more concerned towards my well-being once we're married.'

Any intention of avoiding looking at him fled her mind. '*Married?* Don't you think you've taken this far enough?' she snapped.

'Excuse me?'

'You wanted to humiliate my father. Congratulations, you've made headlines in every single newspaper. Don't you think it's time to drop this?'

His eyes turned into pools of ice. 'You think this is some sort of game?' he enquired silkily.

'What else can it be? If you really had the evidence you claim to have, why haven't you handed it over to the police?'

'You believe I'm bluffing?' His voice was a sharp blade slicing through the air.

'I believe you feel aggrieved.'

'Really? And what else did you *believe*?'

Eva refused to quail beneath the look that threatened to cut her into pieces. 'It's clear you want to make some sort of statement about how you were treated by my father. You've done that now. Let it go.'

'So your father did all this—' he indicated the papers '—just to stop me throwing a childish tantrum? And what about you? Did you throw yourself at my feet to buy your family time to see how long my bluff would last?'

She flung her arms out in exasperation. 'Come on, Zaccheo—'

They both stilled at her use of his name. Eva had no time
to recover from the unwitting slip. Merciless fingers speared
into her hair, much as they had last night, holding her captive as his thumb tilted her chin.

'How far are you willing to go to get me to be *reasonable*? Or perhaps I should guess? After all, just last night
you'd dropped to an all-time low of whoring yourself to a
drunken boy in order to save your family.' The thick con-
demnation feathered across her skin.

Rage flared in her belly, gave her the strength to remain
upright. He stood close. Far too close. She stepped back, but
only managed to wedge herself between the table and Zaccheo's towering body. 'As opposed to what? Whoring myself
to a middle-aged criminal?'

He leaned down, crowding her further against the polished
wood. 'You know exactly how old I am. In fact, I recall precisely where we both were when the clock struck midnight
on my thirtieth birthday. Or perhaps you need me to refresh
your memory?' His smooth, faintly accented voice trailed
amused contempt.

'Don't bother—'

'I'll do it anyway, it's no hardship,' he offered, as if her
sharp denial hadn't been uttered. 'We were newly engaged,
and you were on your knees in front of my penthouse window, uncaring that anyone with a pair of decent binoculars
would see us. All you cared about was getting your busy,
greedy little hands on my belt, eager to rid me of my trousers so you could wish me a happy birthday in a way most
men fantasise about.'

Her skin flushed with a wave of heat so strong, she feared
spontaneous combustion. 'That wasn't my idea.'

One brow quirked. 'Was it not?'

'No, you dared me to do it.'

His mouth twitched. 'Are you saying I forced you?'

Those clever fingers were drifting along her scalp, lazily
caressing, lulling her into showing her vulnerability.

Eva sucked in a deep breath. 'I'm saying I don't want to talk about the past. I prefer to stick to the present.'

She didn't want to remember how gullible she'd been back then, how stupidly eager to please, how excited she'd been that this god of a man, who could have any woman he wanted with a lazy crook of his finger, had pursued *her*, chosen *her*.

Even after learning the hard way that men in positions of power would do anything to stay in that power, that her two previous relationships had only been a means to an end for the men involved, she'd still allowed herself to believe Zaccheo wanted her for herself. Finding out that he was no better, that he only wanted her to secure a *business deal*, had delivered a blow she'd spent the better part of a year burying in a deep hole.

At first his demands had been subtle: a business dinner here, a charity event there—occasions she'd been proud and honoured to accompany him on. Until that fateful night when she'd overheard a handful of words that had had the power to sting like nothing else.

She's the means to an end. Nothing more...

The conversation that had followed remained seared into her brain. Zaccheo, impatiently shutting her down, then brazenly admitting he'd said those words. That he'd used her.

Most especially, she recalled the savage pain in knowing she had got him so wrong, had almost given herself to a man who held such careless regard for her, and only cared about her pedigree.

And yet his shock when she'd returned his ring had made her wonder whether she'd done the right thing.

His arrest days later for criminal negligence had confirmed what sort of man she'd foolishly woven her dreams around.

She met his gaze now. 'You got what you wanted—your name next to mine on the front page. The whole world knows I left with you last night, that I'm no longer engaged to Harry.'

His hand slipped to her nape, worked over tense muscles. 'And how did Fairfield take being so unceremoniously dumped?' he asked.

'Harry cares about me, so he was a complete gentleman about it. Shame I can't say the same about you.'

Dark grey eyes gleamed dangerously. 'You mean he wasn't torn up at the thought of never having access to this body again?' he mocked.

She lifted a brow. 'Never say never.'

Tension coiled his body. 'If you think I'll tolerate any further interaction between you and Fairfield, you're severely mistaken,' he warned with a dark rumble.

'Why, Zaccheo, you sound almost jealous.'

Heat scoured his cheekbones and a tiny part of her quailed at her daring. 'You'd be wise to stop testing me, *dolcezza*.'

'If you want this to stop, tell me why you're doing this.'

'I'm only going to say it one more time, so let it sink in. I don't intend to stop until your father's reputation is in the gutter and everything he took from me is returned, plus interest.'

'Can I see the proof of what you accuse my father of?'

'Would you believe even if you saw it? Or will you cling to the belief that I'm the big, bad ogre who's just throwing his weight about?' he taunted.

Eva looked down at the papers on the table, every last one containing everything Zaccheo had demanded. Would her father have done it if Zaccheo's threats were empty?

'Last night, when you said you and I…' She stopped, unable to process the reality.

'Would be married in two weeks? *Sì*, I meant that, too. And to get that ball rolling, we're going shopping for an engagement ring in exactly ten minutes, after which we have a full day ahead, so if you require further sustenance I suggest you finish your breakfast.'

He dropped his fingers from her nape and stepped back. With a last look filled with steely determination, he picked up the closest paper and walked out of the room.

CHAPTER FIVE

THEIR FIRST STOP was an exclusive coat boutique in Bond Street. Zaccheo told himself it was because he didn't want to waste time. The truth mocked him in the form of needing to cover Eva Pennington's body before he lost any more brain cells to the lust blazing through his bloodstream.

In the dark cover of her family terrace and the subsequent helicopter journey home, he'd found relief from the blatant temptation of her body.

In the clear light of day, the red dress seemed to cling tighter, caress her body so much more intimately that he'd had to fight the urge to lunge for her each time she took a breath.

He watched her now, seated across from him in his limo as they drove the short twenty-minute distance to Threadneedle Street where his bankers had flown in the diamond collection he'd requested from Switzerland.

Her fingers plucked at the lapel of the new white cashmere coat, then dropped to cinch the belt tighter at her tiny waist.

'You didn't need to buy me a coat,' she grumbled. 'I have a perfectly good one back at my flat.'

He reined in his fascination with her fingers. 'Your flat is on the other side of town. I have more important things to do than waste an hour and a half sitting in traffic.'

Her plump lips pursed. 'Of course, extracting your pound of flesh is an all-consuming business, isn't it?'

'I don't intend to stop at a mere pound, Eva. I intend to take the whole body.'

One eyebrow spiked. 'You seem so confident I'm going to hand myself to you on a silver platter. Isn't that a tad foolish?'

There was that tone again, the one that said she didn't believe him.

'I guess we'll find out one way or the other when the sordid details are laid out for you on Monday. All you need to concern yourself about today is picking out an engagement ring that makes the right statement.'

Her striking green eyes clashed with his and that lightning bolt struck again. 'And what statement would that be?' she challenged.

He let loose a chilling half-smile that made his enemies quake. 'Why, that you belong to me, of course.'

'I told you, I've no intention of being your possession. A ring won't change that.'

'How glibly you lie to yourself.'

She gasped and he was once again drawn to her mouth. A mouth whose sweet taste he recalled vividly, much to his annoyance. 'Excuse me?'

'We both know you'll be exactly who and what I want you to be when I demand it. Your family has too much at stake for you to risk doing otherwise.'

'Don't mistake my inclination to go along with this farce to be anything but my need to get to the bottom of why you're doing this. It's what families *do* for each other. Of course, since you don't even speak about yours, I assume you don't know what I'm talking about.'

Zaccheo called himself ten kinds of fool for letting the taunt bite deep. He'd lost respect for his father long before he'd died in shame and humiliation. And watching his mother whore herself for prestige had left a bitter taste in his mouth. As families went, he'd been dealt a bad hand, but he'd learned long ago that to wish for anything you couldn't create with your own hard-working hands was utter folly. He'd stopped making wishes by the time he hit puberty. Recalling the very last wish he'd prayed night and day for as a child, he clenched his fists. Even then he'd known fate would laugh at his wish for a brother or sister. He'd known that wish, despite his mother being pregnant, would not come true. He'd *known*.

He'd programmed himself not to care after that harrowing time in his life.

So why the hell did it grate so much for him to be reminded that he was the last Giordano?

'I don't talk about my family because I have none. But that's a situation I intend to rectify soon.'

She glanced at him warily. 'What's that supposed to mean?'

'It means I had a lot of time in prison to re-examine my life, thanks to your family.' He heard the naked emotion in his voice and hardened his tone. 'I intend to make some changes.'

'What sort of changes?'

'The type that means you'll no longer have to whore out your integrity for the sake of the great Pennington legacy. You should thank me, since you seem to be the one doing most of the heavy lifting for your family.'

Zaccheo watched her face pale.

'I'm not a whore!'

He lunged forward before he could stop himself. 'Then what the hell were you doing dressed like a tart, agreeing to marry a drunken playboy, if not for cold, hard cash for your family?' The reminder of what she wore beneath the coat blazed across his mind. His temperature hiked, along with the increased throbbing in his groin.

'I didn't do it for money!' She flushed, and bit down on her lower lip again. 'Okay, yes, that was part of the reason, but I also did it because—'

'Please spare me any declarations of *true love*.' He wasn't sure why he abhorred the idea of her mentioning the word love. Or why the idea of her mentioning Fairfield's name filled him with rage.

Zaccheo knew about her friendship with Fairfield. And while he knew their engagement had been a farce, he hadn't missed the camaraderie between them, or the pathetic infatuation in the other man's eyes.

Sì, he was jealous—Eva would be his and no one else's. But he also pitied Fairfield.

Because love, in all forms, was a false emotion. Nothing but a manipulative tool. Mothers declared their love for their children, then happily abandoned them the moment they ceased to be a convenient accessory. Fathers professed to have their children's interest at heart because of *love*, but when it came right down to it they put themselves above all else. And sometimes even forgot that their children *existed*.

As for Eva Pennington, she'd shown how faithless she was when she'd dropped him and distanced herself mere days before his arrest.

'I wasn't going to say that. Trust me, I've learned not to toss the word *love* about freely—'

'Did you know?' he sliced at her before he could stop himself.

Fine brows knitted together. 'Did I know what?'

'Did you know of your father's plans?' The question had been eating at him far more than he wanted to admit.

'His plans to do what?' she asked innocently. And yet he could see the caginess on her face. As if she didn't want him to probe deeper.

Acrid disappointment bit through him. He was a fool for thinking, perhaps *wishing*, despite all the signs saying otherwise, that she'd been oblivious to Oscar Pennington's plans to make him the ultimate scapegoat.

'We're here, sir.' His driver's voice came through the intercom.

Zaccheo watched her dive for the door. He would've laughed at her eagerness to get away from the conversation that brought back too many volatile memories, had he not felt disconcerting relief that his question had gone unanswered.

He'd been a fool to pursue it in the first place. He didn't need more lies. He had cold, hard facts proving the Penningtons' guilt. Dwelling on the whys and wherefores of Eva's actions was a fool's errand.

He stepped out into the winter sunshine and nodded at the bank director.

'Mr Giordano, welcome.' The older man's expression vacillated between obsequiousness and condescension.

'You received my further instructions?' Zaccheo took Eva's arm, ignoring her slight stiffening as he walked her through the doors of the bank.

'Yes, sir. We've adhered to your wishes.' Again he caught the man's assessing gaze.

'I'm pleased to hear it. Otherwise I'm sure there would be other banks who would welcome GWI's business.'

The banker paled. 'That won't be necessary, Mr Giordano. If you'll come with me, the jewellers have everything laid out for you.'

It should've given him great satisfaction that he'd breached the hallowed walls of the centuries-old establishment, that he'd finally succeeded where his own father had tried so hard and failed, giving his life in pursuit of recognition.

But all Zaccheo could hear, could *feel*, was Eva's presence, a reminder of why his satisfaction felt hollow. She was proof that, despite all he'd achieved, he was still regarded as the lowest of the low. A nobody. An expendable patsy who would take any treatment his betters doled out without protest.

We shall see.

They walked down several hallways. After a few minutes, Eva cleared her throat. 'What instructions did you give him?' she asked.

He stared down at her. 'I told him to remove all pink diamonds from the collection and instruct my jewellers that I do not wish to deal with diamonds of that colour in the future.'

'Really? I thought pink diamonds were all the rage these days?'

He shrugged. 'Not for me. Let's call it a personal preference.'

The penny dropped and she tried to pull away from his hold. He refused to let go. 'Are you really that petty?' she asked as they approached a heavy set of oak doors. 'Just because Harry gave me a pink diamond…' Her eyes widened when he caught her shoulders and pinned her against the wall. When she started to struggle, he stepped closer, caging her in with his body.

'You'll refrain from mentioning his name in my presence ever again. Is that understood?' Zaccheo felt his control slipping as her scent tangled with his senses and her curvy figure moved against him.

'Let me go and you'll need never hear his name again,' she snapped back.

'Not going to happen.' He released her. 'After you.'

She huffed a breath and entered the room. He followed and crossed to the window, struggling to get himself under control as the director walked in with three assistants bearing large velvet trays. They set them on the polished conference table and stepped back.

'We'll give you some privacy,' the director said before exiting with his minions.

Zaccheo walked to the first tray and pulled away the protective cloth. He stared at the display of diamonds in all cuts and sizes, wondering for a moment how his father would've reacted to this display of obscene wealth. Paolo Giordano had never managed to achieve even a fraction of his goals despite sacrificing everything, including the people he should've held dear. Would he have been proud, or would he have bowed and scraped as the bank director had a few moments ago, eager to be deemed worthy of merely touching them?

'Perhaps we should get on with choosing a stone. Or are we going to stare at them all day?' Eva asked.

Eva watched his face harden and bit her tongue. She wasn't sure why she couldn't stop goading him. Did part of her want to get under his skin as he so effortlessly got under hers?

Annoyed with herself for letting the whole absurd situation get to her, she stepped forward and stared down at the

dazzling array of gems. Large. Sparkling. Flawless. Each
worth more than she would earn in half her lifetime.

None of them appealed to her.

She didn't want to pick out another cold stone to replace
the one she'd handed back to Harry before running after
Zaccheo last night.

She didn't want to be trapped into yet another conse-
quence of being a Pennington. She wanted to be free of the
guilty resentment lurking in her heart at the thought that
nothing she did would ever be enough for her family. Or the
sadness that came with the insurmountable knowledge that
her sister would continue to block any attempt to forge a relationship with her father.

She especially didn't want to be trapped in any way with
Zaccheo Giordano. That display of his displeasure a few
moments ago had reminded her she wanted nothing to do
with him. And it was not about his temper but what she'd felt
when her body had been thrust against his. She'd wanted to
be held there...indefinitely.

Touching him.

Soothing his angry brow and those brief flashes of pain
she saw in his eyes when he thought she wasn't looking.

God, even a part of her wanted to coax out that heart-
stopping smile she'd glimpsed so very rarely when he was
pursuing her!

What was wrong with her?

'Is that the one you wish for?'

She jumped and stared down at the stone that had somehow found its way into her palm. She blinked in shock.

The diamond was the largest on the tray and twice as obscene as the one that had graced her finger last night. No
wonder Zaccheo sounded so disparaging.

'No!' She hastily dropped it back into its slot. 'I'd never
wear anything so gratuitous.'

His coldly mocking gaze made her cringe. 'Really?'

Irritation skated over her skin. 'For your information, I didn't choose that ring.'

'But you accepted it in the spirit it was given—as the cost of buying your body in exchange for shares in Penningtons?'

Icy rage replaced her irritation. 'Your continuous insults make me wonder why you want to put up with my presence. Surely revenge can't be as sweet as you wish it if the object of your punishment enrages you this much?'

'Perhaps I enjoy tormenting you.'

'So I'm to be your punching bag for the foreseeable future?'

'Is this your way of trying to find out how long your sentence is to be?'

'A sentence implies I've done something wrong. I *know* I'm innocent in whatever you believe I've done.'

His smile could've turned a volcano into a polar ice cap. 'I've found that proclamations of innocence don't count for a thing, not when the right palm is greased.'

She inhaled at the fury and bitterness behind his words. 'Zaccheo...'

Whatever feeble reply she'd wanted to make died when his eyes hardened.

'Choose the diamond you prefer or I'll choose it for you.'

Eva turned blindly towards the table and pointed to the smallest stone. 'That one.'

'No.'

She gritted her teeth. 'Why not?'

'Because it's pink.'

'No, it's not...' She leaned closer, caught the faint pink glow, and frowned. 'Oh. I thought—'

A mirthless smile touched his lips. 'So did I. Perhaps I'll change bankers after all.' He lifted the cover of the second tray and Eva stared dispassionately at the endless rows of sparkling jewels. None of them spoke to her. Her heart hammered as it finally dawned on her why.

'Is there any reason why you want to buy me a new ring?'

He frowned. *'Scusi?'*

'When you proposed the first time, you gave me a different ring. I'm wondering why you're buying me a different one. Did you lose it?' Despite the circumstances surrounding his proposal and her subsequent rejection of him, she'd loved that simple but exquisite diamond and sapphire ring.

'No, I didn't lose it.' His tone was clipped to the point of brusqueness.

'Then why?'

'Because I do not wish you to have it.'

Her heart did an achy little dance as she waited for further elaboration. When she realised none would be forthcoming, she pulled her gaze from his merciless regard and back to the display.

He didn't want her to have it. Why? Because the ring held special meaning? Or because she was no longer worthy of it?

Berating herself for feeling hurt, she plucked a stone from the middle of the tray. According to the size chart it sat in mid-range, a flawless two carat, square-cut that felt light in her palm. 'This one.' She turned and found him staring at her, his gaze intense yet inscrutable.

Wordlessly, he held out his hand.

Her fingers brushed his palm as she dropped the stone and she bit back a gasp as that infernal electricity zinged up her arm.

His eyes held hers for a long moment before he turned and headed for the door. The next few minutes passed in a blur as Zaccheo issued clipped instructions about mountings, scrolls and settings to the jeweller.

Before she could catch her breath, Eva was back outside. Flashes went off as a group of paparazzi lunged towards them. Zaccheo handed her into the car before joining her. With a curt instruction to the driver, the car lurched into traffic.

'If I've achieved my publicity quota for the day, I'd like to be dropped at my flat, please.'

Zaccheo focused those incisive eyes on her. 'Why would I do that?'

'Aren't we done? I'd catch a bus home, but I left my handbag and phone at Pennington Manor—'

'Your belongings have been brought to my penthouse,' he replied.

'Okay, thanks. As soon as I collect them, I'll be out of your hair.' She needed to get out of this dress, shower and practise the six songs she would be performing at the club tonight. Saturday nights were the busiest of the week, and she couldn't be late. The music producer who'd been frequenting the club for the last few weeks might make another appearance tonight.

A little bubble of excitement built and she squashed it down as that half-smile that chilled her to the bone appeared on Zaccheo's face.

'You misunderstand. When I mentioned your belongings, I didn't mean your handbag and your phone. I meant everything you own in your bedsit has been removed. While we were picking your engagement ring, your belongings were relocated. Your rent has been paid off with interest and your landlady is busy renting the property to someone else.'

'What on earth are you talking about?' she finally asked when she'd picked up her jaw from the floor and sifted through his words. 'Of course I still live there. Mrs Hammond wouldn't just let you into my flat. And she certainly wouldn't arbitrarily end my lease without speaking to me first.'

Zaccheo just stared back at her.

'How dare you? Did you threaten her?'

'No, Eva. I used a much more effective tool.'

Her mouth twisted. 'You mean you threw so much money at her she buckled under your wishes?'

He shrugged rugged, broad shoulders. 'You of all people

should know how money sways even the most veracious hearts. Mrs Hammond was thrilled at the prospect of receiving her new hip replacement next week instead of at the end of the year. But it also helps that she's a hopeless romantic. The picture of us in the paper swayed any lingering doubts she had.'

Eva's breath shuddered out. Her landlady had lamented the long waiting list over shared cups of tea and Eva had offered a sympathetic ear. While she was happy that Mrs Hammond would receive her treatment earlier than anticipated and finally be out of pain, a huge part of her couldn't see beyond the fact that Zaccheo had ripped her safe harbour away without so much as a by your leave.

'You had absolutely no right to do that,' she blazed at him.

'Did I not?' he asked laconically.

'No, you didn't. This is nothing but a crude demonstration of your power. Well, guess what, I'm unimpressed. Go ahead and do your worst! Whatever crimes you think we've committed, maybe going to prison is a better option than this…this kidnapping!'

'Believe me, prison isn't an option you want to joke with.'

His lacerated tone made her heart lurch. She looked into his face and saw the agony. Her eyes widened, stunned that he was letting her witness that naked emotion.

'You think you know what it feels like to be robbed of your freedom for months on end? Pray you never get to find out, Eva. Because you may not survive it.'

'Zaccheo… I…' She stuttered to a halt, unsure of what to make of that raw statement.

His hand slashed through the air and his mask slid back into place. 'I wanted you relocated as swiftly as possible with a minimum of fuss,' he said.

A new wave of apprehension washed over her. 'Why? What's the rush?'

'I thought that would be obvious, Eva. I have deep-seated trust issues.'

Sadly, she'd reaped the rewards of betrayed trust, but the fierce loyalty to her family that continued to burn within her made her challenge him. 'How is that my family's fault?'

His nostrils flared. 'I trusted your father. He repaid that trust with a betrayal that sent me to prison! And you were right there next to him.'

Again she heard the ragged anguish in his voice. A hysterical part of her mind wondered whether this was the equivalent of a captor revealing his face to his prisoner. Was she doomed now that she'd caught a glimpse of what Zaccheo's imprisonment had done to him?

'So you keeping me against my will is meant to be part of *my* punishment?'

He smiled. 'You don't have to stay. You have many options available to you. You can call the police, tell them I'm holding you against your will, although that would be hard to prove since three hundred people saw you chase after me last night. Or you can insist I return your things and reinstate your lease. If you choose to walk away, no one will lift a finger to stop you.'

'But that's not quite true, is it? What real choice do I have when you're holding a threat over my father's head?'

'Leave him to flounder on his own if you truly believe you're guilt-free in all of this. You want to make a run for it? Here's your chance.'

His pointed gaze went to the door and Eva realised they'd completed the short journey from the bank to the iconic building that had brought Zaccheo into her life and turned it upside down.

She glanced up at the building *Architectural Digest* had called 'innovative beyond its years' and 'a heartbreakingly beautiful masterpiece'.

Where most modern buildings boasted elaborate glass edifices, The Spire was a study in polished, tensile steel. Thin sheets of steel had been twisted and manipulated around the towering spear-like structure, making the tallest building in

London a testament to its architect's skill and innovation. Its crowning glory was its diamond-shaped, vertiginous platform, within which was housed a Michelin-starred restaurant surrounded by a clear twenty-foot waterfall.

One floor beneath the restaurant was Zaccheo's penthouse. Her new home. Her prison.

The sound of him exiting the car drew her attention. When he held out his hand to her, she hesitated, unable to accept that this was her fate.

A muscle ticced in his jaw as he waited.

'You'd love that, wouldn't you? Me helping you bury my father?'

'He's going down either way. It's up to you whether he gets back up or not.'

Eva wanted to call his bluff. To shut the door and return everything to the way it was this time yesterday.

The memory of her father in that hospital bed, strung up to a beeping machine, stopped her. She'd already lost one parent. No matter how difficult things were between them, she couldn't bear to lose another. She would certainly have no hope of saving her relationship with her sister if she walked away.

Because one thing was certain. Zaccheo meant to have his way.

With or without her co-operation.

CHAPTER SIX

EVA BLEW HER fringe out of her eyes and glanced around her. The guest suite, a different one from the one she'd slept in last night, was almost three times the size of her former bedsit. And every surface was covered with designer gowns and accessories. Countless bottles of exclusive perfumes and luxury grooming products were spread on the dresser, and a team of six stylists each held an item of clothing, ready to pounce on her the moment she took off the dress she was currently trying on.

She tried hard to see the bright side of finally being out of the red dress. Unfortunately, any hint of brightness had vanished the moment she'd stepped out of the car and re-entered Zaccheo's penthouse.

'How many more before we're done?' She tried to keep her voice even, but she knew she'd missed amiability by a mile when two assistants exchanged wary glances.

'We've done your home and evening-wear package. We just need to do your vacation package and we'll be done with wardrobe. Then we can move on to hair and make-up,' Vivian, the chief stylist, said with a megawatt smile.

Eva tried not to groan. She needed to be done so she could find her phone and call her father. There was no way she was twiddling her thumbs until Monday to get a proper answer.

Being made into Zaccheo's revenge punchbag...his *married* revenge punchbag...wasn't a role she intended to be placed in. When she'd thought there was a glimmer of doubt as to Zaccheo's threat being real, she'd gone along with this farce. But with each hour that passed with silence from her father, Eva was forced to believe Zaccheo's threats weren't empty.

Would he go to such lengths to have her choose precious gems, remove her from her flat, and hire a team of stylists to turn her into the sort of woman he preferred to date, if this was just some sort of twisted game?

Her hand clenched as her thoughts took a different path. What exactly was Zaccheo trying to turn her into? Obviously he wasn't just satisfied with attaining her pedigree for whatever his nefarious purposes were. He wanted her to look like a well-dressed mannequin while he was at it.

'Careful with that, Mrs Giordano. That lace is delicate.'

She dropped the dress, her heart hammering far too fast for her liking. 'Don't call me that. I'm not Mrs Giordano—'

'Not yet, at least, right, *bellissima*?'

Eva heard the collective breaths of the women in the room catch. She turned as Zaccheo strode in. His eyes were fixed on her, flashing a warning that made her nape tingle. Before she could respond, he lifted her hands to kiss her knuckles, one after the other. Her breathing altered precariously as the silky hairs of his beard and the warm caress of his mouth threw her thoughts into chaos.

'It's only a few short days until we're husband and wife, *si*?' he murmured intimately, but loud enough so every ear in the room caught the unmistakeable statement of possession.

She struggled to think, to *speak*, as sharp grey eyes locked with hers.

'No…I mean, yes…but let's not tempt fate. Who knows what could happen in a *few short days*?' She fully intended to have placed this nightmare far behind her.

His thumbs caressed the backs of her hands in false intimacy. 'I've moved mountains to make you mine, *il mio prezioso*. Nothing will stand in my way.' His accent was slightly more pronounced, his tone deep and captivating.

Envious sighs echoed around the room, but Eva shivered at the icy intent behind his words. She snatched her hands from his. Or she attempted to.

'In that case, I think you ought to stop distracting me so I can get on with making myself beautiful for you.' She hoped her smile looked as brittle as it felt. That her intention to end this was clear for him to see. 'Or was there something in particular you wanted?'

His eyes held hers for another electrifying second before he released her. 'I came to inform you that your belongings have been unpacked.' He surveyed the room, his gaze taking in the organised chaos. 'And to enquire whether you wish to have lunch with me or whether you want lunch brought to you so you can push through?' He turned back to her, his gaze mockingly stating that he knew her choice before she responded.

She lifted her chin. 'Seeing as this makeover was a complete *surprise* that I'd have to *make* time for, we'll take lunch in here, please.'

He ignored her censorious tone and nodded. 'Your wish is my command, *dolcezza*. But I insist you be done by dinnertime. I detest eating alone.'

She bit her tongue against a sharp retort. The cheek of him, making demands on her time when *he'd* been the one to call in the stylists in the first place! She satisfied herself with glaring at his back as he walked out, his tall, imposing figure owning every square inch of space he prowled.

The women left three excruciating hours later. The weak sun was setting in grey skies by the time Eva dragged her weary body across the vast hallway towards the suite she'd occupied last night. Her newly washed and styled hair bounced in silky waves down her back and her face tingled pleasantly from the facial she'd received before the barely there make-up had been applied.

The cashmere-soft, scooped-neck grey dress caressed her hips and thighs as she approached her door. She'd worn it only because Vivian had insisted. Eva hadn't had the heart to tell her she intended to leave every single item untouched. But Eva couldn't deny that the off-shoulder, floor-length dress felt elegant and wonderful and exactly what she'd have chosen to wear for dinner. Even if it was a dinner she wasn't looking forward to.

Her new four-inch heels clicked on the marble floor as she opened the double doors and stopped. Her hands flew to cover her mouth as she surveyed the room. Surprise was followed a few seconds later by a tingle of awareness that told her she was no longer alone.

Even then, she couldn't look away from the sight before her.

'Is something wrong?' Zaccheo's enquiry made her finally turn.

He was leaning against the door frame, his hands tucked into the pockets of his black tailored trousers. The white V-necked sweater caressed his muscular arms and shoulders and made his grey eyes appear lighter, almost eerily silver. His slightly damp hair gleamed a polished black against his shoulders and his beard lent him a rakish look that was absolutely riveting.

His gaze caught and held hers for several seconds before conducting a detailed appraisal over her face, hair and down her body that made the tingling increase. When his eyes returned to hers, she glimpsed a dark hunger that made her insides quake.

Swallowing against the pulse of undeniable attraction, she turned back to survey the room.

'I can't believe everything's been arranged so precisely,' she murmured.

'You would've preferred that they fling your things around without thought or care?'

'That's not what I mean and you know it. You've reproduced my room almost exactly how it was before.'

He frowned. 'I fail to see how that causes you distress.'

She strolled to the white oak antique dresser that had belonged to her mother. It'd been her mother's favourite piece of furniture and one of the few things Eva had taken when she'd left Pennington Manor.

Her fingers drifted over the hairbrush she'd used only yesterday morning. It had been placed in the little stand just as she normally did. 'I'm not distressed. I'm a little disconcerted that my things are almost exactly as I left them at my flat yesterday morning.' When he continued to stare, she pursed her lips. 'To reproduce this the movers would've needed photographic memories.'

'Or a few cameras shots as per my instructions.'

She sucked in a startled breath. 'Why would you do that?'

His lashes swept down for a moment. Then he shrugged. 'It was the most efficient course of action.'

'Oh.' Eva wasn't sure why she experienced that bolt of disappointment. Was she stupid enough to believe he'd done that because he *cared*? That he'd wanted her to be comfortable?

She silently scoffed at herself.

Lending silly daydreams to Zaccheo's actions had led to bitter disappointment once before. She wasn't about to make the same mistake again.

She spotted her handbag on the bed and dug out her phone. The battery was almost depleted, but she could make a quick call to her father before it died. She started to press dial and realised Zaccheo hadn't moved.

'Did you need something?'

The corner of his mouth quirked, but the bleakness in his eyes didn't dissipate. 'I've been in jail for over a year, *dolcezza*. I have innumerable needs.' The soft words held a note of deadly intent as his gaze moved from her to the bed. Her heart jumped to her throat and the air seemed to evaporate from the room. 'But my most immediate need is sustenance. I've ordered dinner to be brought from upstairs. It'll be here in fifteen minutes.'

She managed to reply despite the light-headedness that assailed her. 'Okay. I'll be there.'

With a curt nod, he left.

Eva sagged sideways onto the bed, her grip on the phone tightening until her bones protested. In the brief weeks she'd dated Zaccheo a year and half ago, she'd seen the way women responded to his unmistakeable animal magnetism. He only needed to walk into the room for every female eye to zero in on him. She'd also witnessed his reaction. Sometimes he responded with charm, other times with arrogant aloofness. But always with an innate sexuality that spoke of a deep appreciation for women. She'd confirmed that appreciation by a quick internet search in a weak moment, which had unearthed the long list of gorgeous women he'd had shockingly brief liaisons with in the past. A young, virile, wealthy bachelor, he'd been at the top of every woman's 'want to bed' list. And he'd had no qualms about helping himself to their amorous attentions.

To be deprived of that for almost a year and a half...

Eva shivered despite the room's ambient temperature. No, she was the last woman Zaccheo would *choose* to bed.

But then, he'd kissed her last night as if he'd wanted to devour her. And the way he'd looked at her just now?

She shook her head.

She was here purely as an instrument of his vengeance. The quicker she got to the bottom of *that*, the better.

Her call went straight to voicemail. Gritting her teeth, she left a message for her father to call her back. Sophie's phone rang for almost a minute before Eva hung up. Whether her sister was deliberately avoiding her calls or not, Eva intended to get some answers before Monday.

Resolving to try again after dinner, Eva plugged in her phone to charge and left her room. She met two waiters wheeling out a trolley as she entered the dining room. A few seconds later, the front door shut and Eva fought the momentary panic at being alone with Zaccheo.

She avoided looking at his imposing body as he lifted the silver domes from several serving platters.

'You always were impeccably punctual,' he said without turning around.

'I suppose that's a plus in my favour.'

'Hmm…' came his non-committal reply.

She reached her seat and froze at the romantic setting of the table. Expensive silverware and crystal-cut glasses gleamed beneath soft lighting. And already set out in a bed of ice was a small silver tub of caviar. A bottle of champagne chilled in an ice stand next to Zaccheo's chair.

'Do you intend to eat standing up?'

She jumped when his warm breath brushed her ear. When had he moved so close?

'Of course not. I just wasn't expecting such an elaborate meal.' She urged her feet to move to where he held out her chair, and sat down. 'One would almost be forgiven for thinking you were celebrating something.'

'Being released from prison isn't reason enough to enjoy something better than grey slop?'

Mortified, she cursed her tactlessness. 'I…of course. I'm sorry, that was… I'd forgotten…' *Oh, God, just shut up, Eva.*

'Of course you had.'

She tensed. 'What's that supposed to mean?'

'You're very good at putting things behind you, aren't you? Or have you forgotten how quickly you walked away from me the last time, too?'

She glanced down at her plate, resolutely picked up her spoon and helped herself to a bite of caviar. The unique taste exploded on her tongue, but it wasn't enough to quell the anxiety churning her stomach. 'You know why I walked away last time.'

'Do I?'

'Yes, you do!' She struggled to keep her composure. 'Can we talk about something else, please?'

'Why, because your actions make you uncomfortable? Or does it make your skin crawl to be sharing a meal with an ex-convict?'

Telling herself not to rise to the bait, she took another bite of food. 'No, because you snarl and your voice turns arctic, and also because I think we have different definitions of what really happened.'

He helped himself to a portion of his caviar before he responded. 'Really? Enlighten me, *per favore*.'

She pressed her lips together. 'We've already been through this, remember? You admitted that you proposed to me simply to get yourself into the Old Boys' Club. Are you going to bother denying it now?'

He froze for several heartbeats. Then he ate another mouthful. 'Of course not. But I believed we had an agreement. That you knew the part you had to play.'

'I'm sorry, I must have misplaced my copy of the Zaccheo Giordano Relationship Guide.' She couldn't stem the sarcasm or the bitterness that laced her voice.

'You surprise me.'

'How so?' she snapped, her poise shredding by the second.

'You're determined to deny that you know exactly how this game is played. That you aristocrats haven't practised the *something-for-something-more* tenet for generations.'

'You seem to be morbidly fascinated with the inner workings of the peer class. If we disgust you so much, why do you insist on soiling your life with our presence? Isn't it a bit convenient to hold us all responsible for every ill in your life?'

A muscle ticced in his jaw and Eva was certain she'd struck a nerve. 'You think having my freedom taken away is a subject I should treat lightly?'

The trembling in her belly spread out to engulf her whole body. 'The *evidence* led to your imprisonment, Zaccheo. Now we can change the subject or we can continue to fight to see who gives whom indigestion first.'

He remained silent for several moments, his eyes boring into hers. Eva stared back boldly, because backing down would see her swallowed whole by the deadly volcanic fury lurking in his eyes. She breathed a tiny sigh of relief when that mocking half-smile made an appearance.

'As you wish.' He resumed eating and didn't speak again until their first course was done. 'Let's play a game. We'll call it *What If*,' he said into the silence.

Tension knotted her nape, the certainty that she was toying with danger rising higher. 'I thought you didn't like games?'

'I'll make an exception this time.'

She took a deep breath. 'Okay. If you insist.'

'What if I wasn't the man you think I am? What if I happened to be a stranger who was innocent of everything he's been accused of? What if that stranger told you that every day he'd spent in prison felt like a little bit of himself was being chipped away for ever? What would you say to him?' His voice held that pain-laced edge she'd first heard in the car.

She looked at his face but his eyes were downcast, his white-knuckled hand wrapped around his wine glass.

This was no game.

The tension that gripped her vibrated from him, engulfing them in a volatile little bubble.

'I'd tell you how sorry I was that justice wasn't served properly on your behalf.' Her voice shook but she held firm. 'Then I'd ask you if there was anything I could do to help you put the past behind you.'

Arctic grey eyes met hers. 'What if I didn't want to put it behind me? What if everything I believe in tells me the only way to achieve satisfaction is to make those responsible pay?'

'I'd tell you it may seem like a good course of action, but doing that won't get back what you've lost. I'd also ask why you thought that was the only way.'

His eyes darkened, partly in anger, partly with anguish. She half expected him to snarl at her for daring to dissuade him from his path of retribution.

Instead, he rose and went to dish out their second course. 'Perhaps I don't know another recourse besides crime and punishment?' he intoned, disturbingly calm.

Sorrow seared her chest. 'How can that be?'

He returned with their plates and set down her second course—a lobster thermidor—before taking his seat. His movements were jerky, lacking his usual innate grace.

'Let's say hypothetically that I've never been exposed to much else.'

'But you know better or you wouldn't be so devastated at the hand you've been dealt. You're angry, yes, but you're also wounded by your ordeal. Believe me, yours isn't a unique story, Zaccheo.'

He frowned at the naked bitterness that leaked through her voice. 'Isn't it? Enlighten me. How have *you* been wounded?'

She cursed herself for leaving the door open, but, while she couldn't backtrack, she didn't want to provide him with more ammunition against her. 'My family…we're united where it counts, but I've always had to earn whatever regard I receive, especially from my father. And it hasn't always been easy, especially when walls are thrown up and alliances built where there should be none.'

He saw through her vagueness immediately. 'Your father and your sister against your mother and you? There's no need to deny it. It's easy to see your sister is fashioning herself in the image of her father,' he said less than gently.

Eva affected an easy shrug. 'Father started grooming her when we were young, and I didn't mind. I just didn't understand why that meant being left out in the cold, especially…' She stopped, realising just how much she was divulging.

'Especially…?' he pressed.

She gripped her fork tighter. 'After my mother died. I thought things would be different. I was wrong.'

His mouth twisted. 'Death is supposed to be a profound leveller. But it rarely changes people.'

She looked at him. 'Your parents—'

'Were the individuals who brought me into the world. They weren't good for much else. Take from that what you will. We're also straying away from the subject. *What if* this stranger can't see his way to forgive and forget?' That ruthless edge was back in his voice.

Eva's hand shook as she picked up her glass of Chianti. 'Then he needs to ask himself if he's prepared to live with the consequences of his actions.'

His eyebrows locked together in a dark frown, before his lashes swept down and he gave a brisk nod. 'Asked and answered.'

'Then there's no further point to this game, is there?'

One corner of his mouth lifted. 'On the contrary, you've shown a soft-heartedness that some would see as a flaw.'

Eva released a slow, unsteady breath. Had he always been like this? She was ashamed to admit she'd been so dazzled with Zaccheo from the moment he'd walked into Siren two years ago, right until the day he'd shown her his true colours, that she hadn't bothered to look any deeper. He'd kissed her on their third date, after which, fearing she'd disappoint him, she'd stumblingly informed him she was a virgin.

His reaction had been something of a fairy tale for her. She'd made him out as her Prince Charming, had adored the way he'd treated her like a treasured princess, showering her with small, thoughtful gifts, but, most of all, his undivided time whenever they were together. He'd made her feel precious, adored. He'd proposed on their sixth date, which had coincided with his thirtieth birthday, and told her he wanted to spend the rest of his life with her.

And it had all been a lie. The man sitting in front of her had no softness, only that ruthless edge and deadly charm.

'Don't be so sure, Zaccheo. I've learnt a few lessons since our unfortunate association.'

'Like what?'

'I'm no longer gullible. And my family may not be perfect, but I'm still fiercely protective of those I care about. Don't forget that.'

He helped himself to his wine. 'Duly noted.' His almost

bored tone didn't fool her into thinking this subject had stopped being anything but volatile.

They finished their meal in tense silence.

Eva almost wilted in relief when the doorbell rang and Zaccheo walked away to answer it.

Catching sight of the time, she jumped up from the dining table and was crossing the living room when Zaccheo's hand closed over her wrist.

'Where do you think you're going?' he demanded.

'Dinner's over. Can you let me go, please? I need to get going or I'll be late.'

His brows furrowed, giving him a look of a dark predator. 'Late for what?'

'Late for work. I've already taken two days off without pay. I don't want to be late on top of everything else.'

'You still work at Siren?' His tone held a note of disbelief.

'I have to make a living, Zaccheo.'

'You still sing?' His voice had grown deeper, his eyes darkening to a molten grey as he stared down at her. Although Zaccheo's expression could be hard to decipher most of the time, the mercurial changes in his eyes often spelled his altered mood.

This molten grey was one she was familiar with. And even though she didn't want to be reminded of it, a pulse of decadent sensation licked through her belly as she recalled the first night she'd seen him.

He'd walked into Siren an hour before closing, when she'd been halfway through a sultry, soulful ballad—a song about forbidden love, stolen nights and throwing caution to the wind. He'd paused to order a drink at the bar, then made his way to the table directly in front of the stage. He'd sipped his whisky, not once taking his eyes off her. Every lyric in the three songs that had followed had felt as if it had been written for the man in front of her and the woman she'd wanted to be for him.

She'd been beyond mesmerised when he'd helped her off

the stage after her session. She'd said yes immediately when he'd asked her out the next night.

But she'd been wrong, so very wrong to believe fate had brought Zaccheo to the club. He'd hunted her down with single-minded intent for his own selfish ends.

God, how he must have laughed when she'd fallen so easily into his arms!

She yanked her arm free. 'Yes, I still sing. And I'd be careful before you start making any threats on my professional life, too. I've indulged you with the engagement-ring picking and the makeover and the homecoming dinner. Now I intend to get back to *my* reality.'

She hurried away, determined not to look over her shoulder to see whether he was following. She made it to her room and quickly changed into her going-to-work attire of jeans, sweater, coat and a thick scarf to ward off the winter chill. Scooping up her bag, she checked her phone.

No calls.

The unease in her belly ballooned as she left her suite.

Zaccheo was seated on the sofa in the living room, examining a small black velvet box. His eyes tracked her, inducing that feeling of being helpless prey before a ruthless marauder. She opened her mouth to say something to dispel the sensation, but no words emerged. She watched, almost paralysingly daunted as he shut the box and placed it on the coffee table next to him.

'Would it be too *indulgent* to demand a kiss before you leave for work, *dolcezza*?' he enquired mockingly.

'Indulgent, no. Completely out of the question, most definitely,' she retorted. Then silently cursed her mouth's sudden tingling.

He shook his head, his magnificent mane gleaming under the chandelier. 'You wound me, Eva, but I'm willing to wait until the time when you will kiss me freely without me needing to ask.'

'Then you'll be waiting an eternity.'

CHAPTER SEVEN

ZACCHEO PACED THE living room and contemplated leaving another voicemail message.

He'd already left five, none of which Eva had bothered to answer. It was nearly two a.m. and she hadn't returned. In his gloomy mood, he'd indulged in one too many nightcaps to consider driving to the club where she worked.

His temperament had been darkening steadily for the last four hours, once he'd found out what Eva's father was up to. Pennington was scrambling—futilely of course, because Zaccheo had closed every possible avenue—to find financial backing. That was enough to anger Zaccheo, but what fuelled his rage was that Pennington, getting more desperate by the hour, was offering more and more pieces of The Spire, the building that he would no longer own come Monday, as collateral. The blatant fraud Pennington was willing to perpetrate to fund his lifestyle made Zaccheo's fists clench as he stalked to the window.

The view from The Spire captured the string of bridges from east to west London. The moment he'd brought his vision of the building to life with the help of his experienced architects had been one of the proudest moments of his life. More than the properties he owned across the world and the empire he'd built from the first run-down warehouse he'd bought and converted to luxury accommodation at the age of twenty, this had been the one he'd treasured most. The building that should've been his crowning glory.

Instead it'd become the symbol of his downfall.

Ironically, the court where he'd been sentenced was right across the street. He looked down at the courthouse, jaw clenched.

He intended it to be the same place where his name was cleared. He would not be broken and humiliated as his father had been by the time he'd died. He would not be whispered about behind his back and mocked to his face and called a parasite. Earlier this evening, Eva had demanded to know why he'd been so fascinated with her kind.

For a moment, he'd wondered whether his burning desire to prove they were not better than him was a weakness. One he should *put behind him*, as Eva had suggested, before he lost a lot more of himself than he already had.

As much as he'd tried he hadn't been able to dismiss her words. Because he'd lied. He knew how to forgive. He'd forgiven his father each time he'd remembered that Zaccheo existed and bothered to take an interest in him. He'd forgiven his mother the first few times she'd let his stepfather treat him like a piece of garbage.

What Zaccheo hadn't told Eva was that he'd eventually learned that forgiveness wasn't effective when the recipient didn't have any use for it.

A weakening emotion like forgiveness would be wasted on Oscar Pennington.

A keycard clicked and he turned as the entry code released the front door.

Sensation very close to relief gut-punched him.

'Where the hell have you been?' He didn't bother to obviate his snarl. Nor could he stop checking her over from head to toe, to ascertain for himself that she wasn't hurt or hadn't been a victim of an accident or a mugging. When he was sure she was unharmed, he snapped his gaze to her face, to be confronted with a quizzical look.

Dio, was she *smirking* at him?

He watched her slide her fingers through her heavy, silky hair and ignored the weariness in the gesture.

'Is it Groundhog Day or something? Because I could've sworn we had a conversation about where I was going earlier this evening.'

He seethed. 'You finished work an hour and a half ago. Where have you been since then?'

She tossed a glare his way before she shrugged off her coat. The sight of the jeans and sweater she'd chosen to wear instead of the roomful of clothes he'd provided further stoked his dark mood.

'How do you know when I finished work?'

'Answer the question, Eva.'

She tugged her handbag from her shoulder and dropped it on the coffee table. Then she kicked off her shoes and pushed up on the balls of her feet in a smooth, practised stretch reminiscent of a ballet dancer.

'I took the night bus. It's cheaper than a cab, but it took forty-five minutes to arrive.'

'*Mi scusi?* You took the *night bus*?' His brain crawled with scenarios that made his blood curdle. He didn't need a spell in prison to be aware of what dangerous elements lurked at night. The thought that Eva had exposed herself, *willingly*, to—

'Careful there, Zaccheo, you almost sound like one of those snobs you detest so much.'

She pushed up again, her feet arching and flattening in a graceful rise and fall.

Despite his blood boiling, he stared, mesmerised, as she completed the stretches. Then he let his gaze drift up her body, knowing he shouldn't, yet unable to stop himself. The sweater, decorated with a D-minor scale motif, hugged her slim torso, emphasising her full, heavy breasts and tiny waist before ending a half-inch above her jeans.

That half-inch of flesh taunted him, calling to mind the smooth warmth of her skin. The simmering awareness that had always existed between them, like a fuse just waiting to be lit, throbbed deep inside. He'd tried to deny it earlier this evening in the hallway, when he'd discovered she still sang at Siren.

He'd tried to erase the sound of her sultry voice, the evocative way Eva Pennington performed on stage. He'd cursed himself when his body had reacted the way it had the very first time he'd heard her sing. That part of his black mood also stemmed from being viscerally opposed to any other man experiencing the same reaction he did from hearing her captivating voice, the way he had been two years ago, was a subject he wasn't willing to acknowledge, never mind tackle.

He pulled his gaze from the alluringly feminine curve of her hips and shapely legs and focused on the question that had been burning through him all night.

'Explain to me how you have two million pounds in your bank account, but take the bus to and from work.'

Her mouth gaped for several seconds before she regained herself. 'How the hell do you know how much money I have in my bank account?' she demanded.

'With the right people with the right skills, very easily. I'm waiting for an answer.'

'You're not going to get one. What I do with my money and how I choose to travel is *my* business.'

'You're wrong, *cara*. As of last night, your welfare is very much my business. And if you think I'm willing to allow you to risk your safety at times when drunken yobs and muggers crawl out of the woodwork, you're very much mistaken.'

'*Allow* me? Next you'll be telling me I need your permission to breathe!'

He spiked his fingers through his hair, wondering if she'd ever been this difficult and he'd somehow missed it. The Eva he remembered, before his eyes had been truly opened to her character, had possessed a quiet passion, not this defiant, wild child before him.

But no, there'd never been anything *child*like about Eva.

She was all woman. His libido had thrilled to it right from the first.

Understandably this acute reaction was because he'd been without a woman for over a year. Now was not the time to let it out of control. The time would arrive soon enough.

She tossed her head in irritation, and the hardening in his groin threatened to prove him wrong.

'Since I need you alive for the foreseeable future, no, you don't require my permission to breathe.'

She had the nerve to roll her eyes. 'Thank you very much!'

'From now on you'll be driven to and from work.'

'No, thanks.'

He gritted his teeth. 'You prefer to spend hours freezing at a bus stop than accept my offer?'

'Yes, because the *offer* comes at a price. I may not know what it is yet, but I've no intention of paying it.'

'Why do you insist on fighting me when we both know you don't have a choice? I'm willing to bet your father didn't return a single one of your phone calls last night.'

Wide, startled eyes met his for a second before she looked away. 'I'm sure he has his reasons.'

It spoke volumes that she didn't deny trying to reach Oscar. 'Reasons more important than answering the phone to his daughter? Do you want to know what he's been up to?'

'I'm sure you're about to apprise me whether I want to hear it or not.'

'He's been calling in every single favour he thinks he's owed. Unfortunately, a man as greedy as your father cashed in most of his favours a long time ago. He's also pleading and begging his way across the country in a bid to save himself from the hole he knows I'm about to bury him in. He didn't take your calls, but he took mine. I recorded it if you wish me to play it back to you?'

Her fists clenched. 'Go to hell, Zaccheo,' she threw at him, but he glimpsed the pain in her eyes.

He almost felt sorry for her. Then he remembered her part in all this.

'Come here, Eva,' he murmured.

She eyed him suspiciously. 'Why?'

'Because I have something for you.'

Her gaze dropped to his empty hands before snapping

back to his face. 'There's nothing you have that I could possibly want.'

'If you make me come over there, I'll take that kiss you owe me from last night.' *Dio*, why had he said that? Now it was all he could think about.

Heat flushed her cheeks. 'I don't owe you a thing. And I certainly don't owe you any kisses.'

The women he'd dated in the past would've fallen over themselves to receive any gift he chose to bestow on them, especially the one he'd tucked into his back pocket.

Slowly, he walked towards her. He made sure his intent was clear. The moment she realised, her hands shot out. 'Stop! Didn't your mother teach you about the honey versus vinegar technique?'

Bitterness drenched him. 'No. My mother was too busy climbing the social ladder after my father died to bother with me. When he was alive, she wasn't much use either.'

She sucked in a shocked breath and concern furrowed her brow. 'I'm sorry.'

Zaccheo rejected the concern and let the sound of her husky voice, scratchy from the vocal strain that came with singing, wash over him instead. He didn't want her concern. But the sex he could deal with.

The need he'd been trying to keep under tight control threatened to snap. He took another step.

'Okay! I'm coming.' She walked barefooted to him. 'I've done as you asked. Give me whatever it is you want to give me.'

'It's in my back pocket.'

She inhaled sharply. 'Is this another of your games, Zaccheo?'

'It'll only take a minute to find out. Are you brave enough, *dolcezza*?' he asked.

Her gaze dropped and he immediately tilted her chin up with one finger. 'Look at me. I want to see your face.'

She blinked, then gathered herself in that way he'd always found fascinating. Slowly, she reached an arm around him. Her fingers probed until she found the pocket opening.

They slipped inside and he suppressed a groan as her fingers caressed him through his trousers. His blood rushed faster south as she searched futilely.

'It's empty,' she stated with a suspicious glare.

'Try the other one.'

She muttered a dirty word that rumbled right through him. Her colour deepened when he lifted his eyebrow.

'Let's get this over with.' She searched his right pocket and stilled when she encountered the box.

'Take it out,' he commanded, then stifled another groan when her fingers dug into his flesh to remove the velvet box. It took all the control he could muster not to kiss her when her lips parted and he glimpsed the tip of her tongue.

During his endless months in prison, he'd wondered whether he'd overrated the chemistry that existed between Eva and him. The proof that it was as potent as ever triggered an incandescent hunger that flooded his loins.

Sì, this part of his revenge that involved Eva in his bed, being inside her and implanting her with his seed, would be easy enough and pleasurable enough to achieve.

'I cannot wait to take you on our wedding night. Despite you no longer being a virgin, I'll thoroughly enjoy making you mine in every imaginable way possible. By the time I'm done with you, you'll forget every other man that you dared to replace me with.'

Her eyelids fluttered and she shivered. But the new, assertive Eva came back with fire. 'A bold assertion. But one, sadly, we'll both see unproven since there'll be no wedding *or* wedding night. And in case I haven't mentioned it, you're the last man I'd ever welcome in my bed.'

Zaccheo chose not to point out that she still had her hand in his pocket, or that her fingers were digging more firmly into his buttock.

Instead, he slid his phone from his front pocket, activated the recording app and hit the replay button.

Despite her earlier assertion that she'd grown a thicker skin, shadows of disbelief and hurt criss-crossed her face as she listened to the short conversation summoning her father to a meeting first thing on Monday. Unlike the night before where Pennington had blustered his way through Zaccheo's accusations, he'd listened in tense silence as Zaccheo had told him he knew what he was up to.

Zaccheo had given him a taster of the contents of the documents proving his innocence and the older man had finally agreed to the meeting. Zaccheo had known he'd won when Pennington had declined to bring his lawyers to verify the documents.

Thick silence filled the room after the recording ended.

'Do you believe me now, Eva? Do you believe that your family has wronged me in the most heinous way and that I intend to exact equal retribution?'

Her nostrils flared and her mouth trembled before she wrenched back control. But despite her composure, a sheen of tears appeared in her eyes, announcing her tumultuous emotion. 'Yes.'

'Take the box out of my pocket.'

She withdrew it. His instructions on the mount and setting had been followed to the letter.

'I intended to give it to you after dinner last night. Not on bended knee, of course. I'm sure you'll agree that once was enough?'

Her eyes darkened, as if he'd hurt her somehow. But of course, that was nonsense. She'd returned his first ring and walked away from him after a brief argument he barely recalled, stating that she didn't wish to be married to *a man like him*.

At the time, Zaccheo had been reeling at his lawyers' news that he was about to be charged with criminal negligence. He hadn't been able to absorb the full impact of Eva's betrayal until weeks later, when he'd already been in prison. His trial had been swift, the result of a young, overeager judge desperate to make a name for himself.

But he'd had over a year to replay the last time he'd seen Eva. In court, sitting next to her father, her face devoid of emotion until Zaccheo's sentence had been read out.

In that moment, he'd fooled himself into thinking she'd experienced a moment of agony on his behalf. He'd murmured her name. She'd looked at him. It was then that he'd seen the contempt.

That single memory cleared his mind of any extraneous feelings. 'Open the box and put on the ring,' he said tersely.

His tone must have conveyed his capricious emotional state. She cracked open the small case and slid on the ring without complaint.

He caught her hand in his and raised it, much as he had on Friday night. But this time, the acute need to rip off the evidence of another man's ownership was replaced by a well of satisfaction. 'You're mine, Eva. Until I decide another fate for you, you'll remain mine. Be sure not to forget that.'

Turning on his heel, he walked away.

Eva woke on Monday morning with a heavy heart and a stone in her gut that announced that her life was about to change for ever. It had started to change the moment she'd heard Zaccheo's recorded conversation with her father, but she'd been too shocked afterwards to decipher what her father's guilt meant for her.

Tired and wrung out, she'd stumbled to bed and fallen into a dreamless sleep, then woken and stumbled her way back to work.

Reality had arrived when she'd exited Siren after her shift to find Zaccheo's driver waiting to bring her back to the penthouse. She'd felt it when Zaccheo had told her to be ready to attend his offices in the morning. She'd felt it when she'd walked into her suite and found every item of clothing she'd tried on Saturday neatly stacked in the floor-to-ceiling shelves in her dressing room.

She felt it now when she lifted her hand to adjust her collar and caught the flash of the diamond ring on her finger. The flawless gem she'd chosen so carelessly had been mounted on a bezel setting, with further diamonds in decreasing sizes set in a platinum ring that fitted her perfectly.

You're mine, Eva. Until I decide another fate for you, you'll remain mine.

She was marrying Zaccheo in less than a week. He'd brought forward the initial two-week deadline by a whole week. She would marry him or her father would be reported to the authorities. He'd delivered that little bombshell last night after dinner. No amount of tossing and turning had altered that reality.

When she'd agreed to marry Harry, she'd known it would be purely a business deal, with zero risk to her emotions.

The idea of attaching herself to Zaccheo, knowing the depth of his contempt for her and his hunger for revenge, was bad enough. That undeniably dangerous chemistry that hovered on the point of exploding in her face when she so much as looked at him...*that* terrified her on an unspeakable level. And not because she was afraid he'd use that against her.

What she'd spent the early hours agonising over was her own helplessness against that inescapable pull.

The only way round it was to keep reminding herself why Zaccheo was doing this. Ultimate retribution and humiliation was his goal. He didn't want anything more from her.

An hour later, she sat across from her father and sister and watched in growing horror as Zaccheo's lawyers listed her father's sins.

Oscar Pennington sat hunched over, his pallor grey and his forehead covered in light sweat. Despite having heard Zaccheo's recording last night, she couldn't believe her father would sink so low.

'How could you do this?' she finally blurted when it got

too much to bear. 'And how the hell did you think you'd get away with it?'

Her father glared at her. 'This isn't the time for histrionics, Eva.'

'And you, Sophie? Did you know about this?' Eva asked her sister.

Sophie glanced at the lawyers before she replied, 'Let's not lose focus on why we're here.'

Anger shot through Eva. 'You mean let's pretend that this isn't really happening? That we're not here because Father *bribed* the builders to take shortcuts and blamed someone else for it? And you accuse me of not living in the real world?'

Sophie's lips pursed, but not before a guilty flush rushed into her face. 'Can we not do this now, please?' Her agitated gaze darted to where Zaccheo sat in lethal silence.

Eva stared at her sister, a mixture of anger and sadness seething within her. She was beginning to think they would never get past whatever was broken between them. And maybe she needed to be more like Zaccheo, and divorce herself from her feelings.

Eva glanced at him and the oxygen leached from her lungs.

God!

On Friday night, his all-black attire had lent him an air of suave but icy deadliness reminiscent of a lead in a mafia movie. Since then his casual attires, although equally formidable in announcing his breathtaking physique, had lulled her into a lesser sense of danger.

This morning, in a dark grey pinstripe suit, teamed with a navy shirt, and precisely knotted silver and blue tie, and his hair and beard newly trimmed, Zaccheo was a magnificent vision to behold.

The bespoke clothes flowed over his sleekly honed muscles and olive skin, each movement drawing attention to his powerfully arresting figure.

It was why more than one female employee had stared in

blatant interest as they'd walked into GWI's headquarters in the City this morning. It was why she'd avoided looking at him since they'd sat down.

But she'd made the mistake of looking now. And as he started to turn his head she *knew* she wouldn't be able to look away.

His gaze locked on her and she read the ruthless, possessive statement of ownership in his eyes even before he opened his mouth to speak. 'Eva has already given me what I want—her word that she's willing to do whatever it takes to make reparations.' His gaze dropped to the ring on her finger before he faced her father. 'Now it's your turn.'

CHAPTER EIGHT

'HERE'S A LIST of businesses who withdrew their contracts because of my incarceration.' Zaccheo nodded to one of his lawyers, who passed a sheet across the desk to her father.

Eva caught a glimpse of the names on the list and flinched. While the list was only half a page, she noticed more than one global conglomerate on there.

'You'll contact the CEO of each of those companies and tell them your side of the story.'

Fear flashed across her father's face. 'What's to stop them from spilling the beans?'

Zaccheo gave that chilling half-smile. 'I have a team of lawyers who'll ensure their silence if they ever want to do business with me again.'

'You're sure they'll still want your business?' Her father's voice held a newly subdued note.

'I have it on good authority their withdrawal was merely a stance. Some to gain better leverage on certain transactions and others for appearances' sake. Once they know the truth, they'll be back on board. But even if they don't come back to GWI, the purpose of your phone call would've been achieved.'

'Is this really necessary? Your company has thrived, probably beyond your wildest dreams, even while you were locked up. And this morning's stock-market reports show your stock at an all-time high.' Eva could hear the panic in her father's voice. 'Do I really need to genuflect in front of these people to make you happy?' he added bitterly.

'Yes. You do.'

Her father's face reddened. 'Look here. Judging by that rock I see on Eva's finger, you're about to marry my daughter. We're about to be *family*. Is this really how you wish to start our familial relationship?'

Bitterness pushed aside her compassion when she realised her father was once again using her as leverage for his own ends.

'You don't think this is the least you can do, Father?' she asked.

'You're taking his side?' her father demanded.

Eva sighed. 'I'm taking the side of doing the right thing. Surely you can see that?'

Her father huffed, and Zaccheo's lips thinned into a formidable line. 'I have no interest in building a relationship with you personally. You can drop dead for all I care. Right after you carry out my instructions, of course.'

'Young man, be reasonable,' her father pleaded, realising that for once he'd come up against an immoveable object that neither his charm nor his blustering would shift.

Zaccheo stared back dispassionately. No one in the room could harbour the misguided idea that he would soften in any way.

'I don't think you have a choice in the matter, Father,' Sophie muttered into the tense silence.

Eva glanced at her sister, searching for that warmth they'd once shared. But Sophie kept her face firmly turned away.

Eva jumped as her father pushed back his chair. 'Fine, you win.'

Zaccheo brushed off imaginary lint from his sleeve. 'Excellent. And please be sure to give a convincing performance. My people will contact each CEO on that list by Friday. Make sure you get it done by then.'

Her father's barrel chest rose and fell as he tried to control his temper. 'It'll be done. Sophie, we're leaving.'

Eva started to rise, too, only to find a hand clamped on her hip. The electricity that shot through her body at the bold contact had her swaying on her feet.

'What are you doing?' she demanded.

Zaccheo ignored her, but his thumb moved lazily over her hip bone as he addressed her father. 'You and Sophie may leave. I still have things to discuss with my fiancée. My secretary will contact you with details of the wedding in the next day or two.'

Her father looked from her face to Zaccheo's. Then he stormed out of the door.

Eva turned to Zaccheo. 'What more could we possibly have to discuss? You've made everything crystal clear.'

'Not quite everything. Sit down.' He waited until she complied before he removed his hand.

Eva wasn't sure whether it was relief that burst through her chest or outrage. Relief, most definitely, she decided. Lacing her fingers, she waited as he dismissed all except one lawyer.

At Zaccheo's nod, the man produced a thick binder and placed it in front of Zaccheo, after which he also left.

She could feel Zaccheo's powerful gaze on her, but she'd already unsettled herself by looking at him once. And she was reeling from everything that had taken place here in the last hour.

When the minutes continued to tick by in silence, she raised her head. 'You want my father to help rebuild the damage he caused to your reputation, but what about your criminal record? I would've thought that would be more important to you.'

'You may marry a man with a criminal record come Saturday, but I won't remain that way for long. My lawyers are working on it.'

Her heart lurched at the reminder that in a few short days she would be his wife, but she forced herself to ask the question on her mind. 'How can they do that without implicating my father? Isn't withholding evidence a crime?'

'Nothing will be withheld. How the authorities choose to apply the rule of law is up to them.'

Recalling the state of her father's health, she tightened

her fists in anxiety. 'So you're saying Father can still go to prison? Despite letting him believe he won't?'

The kick in his stare struck deep in her soul. 'I'm the one who was wronged. I have some leeway in speaking on his behalf, should I choose to.'

The implied threat didn't escape her notice. They would either toe his line or suffer the consequences.

She swallowed. 'What did you want to discuss with me?'

He placed a single sheet of paper in front of her.

'These are the engagements we'll be attending this week. Make sure you put them in your diary.'

She pursed her lips, denying that the deep pang in her chest was hurt. 'At least you're laying your cards on the table this time round.'

'What cards would those be?'

She shrugged. 'The ones that state your desire to conquer the upper class, of course. Wasn't that your aim all along? To walk in the hallowed halls of the Old Boys' Club and show them all your contempt for them?'

His eyes narrowed, but she caught a shadow in the grey depths. 'How well you think you know me.'

She cautioned herself against probing the sleeping lion, but found herself asking anyway, 'Why, Zaccheo? Why is it so important that you bring us all down a peg or two?'

He shifted in his seat. If she hadn't known that he didn't possess an ounce of humility, she'd have thought he was uneasy. 'I don't detest the whole echelon. Just those who think they have a right to lord it over others simply because of their pedigree. And, of course, those who think they can get around the laws that ordinary people have to live by.'

'What about me? Surely you can't hate me simply because our relationship didn't work out?'

'Was that what we had—a *relationship*?' he sneered. 'I thought it was a means for you to facilitate your father's plans.'

'*What?* You think I had something to do with my father scapegoating you?'

'Perhaps you weren't privy to his whole plan like your sister was. But the timing of it all was a little too convenient, don't you think? You walked away *three days* before I was charged, with a flimsy excuse after an even flimsier row. What was it? Oh, yes, you didn't want to marry *a man like me*?'

She surged to her feet, her insides going cold. 'You think I staged the whole thing? Need I remind you that you were the one who initiated our first meeting? That you were the one to ask me out?'

'An event carefully orchestrated by your father, of course. Do you know why I was at Siren that night?'

'Will you believe me if I said no?'

'I was supposed to meet your father and two of his investors there. Except none of them showed.'

She frowned. 'That's not possible. My father hates that I sing. He hates it even more that I work in a nightclub. I don't think he even knows where Siren is.'

'And yet he suggested it. Highly recommended it, in fact.'

The idea that her father had engineered their first meeting coated her mouth with bitterness. He'd used her strong loyalty to their family to manipulate her long before she'd taken a stand and moved out of Pennington Manor. But this further evidence showed a meticulousness that made her blood run cold.

'Were you even a virgin back then?' Zaccheo sliced at her.

The question brought her back to earth. 'Excuse me?'

'Or was it a ploy to sweeten the deal?'

'I didn't know you existed until you parked yourself in front of the stage that night!'

'Maybe not. But you must've known who I was soon after. Isn't that what women do these days? A quick internet search while they're putting on their make-up to go on the first date?'

Eva couldn't stop her guilty flush because it was exactly what she'd done. But not with the reprehensible intentions he'd implied. Zaccheo's all-consuming interest in her had seemed too good to be true. She'd wanted to know more about the compelling man who'd zeroed in on her with such unnerving interest.

What she'd found was a long list of conquests ranging from supermodels to famous sports stars. She'd been so intimidated, she'd carefully kept her inexperience under wraps. It was that desperately embarrassing need to prove her sophistication that had led to her boldly accepting his dare to perform oral sex on him on his thirtieth birthday. She'd been so anxious, she'd bungled it even before she'd unfastened his belt. In the face of his wry amusement, she'd blurted her inexperience.

The inexperience he was now denouncing as a ploy.

'I don't care what you think. All I care about is that I know what I'm letting myself in for now. I know exactly the type of man you are.' One whose ruthless ambition was all he cared about.

He regarded her for several tense seconds. 'Then this won't surprise you too much.' He slid a thick burgundy folder across to her. 'It's a prenuptial agreement. On the first page you'll find a list of independent lawyers who can guide you through the legalese should you require it. The terms are non-negotiable. You have twenty-four hours to read and sign it.'

She glanced from him to the folder, her mouth dropping open in shock. 'Why would I need a prenup? I've agreed to your demands. Isn't this overkill?'

'My lawyers go spare if I don't get everything in writing. Besides, there are a few items in there we haven't discussed yet.'

Something in his voice made her skin prickle. Her belly quaked as she turned the first page of the thick document. The first few clauses were about general schedules and routines, making herself available for his engagements within reason, how many homes he owned and her duty to oversee the running of them, and his expectation of her availability to travel with him on his business trips should he require it.

'If you think I'm going to turn myself into a pet you can pick up and hop on a plane with whenever it suits you, you're in for a shock.'

He merely quirked an eyebrow at her. She bristled but carried on reading.

She paused at the sixth clause. 'We can't be apart for more than five days in the first year of marriage?'

The half-smile twitched. 'We don't want tongues wagging too soon, do we?'

'You mean after the first year I can lock myself in a nunnery for a year if I choose to?'

For the first time since Zaccheo had exploded back into her life, she glimpsed a genuine smile. It was gone before it registered fully, but the effect was no less earth-shattering. 'No nunnery would accept you once you've spent a year in my bed.'

Her face flamed and the look in his eyes made her hurriedly turn the page.

The ninth made her almost swallow her tongue. 'I don't want your money! And I certainly don't need that much money *every* month.' The sum stated was more than she earned in a year.

He shrugged. 'Then donate it to your favourite charity.'

Since she wasn't going to win that one, she moved on to the tenth and last clause.

Eva jerked to her feet, her heart pounding as she reread the words, hoping against hope that she'd got it wrong the first time. But the words remained clear and stark and *frightening*. 'You want…*children*?' she rasped through a throat gone bone dry with dread.

'*Sì,*' he replied softly. 'Two. An heir and a spare, I believe you disparagingly refer to that number in your circles. More if we're lucky—stop shaking your head, Eva.'

Eva realised that was exactly what she was doing as he rose and stalked her. She took a step back, then another, until her backside bumped the sleek black cabinet running the length of the central wall.

He stopped in front of her, leaned his tall, imposing frame over hers. 'Of all the clauses in the agreement, this is non-negotiable.'

'You said they were all non-negotiable.'

'They are, but some are more non-negotiable than others.'

A silent scream built inside her. 'If this one is the most important why did you put it last?'

'Because you would be signing directly below it. I wanted you to feel its import so there would be no doubt in your mind what you were agreeing to.'

She started to shake her head again but froze when he angled himself even closer, until their lips were an inch apart. Their breaths mingling, he stared her down. Eva's heart climbed into her throat as she struggled to sift through the emotions those words on the page had evoked.

Zaccheo was asking the impossible.

Children were the reasons why her last two relationships before him had failed before they'd even begun.

Children were the reason she'd painfully resigned herself to remaining single. To spurning any interest that came her way because she hadn't been able to bear the thought of baring her soul again only to have her emotions trampled on.

She wouldn't cry. She wouldn't break down in front of Zaccheo. Not today. *Not ever.* He'd caused her enough turmoil to last a lifetime.

But he was asking the impossible. 'I can't.'

His face hardened but he didn't move a muscle. 'You can. You *will*. Three days ago you were agreeing to marry another man. You expect me to believe the possibility of children weren't on the cards with Fairfield?'

She shook her head. 'My agreement with Harry was different. Besides, he…' She stopped, unwilling to add to the flammable tension.

'He what?' Zaccheo enquired silkily.

'He didn't *hate* me!'

He seemed almost surprised at her accusation. Surprise slowly gave way to a frown. 'I don't hate you, Eva. In fact, given time and a little work, we might even find common ground.'

She cursed her heart for leaping at his words. 'I can't—'

'You have twenty-four hours. I suggest you take the time and review your answer before saying another word.'

Her stomach clenched. 'And if my answer remains the same?'

His expression was one of pure, insufferable arrogance. 'It won't. You make feeble attempts to kick at the demands of your ancestry and title, but inevitably you choose blood over freedom. You'll do anything to save your precious family name—'

'You really think so? After the meeting we just had? Are you really that blind, or did you not see the way my sister and my father treat me? We are not a close family, Zaccheo. No matter how much I wish it…' Her voice shook, but she firmed it. 'Have you stopped to think that you pushing me this way may be the catalyst I need to completely break away from a family that's already broken?'

Her terse words made his eyes narrow. But his expression cleared almost immediately. 'No, you're loyal. You'll give me what I want.'

'No—'

'Yes,' he breathed.

He closed the gap between them slowly, as if taunting her with the knowledge that she couldn't escape the inevitability of his possession.

His mouth claimed hers—hot, demanding, powerfully erotic. Eva moaned as her emotions went into free fall. He feasted on her as if he had all the time in the world, taking turns licking his way into her mouth before sliding his tongue against hers in an expert dance that had her desperately clutching his waist.

Wild, decadent heat swirled through her body as he lifted her onto the cabinet, tugged up the hem of her dress and planted himself between her thighs. Her shoulders met the wall and she gasped as one hand gripped her thigh.

Push him away. You need to push him away!

Her hands climbed from his waist to his chest, albeit far slower and in a far more exploratory fashion than her screeching brain was comfortable with. But she made an effort once she reached his broad shoulders.

She pushed.

And found her hands captured in a firm one-handed hold above her head. His other hand found her breast and palmed it, squeezing before flicking his thumb over her hardened nipple.

Sensation pounded through her blood. Her legs curled around his thickly muscled thighs and she found herself pulled closer to the edge of the cabinet, until the powerful evidence of his erection pushed at her core.

Zaccheo gave a deep groan and freed her hands to bury his in her hair. Angling her head for a deeper invasion, he devoured her until the need for air drove them apart.

Chests heaving, they stared at each other for several seconds before Eva scrambled to untangle her legs from around him. Every skin cell on fire, she struggled to stand up. He stopped her with a hand on her belly, his eyes compelling hers so effortlessly, she couldn't look away.

The other hand moved to her cheek, then his fingers drifted over her throbbing mouth.

'As much as I'd like to take you right here on my boardroom cabinet, I have a dozen meetings to chair. It seems everyone wants a powwow with the newly emancipated CEO. We'll pick this up again at dinner. I'll be home by seven.'

She diverted enough brainpower from the erotic images it was creating to reply. 'I won't be there. I'm working tonight.'

A tic throbbed at his temple as he straightened his tie. 'I see that I need to put aligning our schedules at the top of my agenda.'

She pushed him away and stood. 'Don't strain yourself too much on my account,' she responded waspishly. She was projecting her anger at her weakness onto him, but she couldn't help herself. She tugged her dress down, painfully aware of the sensitivity between her unsteady legs as she moved away from him and picked up her handbag and the folder containing the prenup. 'I'll see you when I see you.'

He took her hand and walked her to the door. 'I guarantee you it'll be much sooner than that.' He rode the lift down with her to the ground floor, barely acknowledging the keen interest his presence provoked.

Romeo was entering the building as they exited. The two men exchanged a short conversation in Italian before Zaccheo opened the door to the limo.

When she went to slide in, he stopped her. 'Wait.'

'What is it?' she demanded.

His lips firmed and he seemed in two minds as to his response. 'For a moment during the meeting, you took my side against your father. I'll factor that favourably into our dealings from now on.'

Eva's heart lifted for a moment, then plunged back to her toes. 'You don't get it, do you?'

He frowned. 'Get what?'

'Zaccheo, for as long as I can remember, all I've wished was for there to be *no sides*. For there not to be a *them* against *us*. Maybe that makes me a fool. Or maybe I'll need to give up that dream.'

His eyes turned a shade darker with puzzlement, then he shrugged. '*Sì, bellissima*, perhaps you might have to.'

And right in front of the early lunch crowd, Zaccheo announced his ownership of her with a long, deep kiss.

* * *

Eva could barely hear herself think above the excited buzz in Siren's VIP lounge as she cued the next song.

She was sure the unusually large Monday night crowd had nothing to with Ziggy Preston, the famous record producer who'd been coming to watch her perform on and off for the past month, and everything to do with the pictures that had appeared in the early-evening paper of her kissing Zaccheo outside his office this afternoon. Avoiding the news had been difficult, seeing as that kiss and a large-scale picture of her engagement ring had made front-page news.

One picture had held the caption *'Three Ring Circus'*— with photos of her three engagement rings and a pointed question as to her motives.

It'd been a relief to leave Zaccheo's penthouse, switch off her phone and immerse herself in work. Not least because blanking her mind stopped her from thinking about the last clause in the prenup, and the reawakened agony she'd kept buried since her doctor had delivered the harrowing news six years ago. News she'd only revealed twice, with devastating consequences.

She almost wished she could blurt it out to Zaccheo and let the revelation achieve what it had in the past—a swift about-face from keen interest to cold dismissal, with one recipient informing her, in the most callous terms, that he could never accept her as a full woman.

Pain flared wider, threatening the foundations she'd built to protect herself from that stark truth. Foundations Zaccheo threatened.

She clutched the mic and forced back the black chasm that swirled with desolation. Her accompanying pianist nodded and she cleared her throat, ready to sing the ballad that ironically exhorted her to be brave.

She was halfway through the song when he walked in. As usual, the sight of him sent a tidal wave of awareness through her body and she managed to stop herself from stumbling by the skin of her teeth. Heads turned and the buzz in the room grew louder.

Zaccheo's eyes raked her from head to toe before settling on her face. A table miraculously emptied in front of the stage. Someone took his overcoat and Eva watched him release the single button to his dinner jacket before pulling out a chair and seating himself at the roped-off table before her.

The sense of déjà vu was so overwhelming, she wanted to abandon the song and flee from the stage. She finished, she smiled and accepted the applause, then made her way to where he pointedly held out a chair for her.

'What are you doing here?' she whispered fiercely.

He took his time to answer, choosing instead to pull her close and place a kiss on each cheek before drawing back to stare at her.

'You couldn't make dinner, so I brought dinner to you.'

'You really shouldn't have,' she replied, fighting the urge to rub her cheeks where his lips had been. 'Besides, I can't. My break is only twenty minutes.'

'Tonight your break is an hour, as it will be every night I choose to dine with you here instead of at our home. Now sit down and smile, *mio piccolo uccello che canta*, and pretend to our avid audience that you're ecstatically happy to see your fiancé,' he said with a tone edged in steel.

CHAPTER NINE

ZACCHEO WATCHED MYRIAD expressions chase across her face. Rebellion. Irritation. Sexual awareness. A touch of embarrassment when someone shouted their appreciation of her singing from across the room. One glance from Zaccheo silenced that inebriated guest.

But it was the shadows that lurked in her eyes that made his jaw clench. All day, through the heady challenge of getting back into the swing of business life, that look in her eyes when she'd seen his last clause in the prenuptial agreement had played on his mind. Not enough to disrupt his day, but enough for him to keep replaying the scene. Her reaction had been extreme and almost…distressed.

Yes, it bothered him that she saw making a family with him abhorrent, even though he'd known going in that, had she been given a choice, Eva would've chosen someone else, someone more *worthy* to father her children. Nevertheless, her reaction had struck hard in a place he'd thought was no longer capable of feeling hurt.

The feeling had festered, like a burr under his skin, eating away at him as the day had progressed. Until he'd abruptly ended a videoconference and walked out of his office.

He'd intended to return home and help himself to fine whisky in a toast to striking the first blow in ending Oscar Pennington's existence. Instead he'd found himself swapping his business suit for a dinner jacket and striding back out of his penthouse.

The woman who'd occupied far too much of his thoughts today swayed to her seat and sat down. The pounding in his blood that had never quite subsided after that kiss in his boardroom, and increased the moment he'd entered the

VIP room and heard her singing, accelerated when his gaze dropped to her scarlet-painted lips.

Before he'd met Eva Pennington, Zaccheo had never labelled himself a possessive guy. Although he enjoyed the thrill of the chase and inevitable capture, he'd been equally thrilled to see the back of the women he'd dated, especially when the clinginess had begun.

With Eva, he'd experienced an unprecedented and very caveman-like urge to claim her, to make sure every man within striking distance knew she belonged to him. And only him. That feeling was as unsettling as it was hard to eradicate. It wasn't helped when she toyed with her champagne glass and avoided eye contact.

'I don't appreciate you messing with my schedule behind my back, Zaccheo,' she said.

He wasn't sure why the sound of his name on her lips further spiked his libido, but he wanted to hear it again. He wanted to hear it fall from her lips in the throes of passion, as he took her to the heights of ecstasy.

Dio, he was losing it. Losing sight of his objective. Which was to make sure she understood that he intended to give no quarter in making her his.

He took a bracing sip of champagne and nodded to the hovering waiters ready to serve the meal he'd ordered.

'It was dinner here or summoning you back to the penthouse. You should be thanking me for bending like this.'

She glared. 'You really are a great loss to the Dark Ages, you know that?'

'In time you'll learn that I always get my way, Eva. *Always.*'

Her eyes met his and that intense, inexplicable connection that had throbbed between them right from the very start pulled, tightened.

'Did it even occur to you that I may have said yes if you'd asked me to have dinner with you?'

Surprise flared through him, and he found himself asking, 'Would you?'

She shrugged. 'I guess you'll never know. We need to discuss the prenup,' she said.

He knew instinctively that she was about to refuse him again. A different sort of heat bloomed in his chest. 'This isn't the time or place.'

'I don't...' She paused when the waiters arrived at the table with their first course. As if recalling where they were, she glanced round, took a deep breath, and leaned forward. 'I won't sign it.'

Won't, not *can't*, as she'd said before.

Bitterness surged through his veins. 'Because the thought of my seed growing inside you fills you with horror?'

Her fingers convulsed around her knife, but, true to her breeding, she directed it to her plate with understated elegance to cut her steak.

'Why would you want me as the mother of your children, anyway? I would've thought you'd want to spare yourself such a vivid reminder of what you've been through.'

'Perhaps I'm the one to give the Pennington name the integrity it's been so sorely lacking thus far.'

She paled, and he cursed himself for pursuing a subject that was better off discussed in private. Although he'd made sure their table was roped off and their conversation couldn't be overheard, there was still more than enough interest in them for each expression flitting across Eva's face to be captured and assessed.

'So we're your personal crusade?' she asked, a brittle smile appearing on her face as she acknowledged someone over his shoulder.

'Let's call it more of an experiment.'

Her colour rose with the passionate fury that intrigued him. 'You'd father children based on an *experiment*? After what you've been through...what we've both been through, you think that's fair to the children you intend to have to be used solely as a means for you to prove a point?' Her voice was ragged and he tensed.

'Eva—'

'No, I won't be a part of it!' Her whisper was fierce. 'My mother may have loved me in her own way, but I was still the tool she used against my father when it suited her. If my grades happened to be better than Sophie's, she would imply my father was lacking in some way. And believe me, my father didn't pull his punches when the situation was reversed.' She swallowed and raised bruised eyes to his. 'Even if I cou—wanted to why would I knowingly subject another child to what I went through? Why would I give you a child simply to use to *prove a point*?'

'You mistake my meaning. I don't intend to fail my children or use them as pawns. I intend to be there for them through thick and thin, unlike my parents were for me.' He stopped when her eyes widened. 'Does that surprise you?'

'I… Yes.'

He shrugged, even though it occurred to him that he'd let his guard down more with her than he ever had with anyone. But she had no power to hurt him. She'd already rejected him once. This time he knew the lay of the land going in. So it didn't matter if she knew his parental ambitions for the children they'd have.

'My children will be my priority, although I'll be interested to see how your family fares with being shown that things can be done differently. The *right* way.'

He watched her digest his response, watched the shadows he was beginning to detest mount in her eyes. He decided against probing further. There'd been enough turbulent emotions today. He suspected there would be further fireworks when she found out the new business negotiations he'd commenced this afternoon.

That a part of him was looking forward to it made him shift in his seat.

Since when had he craved verbal conflict with a woman?

Never. And yet he couldn't seem to help himself when it came to Eva.

He was debating this turn of events as their plates were removed when a throat cleared next to them.

The man was around his age, with floppy brown hair and a cocky smile that immediately rubbed Zaccheo the wrong way.

'Can I join you for a few minutes?' he asked.

The *no* that growled up Zaccheo's chest never made it. Eva was smiling—her first genuine smile since he'd walked in—and nodding. 'Mr Preston, of course!'

'Thanks. And call me Ziggy, please. Mr Preston is my headmaster grandfather.'

'What can we do for you, *Ziggy*?' Zaccheo raised an eyebrow at the furious look Eva shot him.

The other man, who was staring at Eva with an avidness that made Zaccheo's fist clench, finally looked in his direction. 'I came to pay my compliments to your girlfriend. She has an amazing voice.'

Eva blushed at his words.

Zaccheo's eyes narrowed when he noticed she wasn't wearing her engagement ring. 'Eva's my fiancée, not my girlfriend. And I'm very much aware of her exceptional talent,' he said, the harsh edge to his voice getting through to the man, who looked from him to Eva before his smile dimmed.

'Ah, congratulations are in order, then?'

'*Grazie,*' Zaccheo replied. 'Was there something else you wanted?'

'Zaccheo!' Eva glared harder, and turned to Ziggy. 'Pardon my *fiancé*. He's feeling a little testy because—'

'I want her all to myself but find other *things* standing in my way. And because you're not wearing your engagement ring, *dolcezza*.'

She covered her bare fingers with her hand, as if that would remove the evidence of the absence of his ring. 'Oh,

I didn't want to risk losing it. I'm still getting used to it.' The glance she sent him held a mixture of defiance and entreaty.

Ziggy cleared his throat again. 'I don't want to play the *Do-you-know-who-I-am?* card, but—'

'Of course I know who you are,' Eva replied with a charming laugh.

Ziggy smiled and produced a business card. 'In that case, would you like to come to my studio next week? See if we can make music together?'

Eva's pleased gasp further darkened Zaccheo's mood. 'Of course I can—'

'Aren't you forgetting something, *luce mio?*' he asked in a quietly lethal tone.

'What?' she asked, so innocently he wanted to grab her from the chair, spread her across the table and make her see nothing, no one, but him. Make her recall that she had given her word to be his and only his.

'You won't be available next week.' He didn't care that he hadn't yet apprised her of the details. He cared that she was smiling at another man as if *he* didn't exist. 'We'll be on our honeymoon on my private island off the coast of Brazil where we'll be staying for the next two weeks.'

Her eyes rounded, but she recovered quickly and took the business card. 'I'll *make* time to see you before I go. Surely you don't want to deny me this opportunity, *darling?*' Her gaze swung to him, daring him to respond in the negative.

Despite his irritation, Zaccheo curbed a smile. 'Of course. Anything for you, *dolcezza.*'

Ziggy beamed. 'Great! I look forward to it.'

The moment he was out of earshot, she turned to Zaccheo. 'How dare you try and sabotage me like that?'

'Watching you smile at another man like that fills me with insane jealousy. It also brings out the jerk in me. My apologies,' he growled. Her mouth dropped open. 'Close your mouth, Eva.'

She shook her head as if reeling from a body blow.

Welcome to my world.

'Where's your ring?' He stared at her, his control on a knife-edge.

Perhaps sensing the dangerously shifting currents, she pulled up the gold chain that hung between her pert, full breasts. His ring dangled from it.

'Put it on. Now,' he said, struggling to keep his voice even.

Undoing the clasp, she took the ring off the chain and slid it back on her finger. 'There. Can I return to work now or are you going to harangue me about something else?'

He told himself he did it because he needed to put his rampaging emotions *somewhere*. That it was her fault for pushing him to his limit. But when he plucked her from her seat, placed her in his lap and kissed her insanely tempting mouth, Zaccheo knew it was because he couldn't help himself. She *got* to him in a way no one else did.

By the time he pulled away, they were both breathing hard. Her high colour filled him with immense satisfaction, helping him ignore his own hopeless loss of control.

'Don't take the ring off again, Eva. You underestimate the lengths I'm prepared to go to in making sure you stick to your word, but for your sake I hope you start taking me seriously.'

In contrast to the vividness of Zaccheo's presence, the rest of the night passed in a dull blur after he left. By the time Eva collapsed into bed in the early hours, her head throbbed with the need to do something severely uncharacteristic. Like scream. Beat her fists against the nearest wall. Shout her anger and confusion to the black skies above.

She did nothing of the sort. More than anything, she craved a little peace and quiet.

After that kiss in the club, even more eyes had followed her wherever she went. Hushed whispers had trailed her to the bathroom. By the time her shift had ended three hours later, she'd been ready to walk out and never return.

She wouldn't, of course. Working at Siren gave her the free time to write her songs while earning enough to live on. Despite Zaccheo's heavy-handedness, she could never see a time when she'd be dependent on anyone other than herself.

'You underestimate the lengths I'm prepared to go to...'

The forceful statement had lingered long after he'd left, anchored by the heavy presence of the prenuptial agreement in her handbag.

He'd said he wouldn't negotiate. Eva didn't see that he had a choice in this matter. Refusing to marry him might well spell the end for her father, but withholding the truth and marrying him knowing she could never fulfil her part of the bargain would be much worse.

Turning in bed, she punched her pillow, dreading the long, restless night ahead. Only to wake with sunshine streaming through the window and her clock announcing it was ten o'clock.

Rushing out of bed, she showered quickly and entered the dining room just as Romeo was exiting, having finished his own breakfast. The table was set for one and Eva cursed herself for the strange dip in her belly that felt very much like disappointment.

'Good morning. Shall I get the chef to make you a cooked breakfast?' The man whose role she was beginning to suspect went deeper than a simple second-in-command asked.

'Just some toast and tea, please, thank you.'

He nodded and started to leave.

'Is Zaccheo around or has he left for the office?'

'Neither. He left this morning for Oman. An unexpected hiccup in the construction of his building there.'

Eva was unprepared for the bereft feeling that swept through her. She should be celebrating her temporary reprieve. Finding a way to see if she could work around that impossible clause. 'When will he be back?'

'In a day or two. Latest by the end of the week to be ready in time for the wedding,' Romeo said in that deep, modulated voice of his. 'This is for you.' He handed her a folded note and left.

The bold scrawl was unmistakeably Zaccheo's.

Eva,

Treat my absence as you wish, but never as an excuse to be complacent.

My PA will be in touch with details of your wedding dress fitting this morning and your amended schedule for the week.

You have my permission to miss me.

Z

Ugh! She grimaced at the arrogance oozing from the paper. Balling the note, she flung it across the table. Then quickly jumped up and retrieved it before Romeo returned. The last thing she wanted was for him to report her loss of temper to Zaccheo.

Her traitorous body had a hard enough time controlling itself when Zaccheo was around. She didn't want him to know he affected her just as badly when he was absent.

By the time breakfast was delivered, she'd regained her composure. Which was just as well, because close on the chef's heel was a tall, striking brunette dressed in a grey pencil skirt and matching jacket.

'Good morning, my name is Anyetta, Mr Giordano's PA. He said you were expecting me?'

'I was expecting a phone call, not a personal visit.'

Anyetta delivered a cool smile. 'Mr Giordano wanted his wishes attended to personally.'

Eva's appetite fled. 'I bet he did,' she muttered.

She poured herself a cup of tea as Anyetta proceeded to fill up her every spare hour between now and Saturday morning.

Eva listened until her temper began to flare, then tuned

out until she heard the word *makeover.* 'I've already had one makeover. I don't need another one.'

Anyetta's eyes drifted over Eva's hair, which she admitted was a little wild since she hadn't brushed it properly before she'd rushed out to speak to Zaccheo. 'Not even for your wedding day?'

Since there wasn't likely to be a wedding day once she told Zaccheo she had no intention of signing the agreement, she replied, 'It'll be taken care of.'

Anyetta ticked off a few more items, verified that Eva's passport was up to date, then stood as the doorbell rang. 'That'll be Margaret with your wedding dress.'

The feeling of being on a runaway train intensified as Eva trailed Anyetta out of the dining room. She drew to a stunned halt when she saw the middle-aged woman coming towards her with a single garment bag and a round veil and shoebox.

'Please tell me you don't have a team of assistants lurking outside ready to jump on me?' she asked after Anyetta left.

Margaret laughed. 'It's just me, Lady Pennington. Your fiancé was very specific about his wishes, and, meeting you now, I see why he chose this dress. He did say I was to work with you, of course. So if you don't like it, we can explore other options.'

Eva reminded herself that this situation hadn't arisen out of a normal courtship, that Zaccheo choosing her wedding dress for her shouldn't upset her so much. Besides, the likelihood of this farce ever seeing the light of day was very low so she was better off just going along with it.

But despite telling herself not to care, Eva couldn't suppress her anxiety and excitement.

She gasped as the dress was revealed.

The design itself was simple and clean, but utterly breathtaking. Eva stared at the fitted white satin gown overlaid with lace and beaded with countless tiny crystals. Delicate capped sleeves extended from the sweetheart neckline and the tiniest train flared out in a beautiful arc. At the back, more crystals had been embedded in mother-of-pearl buttons that went from nape to waist. Unable to resist, Eva reached out to touch the dress, then pulled herself back.

There was no point falling in love with a dress she'd never wear. No point getting butterflies about a marriage that would never happen once she confessed her flaw to Zaccheo. Her hands fisted and she fought the desolation threatening to break free inside her.

For six years, she'd successfully not dwelt on what she could never have—a husband who cared for her and a family of her own. She'd made music her life and had found fulfilment in it. She wasn't about to let a heartbreakingly gorgeous dress dredge up agonies she'd sealed in a box marked *strictly out of bounds.*

'Are you ready to try it on?' Margaret asked.

Eva swallowed. 'Might as well.'

If the other woman found her response curious, she didn't let on. Eva avoided her gaze in the mirror as the dress was slipped over her shoulders and the delicate chiffon and lace veil was fitted into place. She mumbled her thanks as Margaret helped her into matching-coloured heels.

'Oh, I'm pleased to see we don't need to alter it in any way, Lady Pennington. It fits perfectly. Looks like your fiancé was very accurate with your measurements. You'd be surprised how many men get it wrong…'

She kept her gaze down, frightened to look at herself, as Margaret tweaked and tugged until she was happy.

Eva dared not look up in case she began to *hope* and *wish*. She murmured appropriate responses and turned this way and that when asked and breathed a sigh of relief when the ordeal was over. The moment Margaret zipped up the bag and left, Eva escaped to her suite. Putting her headphones on, she activated the music app on her tablet and proceeded to drown out her thoughts the best way she knew how.

But this time no amount of doing what she loved best could obliterate the thoughts tumbling through her head.

At seventeen when her periods had got heavier and more painful with each passing month, she'd attributed it to life's natural cycle. But when stronger painkillers had barely alleviated the pain, she'd begun to suspect something major was wrong.

Collapsing during a university lecture had finally prompted her to seek medical intervention.

The doctor's diagnosis had left her reeling.

Even then, she'd convinced herself it wasn't the end of the world, that compared to her mother's fight against cancer, a fight she'd eventually lost a year later, Eva's problem was inconsequential. Women dealt with challenging problems like hers every day. When the time came, the man she chose to spend the rest of her life with would understand and support her.

Eva scoffed at her naiveté. Scott, the first man she'd dated in the last year of university, had visibly recoiled from her when she'd mentioned her condition. She'd been so shocked by his reaction, she'd avoided him for the rest of her time at uni.

Burnt, she'd sworn off dating until she'd met George Tremayne, her fellow business intern during her brief stint at Penningtons. Flattered by his attentiveness, she'd let down her guard and gone on a few dates before he'd begun to pressure her to take things further. Her gentle rejection and confession of her condition had resulted in a scathing volley of insults, during which she'd found out exactly why her father had been pressing her to work at Penningtons after graduation.

Oscar Pennington, already secure in his conscript of Sophie as his heir, was eager to offload his remaining daughter and had lined up a list of suitable men, George Tremayne, the son of a viscount, being on the top of that list. George's near-identical reaction to Scott's had hurt twice as much, and convinced Eva once and for all that her secret was best kept to herself.

Finding out she was yet another means to an end for Zaccheo had rocked her to the core, but she'd taken consolation in the fact the secret she'd planned on revealing to him shortly after their engagement was safe.

That secret was about to be ripped open.

As she turned up the volume of her music Eva knew disclosing it to Zaccheo would be the most difficult thing she would ever do.

CHAPTER TEN

ZACCHEO SCROLLED THROUGH the missed calls from Eva on his phone as he was driven away from the private hangar. Romeo had relayed her increasingly frantic requests to reach him. Zaccheo had deliberately forbidden his number from being given to her until this morning, once he'd confirmed his return to London.

His jaw flexed as he rolled tight shoulders. The number of fires he'd put out in Oman would've wiped out a lesser man. But Zaccheo's name and ruthless nature weren't renowned for nothing, and although it'd taken three days to get the construction schedule back on track, his business partners were in no doubt that he would bring them to their knees if they strayed so much as one millimetre from the outcome he desired.

It was the same warning he'd given Oscar Pennington when he'd called yesterday and attempted an ego-stroking exercise to get Zaccheo to relent on his threats. Zaccheo had coldly reminded him of the days he'd spent in prison and invited Pennington to ask for clemency when hell froze over.

No doubt Eva's eagerness to contact him was born of the same desire as her father's. But unlike her father, the thought of speaking to Eva sent a pleasurable kick of anticipation through his blood, despite the fact that with time and distance he'd looked back on their conversations since his release with something close to dismay.

Had he really revealed all those things about his time in prison and his childhood to her?

What was even more puzzling was her reaction. She hadn't looked down her nose at him in those moments. Had in fact exhibited nothing but empathy and compassion. Pushing the bewildering thought away, he dialled her number, gratified when she picked up on the first ring.

'*Ciao*, Eva. I understand you're experiencing pre-wedding jitters.'

'You understand wrong. This wedding isn't going to happen. Not once you hear what I have to say.'

His tension increased until the knots in his shoulders felt like immoveable rocks. He breathed through the red haze blurring his vision. 'I take it you didn't miss me, then?' he taunted.

She made a sound, a cross between a huff and a sigh. 'We really need to talk, Zaccheo.'

'Nothing you say will alter my intention to make you mine tomorrow,' he warned.

She hesitated. Then, 'Zaccheo, it's important. I won't take up too much of your time. But I need to speak to you.'

He rested his head against the seat. 'You have less than twenty-four hours left as a single woman. I won't permit anything like male strippers anywhere near you, of course, but I won't be a total bore and deny you a hen party if you wish—'

'I don't want a damn hen party! What I want is five minutes of your time.'

'Are you dying of some life-threatening disease?'

'*What?* Of course not!'

'Are you afraid I won't be a good husband?' he asked, noting the raw edge to his voice, but realising how much her answer meant to him.

'Zaccheo, this is about me, not you.'

He let her non-answer slide. 'You'll be a good wife. And despite your less than auspicious upbringing, you'll be a good mother.'

He heard her soft gasp. 'How do you know that?'

'Because you're passionate when you care. You just need to channel that passion from your undeserving family to the one we will create.'

'I can't just switch my feelings towards my family off.

Everyone deserves someone who cares about them, no matter what.'

His heart kicked hard and his grip tightened around the phone as bitterness washed through him. 'Not everyone gets it, though.'

Silence thrummed. 'I'm sorry about your parents. Is… your mother still alive?' Her voice bled the compassion he'd begun to associate with her.

It warmed a place inside him even as he answered. 'That depends on who you ask. Since she relocated to the other side of the world to get away from me, I presume she won't mind if I think her dead to me.'

'But she's alive, Zaccheo. Which means there's hope. Do you really want to waste that?' Her pain-filled voice drew him up short, reminding him that she'd lost her mother.

When had this conversation turned messy and emotional?

'You were close to your mother?' he asked.

'When she wasn't busy playing up to being a Pennington, or using me to get back at my father, she was a brilliant mother. I wish… I wish she'd been a mother to both Sophie *and* me.' She laughed without humour. 'Hell, I used to wish I'd been born into another family, that my last name wasn't Pennington—' She stopped and a tense silence reigned.

Zaccheo frowned. Things weren't adding up with Eva. He'd believed her surname was one she would do just about anything for, including help cover up fraud. But in his boardroom on Monday, she'd seemed genuinely shocked and hurt by the extent of her father's duplicity. And there was also the matter of her chosen profession and the untouched money in her bank account.

A less cynical man would believe she was the exception to the abhorrent aristocratic rule…

'At least you had one parent who cared for you. You were lucky,' he said, his mind whirling with the possibility that he could be wrong.

'But that parent is gone, and I feel as if I have no one now,' she replied quietly.

The need to tell her she had him flared through his mind. He barely managed to stay silent. After a few seconds, she cleared her throat. Her next words made him wish he'd hung up.

'I haven't signed the prenup,' she blurted out. 'I'm not going to.'

Because of the last clause.

For a brief moment, Zaccheo wanted to tell her why he wanted children. That the bleak loneliness that had dogged him through his childhood and almost drowned him in prison had nearly broken him. That he'd fallen into a pit of despair when he'd realised no one would miss him should the worst happen.

His mother had emigrated to Australia with her husband rather than stay in the same city as him once Zaccheo had fully established himself in London. That had cut deeper than any rejection he'd suffered from her in the past. And although the news of his trial and sentencing had been world-wide news, Zaccheo had never once heard from the woman who'd given him life.

He could've died in prison for all his mother cared. That thought had haunted him day and night until he'd decided to do something about it.

Until he'd vowed to alter his reality, ensure he had some-one who would be proud to bear his name. Someone to whom he could pass on his legacy.

He hadn't planned for that person to be Eva Pennington until he'd read about her engagement in the file. But once he had, the decision had become iron cast.

Although this course was very much a sweeter, more last-ing experience, Zaccheo couldn't help but wonder if it was all worth the ground shifting so much beneath his feet.

Eva was getting beneath his skin. And badly.

Dio mio. Why were the feelings he'd bottled up for over two decades choosing *now* to bubble up? He exhaled harshly.

Rough and ruthless was his motto. It was what had made him the man he was today. 'You'll be in your wedding dress at noon tomorrow, ready to walk down the aisle where our six hundred guests will be—'

'*Six hundred?* You've invited six *hundred* people to the wedding?' Her husky disbelief made his teeth grind.

'You thought I intended to have a hole-in-the-wall ceremony?' A fresh wave of bitterness rolled over him. 'Or did you think my PA was spouting gibberish when she informed you of all this on Tuesday?'

'Sorry, I must've tuned out because, contrary to what you think, I don't like my life arranged for me,' she retorted. 'That doesn't change anything. I *can't* do this...'

Zaccheo frowned at the naked distress in her voice.

Eva was genuinely torn up about the prospect of giving herself to him, a common man only worthy of a few kisses but nothing as substantial as the permanent state of matrimony.

Something very much like pain gripped his chest. 'Is that your final decision? Are you backing out of our agreement?'

She remained silent for so long, he thought the line was dead. 'Unless you're willing to change the last clause, yes.'

Zaccheo detested the sudden clenching of his stomach, as if the blow he'd convinced himself would never come had been landed. The voice taunting him for feeling more than a little stunned was ruthlessly smashed away.

He assured himself he had another way to claim the justice he sought. 'Very well. *Ciao.*'

He ended the phone call. And fought the urge to hurl his phone out of the window.

Eva dropped the phone onto the coffee-shop table. She'd arrived at work only to discover she'd been taken off the roster due to her impending wedding. Since she had holiday due to her anyway, Eva hadn't fought too hard at suddenly finding herself with free time.

Her session with Ziggy yesterday had gone well, despite her head being all over the place. If nothing else came of it, she could add that to her CV.

Curbing a hysterical snort, she stared at her phone.

She'd done the right thing and ended this farce before it went too far. Before the longings she'd harboured in the last three days got any more out of control.

Deep in her heart, she knew Zaccheo would react the same way to her secret as Scott and George had. He wouldn't want to marry half a woman, especially when he'd stated his expectations in black and white in a formal agreement drafted by a team of lawyers, and then confounded her with his genuine desire to become a father.

So why hadn't she just told him over the phone?

Because she was a glutton for punishment?

Because some part of her had hoped telling him face-to-face would help her gauge whether there was a chance he would accept her the way she was?

Fat chance.

It was better this way. Clean. Painless.

She jumped as her phone pinged. Heart lurching, she accessed the message, but it was only the manageress from Siren, wishing her a lovely wedding and sinfully blissful honeymoon.

Eva curled her hand around her fast-cooling mug. Once the news got out that she'd broken her third engagement in two years, her chances of marrying anyone, let alone a man who would accept her just as she was, would shrink from nil to no chance in hell.

Pain spiked again at the reminder of her condition. Exhaling, she wrenched her mind to more tangible things.

Like finding a place to live.

She weighed her options, despair clutching her insides

when, two hours later, she faced the only avenue open to her. Going back home to Pennington Manor.

Reluctantly, she picked up her phone, then nearly dropped it when it blared to life. The name of the caller made her frown.

'Sophie?'

'Eva, what's going on?' The fear in her voice shredded Eva's heart.

'What do you mean?'

'I've just had to call the doctor because Father's had another episode!'

Eva jerked to her feet, sending her coffee cup bouncing across the table. 'What?'

'We got a call from Zaccheo Giordano an hour ago to say the wedding was off. Father's been frantic. He was about to call you when he collapsed. The doctor says if he's subjected to any more stress he could have a heart attack or a stroke. Is it true? Did you call off the wedding?' The strain in her sister's voice was unmistakeable.

'Yes,' Eva replied. She grabbed her bag and hurried out of the coffee shop when she began to attract peculiar looks. Outside, she shrugged into her coat and pulled up her hoodie to avoid the light drizzle.

'Oh, God. Why?' her sister demanded.

'Zaccheo wanted me to sign a prenuptial agreement.'

'So? Everyone does that these days.'

'One of the terms...he wants *children*.'

Her sister sighed. 'So he backed out when you told him?'

'No, he doesn't know.'

'But... I'm confused,' Sophie replied.

'I tried to tell him but he wouldn't listen.'

'You tried. Isn't that enough?'

Eva ducked into a quiet alley and leaned against a wall. 'No, it's *not* enough. We've caused enough harm where he's concerned. I won't go into this based on a lie.'

'Father's terrified, Eva.'

'Can I talk to him?'

'He's sleeping now. I'll let him know you called when he wakes up.' Sophie paused. 'Eva, I've been thinking…what you said on Saturday, about you not being out to replace me… I shouldn't have bitten your head off. It's just… Father isn't an easy man to please. He was relying on me to see us through this rough patch…'

'I didn't mean to step on your toes, Sophie.'

Her sister inhaled deeply. 'I know. But everything seems so effortless for you, Eva. It always has. I envied you because Mother chose you—'

'Parents shouldn't choose which child to love and which to keep at arm's length!'

'But that was our reality. He wanted a son. And I was determined to be that son. After Mother died, I was scared Father would think I wasn't worth his attention.'

'You were. You still are.'

'Only because I've gone along with whatever he's asked of me without complaint, even when I knew I shouldn't. This thing with Zaccheo… Father's not proud of it. Nor am I. I don't know where we go from here, but once we're through this, can we get together?' Sophie asked, her voice husky with the plea.

Eva didn't realise her legs had given way until her bottom touched the cold, hard ground.

'Yes, if you want,' she murmured. Her hands shook as she hung up.

The last time she'd seen Sophie's rigid composure crumble had been in the few weeks after they'd buried their mother. For a while she'd had her sister back. They'd been united in their grief, supporting each other when their loss overwhelmed them.

As much as Eva missed *that* Sophie, she couldn't stomach having her back under similar circumstances. Nor could she bear the danger that her father faced.

She wasn't sure how long she sat there.

Cold seeped into her clothes. Into her bones. Into her heart.

Feeling numb, she dug into her bag and extracted the pre-nup and read through it one more time.

She couldn't honour Zaccheo's last clause, but that didn't mean she couldn't use it to buy herself, and her father, time until they met and she explained. Despite his own past, he wanted a family. Maybe he would understand why she was trying to salvage hers.

Slowly, she dialled. After endless rings, the line clicked through.

'Eva.' His voice was pure cold steel.

'I...' She attempted to say the words but her teeth still chattered. Squeezing her eyes shut, she tried again. 'I'll sign the agreement. I'll marry you tomorrow.'

Silence.

'Zaccheo? Are you there?'

'Where are you?'

She shivered at his impersonal tone. 'I'm...' She looked up at the street sign in the alley and told him.

'Romeo will be there in fifteen minutes. He'll witness the agreement and bring it to me. You'll return to the penthouse and resume preparations for the wedding.' He paused, as if waiting for her to disagree.

'Will I see you today?' She hated how weak her voice sounded.

'No.'

Eva exhaled. 'Okay, I'll wait for Romeo.'

'Bene.' The line went dead.

The grey mizzle outside aptly reflected Eva's mood as she sat, hands clasped in her lap, as the hairdresser finished putting up her hair. Behind her, Sophie smiled nervously.

Eva smiled back, knowing her sister's nervousness stemmed from the fear that Eva would change her mind again.

But this time there was no going back. She meant to come clean to Zaccheo at the first opportunity and open herself up to whatever consequences he sought.

Just how she would manage that was a puzzle she hadn't untangled yet, but since Zaccheo was hell-bent on this marriage, and she was giving him what he wanted, technically she was fulfilling her side of the bargain.

God, when had she resorted to seeing things in shades of grey instead of black and white, truth and lie? Was Zaccheo right? Did her Pennington blood mean she was destined to do whatever it took, even if it meant compromising her integrity, for the sake of her family and pedigree?

No. She wouldn't care if she woke up tomorrow as ordinary Eva Penn instead of Lady Pennington. And she *would* come clean to Zaccheo, no matter what.

Except that was looking less likely to happen *before* the wedding. Zaccheo hadn't returned to the penthouse last night. She hadn't deluded herself that he was observing the quaint marriage custom. If anything, he was probably making another billion, or actively sowing his last wild oats. She jerked at the jagged pain that shot through her.

Sophie stood up. 'What's wrong?'

'Nothing. How's Father?'

Sophie's face clouded. 'He insists he's well enough to walk you down the aisle.' Her sister's eyes darted to the hairdresser who had finished and was walking out to get Margaret. 'He's desperate that everything goes according to plan today.'

Eva managed to stop her smile from slipping. 'It will.'

Sophie met her gaze in the mirror. 'Do you think I should talk to Zaccheo...explain?'

Eva thought about the conversation she'd had with Zaccheo yesterday, the merciless tone, the ruthless man on a mission who'd been released from prison a mere week ago. 'Maybe not just yet.'

Sophie nodded, then flashed a smile that didn't quite make it before she left Eva alone as Margaret entered.

Any hopes of talking to Zaccheo evaporated when she found herself at the doors of the chapel an hour later.

Catching sight of him for the first time since Monday, she felt her heart slam around her chest.

Romeo stood in the best-man position and Eva wondered again at the connection between the two men. Did Zaccheo have any friends? Or had he lost all of them when her family's actions had altered his fate?

The thought flitted out of her head as her gaze returned almost magnetically to Zaccheo.

He'd eschewed a morning coat in favour of a bespoke three-piece suit in the softest dove-grey silk. Against the snowy white shirt and white tie completing the ensemble, his long hair was at once dangerously primitive and yet so utterly captivating, her mouth dried as her pulse danced with a dark, decadent delight. His beard had been trimmed considerably and a part of her mourned its loss. Perhaps it was that altered look that made his eyes so overwhelmingly electrifying, or it was the fact that his face was set in almost brutal lines, but the effect was like lightning to her system the moment her eyes connected with his.

The music in the great hall of the cathedral he'd astonishingly managed to secure on such short notice disappeared, along with the chatter of the goggle-eyed guests who did nothing to hide their avid curiosity.

All she could see was him, the man who would be her husband in less than fifteen minutes.

She stumbled, then stopped. A murmur rose in the crowd. Eva felt her father's concerned stare, but she couldn't look away from Zaccheo.

His nostrils flared, his eyes narrowing in warning as fear clutched her, freezing her feet.

'Eva?' Her father's ragged whisper caught her consciousness.

'Why did you insist on walking me down the aisle?' she asked him, wanting in some way to know that she wasn't doing all of this to save a man who had very little regard for her.

'What? Because you're my daughter,' her father replied with a puzzled frown.

'So you're not doing it just to keep up appearances?'

His face creased with a trace of the vulnerability she'd glimpsed only once before, when her mother died, and her heart lurched. 'Eva, I haven't handled things well. I know that. I was brought up to put the family name above all else, and I took that responsibility a little too far. Despite our less than perfect marriage, your mother was the one who would pull me back to my senses when I went a little too far. Without her...' His voice roughened and his hand gripped hers. 'We might lose Penningtons, but I don't want to lose you and Sophie.'

Eva's throat clogged. 'Maybe you should tell her that? She needs to know you're proud of her, Father.'

Her father looked to where her sister stood, and he nodded. 'I will. And I'm proud of you, too. You're as beautiful as your mother was on our wedding day.'

Eva blinked back her tears as murmurs rose in the crowd.

She turned to find Zaccheo staring at her. Something dark, sinister, curled through his eyes and she swallowed as his mouth flattened.

I can't marry him without him knowing! He deserves to know that I can't give him the family he wants.

'My dear, you need to move now. It's time,' her father pleaded.

Torn by the need for Zaccheo to know the truth and the need to protect her father, she shook her head, her insides churning.

Churning turned into full-blown liquefying as Zaccheo stepped from the dais, his imposing body threatening to block out the light as he headed down the aisle.

She desperately sucked in a breath, the knowledge that Zaccheo would march her up the aisle himself if need be finally scraping her feet from the floor. He stopped halfway, his gaze unswerving, until she reached him.

He grasped her hand, his hold unbreakable as he turned and walked her to the altar.

Trembling at the hard, pitiless look in his eyes, she swallowed and tried to speak. 'Zaccheo—'

'No, Eva. No more excuses,' he growled.

The priest glanced between them, his expression benign but enquiring.

Zaccheo nodded.

The organ swelled. And sealed her fate.

CHAPTER ELEVEN

'GLARING AT IT won't make it disappear, unless you have superhero laser vision.'

Eva jumped at the mocking voice and curled her fingers into her lap, hiding the exquisite diamond-studded platinum ring that had joined her engagement ring three hours ago.

'I wasn't willing it away.' On the contrary, she'd been wondering how long it would stay on her finger once Zaccheo knew the truth.

The reception following the ceremony had been brief but intense. Six hundred people clamouring for attention and the chance to gawp at the intriguing couple could take a lot out of a girl. With Zaccheo's fingers laced through hers the whole time, tightening commandingly each time she so much as moved an inch away from him, Eva had been near-blubbering-wreck status by the time their limo had left the hall.

Once she'd stopped reeling from the shock of being married to Zaccheo Giordano, she'd taken a moment to take in her surroundings. The Great Hall in the Guildhall was usually booked for years in advance. That Zaccheo had managed to secure it in a week and thrown together a stunning reception was again testament that she'd married a man with enough power and clout to smash through any resistance.

Zaccheo, despite his spell in prison, remained a formidable man, one, she suspected, who didn't need her father's intervention to restore his damaged reputation. So why was he pursuing it so relentlessly? Throughout the reception, she'd watched him charm their guests with the sheer force of his charisma. By the time her father had got round to giving the edifying toast welcoming Zaccheo to the Pennington family, the effort had seemed redundant.

She watched Zaccheo now as the car raced them to the airport, and wondered if it was a good time to broach the subject burning a hole in her chest.

'Something on your mind?' he queried without raising his gaze from his tablet.

Her heart leapt into her throat. She started to speak but noticed the partition between them and Romeo, who sat in the front passenger seat, was open. Although she was sure Romeo knew the ins and outs of the document he'd been asked to witness yesterday, Eva wasn't prepared to discuss her devastating shortcomings in his presence.

So she opted for something else plaguing her. She smoothed her hands on her wedding dress. 'Do I have your assurance that you'll speak on my father's behalf once you hand over the documents to the authorities?'

He speared her with incisive grey eyes. 'You're so eager to see him let off the hook, aren't you?'

'Wouldn't you be, if it was your father?' she asked.

Eva was unprepared for the strange look that crossed his face. The mixture of anger, sadness, and bitterness hollowed out her stomach.

'My father wasn't interested in being let off the hook for his sins. He was happy to keep himself indebted to his betters because he thought that was his destiny.'

Her breath caught. 'What? That doesn't make sense.'

'Very little of my father's actions made sense to me, not when I was a child, and not as an adult.'

The unexpected insight into his life made her probe deeper. 'When did he die?'

'When I was thirteen years old.'

'I'm sorry.' When he inclined his head and continued to stare at her, she pressed her luck. 'How did he—?'

'Zaccheo,' Romeo's deep voice interrupted them. 'Perhaps this is not a subject for your wedding day?'

A look passed between the friends.

When Zaccheo looked at her again, that cool impassivity he'd worn since they'd left the reception to thunderous applause had returned.

'Your father has done his part adequately for now. Our lawyers will meet in a few days to discuss the best way forward. When my input is needed, I'll provide it. *Your* role, on the other hand, is just beginning.'

Before she could reply, the door opened. Eva gaped at the large private jet standing mere feet away. Beside the steps, two pilots and two stewardesses waited.

Zaccheo exited and took her hand. The shocking electricity of his touch and the awareness in his eyes had her scrambling to release her fingers, but he held on, and walked her to his crew, who extended their congratulations.

Eva was grappling with their conversation when she stepped into the unspeakable luxury of the plane. To the right, a sunken entertainment area held a semicircular cream sofa and a separate set of club chairs with enough gadgets to keep even the most attention-deficient passenger happy. In a separate area a short flight of stairs away, there was a conference table with four chairs and a bar area off a top-line galley.

Zaccheo stepped behind her and her body zapped to life, thrilling to his proximity. She suppressed a shiver when he let go of her fingers and cupped her shoulders in his warm hands.

'I have several conference calls to make once we take off. And you…' He paused, traced a thumb across her cheek. The contact stunned her, as did the gentle look in his eyes. 'You look worn out.'

'Is that a kind way of saying I look like hell?' She strove for a light tone and got a husky one instead.

That half-smile appeared, and Eva experienced something close to elation that the icy look had melted from his face. 'You could never look like hell, *cara*. A prickly and challenging puzzle that I look forward to unravelling, most definitely. But never like hell.'

The unexpected response startled her into gaping for several seconds before she recovered. 'Should I be wary that you're being nice to me?'

'I can be less…monstrous when I get my way.'

The reminder that he wouldn't be getting his way and the thought of his reaction once he found out brought a spike of anxiety, rendering her silent as he led her to a seat and handed her a flute of champagne from the stewardess's tray.

'Zaccheo…' She stopped when his thumb moved over her lips. Sensation sizzled along her nerve endings, setting her pulse racing as he brushed it back and forth. The heat erupting between her thighs had her pressing her legs together to soothe the desperate ache.

She hardly felt the plane take off. All she was aware of was the mesmerising look in Zaccheo's eyes.

'I haven't told you how stunning you look.' He leaned closer and replaced his thumb with his lips at the corner of her mouth.

Delicious flames warmed her blood. 'Thank you.' Her voice shook with the desire moving through her. More than anything, she was filled with the blind need to turn her head and meet his mouth with hers.

When his lips trailed to her jaw, then to the curve between her shoulder and neck, Eva let out a helpless moan, her heart racing with sudden, debilitating hunger.

His fingers linked hers and she found herself being led to the back of the plane. Eva couldn't summon a protest. Nor could she remind herself that she needed to come clean, sooner rather than later.

The master bedroom was equally stunning. Gold leaf threaded a thick cream coverlet on a king-sized bed and plush carpeting absorbed their footsteps as he shut the door.

'I intend us to have two uninterrupted weeks on the island. In order for that to happen, I need to work with Romeo to clear my plate work-wise. Rest now. Whatever's on your mind can wait for a few more hours.' Again there was no bite to his words, leaving her lost as to this new side of the man she'd married.

She stood, almost overpowered by the strength of her emotions, as he positioned himself behind her and slowly undid her buttons. The heavy dress pooled at her feet and she stood in only her white strapless bra, panties, and the garter and sheer stocking set that had accompanied her dress.

A rough, tortured sound echoed around the room. *'Stai mozzafiato,'* Zaccheo muttered thickly. 'You're breathtaking,' he translated when she glanced at him.

A fierce blush flared up. Eyes darkening, he circled her, tracing her high colour with a barest tip of his forefinger. Her gaze dropped to the sensual line of his mouth and she bit her own lip as need drowned her.

She gasped, completely enthralled, as he dropped to his knees and reached for her garter belt, eyes locked on hers. He pulled it off and tucked it deep in his inner pocket. When he stood, the hunger on his face stopped her breath, anticipation sparking like fireworks through her veins.

He lightly brushed her lips with his.

'Our first time won't be on a plane within listening distance of my staff.' He walked to the bed and pulled back the covers. He waited until she got in and tucked her in. About to walk away, he suddenly stopped. 'We will make this marriage work, Eva.'

Her mouth parted but, with no words to counter that unexpected vow, she slowly pressed her lips together as pain ripped through her.

'Sleep well, *dolcezza,*' he murmured, then left.

Despite her turmoil, she slept through the whole flight, rousing refreshed if unsettled as to what the future held.

Dressing in a light cotton sundress and open sandals, she left her hair loose, applied a touch of lip gloss and sunscreen and exited the plane.

They transferred from jet to high-speed boat with Romeo at the wheel. The noise from the engine made conversation impossible but, for the first time, the silence between Zaccheo and Eva felt less fraught. The strange but intense feeling that had engulfed them both as he'd undressed her on the plane continued to grip them as they raced towards their final destination. When she caught her hair for the umpteenth time to keep it from flying in the wind, he captured the strands in a tight grip at the base of her neck, then used the hold to pull her closer until she curved into his side. With his other arm sprawled along the back of their seat, he appeared the most at ease Eva had ever seen him.

Perhaps being forced to wait for a while to tell him hadn't been a bad thing.

She let the tension ooze out of her.

Despite the shades covering his eyes, he must have sensed her scrutiny, because he turned and stared down at her for endless minutes. She felt the power of that look to the tips of her toes and almost fell into him when he took her mouth in a voracious kiss.

He let her up for air when her lungs threatened to burst. Burying his face in her throat, he rasped for her ears only, 'I cannot wait to make you mine.'

By the time the boat slowed and pulled into a quiet inlet, Eva was a nervous wreck.

'Welcome to Casa do Paraiso,' he said once the engine died.

Enthralled, Eva looked around. Tropical trees and lush vegetation surrounded a spectacular hacienda made of timber and glass, the mid-morning sun casting vibrant shades of green, orange and blue on the breathtaking surroundings. Wide glass windows dominated the structure and, through them, Eva saw white walls and white furniture with splashes of colourful paintings on the walls perpetuated in an endless flow of rooms.

'It's huge,' she blurted.

Zaccheo jumped onto the sugary sand and grabbed her hand.

'The previous owner built it for his first wife and their eight children. She got it in the divorce, but hated the tropical heat so never visited. It was run-down by the time I bought the island from her, so I made substantial alterations.'

The mention of children ramped up the tension crawling through her belly and, despite her trying to shrug the feeling away, it lingered as she followed him up the wide front porch into the stunning living room.

A staff of four greeted them, then hurried out to where Romeo was securing the vessel. She gazed around in stunned awe, accepting that Zaccheo commanded the best when it came to the structures he put his stamp on, whether commercial or private.

'Come here, Eva.' The order was impatient.

She turned from admiring the structure to admire the man who'd created it. Tall, proud and intensely captivating, he stood at the base of a suspended staircase, his white-hot gaze gleaming dangerously, promising complete sexual oblivion.

Desire pulsed between them, a living thing that writhed, consumed with a hunger that demanded to be met, fulfilled.

Eva knew she should make time now they were here to tell him. Lay down the truth ticking away inside her like a bomb.

After years of struggling to forge a relationship with her father and sister, she'd finally laid the foundations of one today.

How could she live with herself if she continued to keep Zaccheo in the dark about the family he hoped for himself?

Her feet slapped against the large square tiles as she hurried across the room. His mouth lifted in a half-smile of satisfaction. She'd barely reached him when he swung her into his arms and stormed up the stairs.

And then the need to disclose her secret was suddenly no longer urgent. It'd been superseded by another, more pressing demand. One that every atom in her body urged her to assuage. *Now.* Before the opportunity was taken from her. Before her confession once again found her in the brutal wasteland of rejection.

His heat singed where they touched. Unable to resist, she sank her fingers into his hair and buried her face in his neck, eager to be closer to his rough primitiveness.

Feeling bold, she nipped at his skin.

His responding growl was intoxicating. As was the feeling of being pressed against the hard, masculine planes of his body when he slowly lowered her to her feet.

'I've waited so long to be inside you. I won't wait any longer,' he vowed, the words fierce, stamped with decadent intent.

Arms clamped around her waist, he walked her backwards to the vast white-sheeted bed. In one clean move, he pulled her dress over her head and dropped it. Her bra and panties swiftly followed.

Zaccheo stopped breathing as he stared down at her exposed curves.

As he'd done on the plane, he circled her body, this time trailing more fingers over her heated skin, creating a fiery path that arrowed straight between her thighs. She was swaying under the dizzying force of her arousal by the time he faced her again.

'Beautiful. So beautiful,' he murmured against her skin, then pulled her nipple into his mouth, surrounding the aching bud with heat and want.

Eva cried out and clutched his shoulders, her whole body gripped with a fever that shook her from head to toe. He moved his attention to her twin breast while his fingers teased the other, doubling the pleasure, doubling her agony.

'Zaccheo,' she groaned.

He straightened abruptly and reefed his black T-shirt over his head, exposing hard, smooth pecs and a muscle-ridged stomach. But as intensely delectable as his torso was, it wasn't what made her belly quiver. It was the intriguing tattooed band of Celtic knots linked by three slim lines that circled his upper arm. The artwork was flawless and beautiful, flowing gracefully when he moved. Reaching out, she touched the first knot. He paused and stared down at her.

It struck her hard in that moment just how much she didn't know about the man she'd married.

'You seem almost nervous, *dolcezza*.'

Eva struggled to think of a response that wouldn't make her sound gauche. 'Don't you feel nervous, even a little, your first time with a new lover?' she replied.

He froze and his lips compressed for a fraction of a second, as if she'd said something to displease him. Then his fingers went to his belt. 'Nerves, no. Anticipation that a long-held desire is about to be fulfilled? Most definitely.' He removed his remaining clothes in one swift move.

Perfection. It was the only word she could think of.

'Even when you've experienced it more than a few dozen times?'

She gasped when his fingers gripped hers in a tight hold. When he spoke, his voice held a bite that jarred. 'Perhaps we should refrain from the subject of past lovers.'

Hard, demanding lips slanted over hers, his tongue sliding into her mouth, fracturing the last of her senses. She clung to him, her body once again aflame from the ferocious power of his.

Cool sheets met her back and Zaccheo sprawled beside her. After an eternity of kissing, he raised his head.

'There are so many ways I wish to take you I don't know where to begin.'

Heat burst beneath her skin and he laughed softly.

'You blush with the ease of an innocent.' He trailed his hand down her throat, lingering at her racing pulse, before it curved around one breast. 'It's almost enough to make me forget that you're not.' Again that bite, but less ferocious this time, his accent growing thicker as he bent his head and tongued her pulse.

She jerked against him, her fingers gliding over his warm skin of their own accord. 'On what basis do you form the opinion that I'm not?' she blurted before she lost her nerve.

He stilled, grey eyes turning that rare gunmetal shade that announced a dangerously heightened emotional state. His hand abandoned her breast and curled around her nape in an iron grip. 'What are you saying, Eva?' His voice was a hoarse rumble.

She licked nervous lips. 'That I don't want to be treated like I'm fragile…but I don't wish my first time to be without mercy either.'

He sucked in a stunned breath. 'Your *first*… *Madre di Dio.*' His gaze searched hers, his breathing growing increasingly erratic.

Slowly, he drew back from her, scouring her body from head to toe as if seeing her for the first time. He parted her thighs and she moved restlessly, helplessly, as his eyes lingered at her centre. Stilling her with one hand, he lowered his head and kissed her eyes, her mouth, her throat. Then lower until he reached her belly. He licked at her navel, then rained kisses on her quivering skin. Firm hands held her open, then his shoulders took over the job. Reading his intention, she raised her head from the pillow.

'Zaccheo.' She wasn't sure whether she was pleading for or rejecting what was coming.

He reared up for a second, his hands going to his hair to twist the long strands into an expert knot at the back of his head. The act was so unbelievably hot, her body threatened to melt into a useless puddle. Then he was back, broad shoulders easily holding her legs apart as he kissed his way down her inner thighs.

'I know what I crave most,' he muttered thickly. 'A taste of you.'

The first touch of his mouth at her core elicited a long, helpless groan from her. Her spine arched off the bed, her thighs shaking as fire roared through her body. He held her down and feasted on her, the varying friction from his mouth and beard adding an almost unholy pleasure that sent her soaring until a scream ripped from her throat and she fell off the edge of the universe.

She surfaced to feel his mouth on her belly, his hands trailing up her sides. That gunmetal shade of grey reflected deep possession as he rose above her and kissed her long and deep.

'Now, *il mio angelo*. Now I make you mine.'

He captured her hands above her head with one hand. The other reached between her thighs, gently massaging her core before he slid one finger inside her tight sheath. His groan echoed hers. Removing his finger, he probed her sex with his thick shaft, murmuring soft, soothing words as he pushed himself inside her.

'Easy, *dolcezza*.'

Another inch increased the burn, but the hunger rushing through her wouldn't be denied. Her fingers dug into his back, making him growl. 'Zaccheo, please.'

'*Sì*, let me please you.' He uttered a word that sounded like an apology, a plea.

Then he pushed inside her. The dart of pain engulfed her, lingered for a moment. Tears filled her eyes. Zaccheo cursed, then kissed them away, murmuring softly in Italian.

He thrust deeper, slowly filling her. Eva saw the strain etched on his face.

'Zaccheo?'

'I want this to be perfect for you.'

'It won't be unless you move, I suspect.'

That half-smile twitched, then stretched into a full, heart-stopping smile. Eva's eyes widened at the giddy dance her heart performed on seeing the wave of pleasure transform his face. Her own mouth curved in response and a feeling unfurled inside her, stealing her breath with its awesome power. Shakily, she raised her hand and touched his face, slid her fingers over his sensual mouth.

He moved. Withdrew and thrust again.

She gasped, her body caught in a maelstrom of sensation so turbulent, she feared she wouldn't emerge whole.

Slowly his smile disappeared, replaced by a wild, predatory hunger. He quickened the pace and her hands moved to his hair, slipping the knot free and burying her fingers in the thick, luxurious tresses. When her hips moved of their own accord, meeting him in an instinctive dance, he groaned deep and sucked one nipple into his mouth. Drowning in sensation, she felt her world begin to crumble. The moment he captured her twin nipple, a deep tremor started inside her. It built and built, then exploded in a shower of lights.

'*Perfetto.*'

Zaccheo sank his fingers into Eva's wild, silky hair, curbing the desire to let loose the primitive roar bubbling within him.

Mine. Finally, completely mine.

Instead he held her close until her breathing started to return to normal, then he flipped their positions and arranged her on top of him.

He was hard to the point of bursting, but he was determined to make this experience unforgettable for her. Seeing his ring on her finger, that primitive response rose again, stunning him with the strength of his desire to claim her.

His words on the plane slashed through his mind.

Si, he *did* want this to work. Perhaps Eva had been right. Perhaps there was still time to salvage a piece of his soul...

Her eyes met his and a sensual smile curled her luscious mouth. Before he could instruct her, she moved, taking him deeper inside her before she rose. Knowing he was fast losing the ability to think, he met her second thrust. Her eyes widened, her skin flushing that alluring shade of pink as she chased the heady sensation. Within minutes, they were both panting.

Reaching down, he teased her with his thumb and watched

her erupt in bliss. Zaccheo followed her, his shout announcing the most ferocious release he'd experienced in his life.

Long after Eva had collapsed on top of him, and slipped into an exhausted sleep, he lay awake.

Wondering why his world hadn't righted itself.

Wondering what the hell this meant for him.

CHAPTER TWELVE

EVA CAME AWAKE to find herself splayed on top of Zaccheo's body.

The sun remained high in the sky so she knew she hadn't slept for more than an hour or two. Nevertheless, the thought that she'd dropped into a coma straight after sex made her cringe.

She risked a glance and found grey eyes examining her with that half-smile she was growing to like a little more than she deemed wise.

He brushed a curl from her cheek and tucked it behind her ear. The gentleness in the act fractured her breathing.

'Ciao, dolcezza.'

'I didn't mean to fall asleep on you,' she said, then immediately felt gauche for not knowing the right after-sex etiquette.

He quirked a brow. 'Oh? Who did you mean to fall asleep on?' he asked.

She jerked up. 'No, that's not what I meant...' she started to protest, then stopped when she saw the teasing light in his eyes.

She started to settle back down, caught a glimpse of his chiselled pecs and immediately heat built inside her. A little wary of how quickly she was growing addicted to his body, she attempted to slide off him.

He stopped her with one hand at her nape, the other on her hip. The action flexed his arm and Eva's gaze was drawn to the tattoo banding his upper arm.

'Does this have a special meaning?'

His smile grew a little stiffer. 'It's a reminder not to accept less than I'm worth or compromise on what's important to me. And a reminder that, contrary to what the privileged would have us believe, all men are born equal. It's power that is wielded unequally.'

Eva thought of the circumstances that had brought her to this place, of the failings of her own family and the sadness she'd carried for so long, but now hoped to let go of.

'You wield more than enough share of power. Men cower before you.'

A frown twitched his forehead. 'If they do, it is their weakness, not mine.'

She gave an incredulous laugh. 'Are you saying you don't know you intimidate people with just a glance?'

His frown cleared. 'You're immune to this intimidation you speak of. To my memory, you've been disagreeable more often than not.'

She traced the outline of the tattoo, revelling in the smooth warmth of his skin. 'I've never been good at heeding bellowed commands.'

The hand on her hip tightened. 'I do not bellow.'

'Maybe not. But sometimes the effect is the same.'

She found herself flipped over onto her back, Zaccheo crouched over her like a lethal bird of prey. 'Is that why you hesitated as you walked down the aisle?' he asked in a harsh whisper. The look in his eyes was one of almost…hurt.

Quickly she shook her head. 'No, it wasn't.'

'Then what was it? You thought that I wasn't good enough, perhaps?' he pressed. And again she glimpsed a hint of vulnerability in his eyes that caught at a weak place in her heart.

She opened her mouth to *finally* tell him. To lay herself bare to the scathing rejection that would surely follow her confession.

The words stuck in her throat.

What she'd experienced in Zaccheo's bed had given her a taste that was unlike anything she'd ever felt before. The need to hold on to that for just a little while longer slammed into her, knocking aside her good intentions.

Eva knew she was playing with volcanic fire, that the eventual eruption would be devastating. But for once in her life, she wanted to be selfish, to experience a few moments of unfettered abandon. She could have that.

She'd sacrificed herself for this marriage, but in doing so she'd also been handed a say in when it ended.

And it would be sooner rather than later, because she couldn't stand in the way of what he wanted…what he'd been deprived of his whole life…a proper family of his own.

She also knew Zaccheo would want nothing to do with her once he knew the truth. Sure, he wasn't as monstrous as he would have others believe, but that didn't mean he would shackle himself to a wife who couldn't give him what he wanted.

She squashed the voice that cautioned she was naively burying her head in the sand.

Was it really so wrong if she chose to do it just for a little while?

Could she not live in bliss for a few days? Gather whatever memories she could and hang on to them for when the going got tough?

'Eva?'

'I had a father-daughter moment, plus bridal nerves,' she blurted. He raised a sceptical eyebrow and she smiled. 'Every woman is entitled to have a moment. Mine was thirty seconds of hesitation.'

'You remained frozen for five *minutes*,' he countered.

'Just time enough for anyone who'd been dozing off to wake up,' she responded, wide-eyed.

The tension slowly eased out of his body and his crooked smile returned. Relief poured through her and she fell into the punishing kiss he delivered to assert his displeasure at her hesitation.

She was clinging to him by the time he pulled away, and Eva was ready to protest when he swung out of bed. Her protest died when she got her first glimpse of his impressive manhood, and the full effect of the man attached to it.

Dry-mouthed and heart racing, she stared. And curled her fingers into the sheets to keep from reaching for him.

'If you keep looking at me like that, our shower will have to be postponed. And our lunch will go cold.'

A blush stormed up her face.

He laughed and scooped her up. 'But I'm glad that my body is not displeasing to you.'

She rolled her eyes. *As if.* 'False humility isn't an attractive trait, Zaccheo,' she chided as he walked them through a wide door and onto an outdoor bamboo-floored shower. Despite the rustic effects, the amenities were of the highest quality, an extra-wide marble bath sitting opposite a multi-jet shower, with a shelf holding rows upon rows of luxury bath oils and gels.

Above their heads, a group of macaws warbled throatily, then flew from one tree to the next, their stunning colours streaking through the branches.

As tropical paradises went, Eva was already sure this couldn't be topped, and she had yet to see the rest of it.

Zaccheo set her down and grabbed a soft washcloth. 'Complete compatibility in bed isn't a common thing, despite what magazines would have you believe,' he said.

'I wouldn't know.' There was no point pretending otherwise. He had first-hand knowledge of her innocence.

His eyes flared with possession as he turned on the jets and pulled her close.

'No, you wouldn't. And if that knowledge pleases me to the point of being labelled a caveman, then so be it.'

They ate a sumptuous lunch of locally caught fish served with pine-nut sauce and avocado salad followed by a serving of fruit and cheeses.

After lunch, Zaccheo showed her the rest of the house and the three-square-kilometre island. They finished the trek on the white sandy beach where a picnic had been laid out with champagne chilling in a silver bucket.

Eva popped a piece of papaya in her mouth and sighed at the beauty of the setting sun casting orange and purple streaks across the aquamarine water. 'I don't know how you can ever bear to leave this place.'

'I learned not to grow attached to things at an early age.'

The crisp reply had her glancing over at him. His shades were back in place so she couldn't read his eyes, but his body showed no signs of the usual forbidding *do not disturb* signs so she braved the question. 'Why?'

'Because it was better that way.'

She toyed with the stem of her champagne flute. 'But it's also a lonely existence.'

Broad shoulders lifted in an easy shrug. 'I had a choice of being lonely or just…solitary. I chose the latter.'

Her heart lurched at the deliberate absence of emotion from his voice. 'Zaccheo—'

He reared up from where he'd been lounging on his elbows, his mouth set in a grim line. 'Don't waste your time feeling sorry for me, *dolcezza*,' he said, his voice a hard snap that would've intimidated her, had she allowed it.

'I wasn't,' she replied. 'I'm not naive enough to imagine everyone has a rosy childhood. I know I didn't.'

'You mean the exclusive country-club memberships, the top boarding schools, the winters in Verbier weren't enough?' Despite the lack of contempt in his voice this time round, Eva felt sad that they were back in this place again.

'Don't twist my words. Those were just *things*, Zaccheo. And before you accuse me of being privileged, yes, I was. My childhood was hard, too, but I couldn't help the family I was born into any more than you could.'

'Was that why you moved out of Pennington Manor?'

'After my mother died, yes. Two against one became unbearable.'

'And the father-daughter moment you spoke of? Did that help?' he asked, watching her with a probing look.

A tiny bit of hope blossomed. 'Time will tell, I guess. Will you try the same with your mother and stepfather?'

'No. My mother didn't think I was worth anything. My stepfather agreed.'

Her heart twisted. 'Yet you've achieved success beyond most people's wildest dreams. Surely the lessons of your childhood should make you proud of who you are now, despite hating some aspects of your upbringing?'

'I detested all of mine,' he said with harsh finality. 'I wouldn't wish it on my worst enemy.'

The savage edge of pain in his voice made her shiver. She opened her mouth to ask him, but he surged to his feet.

'I don't wish to dwell in the past.' That half-smile flashed on and off. 'Not when I have a sunset as stunning as this and a wife to rival its beauty.' He plucked the glass from her hand and pulled her up.

Tucking her head beneath his chin, he enfolded her in his arms, one around her waist and the other across her shoulders. Eva knew it was a signal to drop the subject, but she couldn't let it go. Not just yet.

She removed his shades and stared into his slate-coloured eyes. 'For what it's worth, I gave away my country-club membership to my best friend, I hated boarding school, and I couldn't ski to save my life so I didn't even try after I turned ten. I didn't care about my pedigree, or who I was seen with. Singing and a family who cared for me were the only things that mattered. One helped me get through the other. So, you see, sometimes the grass *may* look greener on the other side, but most of the time it's just a trick of the light.'

Several emotions shifted within his eyes. Surprise. Shock. A hint of confusion. Then the deep arrogance of Zaccheo Giordano slid back into place.

'The sunset, *dolcezza*,' he said gruffly. 'You're missing it.'

* * *

The feeling of his world tilting out of control was escalating. And it spun harder out of sync the more he fought it.

Zaccheo had been certain he knew what drove Eva and her family. He'd been sure it was the same greed for power and prestige that had sent his father to a vicious and premature death. It was what had made his mother abandon her homeland to seek a rich husband, turn herself inside out for a man who looked down his nose at her son and ultimately made Clara Giordano pack her bags and move to the other side of the world.

But right from the start Eva had challenged him, forced him to confront his long-held beliefs. He hadn't needed to, of course. Oscar Pennington's actions had proven him right. Eva's own willingness to marry Fairfield for the sake of her family had cemented Zaccheo's belief.

And didn't you do the same thing?

He stared unseeing at the vivid orange horizon, his thoughts in turmoil.

He couldn't deny that the discovery of her innocence in bed had thrown him for a loop. Unsettled him in a way he hadn't been for a long time.

For as long as he could remember, his goal had been a fixed, tangible certainty. To place himself in a position where he erased any hint of neediness from his life, while delivering an abject lesson to those who thought themselves entitled and therefore could treat him as if he were common. A spineless fool who would prostrate himself for scraps from the high table.

He'd proven conclusively yesterday at his wedding reception that he'd succeeded beyond his wildest dreams. He'd watched blue-blooded aristocrats fall over themselves to win his favour.

And yet he'd found himself unsatisfied. Left with a hollow, bewildering feeling inside, as if he'd finally grasped the brass ring, only to find it was made of plastic.

It had left Zaccheo with the bitter introspection of whether a different, deeper goal lay behind the burning need to prove himself above the petty grasp for power and prestige.

The loneliness he'd so offhandedly dismissed had in fact eaten away at him far more effectively than his mother's rejection and the callous disregard his father had afforded him when he was alive.

Impatiently, he dismissed his jumbled feelings. He didn't do *feelings*. He *achieved*. He *bested*. And he *triumphed*.

One miscalculation didn't mean a setback. Finding out Eva had had no previous lovers had granted him an almost primitive satisfaction he wasn't going to bother to deny.

And if something came of this union sooner rather than later… His heart kicked hard.

Sliding a hand through her silky hair, he angled her face to his. Her beauty was undeniable. But he wouldn't be risking any more heart-to-hearts. She was getting too close, sliding under his skin to a place he preferred to keep out of bounds. A place he'd only examined when the cold damp of his prison cell had eroded his guard.

He was free, both physically and in guilt. He wouldn't return to that place. And he wouldn't allow her to probe further. Satisfied with his resolution, he kissed her sexy, tempting mouth until the need to breathe forced him to stop.

The sun had disappeared. Lights strung through the trees flickered on and he nodded to the member of staff who hovered nearby, ready to pack up their picnic.

He caught the glazed, flushed look on his wife's face and came to a sudden, extremely pleasing decision.

'Tonight, *il mio angelo*, we'll have an early night.'

The first week flew by in a dizzy haze of sun, sea, exquisite food, and making love. Lots and lots of making love.

Zaccheo was a fierce and demanding lover, but he gave so much more in return. And Eva was so greedy for everything he had to give, she wondered whether she was turning into a sex addict. She'd certainly acted like one this morning, when she'd initiated sex while Zaccheo had been barely awake. That her initiative had seemed to please him had been beside the point.

She'd examined her behaviour afterwards when Zaccheo had been summoned to an urgent phone call by Romeo.

This was supposed to be a moment out of time, a brief dalliance, which would end the moment she spilled her secret to him. And yet with each surrender of her body, she slid down a steeper slope, one she suspected would be difficult to climb back up. Because it turned out that, for her, sex wasn't a simple exchange of physical pleasure. With each act, she handed over a piece of herself to him that she feared she'd never reclaim.

And that more than anything made her fear for herself when this was over.

A breeze blew through an open window and Eva clutched the thin sarong she'd thrown over her bikini. Dark clouds were forming ominously over the island. Shivering, she watched the storm gather, wondering if it was a premonition for her own situation.

Lightning flashed, and she jumped.

'Don't worry, Mrs Eva.' Zaccheo's housekeeper smiled as she entered and turned on table lamps around the living room. 'The storm passes very quickly. The sun will be back out in no time.'

Eva smiled and nodded, but she couldn't shake the feeling that *her* storm wouldn't pass so quickly.

As intense rain pounded the roof she went in search of Zaccheo. Not finding him in his study, she climbed the stairs, her pulse already racing in anticipation as she went down the hallway.

She entered their dressing room and froze.

'What are you doing?' she blurted.

'I would've thought it was obvious, *dolcezza*.' He held clippers inches from his face.

'I can see what you're doing but…*why*?' she snapped. 'You already got rid of most of it for the wedding.' Her voice was clipped, a feeling she couldn't decipher moving through her.

Zaccheo raised an eyebrow, amusement mingled with something else as he watched her. 'I take it this look works for you?'

She swallowed twice before she could speak. When she finally deciphered the feeling coursing through her, she was so shocked and so afraid he would read her feelings, she glanced over his head.

'Yes. I prefer it,' she replied.

For several seconds he didn't speak. Her skin burned at his compelling stare. Schooling her features, she glanced into his eyes.

'Then it will remain untouched.' He set the clippers down and faced her.

Neither of them moved for several minutes. The storm raged outside, beating against the windows and causing the timber to creak.

'Come here, Eva.' Softly spoken, but a command nonetheless.

'I'm beginning to think those are your three favourite words.'

'They are only when you comply.'

She rolled her eyes, but moved towards him. He swivelled in his chair and pulled her closer, parting his thighs to situate her between them.

'Was that very hard to admit?' he rasped.

Her skin grew tight, awareness that she stood on a precipice whose depths she couldn't quite fathom shivering over her. 'No.'

He laughed. 'You're a pathetic liar. But I appreciate you finding the courage to ask for what you want.'

'An insult and a compliment?' she said lightly.

'I wouldn't want you to think me soft.' He caught her hands and placed them on his shoulders. 'You realise that

I'll require a reward for keeping myself this way for your pleasure?'

The way he mouthed *pleasure* made hot need sting between her thighs. Several weeks ago, she would've fought it. But Eva was fast learning it was no use. Her body was his slave to command as and when he wished. 'You got your stylists to prod and primp me into the image you wanted. I've earned the right to do the same to you.' Her fingers curled into the hair she would've wept to see shorn.

He smiled and relaxed in the chair. 'I thought being primped and plucked to perfection was every woman's wish?'

'You thought wrong. I was happy with the way I looked before.'

That wasn't exactly true. Although she'd loved her thick and wild hair, she had to admit it was much easier to tend now the wildness had been tamed a little. And she loved that she could brush the tresses without giving herself a headache. As for the luxurious body creams she'd been provided with, she marvelled at how soft and silky her skin felt now compared to before.

But she kept all of it to herself as he untied the knot in her sarong and let it fall away. 'You were perfect before. You're perfect now. And mine,' he breathed.

Within seconds, Eva was naked and craving what only he could give her, her eventual screams as loud as the storm raging outside.

CHAPTER THIRTEEN

'COME ON, we're taking the boat out today. As much as I'd like to keep you to myself, I think we need to see something of Rio before we leave tomorrow.'

Eva stopped tweaking the chorus of the melody she'd been composing and looked up as Zaccheo entered the living room.

The perverse hope that he would grow less breathtaking with each day was hopelessly thwarted. Dressed in khaki linen trousers and a tight white T-shirt with his hair loose around his shoulders, Zaccheo was so visually captivating, she felt the punch to her system each time she stared at him.

He noticed her staring and raised an eyebrow. Blushing, she averted her gaze to her tablet.

'Where are we going?' She tried for a light tone and breathed an inward sigh of relief when she succeeded.

'To Ilha São Gabriel, three islands away. It's a tourist hotspot, but there are some interesting sights to see there.' He crouched before her, his gaze going to the tablet. Reaching out, he scrolled through her compositions, his eyes widening at the three dozen songs contained in the file.

'You wrote all these?' he asked.

She nodded, feeling self-conscious as he paused at a particularly soul-baring ballad about unrequited love and rejection. She'd written that one a week after Zaccheo had gone to prison. 'I've been composing since I was sixteen.'

His eyes narrowed on her face. 'You've had two million pounds in your bank account for over a year and a half, which I'm guessing is your shareholder dividend from your father's deal on my building?'

Warily, she nodded.

'That would've been more than enough money to pursue your music career without needing to work. So why didn't you use it?' he queried.

She tried to shrug the question away, but he caught her chin in his hand. 'Tell me,' he said.

'I suspected deep down that the deal was tainted. I hated doubting my father's integrity, but I could never bring my-self to use the money. It didn't feel right.' Being proved right had brought nothing but hurt.

He watched her for a long time, a puzzled look on his face before he finally nodded. 'How was your session with Ziggy Preston?' he asked.

She saw nothing of the sour expression he'd sported that night in the club. 'Surprisingly good, considering I'd thought he'd have me on the blacklist of every music producer after your behaviour.'

An arrogant smile stretched his lips. 'They'd have had to answer to me had they chosen that unfortunate path. You're seeing him again?'

She nodded. 'When we get back.'

'*Bene.*' He rose and held out his hand.

She slipped her feet into one of the many stylish sandals now gracing her wardrobe and he led her outside to the jetty.

Climbing on board, he placed her in front of the wheel and stood behind her. She looked around, expecting Zaccheo's right-hand man to be travelling with them. 'Isn't Romeo coming?'

'He had business to take care of in Rio. He'll meet us there.'

The trip took twenty-five minutes, and Eva understood why the Ilha São Gabriel was so popular when she saw it. The island held a mountain, on top of which a smaller ver-sion of the Cristo Redentor in Rio had been erected. Beneath the statue, bars, restaurants, parks and churches flowed right down to the edge of a mile-long beach.

Zaccheo directed her to motor past the busy beach and round the island to a quieter quay where they moored the boat. 'We're starting our tour up there.' He pointed to a quaint little building set into the side of a hill about a quarter of a mile up a steep path.

She nodded and started to walk up when she noticed Romeo a short distance away. He nodded a greeting but didn't join them as they headed up. The other man's watchfulness made Eva frown.

'Something on your mind?' Zaccheo asked.

'I was just wondering…what's the deal with Romeo?'

'He's many things.'

'That's not really an answer.'

Zaccheo shrugged. 'We work together, but I guess he's a confidant.'

'How long have you known him?'

When Zaccheo pulled his shades from the V of his T-shirt and placed them on, she wondered whether she'd strayed into forbidden territory. But he answered, 'We met when I was thirteen years old.'

Her eyes rounded in surprise. 'In London?'

'In Palermo.'

'So he's your oldest friend?'

Zaccheo hesitated for a second. 'Our relationship is complicated. Romeo sees himself as my protector. A role I've tried to dissuade him from to no avail.'

Her heart caught. 'Protector from what?'

His mouth twitched. 'He seems to think you're a handful that he needs to keep an eye on.'

She looked over her shoulder at the quiet, brooding man.

'My father worked for his father,' he finally answered.

'In what capacity?'

'As whatever he wanted him to be. My father didn't discriminate as long as he was recognised for doing the job. He would do anything from carrying out the trash to kneecapping a rival gang's members to claiming another man's bastard child so his boss didn't have to. No job was too small or large,' he said with dry bitterness.

The blood drained from her face. 'Your father worked for the *Mafia*?'

His jaw clenched before he jerked out a nod. 'Romeo's father was a *don* and my father one of his minions. His role was little more than drudge work, but he acted as if he was serving the Pope himself.'

She glanced over her shoulder at Romeo, her stomach dredging with intense emotions she recognised as anguish—even without knowing what Zaccheo was about to divulge.

'That bastard child you mentioned...'

He nodded. 'Romeo. His father had an affair with one of his many mistresses. His mother kept him until he became too much of a burden. When he was thirteen, she dumped him on his father. He didn't want the child, so he asked my father to *dispose* of him. My father, eager to attain recognition at all costs, brought the child home to my mother. She refused but my father wouldn't budge. They fought every day for a month until she ended up in hospital. It turned out she was pregnant. After that she became even more adamant about having another woman's child under her roof. When she lost her baby, she blamed my father and threatened to leave. My father, probably for the only time in his life, decided to place someone else's needs above his ambition. He tried to return Romeo to his father, who took grave offence. He had my father beaten to death. And I...' his face tightened '...I went from having a friend, a mother and father, and a brother or sister on the way, to having nothing.'

Eva frowned. 'But your mother—'

'Had hated being the wife of a mere gofer. My father's death bought her the fresh start she craved, but she had to contend with a child who reminded her of a past she detested. She moved to England a month after he died and married a man who hated the sight of me, who judged me because of who my father was and believed my common blood was an affront to his distinguished name.' The words were snapped out in a staccato narrative, but she felt the anguished intensity behind them.

Eva swallowed hard. Stepping close, she laid her head on his chest. 'I'm so sorry, Zaccheo.'

His arms tightened around her for a heartbeat before he pulled away and carried on up the steps. 'I thought Romeo had died that night, too, until he found me six years ago.'

She glanced at Romeo and her heart twisted for the pain the unfortunate friends had gone through.

They continued up the hill in silence until they reached the building.

They entered the cool but dim interior and as her eyes adjusted to the dark she was confronted by a stunning collection of statues. Most were made of marble, but one or two were sculpted in white stone.

'Wow, these are magnificent.'

'A local artist sculpted all the patron saints and donated them to the island over fifty years ago.'

They drifted from statue to statue, each work more striking than the last. When they walked through an arch, he laced his fingers with hers. 'Come, I'll show you the most impressive one. According to the history, the artist sculpted them in one day.'

Smiling, she let him tug her forward. She gasped at the double-figured display of St Anne and St Gerard. 'Patron saints of motherhood and fertility...' She stopped reading as her heart dropped to her stomach.

Zaccheo traced a forefinger down her cheek. 'I can't wait to feel our child kick in your belly,' he murmured.

A vice gripped her heart, squeezed until it threatened to stop beating. 'Zaccheo—'

His finger stopped her. 'I meant what I said, Eva. We can make this work. And we may not have had the best of role models in parents, but we know which mistakes to avoid. That's a good basis for our children, *si*?' he asked, his tone gentle, almost hopeful.

She opened her mouth, but no words formed. Because the truth she'd been hiding from suddenly reared up and slapped her in the face.

Zaccheo wanted children, not as a tool for revenge, but for himself. The man who'd known no love growing up wanted a family of his own.

And she'd led him on, letting him believe he could have it with her. The enormity of her actions rocked her to the core, robbing her of breath.

'Eva? What's wrong?' he asked with a frown.

She shook her head, her eyes darting frantically around the room.

'You're as pale as a ghost, *dolcezza*. Talk to me!'

Eva struggled to speak around the misery clogging her throat. 'I...I'm okay'

His frown intensified. 'You don't look okay. Do you want to leave?'

She grasped the lifeline. 'Yes.'

'Okay, let's go.'

They emerged into bright sunlight. Eva took a deep breath, which did absolutely nothing to restore the chaos fracturing her mind.

The urge to confess *now*, spill her secret right then and there, powered through her. But it was neither the time nor the place. A group of tourist students had entered the room and the place was getting busier by the second.

Zaccheo led her down the steps. He didn't speak, but his concerned gaze probed her.

The island seemed twice as crowded by the time they descended the hill. The midday sun blazed high and sweat trickled down her neck as they navigated human traffic on the main promenade. When Zaccheo steered her to a restaurant advertising fresh seafood, Eva didn't complain.

Samba music blared from the speakers, thankfully negating the need for conversation. Sadly it didn't free her from her thoughts, not even when, after ordering their food, Zaccheo moved his chair closer, tugged her into his side and trailed his hand soothingly through her hair.

It was their last day in Rio. Possibly their last as husband and wife. Her soul mourned what she shouldn't have craved.

Unbearable agony ripped through her. She'd been living in a fool's paradise. Especially since she'd told herself it wouldn't matter how much time passed without her telling Zaccheo.

It mattered very much. She'd heard his pain when he'd recounted his bleak childhood. With each day that had passed without her telling him she couldn't help him realise his dream, she'd eroded any hope that he would understand why she'd kept her secret from him.

A moan ripped from her throat and she swayed in her seat. Zaccheo tilted her face to his and she read the worry in his eyes.

'Do you feel better?'

'Yes, much better.'

'*Bene*, then perhaps you'd like to tell me what's going on?' he asked.

She jerked away, her heart hammering. 'I got a little lightheaded, that's all.'

His frown returned and Eva held her breath. She was saved when Romeo entered. 'Everything all right?' he asked.

Romeo's glance darted to her. The knowledge in his eyes froze her insides, but he said nothing, directing his gaze back to his friend.

Zaccheo nodded. '*Sì*. We'll see you back at Paraíso.'

The moment he left, Zaccheo lowered his head and kissed her, not the hungry devouring that tended to overtake them whenever they were this close, but a gentle, reverent kiss.

In that moment, Eva knew she'd fallen in love with him.

And that she would lose the will to live the moment she walked away from him.

Their food arrived and they ate. She refused coffee and the slice of *chocotorta* the waiter temptingly offered. Zaccheo ordered an espresso, shooting her another concerned glance. Praying he wouldn't press her to reveal what was wrong just yet, she laid her head on his shoulder and buried her face in his throat, selfishly relishing the moment. She would never get a moment like this once they returned to Casa do Paraíso. He placed a gentle kiss on her forehead and agony moved through her like a living entity.

You brought this on yourself. No use crying now.

She started as the group they'd met on their exit from the museum entered the restaurant. Within minutes, someone had started the karaoke machine. The first attempt, sung atrociously to loud jeers, finished as the waiter returned with Zaccheo's espresso.

Eva straightened in her seat, watching the group absently as each member refused to take the mic. The leader cast his eyes around the room, met Eva's gaze and made a beeline for her.

'No.' She shook her head when he reached her and offered the mic.

He clasped his hands together. '*Por favor,*' he pleaded.

She opened her mouth to refuse, then found herself swallowing her rebuttal. She glanced at Zaccheo. He regarded her steadily, his face impassive. And yet she sensed something behind his eyes, as if he didn't know what to make of her mood.

She searched his face harder, wanting him to say something, *anything*, that would give her even the tiniest hope that what she had to tell him wouldn't break the magic they'd found on his island. Wouldn't break *her*.

In a way it was worse when he offered her that half-smile. Recently his half-smiles had grown genuine, were often a precursor to the blinding smiles that stole her breath…made her heart swell to bursting.

The thought that they would soon become a thing of the past had her surging to her feet, blindly striding for the stage to a round of applause she didn't want.

All Eva wanted in that moment was to drown in the oblivion of music.

She searched through the selection until she found a song she knew by heart, one that had spoken to her the moment she'd heard it on the radio.

She sang the first verse with her eyes shut, yearning for the impossible. She opened her eyes for the second verse. She could never tell Zaccheo how she felt about him, but she could sing it to him. Her eyes found his as she sang the last line.

His gaze grew hot. Intense. Her pulse hammered as she sang the third verse, offering her heart, her life to him, all the while knowing he would reject it once he knew.

She stifled a sob as the machine clicked to an end. She started to step off the stage, but the group begged for another song.

Zaccheo rose and moved towards her. They stared at each other as the clamouring grew louder. Her breath caught when the emotion in his eyes altered, morphing into that darker hue that held a deeper meaning.

He wasn't angry. Or ruthlessly commanding her to bend to his will. Or even bitter and hurt, as he'd been on the hill.

There was none of that in his expression. This ferocity was different, one that made her world stop.

Until she shook herself back to reality. She was grasping at straws, stalling with excuses and foolish, reckless hope. She might have fallen in love with Zaccheo, but nothing he'd said or done had indicated he returned even an iota of what she felt. Their relationship had changed from what it'd been in the beginning, but she couldn't lose sight of *why* it'd begun in the first place. Or why she couldn't let it continue.

Heavy-hearted, she turned back to the machine. She'd seen the song earlier and bypassed it, because she hadn't been ready to say goodbye.

But it was time to end this. Time to accept that there was no hope.

Something was wrong. It'd been since they'd walked down the hill.

But for once in his life, he was afraid to confront a problem head-on because he was terrified the results would be unwelcome. So he played worst-case scenarios in his head.

Had he said or done something to incite this troubled look on Eva's face? Had his confession on the hill reminded her that he wasn't the man she would've chosen for herself? A wave of something close to desolation rushed over him. He clenched his jaw against the feeling. Would it really be the end of the world if Eva decided she didn't want him? The affirmative answer echoing through him made him swallow hard.

He discarded that line of thought and chose another, dissecting each moment he'd spent with her this afternoon.

He'd laid himself bare, something he'd never done until recently. She hadn't shown pity or disgust for the debasing crimes his father had committed, or for the desperately lonely child he'd been. Yet again she'd only showed compassion. Pain for the toll his jagged upbringing had taken on him.

And the songs…what had they meant, especially the second one, the one about saying *goodbye*? He'd witnessed the agony in her eyes while she'd sung that one. As if her heart was broken—

A knock came at his study door, where he'd retreated to pace after they'd returned and Eva had expressed the need for a shower. Alone.

'Zaccheo?'

He steeled himself to turn around, hoping against hope that the look on her face would be different. That she would smile and everything would return to how it was before they'd gone on that blasted trip.

But it wasn't. And her next words ripped through him with the lethal effect of a vicious blade.

'Zaccheo, we need to talk.'

CHAPTER FOURTEEN

EVERY WORD SHE'D practised in the shower fled her head as Eva faced him. Of course, her muffled sobs had taken up a greater part of the shower so maybe she hadn't got as much practice in as she'd thought.

'I...' Her heart sank into her stomach when a forbidding look tightened his face. 'I can't stay married to you.'

For a moment he looked as if she'd punched him hard in the solar plexus, then ripped his heart out while he struggled to breathe. Gradually his face lost every trace of pain and distress. Hands shoved deep in his pockets, he strolled to where she stood, frozen inside the doorway.

'Was this your plan all along?' he bit out, his eyes arctic. 'To wait until I'd spoken on your father's behalf and he was safe from prosecution before you asked for a divorce?'

She gasped. 'You did that? When?' she asked, but his eyes poured scorn on her question.

'Is being married to me that abhorrent to you, Eva? So much so you couldn't even wait until we were back in London?'

'No! Believe me, Zaccheo, that's not it.'

'*Believe* you? Why should I? When you're not even prepared to give us a chance?' He veered sharply away from her and strode across the room, his fingers spiking through his hair before he reversed course and stopped in front of her once more. 'What I don't understand is why. Did I do something? Say something to make you think I wouldn't want this relationship to work?'

The confirmation that this marriage meant more to him was almost too hard to bear.

'Zaccheo, please listen to me. It's not you, it's—'

His harsh laughter echoed around the room. 'Are you *seriously* giving me that line?'

Her fists balled. 'For once in your life, just shut up and listen! I can't have children,' she blurted.

'You've already used that one, *dolcezza*, but you signed along the dotted line agreeing to my clause, remember? So try again.'

Misery quivered through her stomach. 'It's true I signed the agreement, but I lied to you. I *can't* have children, Zaccheo. I'm infertile.'

He sucked in a hoarse breath and reeled backwards on his heels. 'Excuse me?'

'I tried to tell you when I first saw the clause, but you wouldn't listen. You'd made up your mind that I'd use any excuse not to marry you because I didn't want you.'

The stunned look morphed into censure. 'Then you should've put me straight.'

'How? Would you have believed me if I'd told you about my condition? Without evidence to back it up? Or perhaps I should've told Romeo or your PA since they had more access to you than I did in the week before the wedding?'

He looked at her coldly. 'If your conscience stung you so deeply the first time round, why did you change your mind?'

Her emotions were raw enough for her to instinctively want to protect herself. But what did she have to lose? Zaccheo would condemn her actions regardless of whether she kept her innermost feelings to herself or not. And really, how much worse could this situation get? Her heart was already in shreds.

She met his gaze head on. 'You know I lost my mother to cancer when I was eighteen. She was diagnosed when I was sixteen. For two years we waited, hoping for the best, fearing the worst through each round of chemo. With each treatment that didn't work we knew her time was growing shorter. Knowing it was coming didn't make it any easier. Her death ripped me apart.' She stopped and gathered her courage. 'My father has been suffering stress attacks in the last couple of months.' She risked a glance and saw his brows clamped in a forbidding frown. 'He collapsed on Friday after you called to tell him the wedding was off.'

Zaccheo's mouth compressed, but a trace of compassion flashed through his eyes. 'And you blame me? Is that what this is all about?'

'No, I don't. We both know that the blame for our current circumstances lies firmly with my father.' She stopped and licked her lips. 'He may have brought this on himself, but the stress was killing him, Zaccheo. I've watched one parent die, helpless to do anything but watch them fade away. Condemn me all you want, but I wasn't going to stand by and let my father worry himself to death over what he'd done. And I didn't do it for my family name or my blasted *pedigree*. I did it because that's what you do for the people you love.'

'Even when they don't love you back?' he sneered, his voice indicating hers was a foolish feeling. 'Even when they treat you like an afterthought for most of your life?'

Sadness engulfed her. 'You can't help who you love. Or choose who will love you back.'

His eyes met hers for a charged second, before his nostrils flared. 'But you can choose to tell the truth no matter how tough the telling of it is. You can choose *not* to start a marriage based on lies.'

Regret crawled across her skin. 'Yes. And I'm sorry—'

His hand slashed through air, killing off her apology. Walking around her, he slammed the door shut and jerked his chin towards the sofa. He waited until she'd sat down, then prowled in front of her.

'Tell me of this condition you have.'

Eva stared at her clasped hands because watching his face had grown unbearable. 'It's called endometriosis.' She gave him the bare facts, unwilling to linger on the subject and prolong her heartache. 'It started just before I went to university, but, with everything going on with my mother, I didn't pay enough attention to it. I thought it was just something that would right itself eventually. But the pain got worse. One day I collapsed and was rushed to hospital. The diagnosis was made.' She stopped, then made herself go on. 'The doctor said the…scarring was too extensive…that I would never conceive naturally.'

She raised her head and saw that he'd stopped prowling and taken a seat opposite her with his elbows on his knees. 'Go on,' he bit out.

Eva shrugged. 'What else is there to add?' She gave a hollow laugh. 'I never thought I'd be in a position where the one thing I couldn't give would be the difference between having the future I want and the one I'd have to settle for. You accused me of starting this marriage based on lies, but I didn't know you wanted a real marriage. You did all this to get back at my father, remember?'

'So you never sought a second opinion?' he asked stonily, as if she hadn't mentioned the shifted parameters of their marriage.

'Why would I? I'd known something was wrong. Having the doctor confirm it merely affirmed what I already suspected. What was the point of putting myself through further grief?'

Zaccheo jerked to his feet and began prowling again. The set of his shoulders told her he was holding himself on a tight leash.

Minutes ticked by and he said nothing. The tension increased until she couldn't stand it any more. 'You can do whatever you want with me, but I want your word that you won't go after my family because of what I've done.'

He froze, his eyes narrowing to thin shards of ice. 'You think I want you to martyr yourself on some noble pyre for my sick satisfaction?'

She jumped to her feet. 'I don't know! You're normally so quick to lay down your demands. Or throw out orders and expect them to be followed. So tell me what you want.'

That chilling half-smile returned with a vengeance. 'What I want is to leave this place. There's really no point staying, is there, since the honeymoon is well and truly over?'

The flight back was markedly different from the outbound journey. The moment Zaccheo immersed himself in his work, she grabbed her tablet and locked herself in the bedroom.

She threw herself on the bed and sobbed long and hard into the pillow. By the time the plane landed in London, she was completely wrung out. Exhaustion seeped into her very bones and all she wanted was to curl into a foetal position and wish the world away.

She sank further into grey gloom when she descended the steps of the aircraft to find Zaccheo's limo waiting on the tarmac, along with a black SUV.

Zaccheo, wearing a black and navy pinstriped suit, stopped next to her, his expression remote and unfriendly.

'I'm heading to the office. Romeo will drive you to the penthouse.'

He strode to the SUV and drove off.

Eva realised then that throughout their conversation on the island, she'd made the same mistake as when she'd foolishly disclosed her condition before. She'd allowed herself to *hope* that the condition fate had bestowed on her wouldn't matter to that one *special person*. That somehow *love* would find a way.

A sob bubbled up her chest and she angrily swallowed it down.

Grow up, Eva. You're letting the lyrics of your songs cloud your judgement.

'Eva?' Romeo waited with the car door open.

She hastily averted her gaze from the censure in his eyes and slid in.

The penthouse hadn't changed, and yet Eva felt as if she'd lived a lifetime since she was last here.

After unpacking and showering, she trailed from room to room, feeling as if some tether she hadn't known she was tied to had been severed. When she rushed to the door for the third time, imagining she'd heard the keycard activate, she grabbed her tablet and forced herself to work on her compositions.

But her heart wasn't in it. Her mood grew bleaker when Romeo found her curled on the sofa and announced that Zaccheo wouldn't be home for dinner either tonight or the next two weeks, because he'd returned to Oman.

The days bled together in a dull grey jumble. Determined not to mope—because after all she'd been here before—Eva returned to work.

She took every spare shift available and offered herself for overtime without pay.

But she refused to sing.

Music had ceased to be the balm she'd come to rely on. Her heart only yearned for one thing. Or *one man*. And he'd made it abundantly clear that he didn't want her.

Because two weeks stretched to four, then six with no word from Zaccheo, and no answer to her phone calls.

At her lowest times, Eva hated herself for her lethargy, for not moving out of the penthouse. For sitting around, wishing for a miracle that would never materialise.

But the thought of flat-hunting, or, worse, moving back to Pennington Manor, filled her with a desperate heartache that nothing seemed to ease.

Romeo had brought her coffee this morning at the breakfast table. The pitying look he'd cast her had been the final straw.

'If you have something to say, just say it, Romeo.'

'You're not a weak woman. One of you has to take the situation in hand sooner or later,' he'd replied.

'Fine, but he won't return my calls so give him a message from me, will you?'

He'd nodded in that solemn way of his. 'Of course.'

'Tell him I'm fast reaching my tolerance level for his stupid silence. He can stay in Oman for the rest of his life for all I care. But he shouldn't expect to find me here when he deigns to return.'

That outburst had been strangely cathartic. She'd called her ex-landlady and discovered her flat was still unlet. After receiving a hefty payday from Zaccheo, the old woman hadn't been in a hurry to interview new tenants. She'd invited Eva to move back whenever she wanted.

Curiously, that announcement hadn't made her feel better—

'You've been cleaning that same spot for the last five minutes.'

Eva started and glanced down. 'Oh.'

Sybil, Siren's unflappable manageress, eyed her. 'Time for a break.'

'I don't need a—'

'Sorry, love,' Sybil said firmly. 'Orders from above. The new owner was very insistent. You take a break now or I get docked a week's wages.'

Eva frowned. 'Are you serious? Do we know who this new owner is?'

Sybil's eyes widened. 'You don't know?' When she shook her head, the manageress shrugged. 'Well, I'm not one to spread gossip. Shoo! Go put your feet up for a bit. I'll finish up here.'

Eva reluctantly handed over the cleaning supplies. She turned and stopped as the doors swung open and Ziggy Preston walked in.

The smile she tried for failed miserably. 'Ziggy, hello.'

He smiled. 'I heard you were back in town.'

She couldn't summon the curiosity to ask how he knew. 'Oh?'

'You were supposed to call when you got back. I hope that doesn't mean you've signed up with someone else? Because that'd devastate me,' he joked.

Eva tried for another smile. Failed again. 'I didn't sign with anyone, and I don't think I will.'

His face fell. 'Why not?'

She had a thousand and one reasons. But only one that mattered. And she wasn't about to divulge it to another soul. 'I've decided to give the music thing a break for a while.' Or for ever, depending on whether she felt anything but numb again.

Ziggy shoved his hands into his coat pocket, his features pensive.

'Listen, I was supposed to do a session with one of my artists tomorrow afternoon, but they cancelled. Come to the studio, hang out for a while. You don't have to sing if you don't want to. But come anyway.'

She started to shake her head, then stopped. It was her day off tomorrow. The extra shift she'd hoped to cover had suddenly been filled. She could either occupy herself at Ziggy's studio or wander Zaccheo's penthouse like a lost wraith, pining for what she could never have. 'Okay.'

'Great!' He handed her another business card, this one with his private number scribbled on the back, and left.

A couple of months ago, being pursued by a top music producer would've been a dream come true. And yet, Eva could barely summon the enthusiasm to dress the next day, especially when Romeo confirmed he'd given Zaccheo her message but had no reply for her.

Jaw clenched, she pulled on her jeans and sweater, determined not to succumb to the unending bouts of anguish that had made her throw up this morning after her conversation with Romeo.

She wasn't a pearl-clutching Victorian maiden, for heaven's sake!

Her life might *feel* as if it were over, but she'd been through the wringer more than once in her life. She'd survived her diagnosis. She'd survived her mother's death. Despite the odds, she'd mended fences with her father and sister.

Surely she could survive decimating her heart on a love that had been doomed from the start?

Deliberately putting a spring in her step, she arrived at Ziggy's studio in a different frame of mind. Looking around, she repeated to herself that *this* was a tangible dream. Something she could hang on to once Zaccheo returned and she permanently severed the ties that had so very briefly bound them.

Eva was sure she was failing in her pep talk to herself when Ziggy gave up after a third attempt to get her to sample an upbeat pop tune.

'Okay, shall we try one of yours?' he suggested with a wry smile.

Half-heartedly, she sifted through her list, then paused, her heart picking up its sluggish beat as she stared at the lyrics to the song she'd composed that last morning on the island.

'This one,' she murmured.

At Ziggy's nod, she sang the first line.

His eyes widened. 'Wow.' Nodding to the sound booth, he said, 'I'd love to hear the whole thing if you're up to it?'

Eva thought of the raw lyrics, how they offered love, pleaded for for ever and accepted any risks necessary, and breathed deeply.

If this was what it took to start healing herself, then so be it. 'Sure.'

She was singing the final notes when an electrifying wave of awareness swept over her. Her gaze snapped up to the viewing gallery above the booth, where she knew music moguls sometimes listened in on artists. Although the mirrored glass prevented her from seeing who occupied it, she swore she could smell Zaccheo's unique scent.

'Are you okay?' Ziggy asked.

She nodded absently, her gaze still on the gallery window.

'Can you sing the last two lines again?'

'Umm...yes,' she mumbled.

She really was losing it. If she couldn't sing a song she'd written with Zaccheo in mind without imagining she could feel him, smell him, she was in deep trouble. Because as she worked through the other songs Ziggy encouraged her to re-cord, Eva realised all her songs were somehow to do with the man who'd taken her heart prisoner.

She left the studio in a daze and got into the waiting limo. Physically and emotionally drained, she couldn't connect two thoughts together. When she finally accepted what she needed to do, she turned to Romeo.

'Can you take me to Zaccheo's office, please?'

He looked up from the laptop he'd been working on. After a few probing seconds, he nodded.

A wave of dizziness hit her as they waited for the lift at GWI. She ignored the curious glances, and concentrated on staying upright, putting one foot in front of the other as she made her way down the plushly decorated corridor to Zac-cheo's office.

Anyetta's coolly professional demeanour visibly altered when she saw Eva, then turned to shock as her gaze travelled from her head to her toes.

Eva wanted to laugh, but she couldn't be sure she wouldn't dissolve into hysteria. When Anyetta stood, Eva waved her away.

'I know he's not in. I was hoping *you* would email him for me.'

'But—'

'It won't take long, I promise.'

The tall brunette looked briefly bewildered, but her fea-tures settled back into serene composure and she sat down.

'Mark it *urgent*. Presumably, you can tell when he opens emails from you?' Eva asked.

Warily, Zaccheo's PA nodded.

'Good.' Eva approached, pushing back the errant curls obscuring her vision. She folded her arms around her middle and prayed for just a few more minutes of strength.

Anyetta's elegant fingers settled on the keyboard.
Eva cleared her throat.

Zaccheo,

Since you refuse to engage with me, I can only conclude that
I'm free of my obligations to you. To that end, I'd be grateful
if you would take the appropriate steps to end this marriage
forthwith. My family lawyers will be on standby when you're
ready, but I'd be obliged if you didn't leave it too late. I refuse to put my life on hold for you, so take action or I will.

For the record, I won't be accepting any of the monetary
compensation offered, nor will I be seeking anything from
you, except my freedom. If you choose to pursue my family, then you'll do so without my involvement, because I've
done my duty to my family and I'm moving on. I won't let
you use me as a pawn in your vendetta against my father.

You're aware of the state of my father's health, so I hope
you'll choose mercy over retribution.

Regardless of your decision, I'll be moving out of the penthouse tomorrow.

Please don't contact me.

Eva.

'Send it, please,' she said.

Anyetta clicked the button, then looked up. 'He just
opened it.'

Eva nodded jerkily. 'Thank you.'

She walked out with scalding tears filling her eyes. A
solid presence registered beside her and when Romeo took
her arm, Eva didn't protest.

At the penthouse, she dropped her bag in the hallway,
tugged off her boots and coat as her vision greyed. She made
it into bed as her legs gave way and she curled, fully clothed,
into a tight ball. Her last thought before blessed oblivion
claimed her was that she'd done it.

She'd survived her first hour with a heart broken into a million tiny pieces. If there was any justice, she might just make it through the rest of her life with a shredded heart.

CHAPTER FIFTEEN

In the split second before wakefulness hit, Eva buried her nose in the pillow that smelled so much like Zaccheo she groaned with pure, incandescent happiness.

Reality arrived with searing pain so acute, she cried out.

'Eva.'

She jolted upright at the sound of her name. Jagged thoughts pierced her foggy brain like shards of bright light through glass.

She was no longer in her own suite, but in Zaccheo's.

Her clothes were gone, and she was stripped down to her bra and panties.

Zaccheo was sitting in an armchair next to the bed, his eyes trained on her.

And he was clean-shaven.

His thick stubble was gone, his hair trimmed into a short, neat style that left his nape bare.

Despite his altered appearance, his living, breathing presence was far too much to bear. She jerked her head away, stared down at the covers she clutched like a lifeline.

'What are you doing here?' she asked.

'You summoned me. So here I am,' he stated.

She shook her head. 'Please. Don't make it sound as if I have any power over your actions. If I did you would've answered my numerous phone calls like a normal person. And that email wasn't a summons. It was a statement of intent, hardly demanding your presence.'

'Nevertheless, since you went to so much trouble to make sure it reached me, I thought it only polite to answer it in person.'

'Well, you needn't have bothered,' she threw back hotly,

'especially since we both know you don't have a polite bone in your body. Things like *consideration* and *courtesy* are alien concepts to you.'

He looked perturbed by her outburst. Which made her want to laugh. And cry. And scream. 'Are you going to sit there with that insulting look that implies I'm out of my mind?'

'You must forgive me if that's what my expression implies. I meant to wear a look that says I was hoping for a civilised conversation.'

She threw out her hands. 'You have a damned nerve, do you know that? I...' She stopped, her eyes widening in alarm as an unpleasant scent hit her nostrils. Swivelling, she saw the breakfast tray containing scrambled eggs, smoked pancetta, coffee, and the buttered brioche she loved.

Correction. She'd *once* loved.

Shoving the covers aside, she lunged for the bathroom, uncaring that she was half-naked and looked like a bedraggled freak. All she cared about was making it to the porcelain bowl in time.

She vomited until she collapsed against the shower stall, desperately catching her breath. When Zaccheo crouched at her side, she shut her eyes. 'Please, Zaccheo. Go away.'

He pressed a cool towel to her forehead, her eyelids, her cheeks. 'A lesser man might be decimated at the thought that his presence makes you physically ill,' he murmured gravely.

Her snort grated her throat. 'But you're not a lesser man, of course.'

He shrugged. 'I'm saved by Romeo's report that you've been feeling under the weather recently.'

Eva opened her eyes, looked at him, then immediately wished she hadn't. She'd thought his beard and long mane made him gloriously beautiful, but the sight of his chiselled jaw, the cut of his cheekbones, and the fully displayed sensual lips was almost blinding.

'I can't do this.' She tried to stand and collapsed back against the stall.

With a muttered oath, he scooped her up in his arms and strode to the vanity. Setting her down, he handed her a toothbrush and watched as she cleaned her teeth.

Eva told herself the peculiar look turning his eyes that gunmetal shade meant nothing. Zaccheo had probably come to ensure she vacated his penthouse before succumbing to whatever was ailing her.

Steeling her spine, she rinsed her mouth. He reached for her as she moved away from the vanity, but she sidestepped him, her heart banging against her ribs. 'I can walk on my own two feet.'

Zaccheo watched her go, her hips swaying in that impertinent, yet utterly sexy way that struck pure fire to his libido.

He slowly followed, paused in the doorway and watched her pace the bedroom.

Although he'd primed himself for her appearance, he hadn't been quite prepared for when he'd finally returned to the penthouse last night and found her asleep in her suite. All the excuses he'd given himself for staying away had crumbled to dust.

As he'd stood over her, his racing heart had only been able to acknowledge one thing—that he'd missed her more than his brain could accurately fathom. He'd thought the daily reports on her movements would be enough. He'd thought buying Siren and ensuring she didn't overwork herself, or silently watching her from the gallery at Preston's studio yesterday, listening to her incredible voice, would be enough.

It wasn't until he'd received her email that his world had stopped, and he'd forced himself to face the truth.

He was nothing without her.

For the last six weeks he'd woken to a tormenting existence each morning. Each time, something had broken inside him. Something that would probably slot neatly under the banner of heartache. It had nothing to do with the loneliness that had plagued his childhood and led him to believe he needed a family to soothe the ache. It had nothing to do with the retribution he was no longer interested in exacting from Oscar Pennington.

It had everything to do with Eva. Flashes of her had struck him at the most inappropriate times—like the brightness of her smile when he was involved in tense negotiation. The feeling of being deep inside her when he was teetering on the edge of a platform three hundred metres above ground, with no net to catch him should he fall. And everywhere he'd gone, he'd imagined the faintest trace of her perfume in the air.

Nothing had stopped him from reaching out for her in the dead of the night, when his guard was at its lowest and all he could feel was *need*. Ferocious, all-consuming need.

Even the air of sadness that hung around her now wasn't enough to make him *not* yearn for her.

His heart kicked into his stomach, knowing it was his fault she wore that look.

Her throat worked to find the words she needed. He forced himself to remain still, to erect a force field against anything she might say.

'Let's end this now, Zaccheo. Divorce me. Surely you'd prefer that to this mockery of a marriage?'

He'd expected it. Hell, her email had left him in no doubt as to her state of mind.

Yet the words punched him in the gut...*hard*. Zaccheo uttered an imprecation that wasn't fit for polite company.

Give her what she wants. Stop this endless misery and be done with it.

It was the selfless thing to do. And if he needed to have learned anything from the stunning, brave woman in front of him, it was selflessness. She'd sacrificed herself for her family and turned over her innermost secrets when she could've just kept quiet and reaped untold wealth. She'd continued to stay under his roof, continued to seek him out, when fear had sent *him* running.

He *needed* to be selfless for her.

But he couldn't. He walked stiffly to the side table and poured a coffee he didn't want.

'There will be no divorce.'

She glared at him. 'You do realise that I don't need your permission?'

He knew that. He'd lived with that fear ever since she'd announced back in Rio that she didn't want to be married to him any more.

'*Sì,*' he replied gruffly. 'You can do whatever you want. The same way I can choose to tie you up in endless red tape for the next twenty years.'

Her mouth dropped open, then she shut her beautiful, pain-filled eyes. 'Why would you do that, Zaccheo?'

'Why indeed?'

She shook her head, and her hair fluttered over her shoulders. 'Surely you can't want this? You deserve a family.'

There it was again. That selflessness that cut him to the core, that forced him to let go, to be a better man. *Dio mio,* but he wanted her to be selfish for once. To claim what she wanted. To claim him!

'How very noble of you to think of me. But I don't need a family.'

Shock widened her eyes. 'What did you say?'

'I don't need a family, *il mio cuore*. I don't need anything, or anyone, if I have you.' *She* was all he wanted. He'd prostrate himself at her feet if that was what it took.

She stared at him for so long, Zaccheo felt as if he'd turned to stone. He knew that any movement would see him shatter into useless pieces.

But he had to take the leap. The same leap she'd taken on the island, when she'd shared something deeply private and heartbreaking with him.

'If you have *me*?'

He risked taking a breath. 'Yes. I love you, Eva. I've been racking my brain for weeks, trying to find a way to make you stay, convince you to stay my wife—'

'You didn't think to just *ask* me?'

'After walking away from you like a coward?' He shook his head. 'You've no idea how many times I picked up the phone, how many times I summoned my pilot to bring me back to you. But I couldn't face the possibility of you saying no.' He gave a hollow laugh. 'Believe it or not, I convinced myself I'd rather spend the rest of my life living in another country but still married to you, than face the prospect of never having even the tiniest piece of you.'

Her face crumbled and he nearly roared in pain. 'That's no life at all, Zaccheo.'

'It was a reason for me to *breathe*. A selfish but *necessary* reason for me to keep functioning, knowing I had a piece of you even if it was your name next to mine on a marriage certificate.'

'Oh, God!' Tears filled her eyes and he cursed. He wanted to take her in his arms. But he had no right. He'd lost all rights when he'd forced her into marriage and then condemned her for trying to protect herself from his monstrous actions.

He clenched his fists against the agony ripping through him. 'But that's no life for you. If you wish for a divorce, then I'll grant you one.'

'What?' Her face lost all colour. She started to reach for him, but faltered. 'Zaccheo…'

A different sort of fear scythed through him as she started to crumple.

'*Eva!*'

By the time he caught her she was unconscious.

Muted voices pulled her back to consciousness. The blinds in the strange room were drawn but there was enough light to work out that she was no longer in Zaccheo's penthouse. The drip in her right arm confirmed her worst fears.

'What…happened?' she croaked.

Shadowy figures turned, and Sophie rushed to her side.

'You fainted. Zaccheo brought you to the hospital,' Sophie said.

'Zaccheo…' Memory rushed back. Zaccheo telling her he loved her. Then telling her he would divorce her…

No!

She tried to sit up.

The nurse stopped her. 'The doctors are running tests. We should have the results back shortly. In the meantime, you're on a rehydrating drip.'

Eva touched her throbbing head, wishing she'd stop talking for a moment so she could—

She stared at her bare fingers in horror. 'Where are my rings?' she cried.

The nurse frowned. 'I don't know.'

'No…please. I need…' She couldn't catch her breath. Or take her eyes off her bare fingers. Had Zaccheo done it so quickly? While she'd been unconscious?

But he'd said he loved her. Did he not love her enough? Tears brimmed her eyes and fell down her cheeks.

'It's okay, I'll go and find out.' The nurse hurried out.

Sophie approached. Eva forced her pain back and looked at her.

'I hope you don't mind me being here? You didn't call when you got back so I assume you don't want to speak to me, but when Zaccheo called—'

Eva shook her head, her thoughts racing, her insides shredding all over again. 'You're my family, Sophie. It may take a while to get back to where we were before, but I don't hate you. I've just been a little…preoccupied.' Her gaze went to the empty doorway. 'Is…Zaccheo still here?'

Sophie smiled wryly. 'He was enraged that you didn't have a team of doctors monitoring your every breath. He went to find the head of the trauma unit.'

Zaccheo walked into the room at that moment, and Sophie

hastily excused herself. The gunmetal shade of his eyes and the self-loathing on his face made Eva's heart thud slowly as she waited for the death blow.

He walked forward like a man facing his worst nightmare.

Just before she'd fainted, she'd told herself she would fight for him, as she'd fought for her sister and father. Seeing the look on his face, she accepted that nothing she did would change things. Her bare fingers spoke their own truth.

'Zaccheo, I know you said...you loved me, but if it's not enough for you—'

Astonishment transformed his face. 'Not enough for *me*?'

'You agreed to divorce me...'

Anguish twisted his face. 'Only because it was what *you* wanted.'

She sucked in a breath when he perched on the edge of the bed. His fingers lightly brushed the back of her hand, over and over, as if he couldn't help himself.

'You know what I did last night before I came home?'

She shook her head.

'I went to see your father. I had no idea where I was headed until I landed on the lawn at Pennington Manor. Somewhere along the line, I entertained the idea that I would sway your feelings if I smoothed my relationship with your father. Instead I asked him for your hand in marriage.'

'You did what?'

He grimaced. 'Our wedding was a pompous exhibition from start to finish. I wanted to show everyone who'd dared to look down on me how high I'd risen.'

Her heart lurched. 'Because of what your mother and stepfather did?'

He sighed. 'I hated my mother for choosing her aristocrat husband over me. Like you, I didn't understand why it had to be an either-or choice. Why couldn't she love me *and* her husband? Then I began to hate everything he stood for. The need to understand why consumed me. My stepfather was easy to break. Your father was a little more cunning.

He used you. From the moment we met, I couldn't see beyond you. He saw that. I don't know if I'll ever be able to forgive that, but he brought us together.' He breathed deep and shoved a hand through his short hair. 'Possessing you blinded me to what he was doing. And I blamed you for it, right along with him when the blame lay with me and my obsession to get back at you when I should've directed my anger elsewhere.'

'You were trying to understand why you'd been rejected. I tried for years to understand why my father couldn't be satisfied with what he had. Why he pushed his family obsession onto his children. He fought with my mother over it, and it ripped us apart. Everything stopped when she got sick. Perversely, I hoped her illness would change things for the better. For a while it did. But after she died, he reverted to type, and I couldn't take it any more.' She glanced at him. 'Hearing you tell that newspaper tycoon that I was merely a means to an end brought everything back to me.'

Zaccheo shut his eyes in regret. He lifted her hand and pressed it against his cheek. 'He was drunk, prying into my feelings towards you. I was grappling with them myself and said the first idiotic thing that popped into my head. I don't deny that it was probably what I'd been telling myself.'

'But afterwards, when I asked you...'

'I'd just found out about the charges. I knew your father was behind it. You were right there, his flesh and blood, a target for my wrath. I regretted it the moment I said it, but you were gone before I got the chance to take it back.' He brought her hand to his mouth and kissed it, then her palm before laying it over his heart. *'Mi dispiace molto, il mio cuore.'*

His heart beat steady beneath her hand. But her fingers were bare.

'Zaccheo, what you said before I fainted...'

Pain ravaged his face before he nodded solemnly. 'I meant it. I'll let you go if that's what you want. Your happiness means everything to me. Even if it's without me.'

She shook her head. 'No, not that. What you said before.'

He looked deep into her eyes, his gaze steady and true. 'I love you, Eva. More than my life, more than everything I've ever dared to dream of. You helped me redeem my soul when I thought it was lost.'

'You touched mine, made me love deeper, purer. You taught me to take a risk again instead of living in fear of rejection.'

He took a sharp breath. 'Eva, what are you saying?'

'That I love you too. And it tears me apart that I won't be able to give you children—'

His kiss stopped her words. 'Prison was hell, I won't deny it. In my lowest times, I thought having children would be the answer. But you're the only family I need, *amore mio.*'

Zaccheo was rocking her, crooning softly to comfort her when the doctor walked in.

'Right, Mrs Giordano. You'll be happy to hear we've got to the bottom of your fainting spell. There's nothing to worry about besides—'

'Dehydration and the need to eat better?' she asked with a sniff.

'Well, yes, there's that.'

'Okay, I promise I will.'

'I'll make sure she keeps to it,' Zaccheo added with a mock frown. He settled her back in the bed and stood. 'I'll go get the car.'

The doctor shook his head. 'No, I'm afraid you can't leave yet. You need to rest for at least twenty-four hours while we monitor you and make sure everything's fine.'

Zaccheo tensed and caught her hand in his. 'What do you mean? Didn't you say you'd got to the bottom of what ails her?' His eyes met hers, and Eva read the anxiety there.

'Zaccheo…'

'Mr Giordano, no need to panic. The only thing that should ail your wife is a short bout of morning sickness and perhaps a little bed rest towards the end.'

Zaccheo paled and visibly trembled. 'The *end*?'

Eva's heart stopped. 'Doctor, what are you saying?' she whispered.

'I'm saying you're pregnant. With twins.'

EPILOGUE

ZACCHEO EMERGED FROM the bedroom where he'd gone to change his shirt—the second of the day due to his eldest son throwing up on him—to find Eva cross-legged on the floor before the coffee table, their children cradled in her arms as she crooned Italian nursery rhymes she'd insisted he teach her.

On the screen via a video channel, Romeo leaned in closer to get a better look at the babies.

Zaccheo skirted the sofa and sat behind his wife, cradling her and their children in his arms.

'Do you think you'll make it for Christmas?' she asked Romeo. Zaccheo didn't need to lean over to see that his wife was giving his friend her best puppy-dog look.

'*Sì*, I'll do my best to be there tomorrow.'

Eva shook her head. 'That's not good enough, Romeo. I know Brunetti International is a huge company, and you're a super busy tycoon, but it's your godsons' first Christmas. They picked out your present all by themselves. The least you can do is turn up and open it.'

Zaccheo laughed silently and watched his friend squirm until he realised denying his wife anything her heart desired was a futile exercise.

'If that's what you wish, *principessa*, then I'll be there.'

Eva beamed. Zaccheo spread his fingers through her hair, resisting the urge to smother her cheek and mouth in kisses because she thought it made Romeo uncomfortable.

The moment Romeo signed off, Zaccheo claimed his kiss, not lifting his head until he was marginally satisfied.

'What was that for?' she murmured in that dazed voice that was like a drug to his blood.

'Because you're my heart, *dolcezza*. I cannot go long without it. Without you.'

Eva's heart melted as Zaccheo relieved her of their youngest son, Rafa, and tucked his tiny body against his shoulder. Then he held out his hand and helped her up with Carlo, their eldest by four minutes.

Zaccheo pulled them close until they stood in a loose circle, his arms around her. Then, as he'd taken to doing, he started swaying to the soft Christmas carols playing in the background.

Eva closed her eyes to stem the happy tears forming. She'd said a prayer every day of her pregnancy as they'd faced hurdles because of her endometriosis. When the doctors had prescribed bed rest at five months, Zaccheo had immediately stepped back from GWI and handed over the day-to-day running of the company to his new second-in-command.

Their sons had still arrived two weeks early but had both been completely healthy, much to the joy and relief of their parents. Relations were still a little strained with her father and sister, but Oscar doted on his grandsons, and Sophie had fallen in love with her nephews at first sight. But no one loved their gorgeous boys more than Zaccheo. The love and adoration in his eyes when he cradled his sons often made her cry.

And knowing that love ran just as deep for her filled her heart with so much happiness, she feared she would burst from it.

'You've stopped dancing,' he murmured.

She began to sway again, her free hand rising to his chest. She caught sight of her new rings—the engagement ring belonging to his grandmother, which he'd kept but not given her because the circumstances hadn't been right, and the new wedding band he'd let her pick out for their second, family-only wedding—and her thoughts turned pensive. 'I was thinking about your mother.'

Zaccheo tensed slightly. She caressed her hand over his heart until the tension eased out of him. 'What were you thinking?' he asked grudgingly.

'I sent her pictures of the boys yesterday.'

A noise rumbled from Zaccheo's chest. 'She's been asking for one since the day they were born.'

She leaned back and looked into her husband's eyes. 'I know. I also know you've agreed to see her at Easter after my first album comes out.'

Tension remained between mother and son, but when his mother had reached out, Zaccheo hadn't turned her away.

Standing on tiptoe, Eva caressed the stubble she insisted he grow again, and kissed him. 'I'm very proud of you.'

'No, Eva. Everything good in my life is because of *you*.' He sealed her lips with another kiss. A deeper, more demanding kiss.

By mutual agreement, they pulled away and headed for the nursery. After bestowing kisses on their sleeping sons, Zaccheo took her hand and led her to the bedroom.

Their lovemaking was slow, worshipful, with loving words blanketing them as they reached fulfilment and fell asleep in each other's arms.

When midnight and Christmas rolled around, Zaccheo woke her and made love to her all over again. Afterwards, sated and happy, he spread his fingers through her hair and brought her face to his.

'Buon Natale, amore mio,' he said. 'You're the only thing I want under my Christmas tree, from now until eternity.'

'Merry Christmas, Zaccheo. You make my heart sing every day and my soul soar every night. You're everything I ever wished for.'

He touched his forehead to hers and breathed deep. *'Ti amero per sempre, dolcezza mia.'*

* * * * *

PROVOCATIVE ATTRACTION

ALTONYA WASHINGTON

Prologue

Philadelphia, PA

"She's not doing commercials because she's interested in keeping the public informed on what's new at the market, Rook."

Rook Lourdess flexed his fingers once, twice. It was a habit he'd learned had the remarkable tendency to alleviate the need to clench a fist and follow through with connecting said fist to the jaw belonging to the unfortunate soul who'd riled him. Lately, that had been Murray Dean—former friend, former partner and present traitor.

"What are you getting out of this?" Rook asked once the need to punch Murray had passed.

Murray gave a half shrug. "Not a damn thing—"

"Not yet."

Murray's jaw muscles clenched noticeably then. "I'm not blind, Rook, and neither is Viva. She's got a chance in there." He jabbed a thumb over his shoulder toward a long corridor that opened into an expansive main room to the party where most of the guests still mingled.

"You tell me, what were the odds of coming along to one of your boring-ass client events and running into one of the biggest movie producers in the country?" Murray continued.

Rook felt his jaw flex He had no handy remedy to ease the action that reflex usually prefaced. "Did she need you to tell me that?" he queried, his voice low and mildly lethal.

Murray grinned. "She doesn't know I'm out here, but since her getting your attention at a client event is even less likely than her getting it when you're supposed to be *off* the job…" Again, he shrugged. "I thought it'd help to step up."

"Help her? Or help you?"

Murray snorted a laugh through his nostrils. "Me? What am I supposed to get out of it?"

"I don't know." Rook's gaze narrowed, reflecting a jolting amber glint. "It's something, though. You do nothing without a reason."

Bristling at the barb, Murray raised a brow. "Are we getting around to my leaving the security firm, now?"

"Leaving, huh?" Rook rolled a broad shoulder in a casual shrug. "A leave that was followed by your very generous offer to the rest of the guys to come on over to your neck of the woods."

Agitation more noticeable then, Murray rubbed at a clean-shaved albeit weak jaw. "And they threw my offer back in my face," he admitted. At that point, it was useless to deny the unethical moves he'd orchestrated. "What's the problem now, Rook? None of them were willing to jump ship. You're lucky to have a group of very loyal men."

"Yeah, they've all been loyal. All but one. The one I never thought would stab me in the back."

"Because I wanted something for myself?" Murray sounded incredulous.

"No. Because you wanted what belonged to me." Viva Hail, his girlfriend of four years, was an aspiring actress.

"Ahh...and no one takes or even looks at what belongs to Rook Lourdess without paying the stiffest penalties. Guess I should watch my back now after standing up to you about Viva.

"Do you know how on edge she's been about talking to you about Fritz Vossler's production company?" Murray went on when Rook remained silent. "She thought you'd be pissed. Guess she was right."

"To know that, you must've been watching her pretty close." Rook flexed his fingers again, but the fist clenched anyway.

Murray's shrug regained its casual resonance. "Didn't take much watching to know that. Her eyes went back and forth between you and Vossler a good five minutes in there. When you headed off to see to more business, you could all but see how relieved she was."

"Murray."

Both Rook and Murray turned at the sound of the soft but husky feminine voice that had called out.

Viva Hail stood in the foyer where Murray had cornered Rook after Rook's brief chat with his client and security team on hand for the evening's gala event. Rook's client represented a well-known Philadelphia charity that had national appeal to those with ties to the theater and film industries.

Viva shook her head once in Murray's direction.

Murray turned back to Rook. "Listen, man," he began in a tone far more humble than the one he'd used previously. "In spite of everything, I do care about you guys. I was just trying to help." He left Rook with a quick smile, headed to Viva and brushed her arm when he drew near. "I'll be at the bar," he told her.

"I hear you need my attention, is that right?" Rook considered Murray's departing form before looking back to Viva. "I'm only working off his insight, but he seems to have a crap load of it." He made an effort to come down off some of his frustration. "Be straight with me, V. Have I done something to make you afraid to talk to me?"

"No. No, Rook. Please don't think that."

"Then tell me what to think." He threw another look toward the corridor. "When the hell did you and Murray get so close?"

"Since he became the manager of Fritz Vossler's East Coast security division."

Rook ignored the tightening of his jaw muscle then. Word had reached him of Murray snagging the big fish a few weeks back. "What's that got to do with you?"

Viva began a slow walk around the perimeter of the townhome's foyer. The hem of her empire-waist crimson gown swished elegantly about her curvy frame as she moved. "Mr. Vossler and his people are scouting for fresh talent, and anyone they sign is privy to all the perks his West Coast assets receive. Security is one of them."

"Again, what's that got to do with you, V?" His manner proved to her he already had the answer.

"Vossler just asked me to sign with his company."

"Just asked?"

She smiled, understanding. "He asked weeks ago."

Rook smiled then too and commenced his own slow pace of the foyer. "Weeks ago…guess that's what he was talking to you about the other night at Jazzy B's."

Viva inhaled sharper than she realized. Sometimes she forgot how scarily perceptive her boyfriend was. "He goes there a lot when he's in town."

"Right. Looking for new talent and all."

"Rook… Don't make this harder."

"'This.'" Rook stopped his pacing. "Exactly what is 'this,' V? Telling me you signed with a producer? I don't think Murray would've been looking as smug as he was if it was only about that."

Viva watched him, amazed and wondering how he read a person so easily. Resolved, she gathered what remained of her struggling courage and decided to get it over with. "Mr. Vossler offered me a part—not a commercial but a *real* part. Shooting starts in two weeks on location…in Rio."

Rook felt the blow her words dealt him. He forced himself to recover quickly. "Brazil. Congrats."

"Rook—"

"How long will you be gone?"

"Five months," she said after a split second of hesitation. "We head out to Los Angeles right after that to finish filming and postproduction. That'll take another month or so."

Rook resumed his stroll. Then his steps took him in a wide circle around Viva. "That's a lot of prepping to do in two weeks. Shots, passport, your job."

She smiled again. There was no humor in the gesture. She knew what he was getting at. "I've done all that already," she said.

"And at no time was there an opportunity to tell me?"

"I didn't know how—" She bristled anew when he erupted into cold laughter.

"Didn't know how? Hell, V, I guess we've got more problems than I thought."

"I don't want this to ruin us."

The small, bewildered tone of her voice squeezed his heart. "How could you think it wouldn't, babe? Our communication is already in the crapper. You being out of the country for half the year isn't gonna help that."

"I have to take this, Rook. It's what I've been working for."

"Right. After all, you're not just doing commercials because you're interested in keeping the public informed on what's new at the market." At her confused look, he grimaced and shook his head. "So I'm losing you to this?"

"I don't want that." Viva clasped her hands between her breasts and moved to him. "It could work."

"We barely see each other as it is. I'm busy all the damn time getting the firm on point and that's done no favors to our relationship." He paused to smooth a hand across his hair, a mass of soft, close-cropped twists capping his head. "Only thing that's kept us together, V, is you having a less demanding job. That's over now."

Viva felt something chill inside her at his use of the word *over*. Again, she grabbed hold of fledgling courage. "What are you saying? If I take the job, we're done?" she asked.

"Don't put that on me, V. You know how shaky things are between us right now. You know as well as I do that we won't survive another blow. But you can forget about me letting you go. I'm afraid that's a decision that'll be made for us. My actions have already set the path. I guess yours will put us on it."

Her vision was a blur then. He was right. They'd been passing ships for months. Her going to work for Jazmina Beaumont's gentlemen's club had certainly not been the best decision. The fact that he'd become increasingly busy building his firm had taken his mind off the concerns he had with her waitressing there.

They wouldn't survive this, but he was saying that he refused to be the one to put that nail into their coffin. Could she?

"When are you due to leave?"

She barely heard his voice cut through the storm of her thoughts. "End of the week," she said.

Rook had pretty much schooled his expression but the devastation in his entrancing amber stare was unmistakable.

Viva knew she had the answer to her question then. She *could* put that nail in their coffin. She already had.

Chapter 1

Philadelphia, PA
Six years later

Rook Lourdess knew his rich laughter had the tendency to carry whether he was in the midst of absolute silence or chaos. Both environments proved to be appropriate descriptors that night. His laughter carried out from the party still going strong indoors to the terrace that somehow maintained its serene quiet.

"Sounds good," he was saying to whomever he spoke to through the mobile he held to his ear. "Sure you don't need me there?" Rook nodded, listening to the caller's response.

"I guess that'll work, seeing as how I've got that five a.m. conference call…Italy," he added, following a few more seconds of silence.

"Yeah, they sound serious. I keep waiting on them to call and tell me they made a mistake…Ha! I appreciate that," he said once more silence had passed from his end.

"Forget it!" Rook's laughter clung to the words. "I don't care how much you lay on the flattery, you're not goin'…Nah, B, I need you to stay here and hold it all down at the firm, but don't worry, we'll be having that talk soon enough…Yeah…" A somber element crept into Rook's voice then. "Yeah, I'm not looking forward to it either. Listen, man, I better get goin'. Just be ready with that report by tomorrow afternoon. I want to get this all put to bed before I leave… All right, talk to you then." Following another brief stint of silence and more laughter, Rook was easing the phone into a back trouser pocket. He didn't head back to the party, but stood on the terrace and looked out into the night. Moving closer to the stone railing, he inhaled deeply and smiled.

Robust cheer sounded indoors, but Rook resisted the tug of the partygoers and reminded himself that he needed to hit the sack.

His Italian contacts would be speaking with him at 11:00 a.m. their time. He had to be sharp as possible by 5:00 a.m. That wouldn't happen unless he headed for his car and home right then.

Rook was turning to make his exit down the terrace's wide steps when he heard her.

"Italy, huh?"

So much for getting to sleep anytime soon, Rook thought when he saw Viva Hail seated and looking coolly lovely from her spot on one of the cushioned chaises dotting the terrace.

Seeing her never failed to seriously screw with his sleep. Whether it was on the big screen or small didn't matter. Seeing her in person…well, he shuddered to think of what his Italian business associates would think of him when they spoke in eight hours. He wouldn't be getting that full night of sleep he'd hoped for.

"V." His voice was soft, unlike the sound of the blood rushing in his ears.

"Sorry for eavesdropping." Viva lifted a manicured hand a few centimeters from her lap and let it fall back to the beige silk pants she wore. "I was out here when you came to the terrace. I didn't mean to listen in."

"It wasn't anything top secret." He moved closer to where she sat.

"Was it business or pleasure?" Viva didn't close her eyes in mortification when she heard the question trip off her tongue, but mortification rolled in hot and heavy waves all the same. Pleasure was always a given when it involved Rook Lourdess. She knew that well enough, didn't she? Again, she waved. "Sorry to pry."

Rook grinned. "You're not."

"So, um, what part of Italy are you visiting?"

"Belluno."

"Ah…" Viva smiled and closed her eyes as she nodded. "That's not far from Cortina. It's really beautiful this time of year."

"So I hear." Hands hidden in the deep pockets of his dark trousers, Rook strolled closer. "Has your work taken you there?" He somehow resisted asking if her knowledge of the place was on a personal level.

Viva was already nodding. "I did a movie there two

years ago while the show was on hiatus. An ensemble-cast thing. It was fun."

"Ensemble cast, like the show. How's that going?"

"Very well. We've been a truly blessed bunch."

"So no talk of finales anytime soon?"

"If only." Viva threw back her head and sighed. "I was sure we'd be done after season four with everyone so busy with other successful projects, but…" She flexed her fingers over the pants that matched a shimmering blazer. "The audience still loves us, the ratings are dynamite… I'd say we'll be a bunch of kick-ass secret agents well into our nineties."

Laughter hummed around the terrace then.

"So, um, are you visiting Italy on new business for the firm?" Viva figured additional prying couldn't hurt at that point.

"Remains to be seen," was all he could share before the party volume grew to a maddening pitch and tipped over to deafening.

Rook and Viva realized the French doors had opened as chief of detectives Sophia Hail exited with congratulatory cheers behind her.

"There she is!" Rook's voice carried across the terrace as he closed the distance to Sophia and enveloped her in a bear hug. "The news is in the air. Congratulations. It's a good night for the Philly PD," he said and kissed her cheek.

Sophia, the recent recipient of an unexpected promotion to chief of detectives, wore a grin that seemed to make her entire face glow.

"Thanks." Sophia laughed, returning Rook's tight squeeze. "But I can't let any of these accolades go to my head, no matter how good they feel floating up there."

The accolades were well deserved. Sophia and her team had just come leagues closer to wrapping up a complex money-laundering scheme that had implicated several members of the force. Sophia's predecessor was among them.

Viva stepped up to draw her younger sister into a tight squeeze. "Congratulations, sweetie. Are you done for the night?" she asked once they broke from the embrace.

"Hardly," Sophia sighed in a manner that sang with satisfaction. "I just wanted to get back. Mama went to all this trouble to put together this party for me. My people can handle the wrap-up and I'll be back at the job in the morning."

Sophia slid Rook another smile and squeezed his arm. "Think you can fit me in for a quick talk sometime tomorrow?"

"Sure. Might be early. I've got a five a.m. chat to Europe tomorrow."

Sophia whistled, her eyes twinkling. "Good luck with that."

"I'll need it." Rook smoothed a hand over his chest as though the idea pained him. "I should've been in bed hours ago."

"Well, I plan to make it an early day myself," Sophia said. "I'll make time whenever you can drop in."

"Count on it." He nodded before gracing Viva's face with his arresting gaze.

Sophia appeared as though she could read the look. "So, V, I'll just see you inside, okay?"

"No, you stay," Rook said. "I'm the one who needs

to get going." He gave Viva a smile. "Good seeing you. How long before you leave?"

Viva lifted her shoulders and let the move hold a few seconds before she lowered them.

"I'm not sure yet."

"Don't leave without saying goodbye, okay?"

"Count on it," she returned the earlier confirmation he'd given to her sister. With effort, she kept a cool smile in place while he said good-night to Sophia and made his way from the terrace.

"He hasn't changed."

Sophia smiled at Viva's remark. "Did you think he would?" she asked.

The ebony flecks in Viva's warm chocolate stare appeared to sparkle beneath a sudden nudge of emotion. "I prayed he wouldn't after everything that happened. Sophia, um…is he, um…is he seeing anybody?"

Sophia looked off in the direction where Rook had taken his exit. "I'd have to ask Tigo," she said, referring to her fiancé and one of Rook's oldest friends, Santigo Rodriguez. "Far as I know there hasn't been anyone since you."

Viva shot her sister a stunned expression.

"No one *steady* since you," Sophia qualified.

Viva wasn't wholly convinced of that either, but such a statement was easier to swallow than one suggesting there had been *no one* since her.

Rook Lourdess was a presence. He exuded a power that went beyond the obvious potency presented by the striking breadth of his physique. His massive build, combined with a jolting stare and remarkably crafted face, had a talent for unsettling women as thoroughly as it mesmerized them.

Still, it was the subtle aspect of his persona, Viva believed, that was even more alluring. Unarguably, the face and body were difficult acts to follow. The body was a well-honed six and a half feet of solid muscle sheathed in a rich caramel-toned casing that was only rivaled by the face. It was surrounded by a halo of blue-black that, despite the efforts to keep it close-cropped, remained an unruly cap of waves.

The carefully crafted face was accentuated by a heavy-lidded amber stare of such a hue, it seemed almost translucent. The nose emphasized strong, high cheekbones offset by a generous and fully kissable mouth—one Viva remembered was capable of exerting the most extreme forms of pleasure and release.

She cleared her throat, not sure if the moan she'd just given in to had been overheard by her sister or merely an echo in her own head.

"Sure you don't want to catch up to him? He probably hasn't gotten to his car yet."

Viva snorted. "If I punch you, would that be considered assaulting an officer?"

Sophia gave in to a sly grin. "I'd make the charges stick."

Viva countered with a shrug. "I'm sure I could find a lawyer to get me off."

"Mmm… I thought you'd want Rook for that."

A few seconds of silence followed the playfully lurid comment. Then, the sisters gave in to wild laughter that was as much about amusement as it was about happiness over the fact that they were together and that so many troubling aspects of the past were finally being laid to rest. So many...but not all.

"So did I interrupt anything here?" Sophia clasped her hands and eyed the terrace speculatively. "Anything...promising?"

Again, Viva snorted. "If you count small talk promising."

"Ah, honey." Sophia moved close to drop an arm around Viva's shoulders and squeezed. "I'm sorry."

"No need. It's for the best."

"I don't think you believe that." Sophia used her height advantage to drop a kiss to the top of her sister's head. "Are you saying you hold absolutely *no* hope that you guys could have what you once did?"

"It's been a long time."

"And? A lot of time passed between me and Tigo too."

Viva conceded with a smile. "Fair enough, but it still wouldn't be a good idea, Soapy."

"Not a good idea?" Sophia challenged once she'd chuckled over the name Viva had given her before she could correctly pronounce her little sister's name. "You *did* just see the man, right? I'm surprised he walked out of here alone with all the...attention I saw him getting before I had to hustle out of here earlier."

Viva moved to the terrace railing and looked out into the night as though she were seeing Rook there. "There're things I don't want him to know. Ever. Things that might hurt him and that'll make me feel like more of an ass for leaving than I already do."

Intrigued, Sophia's gray eyes narrowed, all teasing elements leaving her face. "Any details you can share?" She joined Viva at the railing. "Is this about Murray?"

"This all happened near the beginning of my career." She slid her sister a sly smile. "I promise there aren't any moves I wish I didn't make. At least none of the truly graphic variety. There are choices I made, though, and later wished I hadn't. Choices I may not have made if working for Jazzy B's hadn't made me immune to certain signs."

"And that's Mom and Dad talking now."

"Maybe," Viva bumped her side to Sophia's. "Parents can make a lot of sense sometimes."

Sophia folded her arms over her chest and turned to lean back against the rail. "So are you going to let these old choices keep you from going back to the man you love?"

"Soap, it's been six—"

"Back to the man who still loves you?" Sophia interrupted. "V, these *things* you mentioned… Murray was with you at the beginning. Are you sure that doesn't have anything to do with this present mess?"

Viva was shaking her head. "This particular choice doesn't have much to do with Murray but some of my other choices… If I hadn't made them, you probably wouldn't have what you need to put your case to bed."

"Hold it, V." Sophia took her sister's shoulders and gave her a slight shake. "I can damn well put my case to bed without drawing you into it."

"Maybe I want to be drawn in." Unshakeable determination sharpened Viva's star-quality features. "I only knew Murray a little through Rook before we started working together at my first production company. It didn't take long for me to see that he could be a shark, but that's a commodity in my world and I didn't shy away from him because I wanted my career and I correctly guessed that he could give me one."

"Hey." Sophia gave Viva another tug. "You're the only one responsible for your career."

"Thanks, Soap, but Murray really is very good at what he does. He made a very successful move from security to talent representation. Over the years, I've come to consider him as a very good friend as well as my agent."

"And that may make it harder for you to believe he could be involved in all the rest," Sophia warned.

"Why'd he do it, Sophia?" Viva tugged her fingers through the light brown coils framing her face. "Why'd he risk doing something that could take away his freedom?"

"Some folks can't resist the sparkle, no matter how much they have. A little more is always a good thing."

"Yeah." Viva thought of how that point had pertained to her when she'd started getting noticed—when the sparkle of real celebrity began to twinkle her way. It should've been enough, but Sophia was right. More always seemed better. She supposed it was the same for Murray. Too bad his quest for more sparkle had turned him into a criminal.

"I have to be part of this, Sophia."

"All right." Sophia nodded. "But if that's the case, I'm going to need you to agree to any and all requests I make pertaining to your own well-being."

Viva bit her lip before acquiescing with a hesitant nod.

"I mean it, V. Take it or leave it."

"Okay...but only on the condition that you don't let any of this newfound power over me go to your head."

"I'll try." To Viva's ears the words held little promise. "But give me any of that A-list actress diva attitude and I'll put you on house arrest."

"Such a hard-ass," Viva accused.

"I'm worse." Sophia waved off the insult. "I'm a bride. I'm about to start getting very anal about things being perfect. Keeping my maid of honor alive goes at the top of that list."

Viva gave herself over to laughter. The gesture was soon being echoed by Sophia and the sisters tucked into another hug.

Rook gave a quick prayer of thanks when he pulled the Suburban into the parking spot outside his condo. The need for sleep had latched on harder and heavier the second his butt had hit the driver's seat.

It was a blessing that he hadn't hit anything or been pulled over for a suspected DUI considering how wiped he was. He'd been looking forward to an exceptional night of sleep, but he now feared that would be a fruitless endeavor. Finding Viva Hail on that terrace had hit him like a brick to his gut.

He'd known she was in town. He'd run into her while his team had supplied security for her sister. Not until that night had the true force of her being back really hit him. She'd always been able to read him so well and he wondered if she could see how out of it he was earlier.

Resting back on the seat, Rook reminisced on how her perception intrigued as well as annoyed him. He wasn't a man who enjoyed having others get inside his head.

Viva Hail wasn't just any *other*. No, she wasn't just any other and how had he honored that so long ago? By giving her an ultimatum. No…it hadn't been a blatant "take it or leave it" ultimatum, but he'd damn well known what he was doing when he gave her that bull about the decision being made for them and that *her* actions would put them on the path his had already set.

He'd let her think the rest was all her decision and whatever the final outcome, it was on her. The simple truth was he just didn't want to see her reaction when he owned up to her dead-on perception that he really was set on them being done if she left. How was he supposed to tell her a thing like that?

Furthermore, how were they supposed to make a relationship work if she'd gone along? Every day she'd regret the choice—the sacrifice—she'd made for their relationship.

Groaning, Rook left the SUV and faintly celebrated the fact that his eyes were still weighted by sleep. He made it to the quiet, understated elegance of the lobby. His condominium complex was an impressive layout of four separate skyscrapers interconnected by a series of moving walkways all joining at the lobby. The walkways were basically for aesthetic purposes—the lobby also housed an elevator bay to accommodate those who opted out of taking the scenic route to their respective towers.

Rook selected an elevator, smiling as the warmth and familiarity of home settled into his bones. Work kept him from arriving during the evening rush; his day job wasn't a normal nine to five after all. He didn't mind as the schedule usually allowed him to arrive once things had settled down.

The place had a way of enveloping him in a solitude he'd felt in few other places that he'd lived. Perhaps that was because it was the place he and Viva had settled in when they'd moved in together all those years ago.

Plush, yet functional carpeting offset by the warm, golden lighting, glowed from mahogany-based sconces against mocha-painted walls. The allure of the place had been Viva's doing. Her presence had lent it the truest sense of warmth and home. Only to himself could he admit he'd do anything to feel that again. His current residence, void of her, was a poor substitute, but better than nothing.

The elevator dinged and sent him on a nonstop ascent to his floor which held only one additional unit aside from his own. He and Viva had happily worked like dogs to maintain the utilities and other incidental expenses associated with such a place. As they'd both come from affluent families, snagging digs at one of the most enviable addresses in the city had raised few brows.

Rook's parents, Kendall and Elise Lourdess, had handled payments on the property. They had fallen as in love with Viva as her parents, Gerald and Veronica Hail, had fallen for Rook.

There was little comment made about them living together unmarried. Assumptions ran high on both sides that nuptials would be forthcoming. Then Viva went to waitress for Jazzy B's Gentlemen's Club and had caught the eye of several men. One introduced her to the camera. Offers for commercials began to flood and their relationship, as Rook saw it, began a slow and terrible transformation that had signaled its end

Chapter 2

"Guess I work better on low fuel."

Burt Larkin chuckled over his boss's insight. "I'll take that to mean the call went well."

"Guess so." Rook held the phone away as he yawned. "We spent the last twenty minutes of the call discussing my trip over there."

"Have I told you how lucky you are?"

Rook laughed. "Only about a million times."

"So will you grace us with your presence today? It's not every day me and the guys see someone as lucky as you."

"How long am I gonna have to put up with these jokes?" Rook said following another few moments of robust laughter.

"Please," Burt sighed. "We haven't even started yet."

Rook countered with a playful groan. "Well, I'll

be in as soon as I leave the cop shop," he told his second in command.

Burt reciprocated the groan. "Should we have bail money handy just in case?"

"Hmph, not this time. I'm only goin' in for a quick talk with the new chief of Ds."

"Ah…this about what went down last night?"

"Not sure. Sophia was kind of vague when she asked for the meeting, but that's probably because Viva was standing right there."

"Well, well." Surprise registered in Burt's twangy voice. "What was that like?"

"I'll give you a hint   it's why I didn't sleep worth a damn last night."

"Right." Burt let the conversation end there, no doubt knowing how touchy the subject was for his boss. "So…at this point, our report is complete and we'll await your input."

"I think from here on out the chief's got her security well in hand. I'll review and sign the report when I get there."

Lourdess Securities, known as L Sec by the clients it handled in the private, public and entertainment sectors, had been hired to provide its coveted brand of protection to Sophia Hail following her recent promotion. The detective's investigation into an ever-increasingly sensational money-laundering scheme had taken root. Threats had also taken root to encourage the insightful detective to back off her inquiries. As a result, Philadelphia DA Paula Starker had sought out Rook and his team to shadow her colleague and friend.

"The rest of the team is in agreement that Chief Hail's normal security detail will be enough, but we're good with maintaining our posts until a certain person of interest is apprehended."

Rook knew what Burt was saying. The team had been on hand the previous evening when several arrests were made in the case. The team knew that Sophia's investigation had led her to Murray Dean.

"According to what I heard last night, our old friend Dean has a role to play in all this." Burt told him.

"Yeah..." Rook's tone was light, but his agreement on Murray's involvement was firm.

"Will this be a new problem for you and Viva, man?"

Rook laughed. "We've had no problems for at least six years, B," he reminded his friend and business associate.

"True, and it'd be a shame to have new upsets weighing in when you're about to pull up stakes for Italy."

"Yeah..." Rook voiced his light agreement once more, but offered no further opinion.

"So I'll see you later?" Burt seemed to take the cue that his boss was all chatted out.

"Yeah, B, thanks." Rook added a goodbye and ended the call.

Setting aside his mobile, he rubbed tired eyes and yawned for what had to be the fiftieth time since he'd awakened that morning. Smirking, he turned the word over in his head... *Awakened.* More like arisen from a troubled bout with his bedsheets.

Dreams had been shoved aside for a night of tossing, turning and images of Viva Hail attacking his subconscious. The sleep he'd hoped to indulge in had flitted away without so much as a toodle-loo when he'd strolled through the quiet, broad space of the condo to the bedroom.

The bed conjured the first of many images—Viva sprawled out on her stomach and sleeping him off after an enthusiastic session of sex, covers twisted with erotic intricacy about her shapely calves and lush thighs. Sleep for him then had become a wish with no possibility of materializing.

Her face and body were irrevocably stamped on his brain. They would never be removed and he wouldn't want them to be. Such a thing was assured when he'd seen her a few weeks earlier rushing into her sister's place. She'd been staying with Sophia while visiting Philadelphia. The image of her had then been reasserted last night. He recalled seeing her on the terrace, knowing how close he was to reaching out to take her to him before they were interrupted.

The body, still curvy and lush, was even more alluring. The added muscle tone was attributed to her active career and the physical demands of the roles she secured. The face was a work of natural glamour enhanced by coils of light brown curls surrounding a honey-toned face.

It was a face that needed no man-made accents. The mouth was a study in erotic art as were the high cheekbones and small nose that upturned just a fraction at the tip. Big brown eyes were offset by ebony flecks that sparkled amid upset or…arousal.

No, getting to sleep last night was an idiot's assumption. And what of Italy? Another assumption? The trip was about more than adding a boost to his business. L Sec was a bona fide success. The investment his parents had made in the dream of their only child had been a smart move. The elder Lourdesses had earned back their seed money many times over.

Rook knew the truth and he suspected most of his executive team knew it, as well. He was running. Two of his best friends had found women with whom they wanted to spend the rest of their lives. It had become too much to remain in the place where he'd lost the woman with whom he wanted to spend the rest of his. The memories that had sustained him for the last six years had at last become a series of ropes knotted into a noose of increasing tightness.

Yes, he was running. Italy was far enough to ease the memories, even if the distance wouldn't totally remove them. Italy, for him, signified freedom. Freedom from a past he was desperate to exorcise.

Of course, all that was before he'd seen Viva again. Rook glimpsed his hand and realized he'd clenched a fist without feeling the move take hold. His temper was elevating to boiling point. It was another of those ropes that were starting to develop choking intensity.

He was considering some time in the gym to trample the blackness clouding his mind, when his phone chimed, reminding him of the meeting with Sophia.

Once more Rook studied his hand. Flexing it slightly, he cast a lingering look toward the door at the end of the hall that led to his home gym. Pivoting then, Rook headed away from the door as though he were being hunted.

* * *

"Are you sure I can't bring you anything, Mr. Lourdess? We've got soft drinks and an array of bottled waters if you prefer that to the chief's coffee."

"I'm good, but thank you." Rook's smile exhibited genuine appreciation when he addressed the attractive brunette from his seat before the wide walnut desk.

"Well, you be sure to let me know if you change your mind."

When the woman left, Rook graced the chief with a look of earnest ease that lent credence to the fact that he had no interest in the magnitude of his appeal.

Sophia's grin was equally earnest as she observed him. "I should apologize for my assistant. She's not always so obvious in her appraisal of my guests."

Rook tossed up a hand, another clear indicator that he thought nothing of the assistant's overt flirting. "It's good to have a talent for making the guests feel special."

"Mmm..." Sophia sipped at her coffee, nodding. "To be on the safe side, I think I'll tell her your heart belongs to my sister."

"Sophia," Rook groaned, leaning back his head a fraction. "Tell me this isn't why you wanted to see me."

"No, not exactly." Sophia studied the steaming liquid in her ceramic mug. "But anyone who saw you guys last night would know there's still love there."

"Does it matter?" Rook asked after a moment's consideration.

Sophia reared back in the scooping burgundy suede chair set behind a desk of impressive breadth befitting the new chief of detectives. "The way you feel about my sister could matter quite a bit in light of what I'm about to ask you."

"Which is?" Shifting a bit in the boxy chair, same color and finish as the one Sophia occupied, Rook felt equal parts expectant and hesitant.

Sophia left her chair to round the desk and ease her hip down to one corner. "V didn't come to town just visiting. She wants to make a statement and testify if need be against Murray Dean."

"What the hell, Sophia?" Rook's voice was a ragged whisper. His arresting gaze was hard and fixed on Sophia then.

"While she's worked with Murray, she's witnessed some things. Things that could tie him up nice and snug to some of Philadelphia's finest who're tangled in this laundering case."

Rook left his chair. Working his square jaw beneath his fingers, he looked as though he were suspended in a state of disbelief. "Is she involved?"

"Viva?" Sophia almost laughed over the absurdity of the question. "No, Rook, that's not it. She's seen him with certain people he'd have a challenging time explaining his connection to."

Rook curbed his desire to question further. He knew there was only so much the detective could share. "Why'd you want to see me today?" he asked instead.

Sophia tugged at a lone curl that dangled from her updo and debated before answering. "*I* want to secure V someplace impenetrable until we can convene a grand jury. We don't know if we can indict Dean on what we have now, but we're determined to pull in as much ammunition as we can."

"And you're okay with that? Letting Viva put her ass on the line like this?"

"I don't need my sister to wrap this, Rook." Sophia's voice held the slightest edge. "Viva came to me with this. What she's got to share could tip the scales a lot more in our favor."

"What'd you mean about putting her someplace impenetrable?"

Sophia's shrug momentarily wrinkled her tailored short-waist black blazer. "I'm sure someone in your... line of work would know of such places. You *or* your men," she quickly qualified. "I'm not trying to put you on the spot here, Rook. You could pass this on to one of your guys. Everyone around here will attest to the great work you guys do. I'm at the head of that line. I need to know my sister's someplace safe if she plans on being involved with this thing."

Rook stalked the spacious office, having resumed his jaw massage. He drew to a complete halt at Sophia's next words.

"Tigo said something about you going to Italy."

It seemed that only Rook's facial muscles were capable of movement then. He used them to fix Sophia with a stunned look.

"This all seems so unreal," Veronica Hail cooed while holding her eldest child in a rocking embrace.

Viva enjoyed the feel of being secure in her mother's arms while her father's arms enfolded them both.

"I know this was sudden," Viva said when her parents allowed her to move out of the embrace just a fraction. "Me just showing up out of the blue, but when I heard about Sophia—"

In unison, the Hails were shushing their daughter.

"It's forgotten, baby." Gerald Hail dropped a kiss to the top of Viva's head. "You never have to apologize for coming home."

"You *never had* to apologize."

Viva heard the stress her mother inserted. "Thank you both." She hugged them again. "You guys were right, you know?" She drew back to fix them with solemn looks. "You warned me against jumping for the first brass ring tossed my way. Hmph. I not only jumped, I threw away my future while I did it." Viva saw the look her parents exchanged and read it well.

"I've seen Rook," she told them.

Gerald Hail looked pleased. Veronica Hail looked elated.

"Stop." Viva raised her hands to ward off their glee. "There's no reason to get all crazy happy here. We didn't rush into each other's arms either time."

"Tell us about these 'either times,'" Gerald urged.

The Hails listened intently as Viva recounted the meeting at Sophia's condo days earlier and the party in Sophia's honor the night before.

"Are you sure it means nothing, honey?" Veronica asked.

"I'm sure and it wouldn't matter either way since he's about to head off to Italy." Viva quickly shared the details of Rook's travel plans.

"And how do you feel about this trip?"

Viva shrugged, hesitating to answer her mother's

question. "I'm in no position to complain. I've been out of his life for six years."

"I don't know, Roni, I'm not so sure she answered your question," Gerald Hail teased.

Viva smiled, fought back the urge to laugh. "Hearing him discuss travel plans was like an arrow through my heart. Am I terrible for saying that? *Dramatic* and terrible?"

"Oh well." Gerald squeezed his daughter close and put a kiss to her temple "I'd say yes to the dramatic. You're an actress, after all." He sent her a sly wink. "I don't think we could convict you of being terrible, though."

"Last night, I wished his business deal would fall through so he wouldn't have to go. Sounds pretty terrible to me."

Gerald caught his wife's eye, smiling when she nodded. "I'm gonna go get our coffee, sugar pea. Smells like it's done," he said to Viva after inhaling the air that held the aroma of rich cinnamon.

"Honey, you know you're entitled to have those feelings about the man you love," Veronica was saying once her husband had left the den.

Viva's expression was then playfully stunned. "How do you and Sophia do that? Just assume love is still involved?"

Veronica pulled Viva with her to a time-worn love seat positioned near the fireplace. "I remember that a wedding seemed to be the way things were heading before all those ships started rolling in for you." She put a hand on Viva's knee and squeezed. "You left to follow opportunity, baby, not because you'd fallen out of love with Rook."

"And that has so much to do with it right there. I chucked it all for fame. How shallow could I get?" Viva leaned forward to scrub her face against her palms. "Rook would be an idiot to forget all that and just take me back on faith."

"But would you want him to?"

"He wouldn't, Mama. I'm sure the man certainly has no shortage of women who'd be willing to stay put for anything he'd ask of them." Viva flopped back against the love seat, a dreamy tint softening her eyes. "You should see him, Mama."

"Oh, I have." Veronica gave a coy smile. "So have several of my friends."

The suggestion roused laughter from both women.

"Listen, sugar pea," Veronica said as she slapped Viva's knee then. "There's only one thing wrong with all these women in Rook's perfect life." She tapped her daughter's nose. "He doesn't love any of them, because they aren't you."

"Take her with me? You're serious here?"

"Oh, please stop, Rook." Sophia rolled her eyes. "I've just given you first dibs at an offer every man in the hemisphere would jump to claim."

"She'd never go for it."

Sophia shook her head as if pitying the fact that Rook truly seemed to have no idea of his appeal to the opposite sex. "You know, I'm sure you could find all sorts of ways to persuade her."

"I'm sure I could," Rook said, finally acknowledging a certain level of his power. "But she's also got a job to get back to. Or has her decision to offer testimony against her agent robbed her of her desire to act?"

"She's between projects, and filming for the show won't resume for another five months." She gave him a teasing look. "Are you trying to tell me you're afraid to be alone with a sexy thing like my sister?"

Rook massaged the bridge of his nose and sighed. "You can still be such a brat sometimes."

"I'll have you know that I don't answer to 'brat' anymore, only Chief of Ds." Sophia gave an indignant sniff.

Rook was moved. "I knew you as 'brat' first."

"Level with me, Soap," Rook said once their laughter had eased. "How serious is this? Do you think someone might go after her?"

"I promise you this is only about me erring on the side of caution here." Her gaze turned steely. "No way would I be making jokes and wasting time trying to convince you to do this instead of citing you with some kind of obstruction if you refused to go along." She dismissed the steely look then to make way for one that skirted about playful wickedness.

"I'm leveling with you here, Rook. No way would that be happening if I thought there was any more we should be doing to keep her safe. But I'd still love it if you'd take the job."

Rook worked his fingers against muscles at his nape that had suddenly bunched. "I won't force her to go along with this," he said.

Sophia appeared satisfied. "Don't worry about it. I've got *no* problems with forcing her."

"Please tell me you're calling from Malibu and not back east."

"I'd be happy to tell you that, if you want a lie." Viva grinned at the sound of the familiar nasal voice on the other end of her mobile.

Artesia Relis groaned. "Do you know what you're putting me through here?"

"You mean by visiting my parents for a little TLC?" Viva colored her words with the hint of a snarky undertone.

"Funny." But Artesia didn't sound amused. "I mean leaving us here with Murray. You know no one but you can deal with him when he's riled up."

Viva set down her tanned leather tote bag, deciding to finish the conversation with Murray Dean's assistant there at her parents' place, instead of outside amid steadily dipping temps.

"What's he riled up over?" Viva asked once she'd slipped into the Hails' spacious laundry room. She heard Arty's dramatic sigh—one she'd heard the aspiring actress deliver on countless occasions. Arty had perfected the gesture over the years and it'd become difficult to tell whether the sigh meant true distress or only mild irritation.

"Well, if *you* don't know, how the hell do you think *I* do? I only called because Murray goes back farther with you than anyone." Arty let the sigh make an encore.

"He's been jumpy, snappish and hard to reach. I

mean that literally *and* figuratively, Veev. Half the time, his clients are calling my line because they can't get through to him on his cell. When they do manage to get in touch, they say he's distant. More than a few of his top names are getting nervous and you know what happens when you guys get nervous."

"Yeah…" Viva was working the bridge of her nose between thumb and forefinger. Folks jumped ship when they got nervous. "And you've got no idea what brought this on?" She played the angle, hoping to plumb information Arty may've cast aside.

The practiced sigh made another appearance. "Hard to say… In this business, there's always one thing or another to get pissy over but he did seem more on edge than usual after that meeting a couple of weeks ago."

"Meeting?" Viva peeked out of the laundry room to ensure her privacy was still intact. "Any idea what that was about?"

"Not much. I didn't even have it listed among his appointments. I can tell you they weren't in the business."

"Meaning they weren't actors?"

"Not actors or anyone else connected with the business. They had an…official look about them."

"Cops?" Viva wondered if Sophia had sent investigators to get a feel for their suspect.

"Not sure. I got the feeling their business didn't skirt the right side of the law. Anyway…" Arty's sigh sounded more natural then. "It was just a feeling," she added.

While Viva didn't need the sharp assistant growing suspicious of her questions, she risked one more.

"Do you think you'd recognize them if you saw them again?"

"Sure I would. Veev? Do you think Murray's okay?"

"I'm sure he is, honey. Don't worry, I'll see what I can find out."

"Thanks. Oh, hey! Be on the lookout for that script and the delivery from wardrobe."

"Thanks for the reminder, Art. Hold down the fort and we'll talk soon." Viva ended the connection, waited a beat and then located the number to place a second call. She muttered a curse when she heard the voice-mail greeting.

"Murray? It's Viva. Give me a call, okay?"

Chapter 3

"So these two and these three?" Sophia tapped her fingers to the two-by-three-inch black-and-white mug shots that coincided with her questions.

"Yeah. Those are all I remember from the bunch." Viva leaned back from the small round conference table in her sister's office.

Sophia nodded firmly, looking pleased. Viva had just positively identified the sons of Sylvester Greenway. The construction entrepreneur, and one of their father's oldest friends, had recently come forward with suspicions of his sons' involvement in the money-laundering scheme that had already deposited so many of Philadelphia's finest in holding cells.

Viva's identification of the Greenways was another direct link. Viva had recalled seeing the men at a Malibu party with Murray Dean. The identification added another layer to the case being built around the security-agent-turned-Hollywood-agent-turned-suspected-money-launderer.

Viva watched Sophia remove the book of mug shots. "Is Murray going to jail, Sophia?" she asked after watching her sister quietly for an extended moment.

"It's not a done deal until there's a verdict." Sophia sat on the corner of her big desk. "But a verdict requires a trial first," she said with an encouraging smile for good measure.

"Doesn't seem like I had that much to offer after all."

"Are you kidding? An eyewitness putting Murray with these guys in Cali with the ones here? It's gonna help the DA build an even stronger case. Police work can be a lot of tedious piecing together, but it often results in one colossal wrecking ball at the end."

Viva responded with an airy laugh. "Thanks, Soap, that helps."

"It's the truth." Sophia vacated her spot on the desk and began to browse the files there.

Viva, meanwhile, walked the perimeter of her sister's new and spacious office digs in the heart of downtown. The building, one of Philadelphia's oldest and most stately, boasted offices befitting what the exterior conveyed.

A person with an eye for interior decorating and design, Viva appreciated the efforts taken to ensure Sophia's office was both warm and functional. The formal blackwood paneling and tables of rich cherrywood were softened by suede furnishings of rich earth tones mingled with a few bolder splashes of color that lent the room an efficient yet appropriately chic appearance.

"I can hear your brain over there, but unfortunately I can't translate," Sophia called once silence filled the room for almost two minutes.

Viva turned from the breathtaking wall of windows that presented a glorious view of the city. She looked at her sister who held a handful of folders over a bottom drawer to one side of her desk.

"Is there anything more I could do here, Sophia? Anything more that you'd want me to do?" Viva asked.

Sophia frowned. "Anything more?"

"I called Murray," Viva blurted, knowing that was the only way she could share what she was sure had been a boneheaded move.

Sophia pushed up slowly to stand. "What the hell, V?"

"I didn't want to risk him running, after I talked to his assistant."

"Viva—"

"The girl was at her wits' end when she called, talking about how out of it Murray was acting. She mentioned something about him having a meeting with folks she knew weren't in the business. She said they looked 'official' but she wasn't sure if they were cops or...worse. I thought maybe they could've been cops and I know you can't divulge all the moves you're making in this case, but she said Murray was acting... off ever since and I—I just wanted to help." Viva took a breath following the long spill, winced and waited for the cop in the room to explode.

Sophia stood hunched over the desk. Her hands were splayed across the surface as she inhaled. She straightened, appearing very calm without leaning the slightest bit toward wanting to explode as Viva expected.

"Making sure that a suspect doesn't run isn't your job."

"I was only—" Viva cut herself off, raising her hands in a look of surrender when Sophia's eyes flashed.

"You've done everything I've intended for you to do." Sophia rounded the desk, her expression schooled. "With that in mind, I think it'd be a good idea for you to stay out of sight for a few weeks."

"I agree." Viva began an eager nod, closing some of the distance between her and Sophia. "That won't be a problem at all. The cast has already discussed taking time off to hunker down with the new script for a long rehearsal—"

"Stop." Sophia glared, waiting for Viva to obey. "Staying out of sight means staying *completely* out of sight, away from anywhere Dean might think to look for you if he's got a mind to. Obviously he's got lots of friends in my neck of the woods." She lifted her hands to gesture at their official surroundings. "Ones I've yet to identify. It wouldn't take much for one of them to discover you're on the witness list."

Viva returned to the chair she'd vacated and leaned on the back. "What have you got in mind?"

Sophia propped her hands to her hips, as if preparing for confrontation. "I thought some time out of the country might be a good idea."

"Well, that's great." Viva gave a solitary clap of agreement. "The cast usually does these rehearsal retreats outside the country. We found this really great place when we were on location in the Philippines."

"Viva!" Sophia gave an exasperated sigh. "Completely out of sight means away from your coworkers too."

"Sophia, please tell me you aren't planning to stash me in some old cabin with only cops for company?"

"Oh, I can do way better than that." Sophia gave a flip shrug and went to settle into her comfortable desk chair. "I'm pretty sure you won't be cooped up in an old cabin, but a snowy chalet, and instead of cops, what do you say to a sexy security specialist?"

Sophia's smile sharpened, as did Viva's glare.

"Still can't believe that fool's getting married."

Rook chuckled when Linus Brooks began to laugh. Enjoying the dig at their friend, Linus indulged in a few additional seconds of laughter before helping himself to a swig of the beer Rook had served up from the wall bar in the living area of his office.

"Sophia's a good match for Tig. Always has been." Linus nodded in apparent appreciation of the savory flavor of the chilled imported brew. "Only thing that makes up for the shame of him letting her walk around free all that time is not wasting any more of it before getting her down the aisle."

"Yeah." Rook observed the mug that held his own serving of the beer. "Some fools *do* wise up given enough time."

As Rook prowled the length of the tall windows behind his desk he felt Linus's eyes on him. "Lotta mess went down between them, but...if *they* could work it out..." Linus trailed off as Rook fixed him with a look. "I'd take that to mean it's never too late, is all I'm saying."

"I'm on my way to Italy in a week," Rook said in a manner to rival the softness of the rain tapping his office window that afternoon.

"A lot could happen in a week," Linus said.

"Not that."

"Rook—"

"Sophia and Tig made a mess of things, but at least they had the time and space to fix it." Briefly, Rook closed his eyes to the dreary view. "How are we ever to fix anything when she's halfway around the world or across the country?"

"Last I heard, *you* were your own boss." Undeterred, Linus swigged down another gulp of the beer. "Educate me on exactly what's stopping you."

"Do you really need me to go into that?" Despite the amount of beer he'd downed, Rook's throat still felt as scratchy as a square of sandpaper.

Understanding pooled in Linus's ebony eyes. "Do you want her back?"

"I never wanted her to go."

"She's here now."

"She is…" Rook seemed to consider the simple truth, but only momentarily. "Trying to work this out with Viva will be messy, Linus. People change and six years is a long time."

The cool understanding on Linus's sculpted dark face meshed with empathy. "You're not a victim to that anymore."

"But it's still in me." Rook tapped the bottom of his mug to a denim-clad knee once he'd taken a seat in front of his desk. "Isn't that what we're always supposed to remember? That it would always be inside us, lurking?" He looked to Linus. "That what we have to focus on now is managing it because we'll never be rid of it?"

With a nod he appeared reluctant to give, Linus set aside his beer. Rook tilted back more of his, knowing he didn't need to say more. Linus understood. After all, Rook reminisced, it had been his old friend who had recognized the signs of Rook's anger morphing into an uncontrollable monster inside him.

It had been Linus who'd bravely forged ahead. He'd refused to let Rook's increasingly hostile mood spook him into doing nothing to help him find the means to battle the darkness carving a spot inside him.

"I don't want her to see that in me."

"You'd never hurt her."

"I know that." Rook's tone was black, yet with a matter-of-fact tinge. "Doesn't mean I want her to see me launch a TV through a plate-glass window because I was aggravated over some ancient drama."

"Might do you both some good. Not tossing a TV through plate glass," Linus clarified with a laugh when Rook glared. "I mean getting this poison out of your system. Finally telling her how what she did made you feel."

Rook shook his head stubbornly. "She wasn't to blame."

"I didn't say she was, but what happened put you in a real bad place—a place you haven't all the way come back from." Linus came to take a chair closest to the one Rook occupied. "You'll never truly manage this crap if you don't share some of that weight with her. Do that at least—even if nothing more comes of it. She'll head back to California and you'll make your moves, but you'll make 'em without a lot of weight from the past dragging at you and dangling like a carrot in front of that monster you need to control."

"Does Eli know you moonlight as a shrink?" Rook teased, referring to Elias Joss, another of their friends and Linus's business partner.

"Aw, he's used to it." Linus gave a playful eye roll. "'Specially if it means the happiness of a friend.

"Look, man," Linus said once laughter was shared. "The last thing I want is for everything you've got pent up to barrel out unexpectedly. Trust me, I know what the consequences of that feels like."

Rook spread his big hands. "What? Am I giving off some kind of dark vibe?"

"No, but I know Viva being back has to be adding some kind of pressure. That added to the fact that you've missed two meetings...and now you're about to take a long trip... Well, I'm a little concerned."

"Don't be." Rook leaned over to slap at Linus's forearm beneath the fleece sleeve of his sweatshirt. "I'm good. I've been good. No reason to think that won't continue."

The phone rang and both men grinned as though the sound were a good omen.

"Yeah, Lind?" Rook greeted his assistant Lindy Peters, by speaker.

"Sorry, Rook, I thought you'd want to take this call. It's Chief Hail."

Linus left his chair, taking his empty beer mug which he used to motion to Rook for another refill.

Rook nodded, appreciating the bit of privacy. "Send

her through." In a few seconds he heard the click on the line. "Soap? Linus is here."

"Hey, Linus!" Sophia called through the speaker.

Rook silenced the speaker once Linus sent his greetings. As Linus busied himself browsing the extensive stock of domestic and imported beers behind the bar, Rook listened to what Sophia had to say. His responses into the phone turned shorter and he couldn't keep frustration from creeping into his voice. Linus must have heard it too, because he returned to his chair and offered an encouraging shrug when the call ended.

"Scratch everything I just said," Rook ordered his friend.

"Viva?"

Her hands going still on the straps of an enormous tan tote bag, Viva turned toward the sound of the vaguely familiar voice that was presently etched with curiosity. Laughter tickled her throat when she saw Burt Larkin standing in the doorway of Rook's office.

"So is it all right to be here in the control room?" Viva asked once she and Burt had exchanged hugs and pleasantries. "Rook's assistant told me to come on in."

"You're fine and besides, it's the best place for you." Burt scratched at a wheat-colored brow. "How'd you get in here without being mobbed anyway?"

Viva gave her tote bag a shake. "Never underestimate the power of a good wig and sunglasses. Sophia told me how to get here but my guess is she regrets that now after ordering me to go along with Rook putting his life on hold to babysit me. I'm sure you know about that."

Burt nodded. "I may've heard something, but I'm sure he doesn't see it as babysitting and putting his life on hold, Viva."

"I'm here to see that he does."

Viva's practiced bravado threatened mutiny when she saw Rook arriving at his office door.

"So I'm gonna head out," Burt said, putting a knowing smile in place. He went to pull Viva into a quick, warm embrace. "Have someone find me before you leave, so I can get an autograph. It'll make me the envy of all my playmates."

"Promise!" Viva laughed.

Burt kept the smile on his attractively weather-beaten face when he sidestepped his boss.

Rook shut the door at Burt's back and was facing it when he began to speak to Viva. "Sophia called, said you might stop by."

"Wow." Viva set aside her tote bag and pretended to be impressed. "Calls announcing my arrival...you and Sophia sure are close these days."

Rook strolled to his desk, which was a fixture of gleaming blackwood in the back of the spacious yet efficient office. Rook allowed himself few comforts when he worked. Even the well-stocked bar and living area radiated Spartan undertones.

"Chief of Ds thinks me and my team do a pretty decent job."

"I'm sure that's true, but you don't need to waste your resources on me."

"Last thing it'd be is a waste." Rook settled onto one corner of the broad, neat desk. "There's no need for a large crew. This is a one-man job."

"Rook, I'm sorry." Viva stopped a few feet before him at the desk.

"Sorry?" He tensed. "What for?"

"Sophia should've never pulled you into this."

"And why is that?" Rook faked a little confusion. "I supply security and you're obviously in need of it."

Viva eased her hands into the side pockets of the teal skirt that showcased her curves and shapely calves where the hem ended just below the knee. "Just what did Sophia tell you?" Suspicion was rife in her slightly husky voice.

"Not much." Rook studied his hands while he rubbed his palms. "Enough to give me a sense of what's going on, but I suspect she's leaving it up to you to share all the...colorful details." He treated himself to a brief but effective appraisal of her body that she felt in every nerve ending. "Sophia gave me the feeling there were several," he added when her eyes met his again.

I'll bet she did, Viva mused silently, feeling the crushing need to act on her threats of bodily harm to her little sister.

Rook made a pretense of straightening the few files lying on his pristine desk. "I've got time to talk now if you want."

"Rook," Viva began in a manner that rarely failed to get her what she wanted. "Listen, I—I don't want you involved with this and I'd appreciate you going to Soap and telling her to put someone else on it."

"No." The response was quick, cold. Rook didn't even spare Viva a glance as he studied the paperwork on his desk.

Viva wasn't surprised by the answer; she knew it'd

been useless to ask the question. She'd only been using the "get me what I want" voice since her name had become a recognizable one. It had proved a successful technique—on most everyone except her sister. Trying it with Rook was just as idiotic. When safety was an issue, he was deaf to any attempt at making light of it.

"So what about your trip to Italy?" she asked then, minus the "get me what I want" emphasis.

"What about it?" He gave her the benefit of his gaze then.

"Are you still going?"

"Yes."

Viva took a quiet moment to process. "Well, how can you do that and watch *me* 24/7?"

He smiled. "I can do that because you're going with me. I'm sure Sophia told you that already."

"I can't."

"You will."

"You'll force me?"

"I've been promised that I won't have to."

"Sophia." Viva hissed her sister's name like it was a curse. "So you already know this involved Murray." She decided it wouldn't hurt to come clean—a little.

Rook tilted his head a fraction, no doubt hoping to shield the sudden and fanatical twitch of a jaw muscle. It was a futile attempt. "I know that."

"And you expect us to just go off to Italy together without that being a problem for us?"

Infuriatingly cool then, Rook leaned forward a tad. "I don't expect that at all," he told her.

"Then what?"

"I expect you to tell me whatever your sister suspects you're keeping from me."

Viva couldn't resist a quick burst of laughter. "What she *suspects* I'm keeping? You're going off the assumption that her suspicions are correct."

"She's a cop. A damn good one. *So* good, she got a promotion most cops don't even bother to dream about at her age." He shrugged. "Yeah, I'm good with assuming her suspicions are correct."

"And did she give you any hints about what she suspects?"

"No. My guess is she's hoping you'll use the time to get into it."

Viva moved closer, resting a hip on the desk when she faced him. "You know she wants me protected because of Murray's involvement with her case."

"I know." A muscle danced wickedly in his cheek. "That alone is enough to make me want in on this."

"And you don't expect this trip to give you any stress and headaches you don't need while you're trying to get your business in order?"

"I expect this trip will give me *a lot* of stress and headaches I don't need, but you're crazy if you think I'd say no to this, V."

With a sigh, Viva studied the low, yet cushioned dark carpeting beneath her pumps. "Rook, you should know that I called Murray. I left a message for him to get in touch. His assistant says he's been acting weird and she thought I could talk him down." Viva thought she saw the carpet blur before her eyes as the explanation spilled out. "I thought it'd be a good idea to call, so he wouldn't run."

Rook watched her like she'd sprouted a second head. "What the hell did you think you were doing?"

"Spare me the lecture," Viva retorted with an airy

wave and eye roll. "Sophia beat you to it and then ordered me to go along with whatever you say. Do you have any idea how frustrating it is to have your baby sister giving you orders like that?"

Rook only grunted a low curse while flexing a fist. "We leave on Thursday," he said.

"Thursday? But that barely gives me time to—" She silenced at the look he sent her way.

"Rook," she pleaded then, hunching over the desk and spreading her hands across the gleaming surface. "See reason here. Murray's my agent. I can't just disappear. What am I supposed to tell him if he calls me back?"

"Do you really want me to answer that?" Rook's insanely desirable face was a study in pure menace.

"Well, I have to tell him something." Viva blew at a curl that bounced between her brows. "He practically has to beg me to take breaks. He'd never believe I just ran off and—"

"Not even if you told him you ran off with me?"

Openmouthed, Viva could only stare.

Rook took advantage of the quiet. "Tell him we're rekindling the flame. Tell him…tell him I threatened to tie you to my bed until you agreed to go along and you believed me. I think that's a threat I've followed through on a time or two, isn't it?"

Viva tried to speak, laugh, something…but she failed at every attempt. She ran her tongue over her lips and tried speaking again. "He'd know that's not true. He'd know I'm lying—"

Any further argument was silenced once he kissed her and her tongue was otherwise engaged with his. Rook had taken command of her wrist and tugged her across the brief space separating them on the desk. Seamless and confident, he settled her across the broad width of his thigh, making her straddle the limb in a ruthless, brazen manner.

The stretchy fabric of her skirt eased up to accommodate the change in her position. Viva didn't care that his manner was raw and hungry so long as he didn't stop. She wasted no time snuggling into the kiss. It was hers to enjoy...or resist.

There was but subtle command at the heart of the way he held her. He was giving her the chance to resist if she wanted, but resistance was light-years away from Viva's consciousness. Nothing could make her withdraw from the wondrous soothing sensation of his tongue stroking and loving her mouth in a way that only *he* could.

Rook apparently felt differently and began to withdraw from the kiss. He didn't leave her cold. Instead, the heated strokes of his tongue cooled to adopt a lazier pace, until he was running the tip along her teeth and the velvety softness of her bottom lip. Then he was kissing her there, pampering the area with whisper-soft, sugary pecks that had her moaning in want of more.

Viva kept her eyes closed, when there was no further pressure against her mouth. She hoped the stimulating pecks—at the very least—would resume. There was nothing. She opened her eyes then, wondering if he felt the thud of her heart as she drowned in the radiance of his amber stare.

Rook used only his thumb to caress her mouth. He smiled, appreciating the unsmudged quality of her petal-pink lipstick. Then he returned his gaze to hers.

"Now you won't have to lie," he said.

Viva let out the breath she hadn't realized she was holding and tried to speak his name. She failed. Gently, Rook set her back where she was.

"Thursday," he said and then left her to head behind his desk.

Swamped by a haze of confusion and unquenched need, Viva managed to snap to. She collected some of her scattered nerves and just managed to leave the room without tripping over herself.

Chapter 4

Tamping down her uneasiness took more time than Viva expected—a thing she realized when she headed out of Rook's office and took the elevator down to the mezzanine level in search of a less direct route outside. From there, it was a short walk down a wide staircase boxed in glossy dark oak and down a set of stairs to the lobby.

The elevator descent and stroll from the mezzanine had proved uneventful enough. That changed when she stepped out into L Sec's bustling switchboard division. Collecting scattered nerves hadn't left her time to remember her disguise.

A surreal moment of uninterrupted quiet set in amongst the inhabitants of the switchboard hub as Viva looked over the once-busy staff. Seconds passed and then the stirrings of hushed conversation eased in like a mist over quiet. The hushed conversation gained volume as acknowledgment took hold. Once the first courageous soul approached the well-known actress, pandemonium ensued.

Despite frazzled nerves, Viva laughed. She didn't mind the attention. She adored her fans. She'd relied on their adoration to pull her out of depressive bouts when they struck more often than she could count.

Signing autographs while making her way through the lobby to the main entrance took all of eighty minutes. Beyond the skyscraper's towering doors, she practically speed-walked to her rental car and fumbled with the key to deactivate the locks. She slipped into the driver's seat, expelling a relieved whoosh of breath once she was concealed behind the car's darkly tinted windows.

The soothing medley of wind chimes gave her cause to jump as her nerves still proved to be unsettled from the kiss. Viva laughed over the self-criticism. It was a kiss, true, but there was no such thing as *only* a kiss when Rook Lourdess was the supplier. Besides… she'd gone without his kisses for far too long.

The phone chimed again and she forced her attention to the screen. Another jolt attacked her senses when her agent's name floated into view.

Closing her eyes, Viva instinctively forced aside all distractions and put herself in character to accept the call. "Hey, Murray," she greeted him in the voice of airy delight that had become her trademark.

"Veev, what's up, love? Everything all right?"

Viva hesitated on her response. She hadn't expected him to ask how she was given how distracted she'd heard he'd been.

"Well, you know how it is… I've been a little out of it lately." She played along, hoping it might encourage him to open up.

"Guess it's weird going home after all this time, huh?"

Viva's smile held a poignant gleam. "Weird, but good," she admitted.

"Glad to hear it." Murray's voice seemed to hold a similar poignancy.

"So are *you* okay? You sound a little drained."

"I am."

"Business?" Viva straightened a little on the suede seat of the sporty BMW. She knew he'd take her query about business to understand that she was referring to show business.

"The outskirts of the business."

"Talk to me, Murray." His distinction encouraged her to probe a little deeper.

Murray evidently needed to vent. "Seems I've got some associates who've decided to try smearing my name."

"Murray, that's terrible. What's going on? Is there anything I can do?"

"Sweet thing—" Murray chuckled "—this is nothing you need to worry your fine self over. I've got it under control. They'll shut their mouths sooner or later. So, um…how's Sophia?"

Viva blinked. "Sophia? Um, fine, fine, she's great. Getting married."

"Ahh, marriage *and* a promotion."

"You—you heard about that all the way out west?"

"News travels, Veev, and I make a point to keep up

with what's goin' on back home, you know? I heard she was working on some money-laundering thing."

"Yeah, she, um…she's close to wrapping it up, actually." Viva debated momentarily and then continued, "She's already made some big arrests. Looks like a winner for her."

"Sounds like she's on top of it."

Viva leaned back on the headrest. "Guess that's why she got the big promotion."

"Mmm…" Murray's silence hung on the line for several seconds. "So how long are you planning to be back east?"

"Not long, actually, um, that's why I called." She cast a quick look across the parking lot in the direction of L Sec. "I'm heading off on another trip, Mur. Just wanted to tell you before I left and to make sure we could stay in touch. I didn't know if you had any big plans or not."

"So where are you heading off to?"

Viva paused for dramatic effect. "I've, um… I've seen Rook since I've been home."

Murray's insightful "mmm…" hit the air again. "Doesn't surprise me, Veev. Even after all this time, there's still a lot of unfinished business between you guys. Makes sense Rook wouldn't want to let any more time pass after doing nothing to stop you from leaving before."

"Murray, stop. The blame isn't all on Rook."

"You're right. You're right, and I hope things work out. You guys got a bad break back then."

"Thank you, Murray." She was genuinely surprised by his words. "Murray, are you gonna be okay? Is there anything I can do?"

"Nothing. Like I said—I'll be fine. There're just some things I need to tidy up. You can call my personal cell if you need to reach me." He chuckled. "You think Rook will let you take calls once he whisks you away?"

Viva was laughing softly. "I'm sure. Jeez, Murray, I'm so on edge about the whole thing…just be available if I call and need to vent."

"You can count on me, Veev, don't worry." Murray was laughing then, but his voice had chilled. "Everything'll be fine once I put some stuff to bed."

The call ended shortly after with goodbyes and more laughter. Viva kept the phone to her ear and turned Murray's words over in her mind. She didn't spend much time on the endeavor, realizing she didn't really want to know what they meant.

Viva's nerves had settled by the time she'd returned to her sister's. When she'd arrived in Philadelphia, Sophia had said there was no reason for her to get a hotel room. As the two of them would be spending most nights talking until the wee hours anyway, they may as well do that someplace more like home.

Viva could've really used Sophia's ear when she arrived at the condo from Rook's office.

Thankfully, her sister was but a phone call away— a fact Viva took advantage of once she'd set aside her disguise bag and changed into loungewear. She contacted Sophia and they rehashed Murray's call while Viva took the edge off the day by indulging in a few glasses of wine.

"Did it sound like he was still in California?" Sophia asked.

Viva swirled the wine in her amber-colored glass and smiled as Rook's similarly colored eyes came to mind. "I couldn't get a sense of where he was."

"'Putting stuff to bed.' That's an odd phrase…" Sophia seemed to be considering that bit of info.

"Yeah, that part freaked me out too." Viva rested back on the sofa, knees raised and bared when the hem of the lounge dress hiked up. "I never heard him talk that way. What do you think it means?"

"Sounds ominous, that's for sure…like maybe he's planning to silence those who could be a threat to him. Do you get it now why I need you to stay out of sight? Murray knows there've been arrests, but he's still set on 'putting stuff to bed,' which could mean he's got more partners out there lurking who could still do damage."

"I get it, Soap," Viva drawled as she downed a bit more of the wine.

"It's just that I've still got folks in my own organization I can't trust," Sophia continued. "I just need you to understand that being with Rook is the safest place you can be."

"I know, Sophia, I know." Viva closed her eyes and rested her head back on the sofa.

"So you went to see Rook, huh?" Sophia asked once another wave of silence hit.

"I tried to talk him out of watching over me."

"I didn't have to twist his arm about doing it, you know. He won't rest until he knows you're safe."

"Yeah." Viva helped herself to another generous swallow of the dry white. "He kissed me," she blurted shortly after.

Sophia gasped and then coughed. "You cold wench! How the hell could you tell me that over the phone?"

"Tried to wait," Viva said as she yawned. "Figured I'd be too wasted to make any sense by the time you got home."

"Well, dammit, stop drinking. I'm on my way."

"He threatened to tie me to his bed if I didn't go along with your plan. I've been tied to Rook's bed before, Soap."

"Mmm...I see. I take it that's a threat you'd want him to make good on?"

"God, yes."

Sophia muttered a playful curse into the phone. "Stop drinking. I'll be there soon."

The connection broke in Viva's ear. "Sure thing," she drawled into the dead receiver. "Soon as I have just a little more." She finished the wine, reached for the half-empty bottle and poured another glass.

"Well, if it ain't the bridegroom!" Rook called to Santigo when he saw him heading for Sophia's condo building around sunset. "Congratulations again, man," he said when they met for handshakes and hugs.

"Time heals all wounds," Tigo said, his darkly handsome face alive with humor and happiness.

Rook winced. "So I keep hearing."

"Well, the statement could stand a little tweaking, I guess," Tigo contemplated aloud. "How about this—wounds heal best when folks stop jabbing at each other."

"Ah...so that's where we've been screwing up."

"Is that 'we' as in you and Viva?"

"Come off it, Tig," Rook said as he and Tigo scanned

their IDs at the sensor just next to the bay of revolving glass doors. "I know your fiancée clued you in to all my new drama."

"Not really. We really haven't had much time together." Tigo slipped his ID into his wallet and appeared playfully crestfallen. "Not much time to get into anything dramatic. Thank God." He grinned.

Rook reciprocated the gesture and appreciated his friend's joy. "Hate to break it to you, but I'm sure that's about to change."

Tigo's steps slowed and he turned. "Anything you wanna just go on and tell me?"

Rook worked the bridge of his nose between thumb and forefinger. "Sophia wants Viva to come with me to Italy."

Tigo whistled. "Jeez, man, that's putting a new spin on business and pleasure."

"Tell me about it."

Both men wore genuine smiles when they paused to greet residential security. The guards in the pine-and-glass-encased booth were especially friendly as they recognized their boss. The men chatted for a while. Tigo took time out to let Sophia know he was there and who he was with. Appreciating the heads-up, Sophia asked them to give her and Viva time to spruce up the place before they came up.

"Looks like L Sec's movin' in," Tigo noted once they were moving beyond the booth toward the elevator bay.

"Looks like." Rook shrugged, his expression reflecting satisfaction. "The building's owners got concerned after what happened to Sophia. They thought they could stand to put more security in place for their residents." He gestured to the ceiling where a magnificent skylight directed weak late-autumn sunlight into the lobby. "Everyone around here seems to like the changes. It's made your wife-to-be a popular girl."

"So are you really good with this—taking V along with you?" Tigo asked once their laughter had eased. "Soap'll understand if it's too much with all that's happened."

Rook leaned against an opposing wall while Tigo hit the button for the elevator. "I know I'm a fool to go along with it, but..." He mopped his face in his palms.

Tigo grinned. "I get it, man. So do you think you guys'll be back for the wedding?"

Rook pushed off the wall. "You guys set a date already?"

"Done wasting time," Tigo said matter-of-factly. "We don't need some huge, crazy event. Right now, we're working to get the folks to go along with that." He laughed. "Guess I've got some drama goin' after all."

"The good kind." Rook clapped Tigo's shoulder as they stepped into an arriving elevator car.

"You want Viva back?" Tigo asked when the car's paneled doors closed with a muffled thud.

"More than anything." Rook relaxed against the paneling and closed his eyes. "And before you say it, yes, I know time isn't on our side."

"There are really only two things you need to ask yourself," Tigo said as he leaned on the wall next to Rook. "Is it worth it and does she feel the same?"

"Do you mean in the physical or mental sense?" Rook's sly smile mimicked his tone of voice. "I can tell you I don't have a clue where her head is."

"So handle your business in Italy and do what you need to in order to settle this between you and V."

Rook gave his old friend a sideways glance. "You know, you're starting to sound like Linus."

"Is that good or bad?"

Laughter filled the ascending car.

"Jeez, V, why couldn't you just listen to me for once in your life? Just believe your little sister knows what she's talking about?" Sophia grumbled when she rushed back into the living room from the kitchen where she'd started a pot of coffee and deposited Viva's emptied wine bottle.

Sophia stooped before Viva, whom she'd found dozing when she got home. She gave her big sister's cheek a quick, light slap. "Come on, girl, the guy of your dreams is on his way up. This is no time for you to be playing the role of the drunken lush.

"V?" She slapped Viva's cheeks again. "Do you hear me?" she queried when her sister groaned. "He's on his way up."

Rousted a bit, Viva's eyes opened to narrow slits. "Up?"

"Rook's coming up."

Viva groaned.

"Come on, V." Sophia added a few more taps to her sister's face.

Viva winced. "You're just doing that to be mean now."

"You know me so well." Sophia pushed to her feet. "Don't go back to sleep!" she called, heading back to the kitchen to check on the coffee. "Locks are off the door, so Rook and Tigo can come on in!"

Viva cradled her head, resting her elbows on her knees as she groaned anew. "Why'd you ask him over?"

"I didn't." Sophia stepped out of the kitchen to answer. "Maybe he wanted to come check and see how you were recovering from that kiss he laid on you earlier."

"You're not helping."

"You'll be okay," Sophia crooned. "You've got several weeks of lavish Italian living coming to you."

"I know what you're doing."

"Oh, yeah? What am I doing?" Sophia returned to the living room with a loaded coffee tray in tow. "Looks like I'm slaving to fix you coffee even after the day I've had." She set down the tray and sighed. "This is why people hate celebrities."

Viva's expression was bland. "People don't hate celebrities."

"They do when they have to deal with 'em in real life."

Viva's misery fully reasserted itself then. "Why couldn't he put up this much effort when I first left?"

"You wouldn't have heard what he had to tell you then." Sophia poured the delicious-smelling brew into an oversize glazed mug depicting a fall scene.

"How do you know that?" Viva tried to pout.

"I know that because I knew you then," Sophia replied as she added cream to the strong black coffee until it turned to an inviting rich beige. "The only thing you loved more than Rook Lourdess was the acting bug."

"So this is my fault?"

"Your words, not mine." Sophia pushed the mug

into Viva's hands. "Drink this." She nodded as her instructions were followed and then moved to prepare her own cup.

"V, we could go back and forth on this all day and into next year, but you only need to remember one thing. Be honest with him." Sophia blew across the surface of the coffee, took a sip and smiled in appreciation of the taste.

"Just tell him whatever it is you think he won't understand," she continued. "You're already apart. There's nothing to lose now, is there?"

Viva started to take another sip of her coffee, but paused. "How easy was all that 'honesty is the best policy' stuff before you and Tig worked it out?"

Sophia savored more of her coffee, her glee apparent in the contented smile and happy shiver she gave. "I never went through anything so hard in my whole life. It wasn't easy—it was hell. Felt like I was walking on coals a lot of the time."

Viva rolled her eyes. "Thanks," she said flatly.

"Anytime." Sophia sipped more coffee and then sighed when she heard a knock at the door.

"I told Tigo to just come on in."

"Why do you keep throwing us together?" Viva set her mug to the stone table before the sofa while Sophia stood to answer the knock. "Do you know how long it's taken me to get over that man?"

Sophia paused a few feet from the door. "I don't know. Why don't you tell me when it happens?"

"I hate you."

Sophia laughed. "You love me."

Chapter 5

"You should've called again," Rook suggested to Tigo once they'd stepped into the condo and saw Viva resting back on the sofa, an arm thrown over her eyes in a picture of woe.

"She started the party without us," Sophia explained as she reclaimed her coffee mug from an end table.

Rook was already kneeling next to the sofa and cupping Viva's jaw. "Is she okay?"

"I'm fine," Viva slurred.

Rook looked to the coffee mug and then gave Viva's jaw a little squeeze. "Didn't you tell your sister that stuff does nothing to perk you up?"

Viva responded with a lazy smile. "It's a cop thing. Coffee's their go-to cure for whatever ails you."

In retaliation, Sophia yanked her sister's hair as she walked past. Tigo soothed the gesture, when Viva cried out, with a kiss to his soon-to-be sister-in-law's brow.

Rook chuckled as the couple headed into the kitchen. "I just wanted to check on you," he told her.

Viva's smile refreshed. "Why? Did you think I'd pass out from the strength of one kiss?"

Rook fingered away the tip of a curl clinging to the corner of her mouth. "It's been known to happen," he said. "Will you let me take you to bed?"

"Mmm…yes…" she purred without hesitation. Instantly she regretted the slip and silently bemoaned the fact that coffee really had no effect on her.

Rook moved in, easily taking her into his arms. "Let's go, I know something that'll work better than coffee."

"Sex?" Viva's tone was hopeful.

Rook laughed. "Sleep."

"I sleep better after sex." She figured she'd already done a fine job of putting her foot in her mouth. No sense stopping now.

Rook played the game in stride. Inside, he wished she'd shut up. In that moment, all he could think of was putting her to bed…with sex. "You already had the wine to help with that," he managed to say.

Viva merely smiled and let her head rest on his shoulder. She enjoyed the security coursing through her in reaction to the broad expanse of muscle supporting her head. Sleepily, she gave him directions to her room.

"Rook," she murmured into his neck, "I miss you."

He grinned then, taking her confession to be alcohol-induced. "I miss you too," he said, playing along. He felt her mouth against his seconds later.

He had no thought to question whether the gesture was alcohol induced or not. He had no thoughts, period—save the fact that they were engaged in a kiss. The second one in over six years.

Somehow, he found the way to her room. One kick from his boot secured the door and sealed them in a cocoon of darkness inside. Rook made no effort to venture any farther beyond the door. He stood, holding her high and close to his chest as the kiss grew more heated and urgent.

The kiss had begun sweetly enough with Viva's lazy exploration of his mouth. Her tongue had grazed his even teeth before curling sensually around his tongue. Now though it turned potent, and Rook's groans mingled with the soft, infectious purrs of pleasure stirring in the back of her throat. Her firm breasts were more than a handful and for that, Rook had no complaints. His only regret was that they weren't filling his hands just then. Cursing raggedly to himself, he drove his tongue against hers.

He moved forward, hoping the bed wasn't too far away. He felt the edge of the mattress nudging him a moment later.

Viva could feel herself lowering and instinctively curved her fingers about his open shirt collar. She was determined to take him down with her.

Rook needed no encouragement on that score. He caged her beneath his wide frame, never once breaking the kiss as he settled between her thighs. The satiny limbs had been bared by the rising hem of the ankle-length lounge dress she wore.

Viva could only gasp when she felt his arousal. His erection was stiffly pronounced, appreciatively wedged against the dampened middle of her panties. Her back bowed as she arched, rubbing against Rook in an attempt to ease away the ache stirred by him there so close to the spot he had been the first to awaken and possess.

It was a possession he still held claim to, Viva admitted in the quiet of her mind. Time had not erased what he and he alone could make her feel with a look or the slightest touch.

There was nothing *slight* about his touch then, however. His crushing weight was a welcome pressure against her body—one that had been so very missed during the six-year drought of their separation. She arched and rubbed against him more insistently. Simultaneously, she engaged her breasts in the lusty interlude.

It was impossible for Rook to ignore the plump mounds crushing into his chest with burgeoning persistence. His palms literally ached with the need to feel the nipples naked against his skin. Yet he resisted, knowing if he indulged, he wouldn't be leaving her until the morning, if then. Clenching his fists, Rook launched an attempt to ease away, to withdraw from the kiss and the haze of pleasure only she had the power to lock him in.

Viva wasn't the least on board with calling a halt to their moment. Her nails grazed the short, cottony waves tapering his nape in a play to keep him close. Even as she continued to move her breasts across his chest, she was freeing her hold at his nape to tug at the ties securing the bodice of her dress.

Rook latched onto the dredges of his willpower and shook his head as he withdrew. "No, V…"

She responded by clutching fistfuls of his shirt and rocking her hips with deliberate insistence. "You don't mean it."

"Damn right, I don't, but it needs to be said."

She gave a throaty laugh, one he'd missed hearing in his ear. Until then, he'd only been able to enjoy the sound from an impersonal distance through a TV or movie screen.

Viva resumed her sweet rocking and the moves had Rook stiffening then to an almost painful state. He surprised them both when he wrenched back. Capturing Viva's wrists, he pressed them above her head, before she could snag his shirt again.

In the weak streams of the streetlights fighting their way past the blinds, he saw her face. The disappointment in her expression broke his heart and for an instant, his temper flared at the idea of her gracing any other man with that look. That look that could render a man incapable of denying her anything. That look that had the power to caress a man's ego, bolster his pride and reduce him to a sex-starved mess all in the same vein.

Considering the idea of her giving that look to another was time poorly spent. That was doubly true for a man currently working to keep a tight rein on his anger. He kissed her sweetly then—a peck to each eyelid. He smiled, noting that she couldn't quickly open them following the kisses, as if they were still weighted down by exhaustion.

"Get some sleep," he murmured next to her ear.

"Stay," she urged.

"I'm not going anywhere," he promised her and realized that he meant it.

"So you're sure your dirty coworkers are as safe as they can be?"

Sophia had just told Rook and Santigo about Viva's call with Murray Dean.

"They're locked up tight," Sophia responded to Rook's question from her snug spot against Tigo on the sofa. "But Murray's words do give us more to consider, like who he might have on the inside that could make my dirty coworkers *less* safe and who we've yet to lock away or put into protective custody before he can 'put them to bed' as he said."

"Hell," Tigo groaned. "How does an agent get tied up in something like this? I mean, I know Hollywood isn't filled with the most angelic souls, but money laundering and using gentlemen's clubs and dirty cops in the mix is quite a stretch."

"The guy was always ambitious," Rook said from his relaxed position in a suede recliner across the room. "Murray wanted the shine and he wasn't above doing what he had to, to get it. Even if it meant pinching off something someone else had already put together."

"Murray worked for you back in the day, right?" Tigo asked.

Rook's nod was a grim confirmation. "He jumped ship without notice to establish his own security firm. Then he added insult to injury when he tried to make off with my staff."

"He's a bold criminal. You have to give him that," Sophia mused.

"You guys think he could've been into all this back then?" Tigo asked.

Rook was first to speak up. "He was ambitious, but I never saw anything that rang criminal."

"They rang unethical though," Sophia said as she shrugged beneath the plum scoop-neck top she'd worn with her blazer that day. "From there, it's not always the biggest leap to the criminal side of things.

"Guess it couldn't hurt to check into what Mr. Dean's got going on behind the scenes on a personal level financially," Sophia suggested once silence held for a time. "Property holdings and things of that nature could provide heavy incentive for certain unethical acts. We've been looking at his current acts, but it could pay to see if our friendly neighborhood agent was living above his legal means and for how long."

"I should've stopped her from going with him." Rook had left the recliner and was pacing. His habitual fist clenching had once again taken hold.

"Easy, man," Tigo soothed. "How could you have known it'd go down this way?"

"I knew," Rook responded blackly. "I probably knew long before Murray pulled his disappearing act and tried to take half my team along for the ride. I should've known something."

"Well, we can change that now." Sophia eased from Tigo's comforting embrace to study Rook. "When this all hits the fan, you can believe Murray's going to be reaching out to all his contacts to rally in defense of his good name. Viva will be right at the top of that list."

"Damn if I let that happen," Rook grumbled, sliding an acid look toward the hallway leading to the bedrooms.

"You're welcome to stay," Sophia told him, no doubt following the path of his glare. "That room's big enough for two."

Her nonsubtle attempt drew a smile to Rook's mouth and he fixed her with a sly look. "How can you be such

a dynamic cop and have such a problem stopping yourself from being so obvious?"

Sophia settled back against Tigo. "When I see trav-
esties, I pull out all the stops to get them corrected."

"Understood, and I love you for trying." Rook eased
a haunted look toward the hallway again. "It's gonna
take more to correct this than us being in the same
place at the same time. I don't know if either of us
is ready for a discussion of how many ways we've
screwed up." He shook his head as if to clear it, turned
and crossed to the sofa where he dropped a kiss to Sophie's forehead.

"Tell her I'll see her tomorrow," Rook instructed
while shaking hands with Tigo. He only nodded at
the concern he saw in the couple's eyes before he left.

"Yeah, this is gonna go over real well... I'll spend
half the season recovering from a broken leg," Viva
grumbled the next morning while giving a skeptical
look to the shoe she held.

The studio that produced the cable crime drama
that she'd been a part for the last five years had delivered the script for the new season. The wardrobe
department had also included a package with the shipment. The spike-heeled pump she held would've easily added at least six inches to her height.

After unpacking about eight pairs of the chic stems,
Viva began an immediate scan of the script to de-
termine what the writers had in store for her tough
and usually no-nonsense character. Apparently, a new
undercover assignment would require her to saunter
around in the bona fide neck breakers over the course
of several episodes.

Viva had nothing against fierce footwear, but filming could last several weeks and hours on end each day. Flouncing around in stilts for much of that time wasn't her idea of a fun work environment. With a resolved, albeit grim smile, Viva slipped into a pair of the intimidating pumps, bracing herself on the boxy arms of the chair she occupied before standing.

Though pumps were familiar staples of her wardrobe, she did exercise a fair amount of discernment when it came to the potential for breaking her behind all in the name of fashion.

"Anyway..." she groaned, taking a tentative step. "For the fans..."

The shoes were to die for, she thought. Pink satin inlaid on white leather straps that crossed over the top of the shoe. The material seemed to glimmer when it captured the light.

Despite the killer height, the shoes felt remarkably comfortable. Viva didn't know if it was her familiarity with heels or that the shoes really were that comfortable, but walking instead of teetering proved more possible than she'd guessed. She could only hope the other stems in the shipment would be just as forgiving.

She was rummaging through the box, trying to decide which pair to try on next, when the entertainment segment of the twenty-four-hour news channel segued in. Her mouth fell open when she heard the name Reynolds Henry. She listened as the broadcaster repeated the headline.

The actor, who had faded into obscurity following a flash of fame and promise, had been found dead in his West Hollywood apartment of an apparent prescription-drug overdose. The broadcaster went on to present a brief montage chronicling Henry's troubled life.

Viva conjured an image of the lanky, blond actor whose biting wit and outspokenness had made him a fan favorite for a time. Her sympathies went out to him and the tragic path his life had taken. She knew that at one point or another, most actors' lives veered along similar stretches. More often than not, those stretches led to ends that mirrored Reynolds Henry's.

Viva had been among the thankful ones who'd managed to overcome the pitfalls and detours that could've made her life hell. Nevertheless, pitfalls and detours had not completely eluded her.

She'd made her own share of mistakes similar to the ones the TV broadcaster presented with such fervor in relation to Henry. She'd made those unfortunate decisions back in the early days, of her own accord. Though she'd certainly been well counseled on the dark situations and shady characters she'd encounter in the life she was seeking, she hadn't listened, hadn't wanted to and had feverishly rebelled against the truths her parents had dished her way. The truths Rook had dished her way...

What would he say if he knew of those mistakes? How would he react to seeing her unfortunate acts broadcasted on a TV screen? She wondered. How would he react were she to tell him?

Grimacing, Viva shook off the possibility. Did they have a chance? A new chance now in this recent turn of events? Did he miss her the way she missed him, or was his acceptance of Sophia's request to look out for her just him doing the right thing? Something that seemed to come so easily to him.

Was it as simple as all that? If not…then did she stand any chance at all of recapturing his heart—his love—if she revealed all to him? Hell, was that even necessary? It was the past—one she had no desire to revisit.

"Stop, V," she told herself, grimacing anew while tapping her nails to her temples. There was no need to torture herself. Best to leave things as they were.

Sophia's case would be closed soon enough. Murray would be dealt with one way or another and she'd be back to her life. Rook would carry on with his. And old truths? Old truths were best left where time had placed them. In the past.

It was foolish for her to even hope for anything fresh between her and Rook. She could accept that.

The bell sounded and she celebrated the intrusion while heading for the door. Seconds after pulling it open, all aspects of her pep talk fled from memory.

Rook stood in the hall.

Chapter 6

"**B**ad time?" Rook wanted to be the first to break the awkward silence.

"No," Viva said once she'd given herself an inward kick to hasten speech.

"You're sure?" He let his amber eyes drift down over her form-fitting black capri yoga pants to the chic high-heeled sandals that showcased her pedicure.

Viva followed the trail of his gaze and winced when discovery bloomed. "Leesi's going undercover," she said, citing the name of her on-screen character, Leesi Errol.

Rook grinned. "Looks like she's gonna be having a good time."

"The camera will make it look that way, but my feet are sure to be screaming the entire season."

"And yet you're using your free time to play around in them."

"Hardly." Viva waved Rook inside. "I gotta practice if I want to look authentic in these things."

Rook watched as she closed the door, approval no doubt lurking in his eyes. "I thought strolling around in those things would be like second nature to you."

"Well, I love heels." Viva gave the shoes a skeptical look. "*Stilts* are another matter altogether." She looked up in time to consider Rook's stare. "Is there a problem?"

"No problem at all." Rook's stare remained fixed.

Hoping for a change in subject, Viva motioned toward the TV. "Sounds like it's getting chillier out there. Can I get you some coffee? Sophia always makes way more than she can drink."

"Sounds good." Rook glanced over his shoulder. "Is she here?"

"She said she was heading to the precinct before going to her office. You could probably still catch her there if you came to see her."

"Actually, it's you I came to see."

Viva noticed the gold envelope he carried.

"Our boarding passes." He handed her the envelope. "I'm taking for granted that your passport's up to date?"

Viva laughed, accepting the packet. "That's an understatement. Yeah, I'm good there."

Rook nodded, his eyes resuming their provocative trek up her body. He could've easily emailed her the flight info, but was quite pleased with himself then for making the decision to come see her in person.

"Oh! The coffee." Viva hurried to the kitchen, teetering a bit on the towering heels. "Do you still take it with sugar and all that cream?"

"That's right." He followed her into the kitchen where he relaxed against the doorway to enjoy watching her move around.

Even in the heels, she still had trouble reaching the larger mugs on the uppermost shelf of the cabinet above the coffeemaker.

Pushing off the doorway, Rook went to help her at the cabinet. Cupping her hip, he urged her to still while he grabbed two mugs.

"Thanks," she said when he handed them to her. "I could've probably used more of this coffee last night instead of all the wine. I know I made a fool of myself. I just can't remember how *much* of a fool."

"That's funny," Rook said, maintaining his stance behind her. "I can't recall you making a fool of yourself either." Dipping his head, he inhaled the airy fragrance following her.

Viva turned then, searching his startling eyes with her own. "If you weren't a stronger man, you'd have woken up in my bed this morning."

"A stronger man…" He massaged the bridge of his nose as if suddenly weary. "A stronger man wouldn't have let you go in the first place." He stepped back, blinking as he suddenly noticed what he'd said. Additionally, he took note of how close he was to touching her—*really* touching her. Touching her the way he thought of whenever she crossed his mind, which was most days and every night.

With Olympian willpower, Rook stepped back. "I didn't come to interrupt you here, only to bring stuff for the trip."

"But—" Viva looked to the counter space "—your coffee."

"I shouldn't stay, V."

"Rook." She caught his wrist and squeezed. "If you insist on taking me with you to Italy, we're gonna be together most days, you know? No time like the present to see if we can handle—" She wasn't given the chance to finish the thought.

Rook had sudden possession of her mouth. The pressure was unforgiving, with a famished intensity, as if he were starving for her. Viva clung to him, her fingers half-curled into the fabric of his shirt. The height of the sandals put her just under his eye level and she could feel the breadth of his broad frame flush against her.

The kiss all but rendered Viva's hands useless, but not so for Rook. His roamed her body with all the familiarity of a skilled and patient lover. He cupped her generous bottom that was appealingly outlined in her snug pants. In the midst of squeezing, he lifted her until he was snug in the V of her thighs.

Viva couldn't deny the moan pressing for release inside her throat. With a subtle urgency to her moves, she worked herself nearer to him in search of heightened sensation.

Rook applied another decisive squeeze to Viva's bottom before he set her atop the counter. Viva's response was to link her shapely calves around his waist in order to keep him close.

She could feel him shifting into retreat mode and she wasn't ready to lose him yet, to lose him again...

Rook eased back, paying more attention to the drill-sergeant-like voice inside his head. The gruff voice warned against him being a slave to his hormones. Just the same, he teetered on the ragged edge of losing what ability he had to resist her when she loosed one of the sweet moans that stroked his ego like mink to the skin.

"V…" He meant for the murmur to evoke precaution. Instead, it held desire in a viselike grip.

Viva eased up from the counter to fuse herself against him. Her breasts crushed into his chest with every effort she made to breathe.

"V…" Rook reached deeper that time, seeking just an ounce of his evasive willpower. He swore he'd hold on to it for dear life once he found it. Hands firm on her waist, he set her back on the countertop and put his forehead to hers.

"I'd say we're even," he panted.

"Not—not really." Viva offered up a breathy laugh. "I at least had the decency to set my love scene in the bedroom."

Light laughter surged for Rook then too, but the gesture was brief. "I should go, V."

"I'm not asking you to."

"You should." He indulged in another whiff of the melon fragrance that clung to her skin and hair. "This isn't what we need."

"It is." She moved her brow against his cheek. "We need *this* and more." In spite of that, she decided to bite the bullet she'd dodged since the party. "We should also talk, Rook. *Really* talk."

"That's not a good idea."

The blunt refusal had her blinking in surprise and confusion.

"It's not a good idea for me." He put distance between them then.

Her confusion mounted, but it seemed Rook had exhausted his explanations.

"I'll be here a couple of hours before our flight leaves," he said and left her alone in the kitchen.

Elias Joss studied two of his four best friends in the world. His vivid blue-green stare was discerning in its steadiness.

"Did he say what this was about?" Eli asked.

"No," Linus said, and idly clinked salt and pepper shakers together, "but my guess is on Viva."

Elias nodded along with Tigo. The men had waited, at Rook's request, in a local bar and grill not far from the downtown headquarters of Joss Construction. The business had been established by Eli's father and was now jointly run between Eli, Santigo and Linus.

The guys didn't have long to wait. Rook arrived about ten minutes after their scheduled meeting time. Following handshakes, hugs, and the placing of food and drink orders, Rook got to the purpose of the gathering.

"She wants to talk," he said in a flat tone and watched his friends trade curious looks.

"Well…" Eli began a slow finger tap against the checkerboard tablecloth. "You know, um, that's a female thing. They…they like to talk. Come to think of it, it's a people thing…"

Laughter gained volume until it carried on a lively chord around the table.

Linus patted Rook's shoulder. "What's up, man? Talk to us."

Rook waited for the server to leave their drink orders. He appreciated the few additional moments to get his thoughts together. He needed them.

"I don't want to talk to her—not about what went wrong between us."

"What's changed, man?" Linus's concern was apparent.

"It's already too much. I can feel it."

At Rook's solemn admission, Tigo and Eli traded knowing looks.

"Are you sure you want us here, man?" Eli asked.

"I'm positive." Rook passed Eli a grateful smile. "I hoped seeing you guys—how happy you are..." He looked to Tigo and then shook his head while massaging the bunched muscles at his nape. "I thought it might change my mind about not wanting to fix things."

"Why wouldn't you want to fix things?" Linus asked.

"We're leaving, um..." Rook traded the neck massage for one that drove his thumb into the center of his palm. "I'm taking her with me on this trip. We'll be alone together for weeks."

"I see...and being together alone is so not the perfect time to talk and fix what's screwed up between you."

Linus's blatant sarcasm drew smiles from everyone, even Rook.

"We'll be alone," Rook reminded his friend once the laughter had eased.

"You wouldn't hurt her."

"I know that." Rook confirmed Linus's words without hesitation. "But talking about it...she'll see what it took me through and I..."

"You'll be stuck there," Eli guessed, "with no place to hide how she hurt you when she left."

"Exactly." Rook's grin was sly when it emerged. "Only she didn't leave—I did. She didn't want us to be over. She only wanted to go after what she'd been working for. It was me who all but said if she left we were done. *I* was the one who put that nail in our coffin."

"So tell her that," Tigo urged.

"And then what?" Rook countered, resting his hands palms up on the big, sturdy table. "Watch her go back to her life when all this is done?"

"She might not want that," Linus said.

Rook's grin meshed with laughter. "I'm about to relocate out of the country, remember? She's just reconnecting with her family. How's all this supposed to work?"

"You're grabbing at excuses," Eli warned.

"You're right." Rook took a moment to mop his face with his palms. "If I tell V all this and I still don't get her back..." He looked to Linus. "It'll be worse than before. I don't want to think about what happens if I can't come back from it. She's already blaming herself—I could see it in her eyes when she said she wanted to talk." He sipped the locally brewed beer he'd ordered.

"Us talking," he continued, "me coming clean about what I went through, what anger did to me... she'll think it was her fault no matter how much I tell her it wasn't."

"So don't take her with you," Tigo blurted. "Between all of us and that warrior squad you've got at L Sec, we can keep her safe until Soap's case is closed and she's out of the woods." He reached across the table, squeezed Rook's wrist. "Go talk to her, spill all this and give her time to deal with it around here with her folks. You go handle your business in Italy. Get all this old drama off your chest and go find out what it feels like to live out from under the weight of it."

Shrugging, Tigo reached for his beer mug and raised it in toast. "Come back here with a new perspective. At the very least, you'll have slayed a demon that's been riding your back for way too long."

There was silence following Tigo's words. After a moment, Eli clapped a hand to his friend's back.

"I swear he's gotten smarter since he's gotten Sophia back by his side where she belongs," Eli teased and joined in when laughter followed.

"Sounds like a damn good plan to me," Linus added.

"It does." Relaxing back in his chair, Rook fixed his friends with an easy smile.

"We could've waited another day or two to do this, you know? You and Rook aren't leaving until—"

"No, Soap, I needed to get this out while I still had my nerve." Viva added a shaky laugh. "Thanks for letting me be involved in this."

"I know it's got to be hard talking about such sticky stuff regarding someone who gave you your big break," Sophia said as she squeezed her sister's arm.

Viva nodded. "Whatever Murray's into needs to come to an end. It's probably weird, but in a way, maybe I'm helping him." She snorted a laugh.

Sophia joined in. "Sounds perfectly sane to me."

Viva sent her sister a skeptical look. "You sure you

want to be using the term 'perfectly sane' and my name in the same sentence?"

"I think we're safe." Sophia left the conference table in her office to top off her coffee and get more hot water for Viva's tea. "You think you'll hear from Murray again?" she asked.

"Not sure." Viva blew at a coiled lock dangling across her brow. "He sounded pretty resolved when we talked."

"I see." Sophia prepped her coffee and added hot water to a new mug for Viva. "Guess that'll leave lots of time for you and Rook to talk, huh?"

"I'm not so sure," Viva said once she'd considered her sister's words for a while. "He came over this morning."

"Well, well..." Playful intrigue sharpened Sophia's features when she turned from the counter with mugs in hand. "You guys pick up from where you left off the night before?"

Viva tried to deny it but couldn't, especially when she betrayed just the faintest flush beneath the light caramel tone of her skin.

Sophia laughed, no doubt noticing her sister's color darken. "I'll take that as a yes."

"Not a *full* yes," Viva argued.

"Now *that* sounds weird." Sophia set down the mugs.

"He pulled away. I mean... I know one of us needed to and I—I certainly wasn't trying—" Viva shook her head, having spied the delight in Sophia's expression. "I told him we needed to talk and he—he said it wasn't a good idea. It wasn't a good idea for him."

"Hmm...more weirdness. Maybe the timing was bad?"

Viva left the table where they'd recorded her statement that afternoon. "I don't think that was it. It sounded more personal than the timing being bad because he was running late for an appointment."

"Will you try talking to him again? Maybe once you guys are in Italy?" Sophia sipped her coffee and watched her sister consider the questions.

"This is something I should tell him before Italy, I think."

"And it's something you don't expect him to take too well."

"I *know* he won't take it too well."

"Just tell him, V." Sophia came around to the side of the table where Viva stood. "Don't worry about whether he thinks it's a good idea or not. Don't even act like you're about to get into it. Just spill it and let the chips fall."

"Yeah." Viva worried her bottom lip between her thumb and forefinger. "That's just what I had in mind, only what he said about talking not being a good idea for him—it unsettled me, Soap."

Concern on her face, Sophia set her mug onto the table. "How?"

"How's he been, Sophia?" Viva fixed her sister with a stern stare. "How's he *really* been?"

"He's been *really* busy and gotten *really* successful."

Viva's resulting laughter was genuine as it bubbled up. "That's good."

"L Sec's been involved with all kinds of big-name clients from all over the world. Much of that happened when Rook added the training end for his clients who wanted their own in-house personnel trained. That got the attention of the sports and entertainment industries—athletes wanting to diversify their workouts, studio types seeing the same for the stunt teams they hired."

"I'm glad for him, Sophia." Viva walked away from the table, picked up her tea on the way past. "But how's *he* been? Beyond all the success of the business, I mean?"

"Honey…" Sophia winced as though she were reluctant to share. "We've gone over this before… You—you know he hasn't been a hermit. No man who looks the way he does would go for long without being noticed by at least fifty women, nor would he shun their advances for long. No matter how in love he is with one of Hollywood's most lusted-after women."

"Well, damn! Did you just compliment me?" Viva faked amazement.

Sophia gave a casual shrug, reached for her coffee. "It's hard, but I'm trying to make an effort."

"Understood." Viva laughed. "But what I'm asking is if you think he's changed. He was always the easygoing sort—laid-back, hard to rile."

"You want to know if your leaving tapped into his temper." Sophia gave an understanding nod. "V, I'd bet my badge that nothing you could tell him would ever break him down so far that he'd put his hands on you that way."

"God, Sophia…" Viva moaned. "That's one of the few things I'm certain of. It's not *me* I'm worried about."

Sophia's expression then was one of renewed realization. "What you have to tell him involves Murray, doesn't it?"

"Not totally." Viva sighed, launched a more determined pace around the office. "But he brushes up against it. I don't want whatever I say to have him lashing out in a way that could hurt him. He doesn't need that—not because of Murray or anyone else I'm connected to. It's not worth it."

"This sounds serious, V." Sophia's face tightened with signs of rigid concern. "Sure it's not something you'd care to share with your baby sis?"

"Hell, Soap, *I* barely want to think about it. Talking it over with my kid sister, my family at all, isn't something I can do without feeling sick inside."

"So why tell Rook?"

"Because my leaving wasn't his fault." Viva pivoted on the chic but sensible peach-colored pumps that accentuated the sharp cuff of the cream trousers she wore. "My leaving would've happened whether or not our relationship had been reduced to us behaving like passing ships. Fact is, things being strained between us made it all easier for me. I left and quickly discovered Rook was so right about the people I left with."

"Listen, V, not to brag, but I do wield a certain amount of power." Sophia set her long legs apart in an intentionally confrontational stance. "Say the word and I'll move mountains to have them arrested."

Viva laughed amid her distress, loving her little sister very much and appreciating her support. "It's not necessary, hon, but thanks."

"But you think Rook would want to kill someone over it?"

"I know he would." Viva hurriedly closed the distance between her and Sophia, grasped Sophia's hands and squeezed out of a sudden need for reassurance. "I know Rook would never hurt me, but he'll damn well hate me once I tell him."

Following the lunch with his friends, Rook decided to put in a quick call to Viva and see if she was free to talk. There was no time like the present, he'd decided, yet his fingers faltered over the screen when he scrolled through his contacts for her number.

Best not to rouse any preconceived notions on her part with a phone call. Best to bite this particular nail right through its rusted head. Rook was tossing the phone to the passenger seat and slipping behind the wheel of the Suburban when the screen lit up with an incoming call. He toyed with not answering, until he glimpsed Burt Larkin's name. He took the call before it transitioned to voice mail.

"Interrupting anything?" Burt queried once the connection was made.

"No, I'm headed back to the office."

"Have you seen Viva today?"

"This morning and, word to the wise, she's gonna start ducking you if you ask for any more autographs."

"Yeah." Burt tried for lightness with the response, but the effort fell flat. "This isn't about that, Rook."

"Tell me." Rook's suspicion niggled its way through fast and deep.

"Has she mentioned a Reynolds Henry?"

"No. Why?"

"He was a client of Murray Dean's and he's dead."

Chapter 7

The talk with Sophia had helped. Viva hadn't realized how much she'd needed to vent about the situation with Rook. It was a situation that, until her return home, had resided very amicably in the recesses of her mind where other events of the past went to languish.

Still, the fact that she very much wanted to have the discussion with Rook was an issue that not even a hearty chat with her sister could extinguish. Yet, Sophia's question had replayed in her head on a loop since she'd left city hall to return to Sophia's condo.

So why tell Rook?

Yes, he deserved to know that she'd gone off half-cocked and made a mistake that solidified the doom of their relationship. Couldn't she just tell him that and leave out all the ugly details? If only…

Viva rushed into the lobby and sent a quick smile to

the desk guards on her way past. Quickly, she doffed the elements of her disguise and was shoving shades and a scarf into her tote. The elevator doors opened and before she could take a step forward, she was escorted none too gently inside.

"Hey—" She caught herself, realizing it was Rook who held her. "Didn't think I'd see you again today."

"Plans have changed." He kept hold of her arm even after the door slid closed with a soothing bump. "Are you packed?"

Viva turned as much as his hold would allow. There was no need to study his face, it was an unreadable mask. "I, um, sure. I haven't been in town long enough to fully unpack so... Rook? What's going on?"

"We leave for Italy in the morning."

She tried to face him more fully then. "Why? What's changed?"

There was no answer from her escort and Viva allowed that scene to play out until they were inside her sister's condo.

"Look, don't get me wrong. I actually find the stony silence sexy." She tossed the tote bag to the sofa and watched him prowl the living room on a security check. "You're still gonna have to come up with some info if you expect me to fly halfway around the world with you tomorrow."

She spread her hands in a silent question that went unanswered when he moved on through the condo, completing his check. "My guess is I won't have time to see my family again before we leave." She folded her arms over the silky peach cargo blouse and tried to match his stony look with her own when he returned to the living room.

His response was not what she'd expected.

"Do you know a Reynolds Henry?"

"Reynolds?" She shed some of her stony veneer. "Well, yeah, I, um, he's an actor. He hasn't worked in a while." She cast a sidelong glance to the flat screen across the room. "If the news I heard this morning is true, he won't have the chance to change that. They say he's dead."

"They were right." Rook's closed expression adopted a grim quality that lent a fiercer element to his caramel-doused features. "Did you know he was a client of Murray's?"

Viva opened her mouth, but no response emerged. Shaky then on her pumps, she settled on to the arm of the nearest chair. "He was... I'd forgotten." The ebony flecks danced in her eyes when she suddenly looked to Rook. "The news reported it was a suicide."

Rook's smile did nothing to diminish his grim expression. "You've been in the business long enough to know how often stories are spun."

"Yeah." Viva studied the carpet without really seeing it. Those words were especially true when the story involved political and entertainment figures. She fixed Rook with a hopeful look. "Do you know what really happened?"

"News said he overdosed on prescription meds, which is true, but word from the lead investigators is that every pill he had was laced with four times the prescribed amount. He would've been dead whether or not he'd taken his meds as instructed."

"But how could you know that already?" Viva pushed off the chair arm. "Even I know it takes longer than a day to get back a tox report." Rook's bland look had her stiffening.

There was a reason his security firm was one of the most sought-after entities worldwide, she reminded herself. Obtaining preliminary details on matters such as these was perhaps among the more unremarkable feats his organization was capable of.

"What are you thinking?" she asked.

"I think you know."

"I don't believe I do." Yet, she stiffened anew when he merely stared. "You can't be thinking Murray would..." She couldn't finish the notion. "Why?" she asked instead.

"What was it he said during your conversation about putting things to bed?"

"By killing his clients? What sense would that make?"

"Oh, I don't know, V. In case they'd seen things that could be hard for him or his more elusive associates to explain away? Who knows?" He stalked the living room, his amber stare seeming more radiant in the wake of agitation. "These clients might take a chance on going to the cops and sharing things that have them concerned, especially if one of them's got a sister on the force."

"Me?" Viva plastered both hands to her chest. "Seriously, Rook? You honestly think he'd come after me that way?" She sounded incredulous, but couldn't ignore the dip her heart took to her stomach.

"Even with all you know and have seen, you still can't bring yourself to believe the worst about the man." Rook shook his head, frustration fixed indelibly on his face.

"That's not it."

"Then what is it?"

"Rook, I—Murray, he—he's got a lot of questionable… He's not… He—"

"Save it." Rook glanced around the living room once more and then sized Viva up with one heated sweep of his stare. "I'll be back in the morning. Use the time to finish packing. I'll make sure you have time to see your folks before the flight. Don't try calling Murray again."

"And if he calls me?" She watched him bow his head and grin a grin that was more malicious than humor filled.

"I know it's hard for you to take my advice seriously when it comes to Murray," he began, "but maybe you could try giving it just a shred of consideration in this case."

He left her then and Viva remained where she stood long after he'd gone.

Belluno, Italy

Rook and Viva arrived in Northern Italy close to 2:00 in the morning. The town of Belluno was a province in the Veneto region. Rook had fallen in love with the neighboring Cortina d'Ampezzo and had decided to own a home there regardless of how his business played out.

As his primary business would be handled in Belluno, the plan was to spend the night at a hotel in town. Rook had arranged to meet with his associates a little earlier than planned, given the change in the arrival date to Italy. Afterward, he and Viva were scheduled to leave for Cortina.

The departure from Philadelphia had been a prompt, teary one filled with goodbyes and light on details. Sophia had, at least, received more insight on the reasons for the change. Viva had sat nearby while Rook shared his findings on Reynolds Henry's passing and how he factored Murray Dean into it all. Viva wasn't surprised that her sister all but carried her to the airport and buckled her into the seat. Rook received the chief of Ds' full blessings to head out of the States with quickness.

Viva didn't mind. Italy was a dreamland in spite of its frigid temps and the generally rainy, snowy and windy climate of the area during that time of year. The environment wasn't such a jolt given the already dipping temps back in the States. Viva found it to be heavenly.

Or…it could've been were it not for Rook's mood, which was proving to rival the region's atmosphere for chilliness. What had triggered his attitude was no surprise nor was it a reaction she could argue. He had every right to be pissed, especially when the topic of their current unrest was the very last thing they'd argued over and what had signaled the demise of their relationship. Viva knew and understood Rook's feelings toward Murray. What she couldn't understand was how he could so easily believe the agent could be capable of murder.

She inhaled the crisp air that swept in from the Schiara mountain range of the Dolomites. Reluctantly, she risked a quick scan of the tarmac in search of Rook. She found him among a circle of suited men, enjoying what appeared to be a rather jovial conversation. With clear, cold air filtering her mind, her voice of reason began to elevate and echo.

If Murray was capable of involving himself in the kinds of things she'd shared with the police less than twenty-four hours earlier, why wouldn't he be capable of murder? Reminding herself that she wasn't dead yet was a weak and hardly reassuring fact.

Could he really be that paranoid? She wondered and found herself replaying the conversation with his assistant. Artesia Relis had believed her boss to be "riled up" enough to contact her. The woman had surely held her job for long enough to handle the infrequent uprisings of a Hollywood agent. Even still, Arty was more than a little agitated over the pressures of her job. She'd sounded downright worried.

Then there was her own conversation with Murray and his assurances that all would be well once he'd put certain things to bed. If she was among them, would he have been so bold as to tell her? Perhaps Reynolds was involved in those aspects of Murray's allegedly illegal dealings. Viva was sure Sophia was at work investigating that very angle.

She shook her head then, realizing she was filling it with too much angst. Much more of that and both her sister and her ex would be agreeing on putting her in an asylum instead of the wonderland beauty of Northern Italy.

With that thought in mind, not to mention the fact that she was lending too much time to worry and not enough to opportunity, Viva got herself in check. After all, Rook's new home was also the place where shopping dreams were made.

Cortina was home to the most drooled-over names in haute couture—Gucci, Bulgari, Benetton. Oh yes, it was a shopper's paradise and she intended to take thorough advantage.

When she felt warm hands on her arms Viva's thoughts pivoted back to Rook. Even through the bulky fabric of her wool peacoat, she recognized his touch. She savored the feel of him as his hands moved up and down her arms.

"You're going to catch your death out here."

Smiling, Viva enjoyed the breadth of his magnificent chest when he pulled her back against it.

"I opt for catching it out here," she sighed. "I like that better than the other places currently vying for the title."

Rook's hands stilled until he was turning Viva to face him. A fierce glint lurked in his dazzling stare then. "Don't you think that," he commanded while giving her a slight shake in the process.

It was hard for Viva to obey. "Why shouldn't I? You believe my own agent might try to kill me."

"Jesus, V." Rook closed his eyes and hung his head for a second or three. "I shouldn't have put that in your head."

"It's not such a far stretch," she said, hearing misery claim her voice. "Makes perfect sense given where things stand."

"I still shouldn't have said it. There are lots of other explanations just as valid. It's just that I can't afford to take any chances."

"But you still believe he's capable of taking a life?" she challenged. "You think he may've taken Reynolds's?"

"I shouldn't have said that either. It was anger talking."

Viva gave a smile that was just as miserable as her former expression. "It's okay to be angry."

"It's not okay for me."

"Signor Lourdess? Are you and the signorina ready?"

The driver's inquiry interrupted Viva's mounting curiosity and her intentions to question Rook's haunted admission.

"Thanks, Luca." Rook sent the man a quick nod and smile before his hands tightened at Viva's arms. Then he was leading her to the waiting limo and getting her settled in the back of the sleek gray vehicle.

"You may want to get out of that coat," he suggested once Luca had shut the car door, securing them inside. "It's over fifteen minutes to the hotel." He looked out the window at the white sky. "We'll probably wake up to snow by morning."

"Thought I saw a few flakes while I waited for you to finish up."

Faint concern dwelled in his eyes. "You should've gotten into the car."

"I didn't mind and it was nice seeing you get acquainted with your new business associates."

Rook raised a brow. "They aren't my associates yet."

"So they're still trying to decide if you can give them what they want?" Viva slipped out of the rich tan-colored wool.

"Oh, they already know that I can," Rook remarked without an ounce of arrogance, only unshakable confidence. "This trip is about whether *I'm* willing to pull up stakes in order to give it to them."

Viva laughed. "Ahh...so *you're* being wooed, huh?"

"Seems so." Rook tossed his brown leather jacket to the long seat opposite the one he and Viva shared.

"And how do your guys feel about that?" She listened as Rook shared his plans.

The executive team would interchange relocation— six months in Italy, six months in the States. Rook explained that the goal was to interview local candidates who would oversee day-to-day operations in the future. Any member of the executive team would be welcome to live there abroad or head back to the States.

"None of them have personal ties that'd prevent them from making the leap if they decided to," he finished.

"So they're loners just like their boss?" Laughter mingled with Viva's words. She watched him smooth a hand across his head, a move her eyes followed with longing. She wished it were her fingers gliding across the close crop of waves.

"They're not like their boss." Rook smirked, appearing quietly amused. "At least they've got *some* semblance of a social life."

"Are you saying you live like a hermit?"

"For the most part, I guess," he admitted, following a moment's consideration. "I suppose that's best."

Shaking her head, Viva tucked her legs up on the car seat. "I'm sure every woman in Philadelphia would disagree with you on that." The interior lighting was a low golden gleam, but enough illumination for her to study him closely then, glimpsing a reaction she'd classify as a cross between regret and resolve. The muscle flexing along his jaw was one she recognized all too well as a signal that his frustration was mounting.

The very last thing she wanted was for either of them to be experiencing frustration there. Sadly, she didn't hold out much hope of them having much chance at avoiding it. At any rate, she hoped they could at least try for one night without it.

With a sigh, Viva uncurled her legs to unzip the chic block-heeled boots she'd worn for the trip. She wriggled her toes indulgently once she tugged off the shoes and tossed them to the opposite side of the dim cabin. She heard Rook's chuckle, a second before she caught his animated expression. "What?" A half smile curved her mouth.

"I see your shoes are still one of the first things you come out of?"

Viva slid an amused look toward the abandoned boots and shrugged. "Ten minutes barefoot sounds like heaven to me."

"Hmph, sounds like you're about to have your work cut out for you." At her confusion, Rook explained, "Getting used to those neck breakers you brought along for the show."

Viva waved off his concern and settled back against the decadent suede cushioning of the seat. "I'm not worried. The camera will mask the majority of my discomfort." She laughed softly. "You'd be surprised by how big an ally the camera can be when you develop a love affair with it. Still..." She gave another indulgent wiggle of her toes. "They're finicky, so you have to know how to sweet-talk them."

Rook's expression was fixed. His stirring gaze appeared even more brilliant given the intensity with which he watched her then. "I don't think you'd have to do much sweet talking. The camera's a slave to what it sees after all."

The unexpected compliment sent arousal plumbing her core with shocking ruthlessness. At any rate, Viva was in no mood to make her needs known only to have him deny her. Instead, she turned, intending to seek solace at the other end of the long, wide seat.

She found herself on her back instead, with Rook's chest against hers. The throbbing at her core became a relentless vibration that seemed to take command of her entire body. Her fingers sank into the luxurious fleece of his midnight-blue sweatshirt in an effort to draw him closer as well as to cease the mad tremble of her fingers.

The effort was basically useless. Sensation had her all but begging him to give her what had been ravaging her dreams for far too long.

Rook's thoughts, however, seemed to be traveling along the same vein as the woman he held. He found the fastening of her dress, releasing it with a dexterous touch. The zipper tab followed from its hiding place snug beneath her arm on the curve-hugging frock.

The move told Viva that he'd most likely scoped out the tab's inconspicuous location the moment she'd arrived in her sister's living room dressed for the trip.

The zipper made barely a sound as he tugged the tab to its lowest point. The material gaped open at Viva's side, providing easy access to her breasts heaving against the lacy, black cups of her bra.

Viva bit her lip to still its quivering, when spasms rocked her as Rook's wide palm covered one of the lace-covered mounds and squeezed. The move was followed by the moan-inducing trip his thumb made around one straining nipple. She wanted so much more than what he was giving her.

Grudgingly, Viva acknowledged that dressing for the weather, not to mention their current location, was going to make a lustier exploration impossible. She treated herself by delighting in the sheer pleasure of having him so near. Rook didn't crush her beneath him, but gave her enough of his considerable weight to bring an approving smile to her mouth.

Viva found her way beneath his sweatshirt. She pouted for a moment when her nails encountered another shirt beneath instead of the taut skin she sought. The shirt hung outside loose-fitting corduroys and she made quick work of fumbling beneath the hem, only to discover a T-shirt tucked neatly inside the waistband.

Hissing a curse, she slammed a fist to his side. "What's with all these clothes?" she grumbled.

"It's cold outside." His reminder was muffled where his mouth was busy at the base of her throat.

"Maybe I should've worn more under my dress," she huffed, "even though my efforts don't seem to be appreciated—"

Her words were smothered by a kiss that sent moans filling the cabin. Viva heard her own voice as well as Rook's. Knowing the moment was to be completely savored, she threaded her fingers through the short, sleek curls of his hair. She smiled, even as her mouth was ravaged by the driving plunges of his tongue.

She had almost—*almost*—forgotten how luxurious his hair was, how taut and unyielding his body was, how sweetly overpowering he felt against her. Viva tried to drive her tongue against his using the same potent thrusts, but she was no match, not against the hunger that fueled his kiss.

He seemed okay with her not being able to do much more than take what he gave her, so Viva didn't see much need to change the status quo. Her strokes in his hair took on a less frantic display. She was roasting inside the dress, despite the fact that he'd already unzipped it. She may have bit her tongue to resist begging him to do more. Happily, her tongue was already engaged in an act she dared not interrupt.

Once Rook had ventured beneath the already hiked hem of her dress, Viva was positively purring beneath him. When he broke the kiss, she gulped in much-needed air and at the same time cursed him for breaking their contact.

"And you talk to *me* about too many clothes?" His voice sounded like a low rumble, yet it was easily decipherable in the quiet confines of the car.

Viva felt his hands at her hips, cradling her bottom encased in a pair of thick tights.

"You only need to tug," she said in a breathy tone that had somewhat become her celebrity calling card, and bumped her hips to his for emphasis.

Rook didn't require the nudge as he was already easing down the tights. He could have cursed the fever that drove him like an inexperienced teen, but just then he was welcoming it. The zeal rushed his veins like some form of adrenaline to which there was no comparison.

He hadn't denied himself a woman's touch since losing Viva. Instead, he'd indulged—overmuch at times. He'd been determined to scour her from the walls of his memory. Those romps had done the trick momentarily. He'd been able to lose himself in lust. But only because he'd refused to acknowledge that the sensation fell far short of what he'd known with Viva.

Rook nuzzled his face deep into the fragrant hollow at Viva's neck, groaning as his palms filled with her derriere. Though the mounds were toned, they maintained the feminine lushness that stiffened his sex, which was straining almost painfully against his button fly.

The low growl of a curse had Viva surfacing from the haze of her arousal. She knew Rook's reaction wasn't in response to the sensuality they were losing themselves in. Thankfully, he didn't give her long to wonder at the sudden change in his mood.

"We're turning off the main road. We'll be at the hotel soon," he said.

Viva didn't bother asking if they had to stop. That answer, though disappointing, was obvious. What wasn't obvious and what she most wanted an answer to, was whether they could finish what they'd started.

Chapter 8

With the exception of the front desk and maintenance staff, the Hotel Oasi was awash in silence when Rook and Viva arrived. The snowfall that had begun at the airport had continued to drift steadily and was dusting the hotel's picturesque grounds by the time they'd exited the car.

In spite of the quiet beauty, Viva felt as though she had a twenty-piece brass section performing inside her head. Sexual frustration had been an aspect of her life that she'd learned to live with. She hadn't exactly lived like a hermit, but she hadn't been the free spirit the media often tried to label members of her world.

There had been a brief…thing between her and her leading man, which had been more to generate buzz for their show than true love. While she and Bryce Danzig were good friends, which made them a provocative on-screen duo, there had been nothing more.

Still, she had made the effort at a real life outside the Hollywood hustle. Sadly, it was the Hollywood hustle that had made sustaining or even acquiring a real relationship impossible or hardly worth the effort.

The seamless check-in process consisted of Rook's signature on a pad. Then, they made their way to the elevator bay to embark upon a smooth ascent in a glass car lit by recessed gold lighting. As her heels sank into thick chocolate carpeting, Viva realized how wiped she was. The mellow environment allowed that fact to seep in. She gave a pronounced blink and fought to keep her eyes open. When she muffled a yawn behind a gloved hand, Rook pulled her into the reassuring shelter of his embrace. Viva shut her eyes and allowed the steady beat of his heart to lead her into escape.

The elevator bumped to a gentle stop and the baggage handler escorted them down another expansive corridor. Rook kept a supportive arm about Viva's waist and she couldn't help but think how that simple touch was more secure than any of the elaborate measures her status deemed her worthy of.

The handler disengaged the locks and double doors opened into a sumptuous suite lit by a single clay-based lamp in a far corner of the palatial living room. Heavy burgundy drapes were parted to reveal the snow falling across the hotel grounds.

Viva took in the beauty of the suite while Rook tipped the handler once the man had returned from placing the luggage in the designated rooms. She continued her tour, approval curving her lips when her hands sank into the back of a plush sofa she passed.

Rich auburn suede gave beneath a mound of softness she envisioned herself sinking into. For the second time that evening, she unzipped her boots and decided there was no time like the present. She sank into the suede sofa, comfort wrapping her in an embrace.

Rook had seen off the handler and was then occupied by his phone when it chimed with a notification. Viva remembered she'd not taken her mobile off airplane mode since they'd landed, so she decided to check her missed calls, as well.

Comfort and serenity fled once the screen activated before her eyes.

Opening his phone to more than ten missed calls was nothing new to Rook. He hadn't as yet, he thought with much relish, developed an emotional attachment to the device. He saw the text from Burt who had also made the ten missed calls. There was a link to a breaking news story. Upon scanning it, Rook's eyes shifted to Viva.

He'd noticed she'd settled onto one of the room's lengthy sofas and was pleased that she might actually get some rest while they were away. Though her clothes and makeup were perfect despite the nine-hour flight, he could still detect the traces of exhaustion in her warm stare. He saw her sit up on the sofa and then stand with the phone clutched in her shaking hand.

"There's nothing you can do for her, V."

Viva turned to Rook as if she were dazed. Her expression revealed that she hadn't wholly deciphered his words to her. She blinked rapidly several times before her eyes tracked to his phone and understanding wedged in alongside devastation.

"I could be there." Her voice was small but determined.

"And be among what, V? Seventy other people already crowding into her hospital room?"

Viva considered his phone with a measuring look. "I only have the info the doctors gave my cast mates. I'm guessing you've got more."

Rook knew that to encourage her to let the subject alone was a waste of his time. He didn't try. Instead, he opened Burt's text. "This'll be breaking within the hour, I'm told. Bevy Ward?" He looked to Viva for confirmation on the name and watched her move from the sofa as she nodded.

"She plays my sister on the show."

Rook nodded as he got a mental image of the actress who played Pamela Errol on the hit show. "She'd just taken the exit off the expressway leading to her place in the Hollywood Hills."

"She must've had a late night out that way," Viva muttered, biting her thumbnail as she paced the area between the sofa and coffee table. "She hates that place."

"Her car hit a guardrail, spun out..." Rook trailed off at the look Viva sent his way. He let an agitated curse die a quick death on his tongue and continued with the story.

"The rest of this hasn't been released to the press. Prelim reports from authorities on scene say marks on the driver's side *could be* consistent with it being sideswiped by another vehicle. There were no other vehicles in the vicinity when Ms. Ward was found. She's got no family, so an attempt was made to contact her agent, Murray Dean. He couldn't be reached. Ms. Ward's costars from her show were then contacted."

Viva let out a whoosh of breath and lost her interest in pacing. She settled back onto the sofa but the cushiony furnishing did little to soothe her that time.

"The reports are preliminary, V," Rook said, in a soft reminder. Silently, he held to the idea that they were more than accurate.

Viva apparently subscribed to that same theory. "Someone ran her off the road, didn't they?"

"I don't need you worrying over this, V—"

"Someone ran her off the road. Bevy is a client of Murray's. Surely you aren't going to try to convince me that this is all one big coincidence?"

"No." Rook set aside his phone. "I won't try to convince you of that."

"I need to be there, Rook." Viva made a shaky attempt to stand.

"Viva—"

"Bev's not just my sister on TV, Rook. There's real closeness there." Emotion fired hotly in Viva's eyes. "You may think that's a bunch of shallow bull, but it's true." She paused, willing back the tears. "When things were at their lowest between me and my family, it was Bev who kept me from going off the deep end."

Smiling reflectively, Viva resumed her slow pacing. She hugged herself as she moved. "She'd always say she was an only child and would've liked to experience some of that sibling angst. 'Only *some*, V,' she'd say… 'I don't think I could handle it three hundred and sixty-five days a year.'" The laughter left Viva's voice and was replaced then by a pleading tone that matched the look she sent to Rook.

"I need to be there."

Rook held firm. "I'm sorry, V."

The pleading look cooled and her gaze went flat.

"Don't let all the permissions my sister's granted you go to your head. I'm only putting up with this 'hiding out' nonsense to make Sophia happy."

"Maybe you should've considered what that would mean before you agreed to it."

Viva burst into quick, harsh laughter. "Like I had any choice!"

"Are you trying to say I bullied you?"

She tilted her head and sneered. "Do you really need to hear me tell you that you did?"

He shrugged. "It's news to me. You never struck me as a woman who reacted well to being bullied. Had I known differently, I may've tried it years ago."

"I know what you're up to." Viva massaged an ache forming near her temples. "This side argument isn't going to make me forget about wanting to go be with my friend."

"Even if it means putting your own life on the line to get there?"

Viva steeled herself against reiterating the fact that Murray wouldn't hurt her—not now. Not when Bev was— God…had he really been responsible for that? She looked to Rook again.

"Does your information say what her condition is?"

Rook's mouth tightened, and he didn't look too eager to share. "She's in bad shape," he confirmed finally. "Broken leg, fractured collarbone. There was some internal bleeding, but they've been able to stop that."

Viva turned her back to Rook when the news reached her ears. She could feel the pressure of tears returning with a vicious intensity. She despised the feel of tears, despised even more anyone seeing her give in to them. Correction—she despised Rook Lourdess seeing her give in to them.

He moved closer, halted within a few inches of touching distance. "You'll know anything I do, the moment I do."

She turned back to him. "And then what?"

"And then you'll know." Rook told himself to let her go when she elbowed past him to leave the room. "V?" he called anyway.

She stopped, but didn't turn to face him.

"Your room's behind the double doors to your left."

Some of the rigidness left Viva's shoulders as despair claimed her. They'd both been of one accord when they'd stepped into the suite. They'd thought of nothing but finishing what they'd started in the car. Now, one more element of unrest between them made that possibility seem more like fantasy.

"Good night, Rook."

He winced at the finality of the statement. Regardless of how unfortunate the evening had turned out, he knew it was best to set out the rest of the ugly cards before they parted ways.

"I know a trip to Italy or anywhere else in the world for you is like going to the post office for others." He smiled grimly when she remained where she was, her back still turned to him. "You can find your way back from here to LA with your eyes closed," he continued.

"I hope you won't do that, but to cut down on the confusion, I thought I'd go on and take this."

Viva turned then, the renewed exhaustion in her eyes making way for a sudden storm to brew as she fixed on what he held—her passport.

"You horse's ass," she spat, bristling when the delicious roughness of his laughter vibrated in the room. She'd heard enough of the gesture to know he was genuinely amused.

"I know you can swear better than that, V. I have the chance to hear it every Saturday night between the hours of ten and eleven."

"Wow." Her smile was chilly. "I'd expect you to be up to more than sitting in front of the TV on a Saturday night."

He responded with a playful roll of his stunning eyes and a lopsided grin. "A man can do a lot in front of a TV. It all depends on what he's watching."

She noticed the glint in his gaze and knew he was teasing her ruthlessly. Realizing that stung. Between the two of them, she was clearly the only one who gave in to pleasuring herself to the memory of their sex life.

Images emerged as those memories surfaced and she was suddenly sweltering inside the already warm dress. She considered him with a look as suspicious as it was measuring.

"I guess you really don't trust me, do you? I gave my word to Sophia, you know?"

"To Sophia—not to me."

"I thought that was understood."

"So did I—once."

She gave an amused snort. "You were right. I didn't think this through before I gave my word. It was so *not* a good idea."

"Well, it's done." He slipped the passport book into a back pocket. "You're stuck with me, so we better make the most of it."

"There was a time when that would've been all I wanted."

He wouldn't let her remark rile him—*couldn't* let it rile him. "A time, huh? When was that? While you were planning your great escape?"

"Like you noticed!" Viva had no problem releasing the tethers on her own temper. "You didn't have a clue until I was practically waving my plane ticket under your nose!" She watched his remarkable gaze flare before he closed his eyes with a slow flutter of unfairly long lashes and bowed his head. It was another move she'd seen often enough—usually when he was stressed over some business matter. Now, she knew the reaction was all for her. Some perverse part of her welcomed the coming explosion.

Such was not to be. Viva watched, fascinated by the way he tamped down the anger as suddenly as it had risen. It was as if he'd made a silent decision against saying anything more. She laughed, unamused when he began to leave the room.

"So even here, even now, we aren't going to discuss this?"

"We aren't going to discuss this," he replied as he stopped and looked at her, "especially not here."

"I'm not afraid of you, Rook." The tiniest sliver of her apprehension eased when his laughter mounted—the one signifying honest amusement.

"I know you're not afraid of me, V. I'm a damn good teacher and I taught you how to defend yourself."

That sweltering feeling returned to place a fiery layer over those memories. Those lessons hadn't been sensual in nature, yet they'd led to events that were of the most carnal variety. She couldn't control her memories and knew by his emerging smile that he could tell his words had taken her thoughts down the route he'd intended.

Viva managed a quiet clearing of her throat and hoped that her voice would cooperate. "I meant I'm not afraid of anything you might say. Chances are high I've probably said the same thing to myself a million times. Rook, we need to put this to rest once and for all, regardless of where it leads...or doesn't lead."

"*You're* not afraid of what I might say, but I am." He swept her with a probing, potent stare. "We aren't getting into this now, V." *Just wait until we're back home*, he silently begged her. *I'll tell you everything you* think *you want to hear.* He knew the only place it would go would be back to the lives they'd led for the past six years.

Viva knew more conversation on the subject would prove useless, but she couldn't resist one last jab. "Once again, it's about what *you* want."

"Guess it's about time I know what that feels like." His smile was a chilly slash across his face and he resumed the trek to his room.

"Don't try making any clever travel arrangements with your phone either. I wouldn't mind having it to keep your passport company," he called over a shoulder.

Viva stood steaming inside her dress and stewing in anger as she watched him stroll from view.

Plain stubbornness kept Viva from venturing outside her room to hunt down breakfast the next morning. By some miracle, she'd been able to fall asleep following the episode—the *latest* episode in the Rook and Viva Show. Unfortunately, she'd awakened after way too few hours of total oblivion. Accepting that additional sleep would not be forthcoming, she performed the morning rituals of washing her face and brushing her teeth. Her plan was to settle back into bed and review the script she'd brought along until she was sure Rook had left the suite to begin his day.

She'd read through three scenes, when knocking sounded at the bedroom door. Rook opened it without waiting on her permission to enter. He stood leaning on the jamb with an amused, knowing smile softening the brutal handsomeness of his face.

"Do diva actresses have something against serving themselves breakfast?" he asked.

Viva continued studying her script, hoping he couldn't see how badly her hands shook. His voice practically reverberated in the room. The effect sent her heart thudding to her throat.

"No," she said with a coolness she didn't at all feel, "but they do find it difficult to stomach breakfast in the presence of cowards."

The word was as stinging as it was unexpected. Rook's reaction to it played all over his expression and he couldn't seem to suppress it.

"Coward?" He gave in to a few seconds of silence before reiterating the insult.

"Mmm..." Viva confirmed, continuing to idly flip through the script.

Rook's chest expanded as he took deep breaths to induce a calm he desperately wanted to feel. He'd expected to hear her call him almost anything but a coward.

"In what way?" He braced himself for her response. She didn't give him the benefit of eye contact.

"You're a smart man, Rook. I don't think an explanation is necessary."

"Maybe not, but why don't you give me one anyway?"

Viva at last put down the script and observed him with bold interest while he stood with his arms folded across his stunning chest.

"So let me get this straight," she began. "*I'm* required to provide explanations while you…get to duck and dodge them like…I don't know…a coward?"

Rook betrayed that the word stung him a second time by giving in to a reflexive jerk of his shoulders beneath the black fleece sweatshirt he wore over a denim shirt of the same color. "Does it matter that I plan to talk through this once we get back to Philly?"

"Ahh…so you're just *afraid* to talk to me *here*?"

"Don't push me, V."

"Rook," she said as she scooted to her knees in the bed, "what's going on with you?" Concern had overruled her anger or the need to pout. "What do all these little comments really mean?" She rolled her eyes and flopped back to the bed while waving off the sigh he uttered in response. "I know, I know…you can't talk about it *here*."

"This isn't easy for me, Viva."

"And you think it's easy for me?" she cried, inwardly cringing at the loss of composure. "There're things you need to know, Rook. Things I need— *want*—to tell you and I—I've waited too long to." She studied her palms as if they held answers to a puzzle she was desperate to solve. "It was easy to live with that when we were on opposite coasts. Just know, Rook, it's as hard for me to keep quiet as it is for you to talk."

She shook her head then, mutinous fire turning her gaze to molten chocolate. "At least *I'm* willing to get over myself and try to get through it."

Rook pushed off the doorjamb then. "This is about more than the two of us trying to get closure over some old drama. You'll have to excuse me if this isn't as *easy* for me as it is for you—"

Viva shoved off the bed and charged. "Damn you, Rook." She shoved at his chest once, then again. Her anger skyrocketed when the push didn't even cause him to stumble.

"Go to hell," she breathed and then gave a regal turn to settle back against the decadent king bed. "Take your cowardice issues with you." She prepared to delve back into her script.

Moments later, the item was yanked from her hands and Viva watched it sail across the room. Her eyes flew to Rook's and she was struck by the raw hunger she found there. She knew what came next—and she welcomed it. He'd be in for a different finale this time, she promised herself.

Rook made good on what his gaze promised. He made no attempt to mask his intentions from Viva. Frustration had all but consumed him. He was a man used to having his plans adhered to and going off without incident. It was what made him such a success in his business.

This wasn't business though. It was a matter all too personal. He'd wanted to hash out everything between them and then have them retreat to their opposing corners for reflection.

Circumstances hadn't allowed for that, however, and now they were in the midst of tension, with her believing him to be a coward of all things. Yes, frustration was tormenting him like a wound rubbed raw and refusing to heal.

Like some injured creature seeking solace from the pain, he was ready to pounce on anything that could prevent it. With the script hurled off to parts unknown, next was the scrap of cotton that had served as Viva's sleep attire the night before.

He had her naked within seconds. But for her heaving breasts and the malice spewing from her dark eyes, she made no other movements.

Rook appreciated the silence challenge.

Chapter 9

Aside from an almost inaudible grunt of surprise, Viva gave no other reaction to Rook's touch. Her nightgown was gone and he'd jerked her down toward the edge of the bed, his fingers curling into the side stitching of her panties. Determined, she refused to give him the satisfaction of letting him see her blink in response as he tugged her free of the delicate white lace. Her eyes remained fixed on his though. The look was challenging and yes, accusing even in their coolness.

Once he'd freed her of the undergarments, Rook tossed them aside as carelessly as he had the script and her sleepwear. Palming her bare hips, he then eased around to knead her lush bottom.

Viva couldn't resist blinking then as she swallowed noticeably. Her heart gave a reactionary lilt when he tugged her closer to the edge of the bed as he knelt there. For long moments, he studied her, his eyes slowly tracking her with desire continuously darkening his vivid stare.

"Coward," she breathed, though the insult had lost much of its kick.

"Right." His voice was a guttural slur as he dipped his head to pamper her inner thighs with firm strokes from the tip of his nose.

Viva bit her lip to resist flinching when his probing reached the folds of her center. There, he skimmed the velvety flesh and inhaled her arousing scent.

"Coward—" She verbalized the taunt again only to have it cut abruptly short when his tongue teased apart her intimate folds and lightly explored the treasure beyond. A shudder rippled through her and she fisted the tangled linens as she cursed her reaction to him. No longer could she deny her need to moan. She gave in to a long, quivering one when his tongue lengthened its exploration into her tight, hot, wet core.

Her hips began a slow writhe only to be stifled from movement when he held her fast and feasted. She melted into the covers, dragging her fingers through her hair and faintly rocking her hips in time to the rhythm he set with his skillful tongue.

Waves of orgasmic pressure turned her into a creature of need, one bent on achieving one goal— pleasure. Rook's head moved this way and that as he alternated speed and deepened penetration. Tentatively, she dropped her hand to trail over the sleek cap of his hair and was further stimulated by the feel of his head bumping her palms.

She tried to speak his name, but the attempt resulted in only a garble of sound. Rook was taking his task seriously, kneading her thighs and keeping them spread to accommodate the breadth of his frame.

Viva continued to melt into the bedding. Orgasm was a fervent pursuer and she was suspended between wanting to deny its effects and totally oblige them. Surrender, she feared, could result in having the man she desired withdraw far too soon. Satisfaction gripped her like a vise then, sending her breath shaking. Renewed spasms jolted, spewing fiery tingles along her nerve endings. She embraced them like the missed sensations they were.

Rook was in tune to her reactions as usual. Slowly he withdrew, but it was only to kiss his way up along her damp skin until he was outlining her breasts with his tongue. He abandoned them though, preferring the sweetness of her mouth. He kissed her, plundering her mouth as thoroughly as he had the rest of her.

Viva accepted the kiss enthusiastically as she attempted to draw every ounce of her taste from his tongue. Her efforts cooled as she achieved her goal. Then, it was on to her next feat.

She had to stifle a smile when she took advantage of Rook's loosened hold. Suddenly, she shoved him off her, and saw his eyes flare with disbelief and simmering temper.

"Thank you for this. It took the edge off." She scanned the bed and then pinned him with a coy look. "But we both know you aren't going to finish what you start and I'm in no mood to be…frustrated again."

Showing off her agility, Viva scooted from under him and rolled to the other side of the bed to lie on her stomach. "Shut the door on your way out, will you?"

Rook's surprise over her sudden turn of the tables had begun to wane. Even his temper—only a subtle flare—had eased back. Frustration, however, had continued to rage hot and heavily. He stood then, watching as Viva lay there, a curvy, caramel-doused picture. She lounged at length, as though she had no care for the state she was leaving him in. He couldn't blame her for torturing him as she was. With that thought in mind, he turned to the door.

Viva heard the slam behind her and fought the urge to curse and plant a fist to the bed. Before she could fully wallow in disappointment over calling his bluff, she felt his crushing weight at her back. Heat engulfed her at once. Rook's mouth was everywhere, skimming her nape, the tops of her shoulders, her spine, his tongue feverishly grazing its dip before he nibbled at the rise of her buttocks. All the while, he tugged the shirt from his back.

Viva arched in reflex, not expecting the path his wicked tongue took as he reacquainted itself with her derriere. Sheer delight had her smiling and softly moaning in high approval of him taking possession of her hips to hold her still for his exploration.

Maintaining that hold, Rook shifted Viva beneath the erotic pressure his mouth delivered. His fingers were just as busy, tormenting her sex with the gentlest caresses before lunging high and deep to become immersed in the moisture there.

Viva turned her face into the nearest pillow and moaned. Rook's beautiful mouth was then at work nibbling the spot where cheek merged with thigh. All the while, his persuasive fingers continued their lusty invasion of her femininity.

"Rook." His name was wrapped up in a shuddering moan.

"Save it." His voice was still little more than a guttural whisper.

Still, Viva pleaded as another climax loomed dangerously close. She didn't want that—not yet anyway.
She wanted more of him and tried to relay that need
through the insistent nudges she made against the
erection straining the button fly of his denims.

She whimpered and he, at last, acquiesced. Viva
sighed when his fingers withdrew. Disappointment
surged as did delight when she felt his hand braced
against the small of her back as he opened his jeans.
Elation wrapped over that delight when she felt the
proof of his need for her resting heavily at her spine.

Viva moaned, hungrily accepting the crushing kiss
Rook subjected her to once he cupped her jaw and angled her to receive it. She had no issue with him taking
such thorough command, especially when he traded
his hold on her face for one at her breast. She smiled,
content and in awe of the unmatched pleasure he could
create with the simplest touch. She did squirm though,
when he left her breast bereft of further exploration.

Mounting impatience gave way to extreme approval
when Viva heard the distinct rip of condom packaging.
Smiling, she snuggled her face into a pillow.

"You came prepared," she purred.

"It's why I came over here in the first place. Now
shut up." His voice was gruff, yet playful.

Viva had only enough time for a single lilt of laughter before Rook's hands were once again smothering
her hips and positioning her to take him from behind.
Her gasp hinged on a shriek of welcome when he filled

her. Instantly, he was stretching her, hastening the climax within a few potent strokes.

"V? Is it too much?"

The query was quiet and given in a manner so sweet, she could've sobbed from the pleasure it added to the moment.

"Yes," she admitted, arching back to take all he had to give. "And if you stop, I'll kill you."

Contentment was like warm syrup gliding through her veins when she felt his chuckles vibrate into her back. That feeling, combined with what he was doing to the rest of her body... Viva didn't think she could hold out against giving herself completely over to it.

"Not yet," he murmured into her hair where he'd buried his face to inhale the fragrance clinging to her coiled tresses.

"Not yet," he repeated, lightly gnawing her shoulder. His perfect teeth grazed the silken flesh he found there.

One big hand remained secure about her thigh, keeping her positioned to enjoy the full extent of his penetration. His other hand had expertly snaked beneath her to once again cradle a pouting breast.

Unashamed and overwhelmed, Viva whimpered as the barrage of sensation claimed her sex. She'd missed him so—his size, the mastery of his hard, big body...

"Not yet, V, please..." Rook could tell she was at her limit in the way her muscles clenched and held him. "Not yet," he chanted as he exquisitely, expertly, incomparably claimed her.

"Not yet," he directed even as he lost control over his restraint and spilled his seed into the condom's thin sheath. Around him, he could feel her sex squeezing his with an almost painful intensity.

The room filled with the sounds of mingled breathing then. Viva felt Rook shift behind her and withdraw once he was spent. Her contentment had no chance to wane, however, as he secured her in a spooning embrace. He kept her there as they drifted into a lengthy and restful doze.

Hours later, Viva woke to find herself tucked cozily beneath the covers. For an instant, she feared it had all been a dream. That was before she shifted on the bed and felt a wondrous discomfort lurking in her muscles and well-used sex. She wanted Rook back, but knew he'd gone to at last get started on his day. It was his real reason for being there, after all.

Yawning, she took a moment to get her bearings and did a bit of quick math in her head. Then, she was reaching for the phone to dial her sister. She estimated it was about 5:00 a.m. in Philadelphia and hoped to get Sophia's voice mail. She wasn't at all surprised when the driven detective answered after three rings.

Sophia laughed. "Lucky for me it's a busy week for both of us. We're trying to wrap up some stuff before the wedding."

"In that case you're forgiven."

"So…" It was Sophia's turn to tease. "Don't you have a soon-to-be-ex ex you need to be smoothing things over with?"

Viva laughed, enjoying the remark. "We're working on it."

"I see… So? Can you share or are the details too obscene?"

"Mmm…" Viva languished between the covers and smiled wickedly. "They may be a bit too…explicit to share over international airspace."

Sophia screamed and Viva basked in her sister's approval before reality set in. "We didn't get around to discussing anything we needed to, Soap."

"Aw, girl, don't be so hard on yourself. Maybe this way you guys can hear each other without all the other…tension getting in the way."

"Here's hoping," Viva sighed. "Sophia, he doesn't seem to want to discuss any part of what went wrong."

"Why do you think that is?"

"He says he *can't* talk about it."

"Can't?"

"Mmm…"

"Well, maybe—" Sophia piped up seconds before shutting herself down.

"Exactly." Viva wasn't surprised by her sister's inability to come up with something to explain Rook's outlook.

"Listen, V, just forget it for now and focus on the bright side. You've gotten closer physically at least. It shouldn't be…*too* hard to enjoy that part."

"Hmm…" Viva adopted some of her sister's light manner. "You could have a point. I guess I could *force* myself to enjoy it." She joined in when Sophia dissolved into a fit of giggling.

"So have you talked to Rook since we left?" Viva was asking a short while later.

"No, why?"

Bracing herself, Viva shared the news about her friend and cast mate Bevy Ward.

"Glad I used my head and insisted on Rook taking

you with him," Sophia quietly complimented herself once Viva had completed her recap.

"It could still be a coincidence, you know?"

"V, come on. You don't believe that any more than Rook does."

"Yeah, well…" Viva began to rub at the sudden pressure along the bridge of her nose. "He doesn't even want to hear me say that this doesn't sound like the kind of thing Murray would do."

"Maybe you're a little too close to Murray to see that it could be."

"I can accept that, Sophia. It's just…a larger part won't let me believe it."

"A person can be capable of all kinds of things if their back is pushed hard enough against a wall." Sophia expressed the observation quietly, as though she knew she was treading on delicate waters.

"I can accept that too, Sophia. Just please don't close yourself off to the possibility that there could be some other explanation for these strange coincidences." Viva pushed up in the bed, "Sophia, promise to keep an open mind on that. There're tons of crimes that go unsolved because the police close themselves off to considering any other explanations aside from the ones *they* want to patronize."

"I got it, I got it and I won't even give you a hard time about preaching since you're a taxpayer."

"Hmph, thanks." Viva realized how rattled she'd become and settled back to the bed. "I'm sorry, Soap. I know Murray's got no one to blame but himself for what's happening, but attacking people who make him money… Well, it just seems weird."

"Have more people than you seen him associating

with folks he shouldn't have been?" Sophia sighed when quiet greeted her question. "Look, *I'll* keep an open mind about Murray, so long as *you* keep an open mind that the possibility exists that he just might try to silence those who could help seal his fate in a not-so-good way."

"I will." Viva gave up trying to massage away the ache between her brows. It was there to stay. "Thanks, Soap. I love you."

"Love you too. Talk to you soon."

Once the connection ended, Viva took a moment to silently rehash the conversation. The endeavor was brief as she was soon shaking her head to ward off the jousting match between her opinion and her sister's.

Viva was inching out from beneath the covers, when she heard a door close near the front of the suite. "Rook?" she called, enjoying the shiver that streaked along her spine when he responded.

When he arrived in her doorway, it was to give her a playfully scrutinizing look. "Still in bed? You're taking this jet-lag thing a bit far."

Viva languished back once more. "I thought you'd be gone longer."

"Disappointed?"

"Mmm…no…" She let her lashes flutter as if she were in the midst of savoring a treat or a memory. "Nope…it's not disappointment I'm feeling. Can you come back to bed?"

His resulting smile expressed distinct regret. "We should get a move on if we plan to make it to Cortina by dark.

"I'm gonna get you settled out there and then come

back to get things started. I'll be back every night before dark though."

Viva didn't want to give in to the twinges of agitation his words stirred, but she couldn't help it. "You'll
be back before dark every night, but you'll make sure
I'm fast asleep before you head for bed, right?"

"Has anything I've said to you mattered, V?" He
sighed. "This talk you want to have so bad? We'll have
it when we're back and that's it."

"And does it matter to you that it's hard to be
around you with this between us like some elephant
in the room? What if it was just me talking?" Her gaze
was as pleading as the hitch in her voice. "You could
save your rebuttal for when we're back."

"Why's this so important to you after all this time?"
He shoved off the door frame with noticeable force.
"Yes, it's crazy with us all of a sudden being around
each other like this, but—"

"You were right," she blurted with a defiant shake
of her head that sent the light brown curls flying into
her pretty face. "You were right about everything—
just like my parents were right. Everything you tried
to warn me I was letting myself in for with Murray
and this life…" She lifted her hands, let them fall back
to the covers in defeat.

Rook had gone rigid. His bright eyes were fixed and
more riveting given the intensity of his stare.

Viva averted her gaze, deciding that *not* looking
at Rook would keep her talking a lot longer. Judging
from the look on his face, she thought he seemed quite
interested in what she had to say. Finally.

"Everything you guys warned me would happen…
it wasn't all bold and in my face, it—it was all very

subtle and after a while I started to think that it really was just all of you trying to stifle me, not wanting me to go after my dreams, to stay where you wanted me, live the dreams *you* had for me." She rolled her eyes wearily and shrugged.

"I forgot all the warnings and let myself be wooed into the life. It wasn't hard. I'd have found a way in even if I hadn't been wooed. But I was and I accepted it all so greedily and then…it was time to prove how much I really wanted it."

Rook could feel the heat rising at his collar to begin a slow but steady streak across his nape. Not a good sign. "We can finish this later, V."

Her head snapped up, eyes flying to his face with pleading intensity. "Rook—"

"Later." He was backing out the door.

"Vossler." The name was soft on her lips, but she knew he heard her when he stopped moving toward the door. "I slept with him."

Rook hung his head, defeat claiming him then, as well. "I'm gonna take a wild stab and guess it wasn't hard for you to be wooed into that either?"

She bristled but accepted the blow and ached as though she'd expected it and needed it.

"Did it make you feel better to tell me that, V?" He moved back into the room. "Did you think it'd give me some kind of sick kick to hear I'd been right about that? About *that* of all things?"

She felt chilled then, not so much by the state of her undress as she was by the monotone of his voice. "I don't know why I told you…only that for so long I felt like I needed to."

"To ease your guilt."

"Maybe."

He was quiet for a long while, smoothing his thumb across the lines in his palm. "I can't speak to your family's motives for saying the things they did to keep you from leaving, V, but I can speak to my own." He waited for her eyes to meet his. "I was grabbing at anything to keep you where you were—that part's true. But it wasn't so you could live by my rules. It was because I knew that where you were going, there'd be no one to look out for you the way that I could."

Viva scooted to her knees and refreshed the pleading warmth of her gaze. "I know you have your problems with Murray, but I need you to know he did right by me. He looked out for me. None of what happened was his fault. I made my own decisions. They were horrible, but they were my own."

Rook grinned, but anger dwelled heavily in his eyes. "Murray Dean can do no wrong by you, can he?"

"Rook—"

"I already knew about Vossler. Maybe when you jump down off the Murray bandwagon you'll ask yourself how it is that I found out." He closed his hand over the doorknob. "Get dressed. We're out in an hour."

The chill attacking Viva's bare skin had her shivering blatantly before the door closed behind Rook.

Chapter 10

Cortina d'Ampezzo, Italy

"It's furnished, but I'm not sure how much of a home
it is."

Viva preceded Rook through a pair of double oak
doors that pretty much dwarfed her. The remarks
about his new acquisition had no effect on her.

In her opinion, the two-story chalet gave off an
unarguably homey feel. Viva moved slowly through
the lower level, her gloved hands reverently tracing
the polished wood surfaces of the bookshelves, message and end tables as well as the rounded cushions of
the sofas and armchairs furnishing the sitting room.

"It's beautiful," she said, her voice quiet, awed.
"Looks like someone's already made a home of it."

Rook was preoccupied with bringing in the luggage from the stone entryway leading to a wide maple-paneled corridor. He seemed too involved in his task to take time to soak in the allure of his new digs.

"The previous owners threw in the furniture," he spared a moment to tell her. "The wife's uncle passed away and left her a fully furnished villa in Morocco or something."

"Nice." Viva's mouth turned down into an impressed smile as she resumed her inspection of the elegant surroundings.

To herself, she noted that the place really only needed a few personal touches to give it a bit of extra warmth. She turned to eye Rook when he entered the room and watched as he shook faint sprinkles of snowfall from the charcoal-brown bomber jacket he wore.

"You made a great choice." She complimented the house when he caught her staring.

Rook took a moment to look around the room as well. "We'll see." His grim tone matched the cool look he directed her way. He motioned toward the ceiling. "Go pick out your room—there're six of them. You're welcome to the master. The others can comfortably sleep up to three grown men."

Viva tried to appreciate his words with a smile, but the effort took its toll. The easily delivered instructions answered one question—they wouldn't be sharing a room. She decided not to waste time berating herself for insisting on sharing past information they both could've done without hearing—or hearing again. He already knew. He knew! Murray had told him…

She shook her head, hoping it hadn't become too

obvious that she'd gotten lost in her thoughts. "You should at least have the master," she urged in a breezy tone.

"I'll have my pick soon enough." Rook headed across the room to stoop before a massive hearth that was framed with hand-carved stone. There, he inspected the screen and wrought-iron fireplace tools set to one side of the long brick foundation.

Viva took pride in not bristling that time. She'd received the answer to yet another question. He was more than ready to be rid of her.

Rook must've sensed how hastily his words came across, for he bowed his head and stood as if the effort weighed heavily upon him. "Chances are I won't have much time to sleep between working and commuting between here and Belluno."

Viva went to the frost-crusted doors leading out to a wraparound balcony. "Why'd you pick this location? It's so remote…" As she studied the range of snowy mountains, her voice turned dreamy.

Rook's tone sounded much the same when he responded. "I think that's why. The agent just showed it to me on the fly." He moved to join Viva at the doors and savored the breathtaking view, as well.

"When I saw it, I thought I could actually *feel* the quiet." The idea had him grinning and he shrugged. "I was sold."

"I believe you." Her eyes were still fixed on the view.

Silence held between them for a time. It was a comfortable quiet in spite of all that had been said.

"Rook—"

He moved suddenly, the sound of her voice seeming to galvanize him into action. "Let me know when you've decided on that room," he said and quickly left her.

Viva soon learned that she was to be left to her own devices. Rook may not have spent much time soaking in all the comfort and solace his new home had to offer, but he had certainly devoted a great deal of time to outfitting its security measures.

Cameras were fixed to every entrance, from those nearest the house to the farthest reaches of the property. There were motion and even heat sensors. The local authorities were but a phone button's push away. They were in such close proximity that Rook didn't feel too agitated over the idea of leaving Viva while he tended to business outside of town.

When Viva teased him that morning about her surprise over him not having a stone fence erected around the property, he grimly confessed that he'd wanted to but was told such a thing would ruin the aesthetics of the landscape. They had shared a quick laugh over the remark, but nothing more. Rook made a hasty departure soon after.

She considered calling Sophia to vent, but decided the woman had far more important things to keep her mind occupied than helping her big sister unravel her affairs of the heart. Besides, it was a priority that whoever was responsible for Bevy's accident and, she suspected, Reynolds Henry's death be stopped.

In spite of everything, she just couldn't make herself believe that Murray was at the bottom of it all. She winced then at the echo of a quiet voice in the back of her mind. The voice was calling her a fool of the highest caliber.

Hadn't she been a witness to what Murray was becoming long before Sophia's investigation put a spotlight on him? Hadn't Rook just confirmed the lengths he'd gone to to ensure the final and immovable nail had been driven into the coffin of their relationship? All that and still she wouldn't believe that Murray Dean had crossed over the line from petty security specialist to something more...monstrous.

"Stop it, Viva. Focus, dammit." She felt a measure of accomplishment when the sound of her voice muffled the one in her head. There was more to occupy her time than thoughts of Murray. She had the script and intimidating six-inch stilts still demanding her mastery.

Those tasks however, weren't nearly as appealing to her as exploring and possibly enhancing her new surroundings. If she was lucky, she mused, she might "enhance" well enough to bring a smile of approval to her host's handsome face. She wouldn't hold out much hope for that though. At the very least, devoting her time to taking on the role of homemaker would perhaps take her mind off what was or *wasn't* happening with her and Rook.

She'd found the chalet to be quite inviting upon first glance. It needed only a few creative accents to add the warmth that shrieked welcome. Viva spent much of the morning roaming the rustic oasis of stone, marble and wood. Windows were in high supply with flower boxes enhancing each of the rectangular holders along the sills. She could almost envision the colorful flora indigenous to the area filling each of the maple boxes with splashes of vibrant color once spring began to grace the environment with new signs of life.

For now, no such enhancements were possible save those of a more man-made variety. Viva went to work on the lamps. Already, she imagined their golden glow filtering out of the numerous windows to give the place the look of a gleaming destination in the midst of a quiet wonderland. The chandeliers were both elegant and unique as they hung from the wood-beamed ceilings of most every room. Still, Viva preferred the cozy invitation only a lamp could offer.

She took advantage of a surprisingly dependable Wi-Fi connection and checked the sites of several local shops. By day's end, she'd put in orders for window treatments and various bathroom accents. One of the shops delivered the first shipment of lamps. The vans were thoroughly checked by the two-man/two-woman security team at the main road. Viva had ordered for the downstairs rooms as well as the two bedrooms she and Rook had claimed. Additional items would arrive over the course of the week and she was certain that her brooding host would notice the minor transformation when he returned.

The hour-and-fifteen-minute commute between Cortina and Belluno gave Rook the time to both clear his mind and return it to its state of cluttered chaos. Luckily, the clearing had taken place as he'd made his way in to meet with the personnel of his European offices and the exclusive clientele he'd be serving there once the deal was closed. The day had been a fast-paced and productive one. So much so, Rook found himself taking the access road to the chalet before the full black of night had descended.

Rook had made small talk with the second shift guard detail and had been surprised, yet pleased to hear about all the activity that had taken place. With any luck, the fact that Viva was making herself at home was a hopeful sign that they could spend more time enjoying the tranquility of his newfound digs instead of the consistent argument about issues long past.

He pulled the Range Rover to a stop several feet from the chalet's main entrance and simply stared. Every window glowed golden bright, a radiant sight against the early evening skies of blues, purples and pinks tinting the horizon to usher in dusk. Easing up on the brakes, he advanced slowly, still in awe of the transformation.

Until that evening, he'd only seen the place lit by the motion and porch lighting, with scant illumination from the indoors. It was a stunning sight. It was the sight of home.

"Guess it's real now," he said to the empty car interior and thought of what that meant.

He wasn't afraid that he wouldn't see his family and friends on a regular basis. He thought of what a kick his mother would get out of telling her friends that she and his dad would be vacationing in Northern Italy. As for Elias and the guys—they were like his brothers. It'd take a lot more than a move halfway around the world to change that.

No, his concern was for Viva. True, things had long since ended between them… He shook his head free of the vivid imagery of them making love less than twenty-four hours ago. Despite that, things between them had ended long ago, but he'd never sensed the finality of it until that moment.

This move to Italy put a new turn on things entirely. After all, there wouldn't be much of a possibility for him to run into her while she was back visiting her parents, would there? Forget living on different coasts, they'd be living in different countries.

"What a mess." He smoothed a hand over his hair and grimaced. He'd finally gotten the courage to begin cutting emotional ties and they instantly engaged to snare him like vises.

Rook shut down the SUV and covered the rest of the gravel drive on foot. Upon entering the house, he reset the security code and was about to call out to Viva when he heard her outburst.

"If you want to fix things between us, this isn't the way!... I don't give a damn if you don't approve. This is my job... Please don't be that way... I didn't ask you here to fight..."

"V?" Frowning, Rook took steady yet cautious steps down the gleaming cobblestone floors of the main corridor. He peeked into the sitting room and the living room, before he found Viva in the den at the rear of the lower level. Discovery dawned and with it came the complete removal of the darkness that had dominated his expression for the better part of the day.

Viva stood in the middle of the den. The room gleamed golden thanks to the newly placed lamps dotting the stout oak end tables flanking thickly cushioned armchairs with their carefully crafted plum upholstery. She held on to a sheaf of papers that Rook immediately identified as her new script and the reason for her intermittent outburst fell into place.

Bracing a shoulder to the den's open doorway, Rook settled in for the show. It was a treat for sure and in more ways than one. The performance was one-sided, but Viva threw a vibrancy into every passage she uttered. It was a chore to look away from her on-screen, he thought. In person, looking away was a futile endeavor for a mere man. It wasn't only a futile endeavor, it was an insane one.

The caramel-toned beauty strutted around in a T-shirt, skintight capri yoga pants and what had to be eight-inch heels like she'd been born in them. Rook inhaled deeply, but kept the intake as soft as he did the exhale while he watched her saunter toward one of the coffee-brown sofas. Somehow, he managed to keep his mouth from dropping open when she plopped down on the sofa in a straddling position and faced the back of the chair.

She kept her eyes on the script and had yet to notice him there using the door frame to support his weight as his legs had become unable to. Viva put her free hand to the sofa, smoothing at the suede with the back of her hand as she might smooth the skin of her lover. Vivid imagery slashed through his mind again and it was he who benefited from the touch he watched her give the sofa with mutinous envy.

The sound of an unintended groan filling the air gave Viva a start and she scooted round on the sofa to find Rook there. Though she was flustered, a slight trace of the practiced naughtiness she'd conjured for the scene still shone through.

"Looks like you've mastered the shoes," Rook said.

Swallowing noticeably, Viva cast a withering look toward the spike-heeled violet satin pumps. The shoes hugged her instep as adoringly as the black and violet ties did her shapely calves.

"It's all about the attitude." The shrug she gave harbored the same withering manner. "Once you master that, the rest is easy."

"If you say so." His stirring eyes traversed the pumps with lingering approval.

"Sorry, I must've lost track of time," she said before their silence grew strained. "I could've done this in my room." She waved the script.

Rook moved from the doorway. "I'd be a fool if I said this wasn't a nice sight to come home to." *Nice.* He silently turned the word over in his head. It was erotic at its finest.

Viva gave a wistful smile then as she scanned the golden-lit room. "I could've saved myself the trouble of all the lamps."

"Glad you didn't." He took the time to observe his den as he moved deeper into the room. "It all hit me as soon as I took the road in. Felt like home."

"Well, then." Viva spread her arms and let her hands fall back to her sides. Her expressive stare pooled with pride and delight. "Guess I accomplished my mission to do at least *that* much." Another goal of that mission had been to improve his mood. As yet, she'd been unable to get a better bead on whether she'd managed that.

Rook moved to join her on the sofa and she scooted to make room.

"That looked like some scene," he said as he nodded toward the script.

"Uh, yeah." Viva ignored the burn in her cheeks. "It's harder when you have to play it alone."

"Trouble in paradise?"

She knew what he meant, and smiled. "Not yet, but the writers are pushing for it so…it's coming."

"So what's up?" He tugged the edge of the script she'd set on the cushion between them. He regarded her slyly. "Or is it a secret?"

She gave in to a more pronounced smile. "I guess I can dish a little." Her expression sobered when she looked to the script. "Leesi's trying to convince Cabot to do something he doesn't want to do," she shared, referring to her on-screen love Cabot Ryan, who was played by Bryce Danzig.

"And what is it that he doesn't want to do?"

"Let her go." Viva watched the muscle flex along his jaw, a reaction she'd anticipated.

"Why would she want him to do that?" Rook's gaze fixed upon the script. His voice had gone softer.

Viva chose to keep her eyes on his killer face instead. "She's got a job to do and she knows he won't be able to handle what she'll have to do to get it done."

Rook responded with a solemn nod. "Maybe he could."

"He'll believe that—for a while."

"So that's it? She'll just assume—"

"She's not assuming. She's got years of their relationship giving her all the material she needs to come to a very informed conclusion."

"So much material that she won't even give him a chance to fix it?"

"She *is* giving him a chance."

"How?" He gave her the benefit of eye contact then. "By asking him to let her go?"

Viva looked to the script then. "I think she hopes he'll follow her. I don't think she even knows that's what she wants, but it is."

"That's a risky game she's playing. They could lose each other for years. Anything could hap—" Rook cut his words short, just as Viva's sharp intake of breath filled the room.

With another shaky breath, she started to shove off the sofa. Rook caught her wrist before she'd done little more than press her hand into the cushions. An instant later, she found herself positioned as she had been while running lines with her imaginary co-star. But this time her knees were planted on either side of Rook's hips, and she knew she had no other choice but to look directly into his exceptional face.

Helplessly, her eyes lowered to his mouth, and memories of its talents shot a blunt throb of need through her core. Reflexively, she moistened her bottom lip and saw the move draw his bright stare to the location.

He stared for a time as though transfixed by the way the pink tip of her tongue darted out to travel across the lush lips accentuated by a light bronze glosser. The sound of his name whispering past them was his undoing.

The hand cupping her hip made a quick ascent until it rested between Viva's shoulder blades. He brought her in closer until he was crushing her velvety mouth against his hard one. Her gasp granted greater depth for his tongue to explore and he did so with sheer relish fueling his moves.

Her hands were weak, yet she just managed to curl them around the lapels of the quarter-length wool jacket he'd yet to remove. Strength may have left her hands but the same couldn't be said of her kiss. Eagerness flooded the gesture to rule choice parts of her anatomy. Gently, she rocked her hips, performing a subtle grind against the ridge of his sex beneath a straining zipper. She moaned while she snuggled deeper into what she craved.

She was on the cusp of begging him to give her more, but her mouth was totally occupied with kissing and not talking. Blindly, her fingers glided from their grip around Rook's jacket lapels to unhook the top fastening of the slate-gray trousers he wore. She had nearly undone the fastening when he smothered her busy fingers beneath a big hand.

"Rook—" She got out just that much before he put her on her back in one seamless, rapid move.

Mouth freed, she begged in earnest then. He was plying the soft, fragrant column of her throat with gentle, wet kisses. Her breasts heaved with mounting vitality the nearer his talented and lovely mouth drew to them. When his lips merely skirted the tops, without so much as an outline around the nipples desperately straining against lacy bra cups, impatience had her cupping the back of his head to snare his sleek curls and offer encouragement.

She sobbed when he covered her free hand and squeezed in his own form of encouragement. Tears stung her eyes and she would've wrenched away, but he held her fast.

"I would've followed if you'd really wanted me to." He inched back when she ceased her struggling.

A mix of longing and regret rippled in his gaze before he squeezed her chin and smiled apologetically. "I would've followed, but you didn't want me to, V. Not then."

With that, he moved to leave her reeling in need and defeat.

Chapter 11

Over the two weeks that followed, Viva threw herself into every task and chore she could devise. Making Rook's house into a home had become less about fixing his mood, which she'd at last deemed a hopeless pursuit, and more about satisfying another personal longing.

The rustic, old-world dwelling underwent a gradual transformation that showcased Viva's flair for interior decorating as well as her love for cozy spaces that epitomized warmth and invitation.

Amid her decorating efforts, she mastered the script. She'd taken to practicing outside her room when Rook was gone, which was quite often. She told herself he had lots to do to get the new leg of his business up and running. That mind-set had sustained her for the first week but not so much going into the second.

She'd accepted that there was nothing she could do

to fix the new layer of trouble laid over their doomed relationship. Her dogged redecorating had been about living a fantasy—one that had not even a snowball's chance of becoming reality.

This was the life she wanted. She knew that. She had known that since long before circumstances had brought them back into one another's lives. He was right. She wouldn't have wanted him to come with her. Not then. Her career and the years she'd spent honing it were not things she resented.

Losing Rook in pursuit of it all, however... Yes, she greatly resented that. Now.

Viva tucked the black quilt beneath her neck and snuggled deeper into the den sofa where she'd lounged for much of the latter part of the afternoon. The snowfall had been a light, but steady drift that was hypnotic and a fabulous soother to her riotous thoughts.

She kept her mobile handy, dreading the call she had to make, but knowing it *had* to be made just the same. With any luck, her sister would be busy and she would get to leave the message she had rehearsed. As she reached for it in her back pocket, the phone jiggled, giving Viva a start. The name on the screen surprised her even as a welcoming grin spread across her face.

"Don't you have a broken leg and fractured collar bone to be mending? Or isn't there someone you should be ordering around? Maybe you're just trying to milk this bed-rest thing for as long as you can." Viva grinned while delivering the playful jibe.

Throaty laughter traveled through the line before an equally rich voice followed. "You know me so well.

I just sent Winnie to bring me a box of those cheese Danish from Reardon's."

"You should be ashamed." Viva shook her head while laughter tickled her throat. "Reardon's is on the other side of town from the hospital. What the hell time is it there anyway?"

"Hey! *She* wanted to!" Bevy Ward's attempt at whining came across instead as a wicked laugh. "Besides…" Her tone mellowed as she seemed to sober. "I needed some alone time to talk to you. Winnie was the only one still hovering and I needed her out."

"How are you, Bev? I know about the injuries."

"Yeah… I'm gonna be out of commission for a while." Hints of stress seeped into Bev's strong voice then. "Anyway… I guess there's a lot to be said for being in fair shape. Doctors are hopeful that the recovery won't be too agonizing. I'm fine though, trying to figure out who I've got to sleep with to keep a steady supply of these painkillers they're giving me. Those things are the ultimate."

Viva had to laugh over her friend's ability to apply comic relief in the direst of situations. "Good to know you've got goals."

"Exactly." Bevy grunted a laugh.

"So what's up?" Viva pushed up on the sofa and switched the phone to her other ear.

"Is it true, V?" Bevy wasted no more time getting to the point of her call. "What they're saying about Murray? Not that the cops are telling us anything," she continued, not noticing that Viva had yet to answer her questions.

"Arty told me they came to Murray's office," Bevy

went on. "She said they came with a warrant after what happened to Fee."

"Fee?" Viva sat all the way up on the sofa then as the image of Fee Fee Spikes began to form inside her head.

"You didn't hear about it yet?" The Southern accent Bevy worked doggedly to mask grew a little more noticeable as concern mounted. "Looks like Fee surprised a burglar and got a broken nose and a few cracked ribs out of the ordeal," she explained.

Viva muttered an oath. The bubbly redhead was a client of Murray Dean's.

"Anyway..." Bev grunted, as though she were moving to a more comfortable spot in her hospital bed. "They say she'll recover. Her manager and agent are screaming bloody murder though after what happened to Reynolds Henry and then me. They—they think someone could be targeting Murray's clients and the cops are hoping someone got a good look at the guy. We won't know till Fee wakes."

"The guy?" Viva gripped the slender mobile in a vise hold. "Not Murray?"

"Well..." Uncertainty filtered Bevy's reply. "I mean... I don't know what *they* think but—well... hell, V, it's *Murray.*"

"Yeah..." Viva left the sofa, tugging at the hem of the T-shirt she'd sported with the hot-pink yoga shorts she'd worn that day. The apparel had pretty much become her primary wardrobe during her unexpected vacation abroad. "Yeah, it's Murray," she sighed.

"V? You don't think Murray—"

"No. No... *I* don't." Viva pushed back a few locks

of her hair and then pressed a finger to the corner of her eye to relieve the pressure building there. "My sister and Rook, on the other hand—"

"Rook?" The weary uncertainty that had gripped Bevy's voice made way for happy curiosity. "Well, well. So for once the gossip rags have it right? Talk about running off with an old flame... Is he as amazing looking as I've heard?"

The turn of conversation had heightened the pressure behind Viva's eyes and she was then massaging a sudden throb at the bridge of her nose. "Yes, he is."

"Weird." Bevy sighed. "Nothing popped off between you guys before as much as I've heard he works with folks in the business."

"Yeah." Viva gave up with the massage, realizing that it was useless. "Weird."

"So? What's it like? Talk to me."

Viva opened her mouth, then closed it. She could honestly offer nothing more to the conversation at that point.

"Ugghh..." Bevy noted from her end of the line. "That bad, huh? Or maybe that good?"

"Too much has happened, Bev. We can't go back to what we were."

"But you want to."

"It's too late."

"And is that what *he* thinks?"

"Our lives are crazy, Bev."

"Lives are always crazy, girl. Love though, *real* love? That shit only comes by once—or maybe twice—if you're lucky."

Viva had to smile then. "Are you biting off Pam's advice?"

Bevy sounded as though she were chuckling over the mention of her on-screen character. Apparently, she'd taken no offense to the accusation. "Hell, I don't see why not," she admitted. "It's damn good advice. Wouldn't hurt you to take it, you know."

"It's more than just a leap of faith here, Bev. He knows things that…they could change things…"

"Things that happened once you split, right?"

"He told me I'd get in over my head back then, Bev. I did."

"And you'll let that stop you from digging your way out?"

"He's made a life, Bev. A good one that's on its way to being a great one." Viva eyed the cozy room with a mix of envy and sadness. "I just had to go and open up all this old drama. It wasn't a good idea and it'll only distract him from what he has to do." She closed her eyes to the distant, snowy mountain view. "When all is said and done, he'll regret all the time he wasted and I'll still be who I am. Nothing there will have changed."

"Boy, you've really thought this through, huh?" Bev's voice held a hint of the playful. "You sound really sure of yourself."

Viva took a refreshing breath and managed a smile. "Nothing here to do but think."

"Well, Winnie should be back with those Danish soon and I think… I think your opinion is bullshit, V."

"Bev—"

"I'm gonna leave you to your thoughts. I think you

should take more time with them. Just call me if you have any more news from your end, okay?"

"All right and you do the same. And, Bev? Thanks."

"Love you, sweets."

"Love you too."

Viva didn't set aside the phone once the connection ended. Instead, she studied it, debating before she dialed out. Her lips thinned with resolve when she heard the voice mail chime through. "Soap? It's me. I need you to call me back when you get this."

"Catch you at a bad time?"

Rook barked a laugh when he heard Linus's query through the phone line. "That's one of those trick questions, right?"

"Ah, no…" Linus groaned, "please don't ruin my fantasies of what it must be like to have a Hollywood starlet all to yourself."

"All right, then." Rook let his silence do the talking.

Again, Linus groaned. "Are you serious here? You guys are a million miles away from everything."

Rook forced a smile, albeit a grim one. "I guess you can never outrun the past."

"Can't you at least set it aside to make room for better stuff?"

"Hell, man, do you think I don't want to? It's *all* I want. *She's* all I want." Tired of pretending his mind was on work, Rook hurled a pen across the desk. "Hollywood starlet or not, she's all I've *ever* wanted."

"So?" Linus let the challenge hold for a moment. "She's there, isn't she? My guess is she wouldn't have gone so quietly, or as quietly as she did, if part of her didn't want to. To hell with what Sophia dictated. Viva's got the means to disappear like that."

Rook heard the man's fingers snapping on the other end of the line.

"She came back for you, kid." Linus's voice was almost a whisper. "You should make use of that. You may not get another chance."

Rook left his desk to stare unseeingly beyond the office picture window that opened to a sea of white. "Maybe I don't think I deserve another chance."

"Bullshit."

"Oh, I get it." Rook turned his back on the snowy scene of the Belluno business park and evaluated his friend's assumption. "Is that what you tell yourself, Line? That all the crap you pulled in the name of having a reaction still means you get another chance? Is it so easy for you to forget that part of the past?" He pushed hard against the back of his desk chair when he passed and sent the furnishing spinning.

"You're right, it's all crap, but I'd take another chance again without hesitation if I had the opportunity to make it right. There's only one thing I regret enough to make the effort, you know? I believe Viva's that one thing for you and I believe you know that." When he only received silence as a response, Linus asked, "You should be getting home now, shouldn't you?"

Home. Rook turned the word over in his head. "Yeah, Line, home sound good."

Rook had been on his way out the door, with intentions to head home, when Linus's call had come through. The call had done a lot of good, despite his reluctance to hear much of his friend's insights. All he'd wanted was to forget; he didn't want to remember the man he'd been back then. The animal he'd been.

His fingers flexed over the steering wheel and he tried to give rising, unsettling memories a mental shove. Useless. There was no real forgetting them. Maybe the trick was to own the past. Viva had owned hers, hadn't she?

What mistakes had she really made though? He wondered. She'd gone after a dream and met up with some nightmares along the way. It wasn't an impossible occurrence. Such was often the case when one chased after the future.

The true mistakes had come in his reaction to what he'd learned. Now, the question was whether telling her about them was really necessary. He'd figured that was a yes, considering how poorly he'd dealt with it all since she'd come back into his life. *That* had roused her questions and she deserved answers—she deserved the truth.

Home appeared around the road's bend in all its welcoming splendor. As per usual when he got there, Rook took the time to just enjoy the view and gather the courage to face his demons. He parked, headed inside and was closing the door seconds before the sense of déjà vu washed over him.

"It's too much…I understand why you suggested it, but we need to find another way…No…No, it only went back to more drama…Don't worry about it, I'll figure something. I've got a costar in the hospital. Remember we told you about Bevy? I should spend time with her anyway. I need you with me on this, Soap. Being here with him is killing me..."

Rook eased the door locks quietly into place and then rested back against the wall as reality hit that this was no instance of déjà vu. He hadn't walked in on Viva rehearsing her script, but into the midst of a scene that was all too true to life. He waited just outside the den until Viva finished the call to her sister.

"Has my hospitality worn thin?"

She turned at the sound of Rook's voice when he entered the room.

"Don't bother using the injured costar excuse," he advised before she could answer. "I'd love to hear the reason you gave to Sophia."

Bowing her head, Viva pressed the tips of her fingers against eyes closed wearily in defeat. "I just don't know what we're doing here."

"I thought it was to save your life."

Her brows lifted as she smiled wistfully. "And does the 'save your life' rate include dynamic sex?"

He was, for a moment, silenced by the unexpected approval that surged in response to her backhanded compliment. He recovered soon enough. "You didn't seem to have a problem accepting the service."

The soft reminder prompted more than the nod she gave. "I hoped we were on our way back to each other."

The admission stopped him again. "You want that?"

She fixed him with a look that was as exasperated as it was accusing. "Of course I want that, you idiot.

I—" She squeezed her eyes shut once more, her cheeks burning over the unintended confession.

"Fortunately, dynamic sex isn't our problem," she professed once a sliver of cool had reasserted itself. "*Unfortunately*, we can't spend all our time in bed, which means at some point, we'll have to talk to each other." She extended her arms, let her hands fall to thighs bared by her shorts. "I don't think there's an argument on how bad we've been doing on that end."

"What does 'on our way back to each other' mean?" Rook was clearly still somewhat dazed by Viva's earlier admission. His rich voice sounded deeper given the soft-spoken manner it had adopted. His striking features were still sharp as he fixated upon her.

"Rook, you—you know what I meant—"

"I want to hear you say it." He closed what distance remained between them.

"Rook, I—I love you," she said quietly, helplessly, as though that single confession was all she was capable of. "I never stopped." She shook her head to put emphasis on the claim. "I want back what we had— what we could've had. I'm sorry I—" She blinked suddenly as though some part of her psyche were reconnecting to reality. "I didn't mean to put all that on you. I know things have changed and you—you can't…want me after I slept with—"

He'd gripped her so suddenly, she gave a tiny shriek before panting out a breath.

"Look at me, V."

For her, the effort was massive. She was close to paralyzed by uncertainty and…fear. Not fear of him, but fear of what she'd see in his eyes.

"Viva? Look at me." He squeezed the bend of her elbow and waited.

Drawing on practiced courage, she met his stunning eyes and gasped over what she saw there. There was no anger—not even a hint of frustration. What she saw instead was awe mingling with the brilliance of hope.

"Not wanting you isn't possible for me Viva. I don't know if it ever will be and I don't much care to find out."

Her lips parted, but Viva had no notion of what she was about to say. That wasn't a problem for Rook as he'd already found a task to occupy her mouth quite thoroughly.

The kiss was as needed as it was seeking. Rook's delivery was a hungry, possessive assault that had Viva instantly moaning and sobbing for more. She could scarcely curve her fingers into the lapels of the leather jacket he wore. No matter, for he kept her high against his chest in the most secure hold.

Needing to feel more of him, Viva wrapped her legs around his waist. Eagerly, she presented her mouth to be explored.

Rook felt as if he were roasting inside the wool lining of his jacket but he refused to relinquish his hold on Viva's bottom to get out of it. He had her flush between himself and the closest wall, in the span of two long strides.

"I'm sorry, sorry…" he groaned, while driving his tongue deep to savor the honeysuckle flavor of her mouth. His kiss drove her head back into the wall.

Viva didn't require apologies. She answered the rough treatment by stripping Rook, none too gently, of his brown jacket before she went to work on the dark shirt he wore beneath it. Silently, she warned herself not to rip the buttons free. Her fingers tingled with the need to stroke his bare flesh.

Those intentions took a backseat when his fingers slipped inside the snug crotch of her shorts. Simultaneous moans echoed in the room. Hers stimulated by his fingers inside her shorts. His by the fact that she wore nothing beneath them.

Rook let his forehead rest on her shoulder. He absorbed the shudders rippling through her curvy frame—a response to the erotic torment that stimulated moisture and held his fingers in the tight clench of her intimate muscles.

Viva found no need to hold on to his breathtaking shoulders. This, despite the fact that he only supported her with the forearm that cradled her bottom. She felt completely secure and she took advantage of that fact by focusing her efforts on the buttons yet to be undone. Once she had his shirt open, she splayed her hands upon the thick slabs of his muscular chest. Her lips were gliding down the chiseled length of his neck, across collarbone and sternum, until she was taking a pebbled male nipple into her mouth.

Rook grunted as sensation slammed into him. For several seconds he endured the pleasurable assault, then he was cursing viciously and bringing an end to the spectacular attention she was giving his chest.

"What?"

Her hushed query stirred his laughter and then he was kissing the corner of her mouth. "Come with me," he said.

* * *

Protection hadn't occurred to her. Viva wondered whether she'd have called attention to its absence if it had. Sure, there was lots more she wanted to do before she said goodbye to her career. Having Rook Lourdess's child was a choice she would have made her career work around.

"We could've stayed downstairs, you know?" She purred the words while tracking the end of her nose along his collarbone.

"We were missing some things," he said as he sheathed himself. Then he took her in his arms. A low sound of animalistic male pleasure thrummed from his throat as he took her with deliberate purpose.

Viva knew there was no need to muffle the sounds of her delight, yet she turned her face into a pillow anyway. She eased her hands beneath its cool cotton texture as her hips dipped and rolled to a rhythm honed by instinct, by want.

Another of Rook's quiet, satisfied rumbles emerged and his slow strokes were moments of pure bliss for Viva. She let out a choked sob when his beautifully shaped mouth took one nipple hostage in an achingly sweet suckle that sent need pooling between her thighs. Somehow, she held back the final barrier on her release.

She wanted more and wouldn't take for granted that what they shared in that moment would soon be repeated. Working then to, in some way, reciprocate his attention to her chest, she dragged a shaky hand up his sweat-slicked abs and rib cage until she was cupping a bulging pec. She caressed his nipple beneath her thumb.

Rook shuddered, his divine mouth still full of her breast. Viva seized the opportunity to turn the tables then and she had him on his back moments later. Their connection never broke; it had no chance to. Viva's hips were smothered in his hands, his hold so secure, it almost allowed for no movement.

Sensually slow, her body rocked in a fashion that sent orgasmic shudders ricocheting through her in thick, unapologetic waves. Her hands glided, coasting up her taut, trim torso. She made a brief stop to cup her breasts before moving on to drag her fingers through her hair and let the mass tumble around her enchanting face.

Rook received almost as much pleasure from the sight of her as he did from the feel of her squeezing the erection that showed no signs of losing its intensity anytime soon. When he sensed her needs were getting the better of her, he added more pressure to his hold at her hips in hopes of preventing her from taking him over the edge with her. Not yet, he told himself. Not yet.

Viva's shudders grew fiercer and Rook knew she was indeed at the limit of her resistance. He wanted more though and he meant to have it. Viva collapsed atop him, yet she still moved with an overt eroticism that would've made him come were it not for how greedy he still was for her.

Viva's smile reflected complete contentment. She felt oh so pampered when his lips brushed her brow for a tender kiss. Yes, she felt wholly content, or at least she *thought* she was, until he put her beneath him again.

This time, she was on her stomach with Rook's considerable weight more stimulating than it was crushing as he took her from behind. Spent as she was, Viva still latched onto a new wave of arousal. She arched up to receive him, gasping eagerly and panting while her intimate folds contracted in a desperate attempt to keep him still to savor.

Rook calmed his enthusiastic captive with quick, soft kisses to her ear and whispered, "Easy...it's my turn now..."

Chapter 12

"I was watching the show one night. You and what's his face were having…a moment."

Viva giggled. "Wholly content" seemed a poor way to describe the way she felt. While the sex had been supreme, the aftermath was hot on its heels. Snuggling into the perfection that was Rook's chest, she sent up a quick prayer for this time to be among the first of many.

"Bryce Danzig." She gave him the name of her leading man. "He's gay, you know?"

Rook snorted. "Hard to tell judging from his scenes with you."

Viva felt the urge to laugh again, knowing the emotion was brought on by more than Rook's teasing. It was from the true happiness coursing through her veins.

The only light glowed from the fireplace. The master suite was dark, even with the moon's illumination. It shone faint that night as it streamed in through windows yet to be covered by drawn drapes.

"Anyway..." Rook continued, snuggling his head deeper into the cradle provided by his arm tucked beneath it. "You were very into what he was doing and I..."

Viva pushed up on her elbow then to look down at him. "The show's director, Jake Hough, had to work a lot with us—me and Bryce—in the beginning. My acting experience was still very limited and Bryce's... sexual preference was a challenge. He'd never acted opposite a woman as a romantic lead before."

Viva rested back into the sheets when she saw she had Rook's attention. "Jake's advice to us was to see the person we most wanted to be with in the world. 'Every move you make, every sound you utter is for them,' he said." She grazed her knuckles against his jaw when he raised up over her.

"Every love scene I've ever done has been with you in my head," she said.

Rook's sly smile defined his features into a more devastating picture. "That was some pretty handy advice."

"Yes, yes, it was." Viva chuckled the words. "Hard to believe the man is four times divorced."

Laughter mingled with the pop and snap of the fire-engulfed logs in the hearth.

"That night I watched you with him," Rook continued, "and I heard you, um...responding to him. I thought about us, thought about you sounding that way for Vossler...and I lost it."

"Rook—" Viva didn't realize she was holding her

breath until he eased his staggering gaze her way. She didn't know what to say. There was no need for more.

"Let me finish," he soothed.

Viva allowed the breath she'd been holding to expel in a slow flow and somehow she managed to keep her gaze from faltering.

Rook sat up then, one arm hanging over a raised knee as he looked toward the fire. "My crew had been on a pretty rough case—it was a domestic thing. The client's daughter was trying to get out of a bad marriage. The ex rubbed the whole team the wrong way. The client hired us to watch her and make sure the fool didn't come around." He brought a hand to his jaw, massaged there for a moment as the buried memories began to surface.

"She'd served the jerk with papers the week before and her father—my client—wanted us to keep an eye out."

Viva decided to sit up then as well, but felt it best not to initiate contact. She could see the muscles in his wide back were rigid with tension.

"That night I saw you on TV...being there in the apartment, *our* apartment...it was too much." He squeezed his eyes shut, gave a quick shake of his head. "I went to relieve whomever was on shift. I just needed to get out of the house and take my mind off stuff—off you..." He passed Viva a sidelong smile, but didn't look her way.

"I went to the daughter's house, talked a little bit with my guys. I was going to take a walk around the grounds. My team was about to pull off when I heard her scream. It was a big place, so we didn't know how long he'd been in there with her before we heard her.

My people are obsessive about their jobs..." He shook his head again. "No way the bastard got past them, but there he was inside. Turned out, he talked his way in. Lied to her about wanting to put the past to rest— that's what she was able to tell me...later. Hmph...put *her* to rest was more like it. She was hurt pretty bad by the time we got him off her. My guys were calling the cops, so all I had to do was restrain him and let him cool his heels until they got there. I didn't."

Viva watched Rook's fists clench. She resisted drawing the sheets over her suddenly chilled skin.

"It just came over me," he said, and then studied his fists, as well. "Like a fever and I... I couldn't—" His sigh was loud over the wood crackling amid the fire.

"It's ironic." He laughed shortly, quietly then. "I beat the guy almost half to death—a guy who lost it when his ex just shook hands with another man and there *I* was on the verge of killing him because I couldn't handle seeing my—my ex...acting out a love scene."

"You know you were dealing with more than that." Viva tentatively voiced the reminder.

Rook angled his head, but still didn't give her the full benefit of his gaze. "It wasn't enough to justify what I did to that guy. No one blamed me for it, but they were plenty ready to lay blame by the end of a few more weeks. Thank God for Linus," he groaned, burying his face in his hands.

"Linus Brooks?" Viva frowned.

"He was the one who got me to include the fight-training service end to my business." He smirked. "Once I dealt with the crap load of anger that had me in danger of losing every friend I had in the world. I, um… I've come a long way on that end, but I've still got a long way to go. Which is why—"

"You kept giving me the brush-off on talking about it," she finished.

He smoothed both hands over his nape. "Right." He then worked the heels of his hands into his eyes while resting back onto the bed.

"So? What now?" Still sitting, Viva turned to study him where he lay.

Rook was quiet for a long time. "You have to know I tried everything to stay away from you. Over the years…there were a lot of times I could've changed that. I didn't and I'm sorry."

Viva returned the lopsided grin he sent her. "I could say the same, you know? What's done is done, right?"

Rook folded her hand into his. "You're gonna have to forgive me if I'm hard to shake after all this." He considered her fingers as if each was a unique source of fascination. "I knew if you ever came back into my life, I wouldn't be up for letting you go again."

"That doesn't sound so bad to me." Viva scooted round to face him more fully.

His expression was a sober one. "I haven't evolved all that much, V. I'm still that guy you had to walk away from."

"I was really in love with that guy, you know?" She straddled him on the bed.

"Really?" Rook fought to suppress a smile. "He was pretty overbearing, kind of a know-it-all."

"Mmm…yeah…yeah, he could be those things. But his body is amazing and he's quite stunning in bed."

Rook had to laugh then. "We can't spend all our time in bed, though, remember?"

She shrugged. "Well, it's not a deal breaker and like I said...I love you, remember?"

"I remember." He'd been spanning the lush length of her thighs with his palms. They traveled up to curve about her waist and he tugged to set her nice and neat against a renewed erection.

Viva wanted to melt, even as her heart sank in reaction to the fact that he'd yet to reciprocate her emotional confession. Still, happiness continued to mount and she forgot her disappointment when he nudged her close for a kiss.

"I love you," he said softly, simply against her mouth.

Her sinking heart was suddenly in her throat and the resulting kiss was more than a greedy claiming. It was a confirmation that their hearts were again as one.

Words of promise and love renewed were whispered deep into the earliest hours of the morning. This, followed by more lovemaking, interrupted by lengthy bouts of sleep, followed by more lovemaking.

Rook didn't make a move to head into work that morning and Viva wasn't about to call his attention to the fact. Sunlight was reflecting blindingly bright off the snow-capped landscape around ten that morning when they decided it might finally be worth checking out another area of the house besides the bedroom.

While Rook went to the kitchen to begin breakfast, Viva returned to the den and set the coffee table. The plan was to eat there with the splendid mountain scenery before their eyes. With the table set, Viva returned to the kitchen to watch Rook put his culinary skills to the test. Watching the man cook was only an added benefit. Viva was more interested in watching him cook wearing only the nylon basketball shorts he'd tugged on before leaving bed. She grabbed her cell as she passed the lamp table where she'd left it last night. By the time she got to the kitchen, she was frowning into her phone.

"Trouble?" Rook had spied the look she wore when she took a seat at the other end of the wide wood-grained cooking island.

"Not sure...there're about ten missed calls from Stanton Giles. He's Bryce's agent."

The news had Rook's hand hovering over the bowl of eggs waiting to be cracked. Viva pulled a trembling hand through her hair and gave the phone a foreboding look.

"I can't take much more of this," she said. "If Stan tells me something's happened to—"

"Hey, hey, stop." Rook turned to wave off her predictions. "Find out what the man wants before you take your trip off the deep end, okay?" His stern expression softened when he saw her decisive nod.

"You're right." Viva continued to nod while she eased off the island's bar seat. She disregarded the time; the man had left ten calls, after all.

Rook forgot his breakfast duties, his focus instead on Viva across the big kitchen. Slowly, approvingly, his gaze roamed her legs bared beneath the hem of an extralarge midnight-blue sweatshirt. All she wore beneath were a pair of pink bikini briefs and the knowledge of that pleased him to no end.

Viva was greeting Stan Giles a few moments later. Rook half listened. His attention gradually returned to his cooking task as he took in the obligatory open-

ing chatter and the series of "mmm-hmms," "okays"
and "rights" Viva uttered for her part of the conversation. Her sudden gasp and hushed "what?" followed
by "Are you serious?" had Rook pausing once again
over the food.

When she screamed, his first instinct was to go to
her. Then he saw the scream followed by five seconds
of excited jumping and a hand covering her mouth to
muffle more screams. He understood. The news was
good. He focused on whipping the eggs into a creamy
yellow froth.

"Oh?...Yeah...No, yeah, yeah, I get it. I, um, how'd
he—how'd he sound, Stan?...Right...Right, no, I—I
get it...Yeah, yeah I *am* excited." She turned, met
Rook's gaze and smiled brighter. "Right," she said into
the phone. "Yeah, okay, Stan, thanks...Okay, sounds
good...All right...All right. Talk to you soon...Bye."

"Good news?" Rook was adding chopped scallions
to a bowl of chopped green peppers and spinach.

"The show..." Viva began as if dazed. "Sounds like
we're popular enough for a movie."

Laughter was brightening Rook's remarkable face
even before the sound tumbled full and rich from his
throat. The explosion of good cheer was followed by
words to that effect and he came around the cooking
island to grab Viva into a bear hug that took her off
her feet.

"It's pretty cool, huh?" Viva's words were practically swallowed up by her laughter.

"Probably old hat for someone who's no stranger
to the big screen," Rook said as he set her to her feet.

"Are you kidding?" Viva shuffled back to the island
and set the phone on the counter. "The show was my

first real leading role. To know it's become so popular with the audience and that the audience is big enough to get the attention of a well-respected studio…it's like a dream that keeps on morphing into something more amazing."

"Okay." Rook nodded, tilted his head as if measuring her expression. "So why do you seem sort of down about it?"

Viva let her smile carry only a few seconds longer before letting it slip. She didn't know why it still surprised her how well he knew her.

"Stan reached out to me because Murray asked him to. Stan is Bryce's agent, not mine."

"So?" Rook went back to his place at the stove.

"So why give a damn whether I hear about this or not if he plans to kill me? He asked Stan to take me on as a client. Why do that?"

"To put you at ease, maybe?" Rook gave the eggs a few more seconds of unnecessary beating. "To have you focused on good fortune instead of the threat at your back? Do you really not get that, V?" He pushed the eggs aside.

"I just don't…"

"Don't what, V? Believe he'd ever do anything so foul? I get it."

"Rook, I—I don't want to fight."

"Neither do I." He took up the egg bowl again. "I'll call you when breakfast is ready."

Viva used another minute to study him. The rigid set of his shoulders was more than a little noticeable. She agreed it was best to wait out the breakfast prep elsewhere. Before she cleared the kitchen's entryway, she heard his voice.

"He enjoyed it," Rook spoke over his shoulder, sorrow clinging to every word. "Murray. He told me to my face. I think he made a special trip back just to do it. He enjoyed telling me about you and Vossler. Grinned like an idiot the whole time he was giving me the details. He knew I was too out of it to beat the hell out of him like I otherwise would've done. He finished up by telling me that his only regret was that he couldn't tell me how much you enjoyed yourself. He must've had a conversation with Vossler about it. According to the man himself, you were very eager to please."

Viva was glad Rook kept his back turned. Her face was shining with tears that blurred her vision as they streamed her cheeks. She left the kitchen soundlessly.

Rook remained motionless until the mutinous anger engulfing him had backed off.

Breakfast was a quiet affair. Rook and Viva managed to enjoy it in the same room, though Viva wondered if that was because they ate in the den and not in a more formal setting at an actual dining table. Aside from requests to pass the fruit bowl or nods for coffee to be topped off, there was no real conversation.

They parted ways soon after the meal. Rook handled the dishes. Viva had said something about getting dressed and then reviewing her script again. She tried to close out the replay of the run-in with Murray that Rook had mentioned. But it was useless.

After she left home—the *way* she left home—there had been no one, no family. There was only Murray— *he'd* been her family. He'd been there for her through everything. Everything. From the early career disappointments, to giving her a shoulder to cry on when she continually mourned the end of her relationship with Rook.

"God…" she moaned, holding her head in her hands as she leaned against the window in the parlor.

Murray had done it. Rook was telling the truth about what he'd been told. Even all the rest, the curious accidents that had befallen others over the last several weeks… He was most likely responsible for them, as well. Most likely? Most definitely. She knew that and she just couldn't bring herself to admit it.

Knocking caught her attention. Quickly, she blinked water from her eyes and turned on the padded window seat where she'd been pretending to review the script for the past few hours. The routine had not changed much over the last day and a half. She and Rook had spent much of that time moving around each other in quiet caution. She guessed they were both afraid of saying more of the wrong thing.

Rook leaned on the doorway, his expression soft. It was the hint of playfulness she saw in his amber eyes that had her dark ones narrowing from curiosity and relief that the tension between them might be easing.

"It just occurred to me that I haven't spent this much time in the house since I brought you here." He inhaled and gave the room a speculative appraisal. "Had no idea how quiet it gets around here."

Viva smiled and waved the script. "I'm gonna know my part and everyone else's by the time we start filming. The quiet really is great for concentration." Her smile widened at his theatrical sigh.

"It's been less than forty-eight hours and I'm about to go into noise withdrawal."

Enjoying his mood, Viva laughed. "Is that a bad thing?"

"Don't know... I've never experienced it before, but I don't think I want to take any chances."

Rook lifted a finger as if to excuse an interruption. Viva watched him take the mobile from his back jeans pocket.

"So are you hinting that we need to make some noise?" she asked once he was done reading the screen.

"I think it can be arranged." He pushed off the doorway and left the parlor.

Curiosity at its height, Viva followed and drew to a tentative stop when she found him relaxed against the wall beside the front door.

"Rook—"

"I think our noise is here." He hiked a thumb toward the door.

Steps still uncertain, Viva moved to the door, opened it a crack and stepped out to the wide entryway.

At first, she saw nothing to indicate the noise Rook had promised. Then, rising snow in the distance brought a suspicious flash to her face. Three SUVs approached.

"What'd you do?" she breathed.

"Not a thing." Rook came out to watch the SUVs roll foward. "I'm totally innocent. Ask the cops if you don't believe me."

Viva laughed when she looked to the stopped SUVs and saw the cop in question step out the back of one.

Laughter then mingled with happy tears as Viva raced from the chalet's entrance to throw herself against her sister in a stifling hug.

Chapter 13

The promised noise had been delivered on once the guests exchanged the plush warmth of the SUVs that had transported them from the airport for the plush warmth of the chalet set amid a landscape of wintry white.

On hand were Tigo and Sophia, along with Linus as well as Elias Joss and his love match, Clarissa David. Rounding out the guest list was Sophia's longtime friend and Philadelphia's DA, Paula Starker.

Viva hadn't realized how starved she was for a bit of noise until she was in the middle of hearty conversation and laughter.

"I can promise you that he had no idea." Sophia confirmed Rook's plea of innocence. "We've been planning this for weeks. Everyone's had their schedules cleared—even Paula. Rook didn't know a thing until we called before leaving for the airport."

Viva squeezed a pillow to her chest and beamed at her sister from the bed. The chalet's six bedrooms were all claimed. Rook had taken the guys out to walk the property before dinner, leaving the girls to get settled in.

"Was it our conversation?" Viva asked.

"Mmm…that's what made us up our plans." Sophia hung up the last sweater from her garment bag and then rested against the entryway of the walk-in closet she would share with her fiancé. "I didn't like the way you sounded, *but…*" Slyness crept into her gray eyes. "Was it my imagination or did you and Rook look like you'd worked things out on that end?"

"For the most part." Viva tried, failed to keep the light bright in her gaze. "Like everything else between us, it's all extraordinarily complicated."

"Care to share any details?" Sophia moved toward the bed.

Viva obliged, taking advantage of the chance to vent to her sister face-to-face. "You can save yourself the trouble of telling me that you see Rook's point," she said upon completing her explanation.

"You know, I really do get it. Your loyalty to Murray. He was there for you at a time when the rest of us couldn't be."

"Is there any more news about him?"

"Not a peep." Sophia unwound a gray cashmere scarf from her neck and let it pool on the edge of the bed once she'd taken a seat on the corner. "Guess he was serious when he told you he was putting things to bed—including himself."

"Is your case still strong without him?" Viva sat

up, folded her legs beneath her while keeping possession of the pillow.

"Having him, having him *talking*, may've given us access to who's at the head of this thing. Your identification of the Greenways strengthens the connection between Murray and my colleagues currently cooling their heels in a cell." Sophia gave an exaggerated shrug while rubbing her hands one inside the other.

"We've managed to pull a few dirty cops off the streets, but the real endgamers…chances are they'll be in the wind if we can't turn Murray. Gotta catch him first, though."

"I'm sorry, Soap."

"Don't be." Sophia gave a contented grin and reached over to squeeze Viva's ankle. "We got a lot of good work done. I only hate it's put you and Rook back in a bad spot."

"A bad spot…" Viva spoke the phrase in a whimsical manner. "That's a spot we're both familiar with."

"I'd hoped the time away would give you a chance…a real one."

"I think it has."

"But Murray's still between you?"

Viva relaxed back onto the bed, her whimsical smile merging with something more stoic. "You know what, Sophia? I've got a feeling he always will be."

"I'd never even think about the office if it meant leaving this place."

Rook raised a long, sleek brow toward Elias and then traded looks with Linus and Santigo. Coming from the workaholic construction entrepreneur, the statement was very much out of character.

"Tell me when your true self decides to make an appearance," Rook urged Eli.

There was a round of laughter then. The guys had returned from their trek about the snowy grounds, but opted for a bit of conversation. The fire pit built into the back deck served as the perfect location.

"Rook, my friend, this is Eli Joss *after* a dose of Clarissa David."

Grinning, Rook settled back on the thick cushions of the wood-framed deck chair he'd selected. "So, what's up, E? Is love to blame?"

"Not a bit." Eli gave a defiant shake of his head, then caving, shrugged. "Maybe...*partly* to blame."

"So how are things goin' here?" Linus asked Rook once waves of the serious had seeped in amid the rousing laughter that had followed Eli's admission. "I thought Viva would be looking more pissed off about being babysat."

One corner of Rook's mouth lifted in a rueful smile. "We've had some breakthroughs...and some setbacks. I told her I knew about Vossler."

There was no need for further details on that score. The guys knew of their friend's struggles following Viva's departure.

"Even after I told her about that, I still think she refuses to see Murray for what he is."

"Sophia says no one's heard a thing from him," Tigo offered.

"Maybe just as well." Rook leaned forward to rest his elbows on his knees and warm his hands near the fire. "But as long as that joker's in the wind..."

"You really think he'd kill her to shut her up?" Eli asked, disbelief in his every word.

Rook let his sigh serve as his initial response. "The angry ex-boyfriend says yes." He participated when his friends laughed.

"And what does the security expert who Italy's willing to shell out a small fortune to think?" Linus asked.

"That guy..." Rook rubbed a warmed hand across his jaw. "That guy thinks she's still in trouble too."

"But not from Murray?" Tigo asked as though he'd already mapped his friend's thoughts.

Again, Rook shook his head. "No, not from Murray, but possibly from people who want to shut him up tight as they do everyone he knows."

Dinner was a hilarious and lively event. Rook had passed off his chef's cap to Sophia and Paula who whipped up a veritable feast. Conversation ran high with compliments and a fair amount of amused surprise over the culinary talents of the DA and chief of Ds. Afterward, it was a game of pool for the guys, while the girls made their way to the cozy parlor for drinks and more talking.

"Linus?" Viva called as she saw the man about to take the corridor to the billiards room. She moved close to squeeze one of his hands into both of hers. "I just wanted to thank you for coming."

"Are you kidding?" Linus's dark eyes sparkled with playful devilment and accentuated his features. "There was nothing Eli could've said, done or *threatened* to do that would've kept me away!" He laughed along with the women and then tugged the fitted sleeve of Clarissa's casual navy jumper. "Tell Eli I said that and I'll deny every word."

Clarissa pressed a hand over her heart. "He won't hear it from me." She laughed out the promise.

"I especially wanted to thank you for everything you did for Rook...before." Viva's eyes were soft, her gaze appreciative.

Linus nodded slowly while a shadow ghosted across his dark face. His gaze moved to Paula then and the woman's intake of breath was overheard by everyone nearby. Apparently, satisfied by the reaction he got, Linus looked to Viva again.

"I know what it's like to let rage take you somewhere you never meant to go. I wasn't about to let my boy experience that if I could help it." He squeezed Viva's elbow, shifted a last quick look to Paula and then continued on his path down the hall.

The satisfying meal had not only filled their stomachs, it had spurred on the need for sleep of the deepest variety.

Viva was true to her duties as hostess once everyone had turned in for the night. She made sure everything was in its place downstairs before she headed up. The parlor was her last stop. She tossed a few pillows back to their places on the love seats and was turning for the door when she saw the shadow filling the entryway.

"It's me." Rook heard her muffled curse of surprise. "Didn't mean to scare you."

"I forgot how quiet you can be." Viva coughed to relieve her voice of its quivering.

"Habit of the job," he said.

Viva could only nod as she was unable to form words with her heart lodged as it was against her larynx. In the dark, she could see Rook move steadily closer. He took her hand, squeezing it when but an inch separated them.

"I'm sorry about what happened, after your call about the movie," he was saying. "You've got a right to your opinion of Murray."

"So do you." Her heart stuttered when she felt him squeeze her hand again.

"Think we could leave this discussion alone?"

The request opened a floodgate of relief. "I'd like that," she said.

"On your way to bed?" Rook asked once silence carried between them for scarcely a second.

Viva took the olive branch to shift the conversation. "Yes, I'm beat," she sighed.

"Where're you sleeping?"

"Wherever you are." The response rushed out before she could stop it.

Rook felt the grin spread across his face when her muffled curse followed the unintended reply. "That's too bad." Playful regret hugged his words.

Again, Viva cursed herself for speaking her mind. In no mood for further humiliation, she tugged her hand free of his and moved to inch by him.

"That's too bad," he repeated, curbing the rest of his statement until he saw her steps slow and halt. "Because I'm not really sleepy right now."

Viva turned then, tilting her head and trying to gauge his expression in the dark. "I, um… I'd hate to leave you up by yourself."

"I'd hate it if you did that too."

"Guess we should go on up?" Slowly, she shaved off the distance she had put between them.

"No need to go up."

Viva's heart was then swan-diving to her stomach when she felt herself being hoisted up. The night was especially black. Even with the open floor plan and tall windows filling the space, the area remained in shadow that evening. Something about that played at the edges of her arousal. The feeling wasn't unnerving. It was electric.

The simple lounge dress she'd worn that evening was soon pooled around her feet in waves of violet cotton. Rook's every move was as enticing as it was unexpected. No chair or sofa in the parlor could comfortably accommodate his height, so he took them to the floor.

Her heart was promising to beat out of her chest as anticipation had its way with her. It was a dual assault, what with Rook plying every inch of skin he uncovered with lazy, openmouthed kisses. Just when she thought she'd predicted the path of his moves, he'd switch gears on her.

The rug offered more than enough cushion for her back and was a soothing pallet for her bare skin once he'd stripped her of every stitch. The lazy kisses resumed their travels, adoring the firm, plump breasts he cupped while his nose skimmed the satiny tops and sides.

Viva sucked in a breath when his tongue encircled a nipple that he drew into a hard suckle. The move sent her hips bucking against the pressure of a ruthless need. Her hands moved up to his and she whimpered over the heat blooming where his thumb teased the nipple he'd yet to take into his mouth.

Her whimpers gained volume when he moved on,

his sculpted mouth brushing her rib cage. He made a brief, but memorable stop to tongue her belly button and Viva couldn't smother the tiny cry that escaped into the air. Her breath hitched when his big hands slipped under her thighs and up to cradle her bottom in his palms.

Aching, Viva offered herself before she even felt him claim her, which he did with a plundering, exploring kiss that pulled a sound that was half cry, half moan from her throat. Tremors and goose bumps riddled her body in unison. His breath was lilting across her skin when he shushed her resulting outbursts. It was useless on Rook's part, especially when he began to feast on the heart of her.

Being quiet was out of the question. Viva tried, but it was pointless to try when his tongue was capable of such incredible things. Her next uninhibited cry had Rook blindly searching for one of the throw pillows she'd moved during her earlier tidy-up session in the room.

He grabbed the small accent pillow and used it to drop a few playful slaps to the side of Viva's head. Laughter mixed with her pleasure-induced sobs then. Still, she complied with his request and turned her approving cries into the pillow instead of letting them fill the guest-packed house.

Rook's feasting showed no signs of curbing. He was truly hungry for her and knew the insatiable craving wouldn't be soothed until he'd claimed her with a more potent part of his anatomy.

Viva could hear the faint crinkle of packaging and, still breathless from his handling, moved the pillow aside. She inched up on her elbows to see that he held a condom, one of several that had fallen from the jeans he'd doffed, while she was still writhing with the memory of his enthusiastic kiss. She pushed up until she was sitting and reached out to offer her assistance with their protection.

The sweetness in the gesture was more than Rook could stand. With lust and love taking over, he took possession of Viva's hips and all but yanked her to straddle his lap. He kissed her with a hunger that had her gasping when he finally let her gulp in air.

He took her in one swift stroke, bringing her down over the wide length of his erection. Viva had the foresight to know her cries would wake the house. She'd already turned her face into his neck, using the area to absorb the volume of the screams that flooded forth when he filled her.

They were entwined with each other, curled in a lover's embrace that sent low moans and hushed cries into the darkened room. Time lost all relevance as the giving and receiving of pleasure took precedence.

"I really think we should go on up now," Viva was saying later as she and Rook lay in a tangle of limbs and clothes. She joined in when he began to laugh.

"It'd be pretty inhospitable for our guests to find us sprawled out naked in the parlor," she managed to say once she'd recovered from the bout of amusement.

There was more laughter in the dark and then Rook was rolling over. Viva couldn't see him very well, but she felt his touch strongly enough. His fingertips glided across her brow and seemed more perfectly amplified in light of the fact.

"Our guests." His mouth followed the trail of his fingers across her skin. "I like the sound of that."

"You do?" Viva could barely form the words as elation squeezed her heart.

"Very much." He rested his forehead to hers, sighed. "V, about Murray—"

"Wait." She caught his hand and brought his fingers to her mouth. "Didn't we say we'd forget that and just accept each other's opinion?"

"What if I told you I thought your opinion was more right than I let on?"

"You—you do?" She cleared her throat at the repeat of her earlier words.

Rook felt the grin spread over his face. "I think maybe you had the chance to know Murray better than I ever did. I've been in this business of mine long enough to know there's always another side to the situation. Not to say the other side is right—only that it bears looking into."

"That sounds pretty mature... Do you think we're finally growing up?"

Her question sounded small in the dark. Rook's smile renewed and he leaned down to brush his mouth to her temple.

"Feels like it," he told her, his mouth then gliding down to travel over her small uptilted nose and over her cheekbones to the curve of her jaw.

Then his lips were melding with hers and they were engaged in a delicate, seeking kiss that harbored a sweltering undercurrent of desire. Tangled limbs moved into new positions as the kiss intensified. The lovers were unconscious of the articles of clothing that became more entwined between their bodies.

During the kiss, Rook chuckled softly. "Your panties are around my ankle."

"Of course they are," she purred. "I have to find *some* way to bind you to me."

He nuzzled her neck. "You don't need them. You've always had my heart and always will."

Their kiss resumed, delicacy and desire humming more urgently then.

"Rook?"

"Mmm…" His tongue tangled lazily with hers and then took full possession of her mouth once again.

Groaning, Viva gave in to more kissing. "Rook…" she managed after more deliciously languid seconds had passed. "You're vibrating."

"Damn right I am." He mouthed another curse though when he felt the vibrations and realized it was his phone.

"Should you get it?"

Rook was more interested in exploring the valley between her breasts. "Somebody just hasn't gotten used to the time change yet. Now stop talking…"

Kissing resumed, along with the vibrations moments later. Giggles overwhelmed Viva, happiness and passion for the man she loved mounting inside her. She kissed his cheek and then spoke against it. "Maybe you should answer and tell whoever it is that people here are trying to sleep…and do other things." She bit down softly on his earlobe.

"I'd like to be doing other things besides answering the phone," Rook grumbled, but took the call when the vibrations set in once again.

Viva stretched, smiled in the dark while waiting for Rook to handle the call. When a lengthy quiet followed his initial clipped greeting to the caller, the tone in his next response piqued Viva's curiosity. She was sitting up by the time his voice crept into a more lethal octave.

"What is it?" She'd watched him in the weak moonlight and could tell when he'd pulled the phone from his ear. "Rook?"

"That was the gate."

"What's wrong?" She heard the rustle of fabric and knew he was getting into his jeans. His words had sent a dull shiver racing up her spine.

Soon, golden light pooled the room from a lamp that Rook had turned on. He continued to dress while Viva squinted to adjust to the unexpected illumination.

"Looks like we gave your friend the benefit of the doubt too soon. They've got Murray outside."

Stunned, Viva could only sit unmoving on the rug as she tried to make sense of the dizzying turn of events. When she finally snapped to, she realized Rook was gone.

Chapter 14

"Sophia...authority agrees with you." Murray Dean's attractive features were relaxed, whether from relief that he wasn't dead of frostbite or by Rook's hand, it wasn't certain.

"You may not feel so cordial later." Sophia's expression was as bland as everyone else who joined them in the room.

Rook had instructed his staff to transport Murray to the house where he'd been heading before he was spotted.

"What the hell are you doing here, Murray?"

Waves of tension surged at Viva's question. The house had awakened shortly after Rook left to meet the crew en route with Murray.

Sophia sent a nod in her sister's direction. Anything Murray said needed to be shared during an official police interview. Viva knew the nod meant that her sister was willing to forgo procedure just then.

"Did you come here to kill me, Mur?" Viva asked when there was no response to her prior question.

The query sparked a flash in Murray's observant walnut-brown eyes. "Hell no, Viva! No, never. I—"

"Never? And what about what happened to Reynolds and Bevy? And these supposed burglars that Fee Fee Spikes walked in on? All a coincidence?"

"Fee...? Reynolds and Bev? Jesus, V, how could you think I—"

"Answer her, Murray." Rook's order earned him a glare from his trespasser.

"You'd like that, wouldn't you?" Murray's sneer accompanied the accusation in his glare. "You'd love to make her second-guess me, wouldn't you?"

"It's not him who's making me do that, Murray."

Viva's admission had Murray slumping in the chair Rook had shoved him into when the guards brought him in.

"I didn't do this, V." His voice was weary.

"But you know who did," Rook countered.

Again, Murray glared at him accusingly but the look didn't hold. Instead, he nodded.

"What's going on with you, Murray?" Arms folded over the powder-blue PJ top she'd changed into, Viva moved closer to her agent. "What are you doing *here*? You had to know Rook would have mad security. You had to know you were walking into certain capture."

"I owed you an explanation." Murray's eyes were soft upon Viva, and then sobered with caution when he glanced toward the others in the room. "I had to try. Chances are I wouldn't get the opportunity...later.

I wasn't trying to kill you, Veev. I'd never do a thing like that no matter what type of screwy crap you've been told I'm into."

"Are you here to tell us you're innocent?" Cold laughter caged Rook's words.

"Far from it." Murray snorted and rubbed both hands across his shaved head. "I knew what I was doing."

"Why, Murray?"

Murray at first shrugged at Viva's quiet, confused question. "I wanted the gloss," he said at last. Simply. "I wanted it fast. Who could blame me?" he asked then to no one in particular. "Who could deny the attraction to it?" He studied his fingers resting idly along the edge of the table. "The life, the lifestyle…" He observed the table as though it showed the lifestyle he then imagined.

"The way those people live is insane—cars, boats, houses. And they have them just—just because… So much money…" He brought both hands to his temples and seemed to go ashen beneath his light honey complexion.

"They've got so much money and no clue what to do with it. I only wanted a piece—only a piece of that life. The great car, the eye-popping house…that would've been enough. I swore to myself that'd be enough, that I'd never be like the others, never take it all for granted.

"They did, you know?" Murray looked up to Viva then, punctuating the query with a knowing smile. "The cars and all that did nothing for them after a while. It lost its mystery, didn't grab them at all after a while." A sadness eased in alongside the acknowledgement.

"Because of that," he sighed, "they were looking for a new fix. For most of them, it wasn't even about making more money and that's when I knew the attraction wasn't in the things themselves, but in the ownership—the sheer will to acquire, the control, the power of it all.

"I'd made ins with folks on the force when I first came out to LA. My business was security and all, so our paths crossed from time to time." He looked to Sophia. "Unfortunately, my path crossed with some of your colleagues who weren't so loyal to what the badge stood for. Some actually sought me out when they heard I was from Philly. Wasn't long after that I was tied into a more direct pipeline and dealing with folks you probably shook hands with every day, Sophia."

Murray sighed, stretched his long legs beneath the table. "Mix in my studio contacts looking to dabble into more than property and vehicle acquisitions…and it was the start of a beautiful friendship."

"So they were laundering the money through the studios?" Sophia sounded incredulous.

"*Some* but those execs had their hands in lots of pies. There were tons of opportunities and tons of places to wash cash."

"And did that get you any closer to what you wanted?" Viva asked.

Murray seemed to be contemplating his answer. "For a while…yes, it did."

"And then?"

Murray looked to Clarissa seated next to Elias at the opposite end of the long table where everyone had gathered. "The tiniest ripple had a chain reaction no one could've guessed," he said. "Your aunt was as smart as she was lovely, Ms. David."

"She was." Clarissa confirmed the words, her smile fueled by the memory of Jazmina Beaumont.

"People with money like your aunt's usually leave their financial concerns to others. She and Mr. Cole were very tight." Murray crossed middle finger over index to insinuate Jazmina's close relationship to her then business manager Waymon Cole.

"He never caught a whiff that she was looking over his shoulder," Clarissa said. "My aunt's been on her own since she was fourteen, Murray. No one watched her back better than she did."

Murray gave a reverent nod. "Whatever bread crumbs she left for you to follow upset the status quo for damn sure."

"Upset, but didn't topple," Sophia noted. "There're still a few of your partners who we'd like to upset to the tune of a jail cell."

"I'd like to see that too, Chief." Murray smirked, having noticed the looks of subtle surprise that appeared on the faces of his audience. "My...*partners* are making it personal by attacking my clients."

"Threatening to kill us if we talk about anything we may have seen?" Viva asked.

"No, sweetness." Murray's smile was apologetic. "Threatening to take out all of my clients if *I* don't talk. If I don't talk and spin the story they deem acceptable, they'll keep going after my clients."

Viva blinked, her back stiffening. "They want you to confess to it all."

Murray chuckled. "As if anyone would believe the

buck stopped with me on a take that substantial. Hell, if that was the case, I'd have a whole fleet of associates handling you guys while I chill on a beach." He shook his head, winced. "Anyway, that's how they wanted it. I've been ducking and dodging, trying to stay under the radar until I could find a time and place to get Sophia's ear." He looked at the chief of detectives then. "I knew I couldn't just talk to you in Philly, so I kept an eye on your movements hoping for a chance."

"You've been following her." It wasn't a question. Tigo's voice, as dark as his expression, left no doubt as to the murderous trail of his thoughts.

"Old habits, man." Murray raised his hands defensively. "Security was once my job and surveillance was a huge part of it. She was never in any danger from me, Santigo. I only wanted a chance to tell her what I was dealing with and see if she could help me."

"Help you get out of it?" Eli asked, his voice and expression as dark and menacing as Tigo's.

Murray was already shaking his head. "Help me, by accepting the story I'll give you. The one that lays all this at my feet."

"You'd do that?" Rook's expression was more curious, not quite as dark as the ones worn by his friends.

Again, Murray was responding before the query was complete. He nodded. "My clients are my dearest friends—my only friends. Some are like family." He looked to Viva. "They are family."

Viva didn't dare blink, knowing the movement would send the water pooling in her eyes streaming down to wet her face.

"You know I can't do that, Murray," Sophia said. "These people are serious. They laced Reynolds's drug stash to make it look like he OD'd." Murray shifted pleading eyes to Viva. "Bevy isn't supposed to be in the hospital. She's supposed to be dead." He managed a grim smile. "Guess those defensive driving classes she had to take to prep for her role on the show paid off. But she should be dead, Viva." He returned his gaze to Sophia.

"These people are serious," he insisted.

"So am I." Sophia's eyes glinted fiercely. "I want the truth, Murray."

"Dammit, aren't you listening to me?" Murray brought his fists down on the table. "Do you think they'll let Bev live once she's out of the hospital?"

Sophia wouldn't relent. "You telling me the truth is the only way we'll get these snakes off the street. You say you care about your clients. Do you care enough to give me the truth?"

Murray regarded his hands for a long time and then he was looking back to Viva. "I never meant for this to happen."

"Oh, Murray." Going to him, Viva gathered the man's trembling hands and squeezed. She smiled when he squeezed in return, bowed his head and kissed the backs of her hands. "Do you remember the time you came to drag me out of that party Reynolds threw?"

In spite of his distress, Murray gave in to a brief laugh. "Yeah, he promoted the hell out of that party. 'Wear your white to drink the white.' Rumor was he'd gotten the liquor flown in special from his cousins in West Virginia."

Viva laughed then too. "Well, it sure tasted like the real deal." She sobered some, but a soft smile remained. "Do you remember what you told me that day?"

Murray's lips thinned and he nodded. "I told you you were better than this. Rumor also had it that Reynolds's career was circling the drain. I thought I could prevent that when he came to me looking for representation. Reynolds and most of the folks he associated with were talented as hell, but they couldn't get or keep jobs because they were too busy sleeping off highs and hangovers for most of the day.

"You'd already made a lot of mistakes in a short span of time," Murray recalled. "Out of my own selfishness, I let you because I hoped it meant you were buying into your life out there." He flicked a glance toward Rook.

"Then I realized you weren't buying in. You were trying to be something—some*one*—new. I told you that who you are got you everything you'd become and that you didn't owe anyone else for that, but you. I still believe that."

Viva nodded, recalling the old lecture that had somehow penetrated the edges of her moonshine-soaked brain. "Do you remember what else you said?"

"I said this was the coward's way out."

Viva gave his hands another tight squeeze. "You do realize these bastards are playing on your fear, don't you?"

"They're powerful people, sweetness. Your career—"

"Is one *I've* made. I don't owe anyone else for that but *me*. Knowing that, I can be brave enough to handle whatever this dishes out. Can you? Can you be brave enough to live by your own words, Mur?"

His weary expression made a slow transformation into one that showed fleeting glimpses of amusement and resolve. "I didn't realize you'd paid so much attention to what I'd said that day."

"People tend to pay attention to the truth." She gave his hands another squeeze. "They'll pay attention, Murray." She looked to Sophia, standing next to Paula, and nodded before turning back to Murray. "Give them that."

A nod gradually took hold of Murray and then he inhaled hugely as if the gesture had added fortification to his resolve. Viva cupped his cheek and he moved to cover her hand with his.

"Do you forgive me, Veev?"

"There's nothing to forgive." She squeezed her eyes against stinging tears when he drew her in for a fierce hug.

Viva warmed her hands about the porcelain mug and delighted in the tea's soothing aroma while she studied the scene beyond the windows.

Eager to get a head start on his day, Murray had insisted on going on record then and there. Sophia didn't want any more liberties taken with the man's rights than there had already been. Yet Murray insisted on at least giving the chief of detectives the names that would prove vital to her case.

The reason for Murray's insistence was no mystery. He wanted the names on record in the event that he didn't make it back to Philadelphia alive. As the man had yet to lawyer up, Sophia decided to accept the information being offered and use her mobile to record the statement.

Bundled in hats and jackets, they walked the snowy acreage behind the chalet. The mountains loomed in quiet majesty. Keeping an appropriate distance were Tigo, Linus and Eli. To maintain an additional air of propriety, DA Paula Starker remained absent from the informal proceedings. She and Clarissa met in the den to program films for an afternoon of movie watching that would begin following Sophia's chat with Murray.

Viva sipped more of the calm-inducing tea and smiled when Rook walked into the kitchen. He retrieved a liter bottle of juice from the fridge and indulged in a generous gulp once he was standing next to Viva at the sink.

"Don't worry, I'm sure Murray's safe," he said as he observed the meeting from the window. "He's got three bodyguards to make sure Sophia doesn't try anything."

Viva sipped her tea, smiled. "Tell them I appreciate it. My little sister can be lethal. I've had enough fights with her to know."

Once the soft laughter had settled, Rook rested a hip along the counter and faced Viva. "I'm sorry about giving you such a hard time about this, V. About Murray."

"Rook, we've been through this." Viva set her mug on the counter. "No more apologies, remember?"

"Can I at least tell you why I gave you such a hard time about it?"

"Haven't you done that already?" She faced him fully, mimicking his leaning stance against the counter.

"Not all of it."

"What's...all of it?"

"I was afraid you wouldn't be right and I wanted you to be right." He focused on the juice bottle and launched a slow pace of the kitchen.

"I've been in love with security in one way or another for as long as I can remember. Think it was since my mom first took me to the bank and I met a real live security guard up close." He smiled on the memory. "Back then, my folks thought I was so infatuated because those guys got to carry guns, but that wasn't even close to being it. Their job was to observe, to figure who needed to be watched and who was okay.

"I was fascinated by that and I tried to get as good at figuring that out as I could." His steps around the kitchen slowed. "I did get good at it. I got damn good at it. I got so good scoping things far off, it got hard to see what was right under my nose." He sighed, buried his face in his hands and then folded his arms across the burgundy shirt he wore.

"I never saw Murray coming. When he left the company and took you with him—" he raked Viva's face and body several times beneath his bright eyes "—it felt like a rock through my stomach and then the rage came and that…that was worse because it just sat there festering like some oozing sore. Hearing about you and Vossler was the lance that sent it all spewing.

"To know I was *that* wrong about someone *that* close to me…it was a devastation that had me second-guessing everything. My career was all I had. It was the only thing that made me keep getting up once you were gone. It was a half existence most of the time with the possibility of poor judgment always hanging over my head."

He turned to take another look out the window, his

expression unreadable. "This morning I discovered I hadn't misjudged him. Yes, he let himself be blinded and swayed by dazzle, but he stuck when it counted. He recognized you were in line to destroy yourself and he helped to prevent it. If I'd been wrong about him and who he was at the core, he wouldn't have told you what he did at that party. He wouldn't have given a damn about you. It's why I gave you hell every time you defended him." He smiled her way then. "I didn't want to let myself...I don't know...hope?"

Rook studied the juice bottle as if it were helping him to test the validity of the word and then he nodded. "Yeah, I—I didn't want to let myself hope and be wrong, knowing this time a misjudgment like that could've meant your life."

Viva came up behind him, smoothed her hands between his shoulder blades. "Murray betrayed you in business *and* friendship. It's not something you're expected to get past overnight, no matter how many names he gives Soap for that recording she's making out there."

Rook turned then, gathering Viva tightly against him. "What was it you said about us growing up? Maybe you had something there."

"Told you," Viva said, going to her toes to brush a kiss to his jaw until he lifted her higher for something more substantial.

Chapter 15

The day ended quietly enough. There was talk about putting Murray in the guest cottage half a mile away from the chalet, but Sophia opted for another plan. At Rook's suggestion, she decided the loft bedroom would be a better fit. Rook had been playing with the idea of turning the area into an office. It would be better suited to Murray Dean for the remainder of his stay, which was slated to be no more than another forty-eight hours at best. Time enough for Murray's official travel companions to arrive from the States to assist in his return.

The tensions of the day had leveled out as feelings of closure started to edge in. By late afternoon into early evening, the nice vibes that had permeated everyone at the onset of their visit were back on track. That had a great deal to do with the host and hostess.

There was no denying that love was vibrating powerfully between Rook and Viva.

The two had bowed out of the movie night, and early morning found them engaged in a sensual scene on the enclosed, heated veranda outside Rook's room. Snow pelted the tinted glass. The quiet tapping created a hypnotic melody that mingled nicely with the uninhibited sounds of passion filling the space. The erotic session, playing out on an oversize armchair beneath a blanket of white fleece, showed no sighs of an immediate cooldown.

When release crested in unison, Viva all but collapsed onto Rook's stunning chest. Laughter mounted in a wave of emotion consisting of satisfaction, happiness and hope.

"I wish we could stay here forever." She sighed, feeling no unease about making the admission. The words were true ones.

"Guess we'll all be following Murray's lead after the wedding." Rook placed a kiss on the top of her head.

During the previous night's dinner, Tigo and Sophia clued everyone in to what was in store for the second leg of their trip. The couple had decided to return to the States as newlyweds. Once the bride's official business was finished, the party would hit the road once again. The destination—Mexico. A private strip of beach would be the setting for the nuptials and home to the wedding party for at least a week.

"Think Sophia will kill me if I miss the wedding?" Viva curved her body tighter into Rook's chest.

"I believe your sister would take great pleasure in the chance to kick your ass for a thing like that."

Viva sighed. "Everything's such a mess, Rook."

"Not as much of a mess as it's been."

"You're in Philadelphia and I'm still in LA. Correction—I'm still in LA and you're a new home owner in Italy. And now there's filming for the show and with all the other projects I've got going…" A haunted look cooled her warm gaze. "We were busted up by our careers before and *that* was before we even got our careers started."

"Hey?" He cupped a hand to her cheek, waited for her to look at him. "Put the blame where it belongs, okay? Not on our careers, but on us." Resting back, he tugged her closer. "Truth is, we didn't bother to work hard enough to keep it together. We could've been fry cooks and not had a better outcome."

Viva laughed, kissed the pec that bulged nearest her lips. "There's a lot to be said for the simpler ways of making a living. Do you think we can handle the distance?"

"Don't know. I know I'm ready to stop guessing and wondering it all into a watery grave." Rook tipped her chin. "You know where I am when you decide to stop doing the same."

Before she could speak, he silenced her with a kiss that sweetly wiped everything from her mind.

Rook left Viva sleeping, pleased to see her catching up on her rest. He knew the last several hours had been a brutal ordeal but one he hoped might be the beginning of a path rebuilding between them.

He'd meant what he had told her. He'd be ready when she was ready. Something told him that he might not have long to wait.

It seemed his guests had similar plans to sleep in that morning. Rook decided to head into Belluno and tend to what had gone undone as a result of the previous day's upset. He took the time to stroll the house. He'd had Viva to thank for making it a home. She'd taken a construction of stone, brick and wood, and had given it life, warmth and the potential to be spectacular. She'd done it for him.

The view from the living room stopped him as it always did when the mountains, in all their snowy scope, stunned him with their majesty.

Though he'd claimed little more than a half hour earlier that he was done guessing and wondering, he couldn't resist wondering how long he could go without Viva until need and pure want had him going after her. If it came down to that, he believed he might actually be forced to beg.

The idea had him grinning as he made his way from the living room to the kitchen. There he found Murray Dean.

Murray choked on the coffee he'd just sipped when he saw Rook in the curved brick entryway of the kitchen. The deep flush beneath his fair complexion betrayed the effects of the steaming coffee.

"Rook—" His voice sounded gravel laden, possibly from the hurried swallow of the hot liquid. The effects could've just as easily been a reaction to the unease Rook Lourdess could instill without saying a word.

"Sorry," Murray said, his tone then a humble one as he regarded the larger man.

Rook was waving off the apology. "You're entitled to food and water—or coffee," he said as he gestured toward the mug Murray cradled between his hands.

A small, relieved breath slipped past Murray's nostrils, but he didn't appear completely at ease. "Chief of Ds gave me the go-ahead" he saw fit to share.

Smiling faintly, Rook poured himself a mug of the aromatic blend. "Wonder if the chief had to square it with her big sister first?"

Rook's demeanor must have relaxed Murray for he grinned. "I think that's who told her to tell me it was okay." Murray indulged in a little more laughter, but soon the gesture was waning as concern took hold.

"Do you think she'll forgive me, Rook?"

"I could've sworn I heard her say she did yesterday." Rook toasted with his mug and then took a sip.

"Yeah." Murray merely studied the contents remaining in his mug then. "I, um… I wasn't talking about that exactly. By now, I'm guessing you told her you know about Vossler and that I was the one who told you."

"You're sure of that?" Rook gave off a sense of maddening calm while observing Murray over the rim of his mug.

"She'd planned to tell you." Murray nodded once when he saw surprise register on Rook's face. "It was all she could talk about and that was long before she ever went to see her family back home."

"All she could talk about…" Rook set his mug to the counter.

"What happened with Vossler…" Murray worked the bridge of his nose between his fingers. "That drama took its toll on her. He didn't hurt her." Murray had looked up in time to glimpse the ferocity in Rook's eyes. "It was how she regretted it." He took a slow turn around the kitchen, the ripped cuffs of his jeans dragging on the glossy floor as he moved.

"She regretted doing it, but *why* she did it... I think that's what really—I don't know—what really wounded something inside her. And I—hell." He began to rub his hands over his head. "I felt like scum for ever putting that mess in her head about Vossler being a top guy. All so I could climb the success ladder quicker."

Rook could feel his palm tingling with a need to draw a fist. He smiled when the tingle and the accompanying upset passed. Moving to the sink, he dashed out what remained of his coffee.

"You didn't force her to do it. She knows that, so do you." *Progress.* Rook said the word silently, triumphantly.

"No, I didn't force her, but I sure as hell didn't try to change her mind about the prick either." Murray came over to toss out his coffee, as well.

Rook sent his former colleague a sideways glance. "You know we could stand here all day going back and forth over who's more at fault, right?"

Murray nodded, grinned. "You're right." Through the window above the sink he studied the almost blinding beauty of the sun reflecting against the sea of snow that served as Rook's backyard. "I'd never ask your forgiveness for this mess, Rook, but I am sorry." His tone was cautious, measuring as he spoke. "I'm sorry and that's not me going back and forth over who's more at fault here. That's me owning it."

Murray squeezed his eyes against the brilliant outdoor view as though it had in fact blinded him. He turned, leaning on the counter while massaging his hands over his head as if to clear it.

"Feeding you all that crap," he began, "it was a punk's move. It wasn't even about you. Not—not completely." Murray's shrug betrayed a helplessness.

Rook moved from the sink. He didn't begrudge the tingle he felt in his palm that time and accepted that, for him, certain triggers would never be totally silenced.

"You and Viva...the way you guys live, hell, the way you both grew up..." Murray's eyes gleamed in acknowledgement of something unseen. "Hell, man, I've wanted that kind of life forever and a day."

Rook frowned, the reaction more about confusion than temper. "What kind of life are you talking about?"

"To be rich." Murray's tone was matter-of-fact. "The kind of rich that makes people take notice when they hear your last name. The way they do with your dad and Viva's."

"Murray, it's natural to want that kind of success. *I* want it, but when you sell your soul to get it...that's when you've got trouble, that's when you know you should be backing off."

"Easy for you to say." Murray failed at producing the grin he strived for. "For people who live the life and always have, there's no mystery, no allure—"

"No attraction?" Rook recalled what the man had said the night before.

Murray nodded then in spite of himself. "Would've been great if I'd realized that before I went and made such an ass of myself."

"Sounds like we're all growing up." Rook felt the smile at his mouth when Viva's words came back to him.

"I pray I'll have the chance to find out if that's true." Murray shed the effects of his musings and turned. "I just wanted you to know I regret my part in what happened. The one thing I pray will come out of all this is for you and V to find your way back to each other."

Murray extended a hand and waited on Rook to decide whether he would take it. The decision didn't take long and soon the men were equal participants in an enthusiastic shake.

Costa Alegre, Mexico
One week later

After having endured another week of snowy seclusion, Viva was more than ready for a little sun and fun. The fact that there was a wedding to go along with it all made the journey that much more unforgettable.

The group had taken the first few days to marvel at the turquoise waters of the Bay of Tenacatita. Costa Alegre boasted miles of unpopulated beach, perfect for supreme meditation. The intimate guest list resided in an exclusive resort that Viva's connections had secured for the affair. The last-minute change in plans hadn't been a bother for Viva. As maid of honor, she'd felt it was the least she could do.

As the bride and groom had no interest in waiting to speak the vows they had planned to utter long ago, upping their wedding date had been a joy. None of the guests had had an issue with the change. Cozy three-room cottages dotted the seaside resort and were

well-stocked for the visit. The setting was as quaint
as it was exotic.

Viva toyed with the idea of lingering a few more
days once the wedding was over and the newlyweds
set off on their honeymoon.

"Think it's too soon for me to tell my clients I need
a vacation?"

Rook's question prompted laughter that Viva
couldn't resist giving in to. "I see our thoughts are on
the same track."

"Really?" He settled down next to where Viva sat
near the fire pit nestled in the midst of low-sitting
beach chairs. The sun was setting and, with the chilly
breeze blowing in off the water, the fire was a welcome treat.

"I've been trying to talk myself out of it."

Viva gave a curious frown. "Out of taking time
off? Why?"

"Wouldn't be any fun without you around."

"Aw..." She took his admission for a tease. "Well,
I'm sure you wouldn't be alone for long."

Viva's outlook was most likely accurate. The resort hostess and the rest of her female staff had given
Rook, Eli, Tigo and Linus an appraising once-over
upon their arrival.

"It wouldn't be the same," he was saying, stretching
out his long legs and moving his sandaled feet closer
to the fire. "Damn sure wouldn't be the way I'd want
it. I love you too damn much, V."

"I love you." She reciprocated the proclamation on a
gasp, emotion swelling when he slipped an arm about
her waist and scooped her from the low chair.

Once Viva was straddling his lap, Rook simply

waited until her eyes were locked with his. "I love you too." Conviction hugged the words. "I never stopped. I never want to lose you again. I never intend to."

A sob spilled out along with Viva's watery laugh. Then she was cupping Rook's face and kissing him with everything she had.

"Now that we've traveled halfway around the world and back again, I'd say we've paid our dues." For a moment, Rook let his gaze linger on the remarkable sky of iridescent colors.

Turning in his loose embrace, Viva rested back against the man she loved and drank in the view, as well. "I'd have to agree. Do you think we could skip all the other boring stuff we're supposed to do while we work it all out and just get right to the all-is-well stage?"

"Mmm..." Rook faked a wince. "That might be tough for me. I was kinda looking forward to all the make-up sex we're supposed to have."

Viva laughed, fearing she would be unable to quell the desire to do so, she was so extraordinarily happy. "I was definitely *not* talking about the make-up sex. Do you think we could get right to *that* and skip all those long boring talks we're probably supposed to have?"

"Hmm..." Again, Rook winced. "There was actually one conversation I was looking forward to."

Confused then, Viva waited.

"Actually, it was more of a sentence."

Carefully, she turned in his lap, abandoning the sky view to study his amazing eyes. "I guess I could handle a sentence. That's not so—"

"Marry me."

Her eyes widened in tandem with her gasp. "You, uh, you know that's actually a phrase? A, um, a question phrase…"

"So it is." He bundled her closer, his expression all serious. "Do you have an answer for me?"

"Will a 'yes' do?" Her response was immediate and she adored the way it caused him to blink in surprise and then glee.

Rook nodded slowly, smiled softly. "Yeah, um…" He cleared his throat in hopes of moving the emotional lump lodged there. "'Yes' will do just fine."

He crushed her mouth with his in a kiss that had Viva humming all the way to her toes.

"So can we get to the make-up sex now?" she asked, once he'd let her up for air.

"We can get to the make-up sex now." Rook was already moving to stand with Viva in his arms where cords of muscle flexed in caramel brilliance against the late sun.

Laughter flowed as the lovers disappeared into their tiny reserved cottage. There, love was made and, at long last, a future was planned. A future together.

* * * * *

TO WEAR HIS RING AGAIN

CHANTELLE SHAW

CHAPTER ONE

'This is the address you asked for. Grosvenor Square W1.'
The taxi driver glanced over his shoulder at his passenger, who was still sitting on the back seat, puzzled that she
hadn't climbed out of the car. 'Is this where you want to
go, love? Or do you want me to take you somewhere else?'

Butterflies danced in Isobel's stomach as she stared out
of the black cab, and for a moment she was tempted to ask
the cabbie to drive on. The Georgian town house looked
exactly the same as she remembered; the four storeys of
mullioned windows gleamed in the spring sunshine, reflecting the trees in the park opposite. She had loved the
house when she had lived there with Constantin, but now
its elegant grandeur seemed to mock her.

She was surprised by how emotional she felt to return,
two years after she had walked out of the front door for
the last time and turned her back on her marriage. Perhaps
she should just sign the divorce petition burning a hole in
her handbag and post it back to Constantin's lawyer. What
was the point in seeing him again after all this time and
dredging up the past?

The truth was that she had never really known her husband. When they had met three years ago, she had been
dazzled by his charm and seduced by his smouldering sexuality. At first, their relationship had been a roller coaster

of sizzling passion, but after their wedding Constantin had changed into a remote stranger. With hindsight, she realised that she had never truly understood the enigmatic Italian who went by the exotic title of Marchese Constantin De Severino.

She visualised the legal document in her handbag with the heading in stark black typeface: *Affidavit in support of divorce—desertion*, and felt a rush of anger at the reason Constantin had given for seeking a divorce. It was true that she had been the one to leave the marriage, and so technically she supposed she *had* deserted him. But he had given her no option but to leave him. He had driven her away with his coldness and his uncompromising attitude towards her career.

She frowned. *Desertion* was such a damning word and, ironically, it contained more emotion than Constantin had ever revealed during the one year of the marriage that they had spent together.

Who was she kidding? When she pictured his hard, sculpted features it was impossible to believe he had a vulnerable side. Constantin did not *do* emotions. It was far more likely that the reason he had given for seeking a divorce had been coldly calculated. But she *would not* take all the blame for the failure of their marriage, Isobel thought fiercely. Constantin needed to realise that she was not a pushover as she had been when he had married her, and he *couldn't* have things all his way. Once, she had been overawed by him. But she was determined to end their marriage as his equal.

'This is fine, thanks,' she told the taxi driver as she stepped onto the pavement and leaned down to the cab window to pay the fare. The breeze lifted her honey-blonde hair from her shoulders.

Recognition dawned on the cabbie's face. 'I know who

you are! You're that singer Izzy Blake from the Stone Ladies. My daughter is a big fan.' He thrust a notepad into Isobel's hand. 'Can I be cheeky and ask for your autograph for my Lily?'

She took the pen he handed her and signed her name. Being recognised by the public was something Isobel doubted she would ever be entirely comfortable with, but she never forgot that the band owed their success to their many thousands of fans worldwide.

'Are you in London to give a concert?' the cabbie asked her.

'No, we finished our European tour in Berlin last week, but I think we're due to play in London in the autumn.' She had given up trying to remember the exact details of the band's hectic schedule. For the past two years, her life had been a blur of airport lounges and hotel lobbies in whichever town, state, continent where the band was performing. She tore a page out of the cabbie's notebook. 'Give me your email address and I'll make sure you're sent a couple of tickets so you can take your daughter to the Stone Ladies' next concert.'

The taxi driver thanked her, and when he drove away Isobel unconsciously clenched her fingers around the strap of her bag as she climbed the front steps of the house and rang the doorbell. Despite her determination to remain cool and calm, she could feel her heart thudding painfully hard beneath her ribs. She was not *nervous* at the prospect of seeing Constantin again, she assured herself. She thought of the divorce petition he had sent her, and the accusatory, condemning word *desertion* had the same effect on her temper as a red rag to a bull.

'Damn you, Constantin,' she muttered beneath her breath, just before the door was opened by a familiar figure.

'Madam,' Constantin's butler greeted her gravely, his

measured tone and imperturbable features revealing no hint of surprise at her sudden reappearance after two years.

'Hello, Whittaker. Is my…husband…at home?' She was annoyed by the huskiness in her voice as she stumbled over the word husband. He wouldn't be for much longer and she would be free to move on with her life.

She had read in a newspaper that Constantin was in London to attend the opening of a new De Severino Eccellenza store—more commonly known by the company's logo DSE—in Oxford Street, and she had planned her visit for Sunday morning because, even though he was a workaholic, it was unlikely that Constantin would have gone to the office on a Sunday.

'The Marquis is downstairs in the gymnasium.' The butler stepped back to allow her to enter the house. 'I will inform him on the internal phone that you are here.'

'No!' Isobel stopped him. She wanted to retain the element of surprise. As Whittaker's brow pleated in a faint frown she added quickly, 'He…he's expecting me.' It was the truth of sorts, she assured herself. No doubt Constantin was waiting for her to meekly sign the divorce petition, but he probably did not expect her to deliver the document in person. She hurried along the hall towards the stairs that led down to the basement.

Constantin had had the gym installed soon after their marriage so that he could work out at home rather than stop off at his private health club after he'd spent all day at the office. Descending the stairs, Isobel could hear a rhythmic pounding noise. The door to the gym was open, and she had a clear view of him slamming his fists into a punchbag. He was totally focused on what he was doing and did not notice her.

Her mouth ran dry as she stood in the corridor and studied him. She had forgotten how *big* he was! He owed his six-feet-plus height to his American mother, who—on one of the rare occasions when he had spoken about his family—Constantin had told Isobel had been a successful model before she had married his father.

She guessed his slashing cheekbones and classically sculpted features were also a result of his mother's genes, but in every other way he was pure Italian male, with exotic olive skin and dark, almost black, glossy hair that grew in luxuriant waves and refused to be completely tamed by the barber's scissors. His shorts and gym vest revealed his powerful thigh and shoulder muscles, and the curling black hairs on his chest were damp with sweat as he powered his fists into the punchbag.

He would need to take a shower after his punishing workout, Isobel mused. An unbidden memory slid into her mind of the early days of their marriage when she had often come down to the gym to watch Constantin work out, and afterwards they had shared a shower. The two years that they had been apart melted away as she remembered running her hands over his naked, muscular thighs and stretching her fingers around his powerful erection while he smoothed a bar of soap over her breasts and continued down her quivering, shivering body until she begged him to end the torment and take her hard and fast, leaning against the wall of the shower cubicle.

Dear heaven! Scalding heat swept through her veins, and she could not repress a choked sound in her throat that immediately alerted Constantin to her presence. His head shot round, and for perhaps thirty seconds Isobel saw a stunned expression on his face before his chiselled features hardened and became unreadable. He pulled off his boxing gloves and strolled towards her.

'Isabella!'

His deep voice was as sensuous as bittersweet chocolate, and his use of the Italian version of her name evoked a flood of molten desire in the pit of Isobel's stomach. How could he have such a devastating effect on her after all this time? Working in the music industry, she was often in the company of good-looking men, but she'd never felt a spark of desire for anyone she'd met. She had put her lack of interest down to the fact that she was still legally married—for although she and Constantin had parted on bad terms she believed in fidelity within marriage. But with a flash of near despair she realised that no other man excited her as her husband did. For the past two years her sexual desires had lain dormant, but one look at Constantin was all it had taken to arouse her body to a fever pitch of lustful longing.

Utterly thrown by her reaction to him, she felt an urge to turn and flee back up the stairs. But it was too late; he halted in front of her, standing unnervingly close so that she inhaled the sensual musk of his maleness.

Beads of sweat glistened on his skin. Isobel found herself wanting to run her fingers through the lock of sable hair that had fallen forwards onto his brow and trace the close-trimmed black stubble that shaded his jaw and upper lip. Every muscle in her body tautened defensively as she fought the effect he had on her. She was unaware that she reminded Constantin of a nervous colt who might bolt at any second.

'Don't hide in the shadows, *cara*,' he drawled. 'I don't know why you're here, but I assume you have a very good reason to let yourself into the house, two years after you ran away.'

His cynical tone hurtled Isobel back in time to the dying days of their marriage when they had been at constant loggerheads.

'I didn't run away,' she snapped.

His heavy black brows rose, but it was his eyes that held her spellbound. The first time Isobel had met him—when she had been a temporary secretary sent by the agency to work for the CEO at the London office of the exclusive jewellery and luxury goods company, De Severino Eccellenza—she had been mesmerised by Constantin's brilliant blue eyes that were such an unexpected contrast to his swarthy, Latin looks.

He shrugged. 'All right, you didn't run. You *sneaked* out while I was on a business trip. I came home to find your note informing me that you had gone on tour with the band and wouldn't be coming back.'

Isobel gritted her teeth. 'You knew I was going to go with the Stone Ladies—we had discussed it. I left because, if I hadn't, we would have destroyed each other. Don't you remember the row we had the morning before you went to France, or the argument we'd had the day before, or the day before that? I couldn't take it any more.' Her voice shook. 'We couldn't even be together in the same room without tension flaring. It was time to end our train wreck of a marriage.'

A throb of pain shot across her brow, causing her to draw a sharp breath and reminding her of the tension headaches she'd suffered during her marriage. She and Constantin were arguing already, mere moments after meeting each other again.

'Besides, I didn't let myself into the house,' she said in a carefully controlled voice. 'I left my door key with my wedding ring on your desk two years ago.' The symbolic gesture of pulling her gold wedding band from her finger had dealt the final devastating blow to her heart, Isobel remembered painfully. 'Whittaker let me in.' She opened her handbag and pulled out the divorce petition. 'I came to return this.'

Constantin flicked his eyes to the document. 'You must be in a desperate hurry to officially end our marriage, if you couldn't wait until tomorrow to put the paperwork in the post.'

Riled by his mocking tone, she opened her mouth to agree that she was impatient to sever the final links between them. She was wearing four-inch heels but Constantin towered over her and she had to tilt her head to meet his cobalt-blue gaze. It was an unwise move, she realised as her eyes dropped to his sensual, full-lipped mouth and her pulse quickened. Her tongue darted out to moisten her suddenly dry lips, and she glimpsed a dangerous glitter in his eyes as he followed the betraying gesture before he roamed his gaze over her in a leisurely inspection that made Isobel's skin tingle.

'You're looking good, *Isabella*,' he drawled.

Her stupid heart performed a somersault, but she managed to respond coolly, 'Thank you.' The old Isobel had struggled to accept compliments graciously, but maturity had given her the self-assurance to be able to look in a mirror and acknowledge that she was attractive.

That did not mean she hadn't spent ages debating what to wear for her meeting with Constantin. Her aim had been to look sophisticated yet give the impression that she hadn't tried too hard and she had eventually settled on dark blue jeans from her favourite designer, teamed with a plain white tee shirt and—for a confidence booster—a pillar-box-red jacket. She had left her long, layered hair loose, and wore minimum make-up—just mascara to emphasise her hazel eyes, and a slick of rose-coloured gloss on her lips.

She saw Constantin glance at her handbag. 'From the new De Severino Eccellenza collection,' he noted. 'Rather ironic, seeing that you always made a fuss when I gave you DSE items while we were together. When you bought your bag I hope you explained that you are my wife, and asked for a discount.'

'Of course I didn't,' Isobel said stiffly. 'I can afford to pay the full price.'

There seemed no point trying to explain that when they had been together she had felt guilty when Constantin had given her DSE jewellery and accessories because everything in the collection was incredibly expensive, and she hadn't wanted to seem like a gold-digger who had married him for his money.

In the last two years her successful singing career had earned her an income that was unbelievable to a girl who had grown up in an ex-colliery village in the north of England, where poverty and deprivation had sucked the life and soul out of the men who had been unemployed since the pit had closed a decade ago. She doubted Constantin would understand how good it made her feel to be able to pay for her own clothes and jewellery after the shame she'd felt as a teenager, knowing that her family relied on handouts from the state.

She glanced at his autocratic features and her heart sank. She had always been conscious of the social divide between them. Constantin was a member of the Italian aristocracy, a man of noble birth and incredible wealth and sophistication, and it was perhaps unsurprising that a miner's daughter had struggled to fit into his exclusive lifestyle. But she was no longer plagued by the insecurities of her youth. Her successful career had given her a sense of self-assurance and pride.

'I don't want to rake up the past,' she told him firmly.

His eyes narrowed appraisingly on her face, and she sensed he was surprised by her new confidence. 'What *do* you want?'

Isobel's intention had been to make it clear that she would not accept responsibility for the collapse of their marriage. But her fiery words were replaced by a different kind of fire in her belly as she watched him pick up a towel and rub it over his arms and shoulders. He pulled off his gym vest and dragged the towel across the whorls of sweat-damp dark hairs that grew thickly on his chest and arrowed down over his flat abdomen.

She jerked her eyes guiltily from where the fuzz of hairs disappeared beneath the waistband of his shorts, and clenched her hand to prevent herself from reaching out and skimming her fingers over his rock-hard abdominal muscles. She had often thought about him in the past two years, but her memory had not done him justice. He was so gorgeous he made her insides melt.

Her skin prickled as every nerve-ending on her body became acutely attuned to Constantin's raw sex appeal. Something primitive and purely instinctive stirred in the pit of her stomach. Her brain sensed that he represented danger, but the alarm bells ringing inside her head were obliterated by the sound of her blood thundering in her ears.

Silence quivered between them like an overstretched elastic band. Constantin frowned when she failed to respond to his question, but he glimpsed the unguarded expression in her eyes and his lips curled into a predatory smile.

'Ah, I think I understand, *cara*. Were you hoping we could get together for old times' sake, before we make our separation legal?'

'Get together?' For a moment Isobel didn't understand. She could not control the heat that surged through her when Constantin's gaze lingered on her breasts, and to her horror she felt her nipples harden and prayed he could not see their jutting points outlined beneath her clingy tee shirt.

'There were no problems with one aspect of our marriage,' he murmured. 'Our sex life was so explosive it was off the Richter scale.'

He was talking about *sex*! Her eyes clashed with his glittering gaze and her fingers itched to wipe the mockery from his face. 'You think I came here to…*proposition* you? In your dreams,' she told him furiously.

Her blood boiled. How dared Constantin suggest that the reason for her visit was because she wanted to sleep with him—*for old times' sake*? But her treacherous mind responded to his provocative suggestion and she visualised them naked and writhing on the gym mat, limbs entangled and their skin damp with sweat as he drove his body into hers in a relentless rhythm.

Heat scalded her cheeks, and she did not trust herself to say anything else to him that wouldn't result in them having one of the vicious arguments that had been a regular feature of the last months of their marriage. Dignified silence seemed her best strategy, but as she swung away from him his gravelly, accented voice stopped her from marching up the stairs.

'You have often been in my dreams these past two years, Isabella. The nights can be long and lonely…can't they?'

Could she possibly have heard regret in his voice? Was there any chance that he had missed her even half as much as she had missed him? Slowly, she turned back to face him, and immediately realised that she had indulged in wishful thinking. He was lounging in the doorway, bare-chested, beautiful and totally aware that he turned her on.

How could she have thought that Constantin might hide a vulnerable side beneath his arrogance? The idea that she had hurt him when she had left two years ago was laughable, Isobel thought bitterly. If he had a heart, he kept it locked behind a wall of impenetrable steel that nothing and no one could breach.

'I don't imagine you have spent many nights alone,' she said tautly, 'not if the stories in the tabloids linking you with numerous beautiful models and socialites are to be believed.'

He shrugged. 'There were occasions when it was necessary for me to invite women to social events—' he sent her a piercing glance '—since my wife wasn't around to accompany me. Unfortunately the gutter press thrive on scandal and intrigue, and if none exist they fabricate lies.'

'Are you saying that you didn't have affairs with those women?'

His mocking expression gave nothing away. 'If you're trying to lead me into admitting adultery as a reason for us to divorce—forget it,' he said coolly. 'You're the one who walked out of our marriage.'

Frustration surged through Isobel and she wanted to demand a straight answer from him. The idea that he had slept with the women he had been photographed with made her feel sick with jealousy. But as Constantin had pointed out, *she* had been the one to leave, and she had no right to ask him about his personal life. He was a red-blooded male with a high sex drive, and common sense told her that he was unlikely to have remained celibate for the past two years.

The adrenalin that had pumped through her veins when she had psyched herself up to see Constantin drained away, and she suddenly felt weary and strangely deflated. It had been a stupid idea to come here.

She looked down at the divorce petition in her hand and calmly ripped it in half.

'I want a divorce as much as you do, but for the reason that we have lived apart for more than two years. If you continue to state my desertion as a reason, I'll begin divorce proceedings against you, citing your unreasonable behaviour.'

He jerked his head back as if she had slapped him and his eyes glittered with anger. '*My* behaviour? What about how you behaved? You were hardly a devoted wife, were you, *cara*?' He made the endearment sound like an insult. 'In fact you went out with your friends so often that I almost forgot I had a wife.'

'I saw my friends because, for some reason that I have never understood, you had turned into the ice man. We were two strangers who happened to live in the same house. But I needed more, Constantin. I needed you...'

Isobel broke off as the hard gleam in Constantin's eyes told her she was wasting her breath. 'I refuse to take part in a slanging match,' she muttered. She gave a hollow laugh. 'It's a telling indictment of our marriage that we can't even agree on how we're going to end it.'

She swung away from him and marched up the stairs, her back ramrod-straight. Reaching the ground-floor level, she hurried towards the front door but was forced to halt as the butler finished speaking on the house phone and moved to stand in front of her.

Whittaker held open the door to the sitting room. 'The Marquis requested that you wait in here while he takes a shower, and he will join you shortly.'

She shook her head. 'No, I'm leaving.'

Whittaker's polite smile did not falter. 'Mr De Severino hopes that you will stay and continue the discussion you began a few minutes ago. Shall I bring you some tea, madam?'

Before she could argue, Isobel found that she had been

steered into the sitting room, and there was a faint click
as Whittaker departed and shut the door behind him. She
didn't understand what Constantin was playing at. It was
clear they had nothing to discuss that could not be dealt
with by their respective divorce lawyers. Her immediate
thought was that she was not going to be a puppet controlled by the master puppeteer as had so often happened
during their marriage.

She reached for the door handle just as the door opened
and the butler entered carrying a tray with a silver teapot
and a cafetière.

'I remembered that you prefer Earl Grey tea, madam,'
he said, smiling as he held out a cup and saucer.

Good manners prevented Isobel from storming out of
the house. She had always got on well with Whittaker, and
her problems with her marriage were not the elderly butler's fault. Suppressing her irritation that Constantin had
got his own way as he had so often done in the past, she
wandered over to the window. The view of the park was
familiar and evoked painful memories.

'I've just spoken to my lawyer and instructed him to
send a new divorce petition for you to sign. You'll also
have to give a written statement saying that we have lived
apart for two years.'

At the sound of Constantin's clipped voice Isobel jolted
and slopped tea into her saucer. She spun round, disconcerted to find him standing close to her. For such a big man
he moved with the silent menace of a panther stalking its
prey, she thought ruefully. The black jeans and polo shirt
he had changed into emphasised his lethal good looks.
His hair was still damp from his recent shower and the
citrusy fragrance of soap mixed with his spicy cologne
teased her senses.

'Giles still thinks I have good grounds to divorce you

for desertion.' Constantin's anger that she had thwarted him was evident in his harsh tone. 'But the legal advice is that it will be quicker to go with the fact that we have been separated for two years. The one thing we *can* both agree on is that we want a swift end to our marriage,' he drawled sardonically.

Determined to hide the pang of hurt that his words evoked, Isobel turned her gaze back to the window and stared once more at the pretty park at the centre of Grosvenor Square.

'When I was pregnant, I often used to stand here and imagine pushing our baby in a pram around the gardens,' she said softly. 'Our little girl would have been almost two and a half now.'

The shaft of pain in her chest was not as sharp as it had once been, but it was enough to make her catch her breath. Coming back to the house where she had lived when she had been pregnant had opened up the wound in her heart that would never completely heal. She had chosen one of the bedrooms at the back of the house for a nursery, and had been busy planning the colour scheme before she and Constantin had made that fateful trip to Italy.

She watched him pour himself a cup of coffee and felt a surge of anger that he had not reacted to the mention of their daughter. Nothing had changed, Isobel thought grimly. When she had lost their baby, twenty weeks into her pregnancy, she had been numb with grief. A few times she had tried to talk about the miscarriage with Constantin, but he had rebuffed her and become even more distant, and eventually she had stopped trying to reach him.

'Do you ever think about Arianna?' The nurse at the hospital had advised them to choose a name for their baby, even though she had been born too early to survive.

He sipped his coffee, and Isobel noted that he did not

meet her gaze. 'There's no point dwelling on the past,' he said shortly. 'Nothing can change what happened. All we can do is move forwards.'

Two years ago, she had been chilled by his lack of emotion, but as she looked closely at him and saw a nerve flicker in his cheek she realised that he was tenser than he appeared.

'Is that why you've begun divorce proceedings? You want to bury the past?'

He winced at her deliberate use of the word *bury*, and Isobel wondered if his mind pictured, as hers did, the small white marble tombstone in the grounds of the chapel at Casa Celeste—the De Severino family's historic home on the shores of Lake Albano—where they had laid Arianna to rest.

Constantin's eyes narrowed. 'Is there a point to this conversation? I haven't heard a word from you in two years. Why have you turned up out of the blue?'

He did not try to disguise his frustration. He had not anticipated this meeting with his soon-to-be ex-wife, and Constantin hated surprises. His shock when he had caught sight of Isobel standing in the doorway of the gym had sparked his anger that she had left him—even though he acknowledged that he had driven her away. She had a hell of a nerve to stroll back into the house, looking so beautiful that he'd been instantly and embarrassingly aroused.

His temper was not improved when he felt his hand shake as he lifted his cup to his lips and gulped down his coffee, scalding the back of his throat in the process. He did not want her here, stirring up memories of the past that he had successfully kept locked away. An image flashed into his mind of their tiny, perfectly formed baby girl who had never lived. Pain flared inside him, but he controlled it as he always did, by force of will, and blocked out the memories.

Harder to control was his body's reaction to Isobel. Unwanted memories were not the only thing she was stirring, Constantin acknowledged self-derisively as he shifted position in an effort to hide the bulge of his arousal. No other woman had ever turned him on as hard and fast as Isobel.

He remembered the first time he had met her. She had hurtled into his office half an hour late for work, a flurry of honey-blonde hair framing a strikingly beautiful face, and announced that she had been sent by the temp agency to cover for his office assistant who was on maternity leave. He'd cut short her explanation of why she was late, but his impatience had died when he had looked into her wide hazel eyes and felt a shaft of desire so strong that it had literally taken his breath away.

From that moment his sole aim had been to take her to bed, a feat he'd achieved within the month. Discovering that he was her first lover had elicited emotions he had not believed himself capable of. The weekend they had spent together in Rome had been the best—and worst—of his life.

It had been the beginning of the nightmares that had haunted him ever since he'd woken in the middle of the night, sweating and shaking, and utterly appalled by the truth that his dream had revealed. He had looked at Isobel sleeping innocently beside him, and realised that for her safety he could not allow their relationship to continue.

CHAPTER TWO

THE SUN GLINTING through the windows turned Isobel's hair to spun gold. A sensation he could not define tugged in Constantin's chest, but he ignored it and forced himself to study her objectively.

Her clothes bore the hallmarks of superb design; the close-fitting jeans drew his attention to her endlessly long legs and her tee shirt snugly moulded her firm breasts. A gold chain around her neck was her only item of jewellery. His mouth thinned as he glanced at her bare left hand and pictured her wedding ring and diamond engagement ring that she had left behind when she had abandoned their marriage to pursue her career.

Her physical appearance had changed little in two years. Her face, with its high cheekbones and firm jaw that gave a clue to her determined character, was as beautiful as he remembered, and her hazel eyes fringed with long lashes were clear and intelligent. Her natural blonde hair was sexily tousled, and the just-got-out-of-bed style made him want to run his fingers through the silky layers.

His eyes sought hers, and he was intrigued when she met his gaze with calm self-assurance where once she would have blushed and looked away. There was something very alluring about a woman who was comfortable in her own skin and Constantin felt an ache of desire in his groin, but, perversely he was irritated by the self-confidence that she had developed after she had left him.

'I'm not the only one of us to have featured in the press,' he said abruptly. 'The Stone Ladies' success has been meteoric and the band has won a raft of music awards. How does it feel to be a famous star?'

Isobel shrugged. 'Frankly, it seems unreal. In two years the band has gone from playing small gigs in pubs to performing in huge arenas in front of thousands of people. Success is amazing, of course, but if I'm honest I find the media interest in my private life hard to deal with.'

'Particularly as the paparazzi are fascinated by your relationship with one of the male band members,' Constantin said sardonically. 'I'm guessing the record company want the band's image to be squeaky clean for your teenage fans, which is why your profile on social media sites makes no mention of the fact that you are married.'

Isobel sighed, sensing that they were heading towards an old argument. 'I've explained that Ryan is just a friend. I'm close to everyone in the band. We grew up together and Ben, Carly and Ryan are like my family. You never understood how important they are to me and I know you resented my friendships, but the truth was that the more you pushed me away, the more I needed to be with people who cared about me, people I could trust.'

Constantin frowned. 'I never gave you any reason not to trust me.'

'I don't mean I suspected you of seeing other women behind my back.' In a way, if he had been unfaithful it would have been easier to understand, Isobel thought painfully. She would have been hurt, but she would have accepted that she'd made a mistake by marrying a notorious playboy, and eventually she would have got over him.

She stared at his handsome face and her heart clenched.

She had written songs about falling in love at first sight but she'd never really believed it could happen—until she'd met Constantin.

When she had hurried into his office on her first day at her new job, her eyes had crashed with his cobalt-blue gaze, and the world had tilted on its axis. She had expected the CEO of a world-famous company to be older, possibly with thinning hair and a thickening waistline, but Constantin was a superb example of masculine perfection, with exotic film-star looks and the commanding presence of a world leader. She had felt intimidated by his height and powerful build, by his smouldering sensuality that made her acutely aware of her femininity. But then he had smiled and she had felt a yearning ache in the pit of her stomach that she had instinctively known only he could assuage.

Constantin put his coffee cup on the tray, and his eyes narrowed on Isobel's flushed face as he wondered what thoughts she was trying to hide behind the sweep of her long eyelashes. She looked amazing, he acknowledged. Following the miscarriage she had barely eaten and had lost weight dramatically, but now her slim figure was firm and toned. Did she have a lover? The thought oozed its poison into his head. She was a beautiful, sensual woman, and it was difficult to believe she had lived like a nun for the past two years.

He had seen her photograph on posters advertising the Stone Ladies' new album. There were pictures of her on giant billboards around London wearing a skirt that was barely more than a wide belt, which showed off her lissom thighs. She was a pin-up girl, a male fantasy, but he had no need of fantasies when he had X-rated memories of making love to her.

Those memories crowded his mind and his arousal became a potent, throbbing force. The atmosphere in the sitting room altered subtly. He heard the quickening sound of his breathing, or was it Isobel's? He looked into her eyes and watched them darken as her pupils dilated, and he knew she was remembering the white-hot hunger that had consumed them in the past and was simmering between them now.

Goosebumps prickled on the back of Isobel's neck when she saw the hard glitter in Constantin's eyes. The realisation that he still desired her filled her with panic and undeniable excitement. She tore her gaze from him and stared desperately at the empty teacup and saucer in her hand, suddenly realising that she was gripping the delicate bone china so tightly it was in danger of breaking. She took a step towards the coffee table, intending to put the cup and saucer on the tray, but her heel caught on the edge of the rug and she stumbled. Immediately two strong arms caught her, and when she regained her balance she found herself standing so close to Constantin that the tips of her breasts grazed his chest.

'Thanks.' She groaned inwardly when her voice emerged as a husky whisper. Her throat felt dry and her senses were swamped by the evocative scent of the spicy aftershave that he always wore. Her common sense told her to move away from him but she seemed to have lost control of her limbs as her mind flew back to the first time he had kissed her.

He had given her a lift home from work. Sitting next to him in his sleek sports car, she had felt even more overwhelmed by him than she did at the office. Her position as an assistant to his PA meant that her conversations with him had been mainly work related, and she had assumed that he barely noticed her. His request as they drove across the city for her to tell him about herself had thrown her into a panic, but he was her boss so she had obediently related the unexciting details of her life growing up in a small Derbyshire village.

When he had finally parked outside her flat, he'd turned to her, and his smile had made her heart skip a beat. 'You're very sweet,' he'd murmured.

His words had rankled. She hadn't wanted him to think she was a *sweet*, silly girl; she'd wanted him to think of her as a woman. Perhaps her feelings had shown in her eyes, because he had given a faint sigh before he'd lowered his head and covered her mouth with his.

Her body had come alive instantly. It was as if he had pressed a switch and awoken her sensuality that had been untested until that moment. Constantin had kissed her as she had imagined a man would kiss a woman, as she had dreamed of being kissed. She had been intoxicated by his mastery, and responded to his passionate demands with a fervency that had made him groan.

'Very soon I will make you mine, Isabella,' he'd warned her softly.

'How soon?' she'd replied, not caring that her eagerness revealed her lack of sophistication.

Now Isobel was three years older, but she was trapped by Constantin's sexual magnetism and felt as though she had flown back in time to when she had been a shy junior secretary who had been kissed senseless by the most exciting man she had ever met. Her heart jerked against her ribs as she watched his head descend, but her stomach plummeted with disappointment when he halted with his lips centimetres from hers.

'Why did you walk out on me?' he said harshly. 'You didn't even have the decency to tell me to my face that you were clearing out. All I got was an insultingly brief note to say that *you* had decided we should end our marriage.'

Isobel swallowed. It was impossible to think properly

when his lips were tantalisingly close, and even more impossible to believe that she had heard a note of hurt in his voice. She longed to close the gap between them, to slide her hand into the silky dark hair at his nape and urge his mouth down on hers. It took all her will power to step away from him.

'Why did you marry me?' She countered his question with one of her own. 'I've often wondered. Was it only because I was pregnant with your child? I believed our relationship was based on more than sexual attraction, but after I had the miscarriage you were so distant. I couldn't get close to you, and you never wanted to talk about... about what had happened. Your coldness seemed to indicate that you wished I wasn't your wife.'

Constantin had always been able to read the emotions on Isobel's expressive features and the pain reflected in her hazel eyes caused him a pang of guilt. He knew he had not given her the support she had needed when she'd lost the baby. He'd been unable to talk about it, and had dealt with his emotions the way he always did, by burying them deep inside and concentrating on running a global business empire. He could hardly blame her for turning to her friends, but he had felt jealous of her closeness to the other members of the band, and in particular her obvious affection for the guitarist, Ryan Fellows.

The cover of the Stone Ladies' new album was an arty black and white picture of the two most photogenic band members—Isobel and Fellows—riding a unicorn. No doubt the romantic image would appeal to the band's thousands of fans, but when Constantin had seen the album cover he'd felt an overwhelming desire to rearrange the guitarist's pretty-boy features with his fist.

The idea that Isobel and Fellows might be lovers evoked a corrosive acid burn in his gut. Isobel had accused him of resenting her friends, and he acknowledged it was the truth. He had been unable to control his possessive feelings, which in turn had made him afraid that he had inherited his father's dangerous jealousy.

He looked at her tense face. It must have taken a lot of guts for her to have come back to the house that he knew held poignant memories for her. He thought of the mural of farm animals that she had been painting on the walls of the nursery. The mural was unfinished and the room was empty. He'd sent the cot and nursery equipment back to the shop and never went into the room that had been destined for their daughter.

The miscarriage had broken Isobel, and it was a measure of her strength of will that she had recovered to be this beautiful, self-assured woman—although close scrutiny revealed faint shadows in her eyes that Constantin guessed would never completely fade. One thing was certain. She deserved his honesty.

'Three years ago we were lovers briefly. The weekend we spent at my apartment in Rome was fun, but...' he shrugged '...I had no desire for a prolonged relationship—and I thought you understood that.' When he had ended the affair shortly after they had returned to London he had assured himself it was for the best to call a halt before things got out of hand. Isobel had needed to understand that the words long-term and commitment were not in his vocabulary.

He exhaled heavily. 'But then fate dealt an unexpected card. When you told me you were pregnant you must have realised that I would not allow my child to be born illegitimate. Marriage was the only option. I could not neglect my duty to my child or to you.'

Isobel flinched. *Duty* was an ugly little word. The realisation that Constantin had proposed marriage because he had felt responsible for her evoked a bitter taste in her mouth. She had told Constantin she was pregnant with his baby because she'd believed he had the right to know. She had been stunned when he'd asked her to marry him. After all, it was the twenty-first century, and being a single mother was no longer regarded as unusual or shameful. When he had proposed, she had convinced herself that he must have some feelings for her. But the stark truth was that she had seen what she had wanted to see.

Yet her stubborn nature still refused to give up the idea that they had shared something meaningful. 'We had some good times in the beginning,' she reminded him.

'I don't deny it. We were going to be parents, and for our child's sake it was important to build an amicable relationship with each other, additional to our sexual compatibility.'

Isobel swallowed the golf ball that had become lodged in her throat. Had Constantin simply been building an *amicable* relationship with her when he had filled the house with yellow roses after she had mentioned that they were her favourite flower? Had she imagined the closeness between them that had grown stronger every day of their three-week honeymoon in the Seychelles?

She stared at his chiselled features and wondered why she had ever believed she had seen warmth in his eyes that glittered as hard and bright as sapphires. What a fool she had been. Despite everything that happened, his coldness to her in the last months of their marriage, deep down she had believed there was a chance that they might one day get back together. That fragile sense of hope had now gone and she was shocked by how badly it hurt.

She turned her head towards the window. The sun streaming through the glass was so bright, and surely it was the glare that was making her eyes water? As if she were looking through a kaleidoscope, she saw the fractured images of a woman pushing a pram through the park with a tall, handsome man at her side. But when she blinked, the vision disappeared, just as her dreams had done.

Somehow she marshalled her thoughts and emotions, and even managed a cool smile when she looked back at Constantin.

'In that case there's nothing more to be said. I'll wait to receive a new divorce petition from your solicitor, which I will sign and return immediately. I understand that the legal proceedings are straightforward in an uncontested divorce.'

'I've instructed my lawyer to offer you a financial settlement.' Constantin frowned when she shook her head. 'I don't understand why you insisted on signing a prenuptial agreement that awarded you absolutely nothing.'

'Because I want nothing from you,' Isobel told him fiercely. 'I'm lucky to be able to earn a high income, but even if the band hadn't become successful I wouldn't have accepted a handout from you.'

Impatience glittered in his eyes. 'I see you've lost none of your prickly independence. You're the only woman I've ever known who got annoyed if I bought you presents.'

She hadn't wanted expensive gifts. What she had wanted he had been unable or unwilling to give her—love, his heart in exchange for hers, a marriage that was a true partnership. Did such a thing even exist? She'd seen little evidence of it in her parents' marriage, Isobel thought wryly. Perhaps her father had been right during one of their many rows about her doing homework rather than writing songs, when he had accused her of wasting her time chasing rainbows. Maybe happy-ever-after only happened in fairy tales.

Of their own volition her eyes fixed on Constantin's

face as she committed his sculpted features to her memory. The faintly cynical curve of his lips evoked a visceral ache in her belly.

She had to get out of the house *now*, before her wafer-thin composure cracked. Never had she been more thankful for the illusion of supreme confidence that performing with the band had given her. She walked unhurriedly across the room and glanced back at Constantin from the doorway. 'I'll instruct my lawyer to reject any financial offer from you.'

'*Per l'amor di Dio!*' He swore beneath his breath as he crossed the room with long strides. 'Dammit, Isobel, you are entitled to receive a settlement from me. The music industry can be fickle, and, although the band is riding high at the moment, no one can say what the future holds.'

Wasn't that the truth? Isobel thought emotively as the image of her tiny baby daughter flashed into her mind. Coming back to the house where she had dreamed of living as a happy family with Constantin and their child, she felt as though a protective layer had been scraped away from the scar tissue surrounding her heart

'There's no reason any more for you to feel responsible for me,' she said tautly.

Her eyes clashed with his, and something in his brilliant blue gaze sent a warning signal to her brain. She sensed that he was mentally stripping her naked, and she was furious with her treacherous body as heat stole through her veins. He had always had the ability to decimate her equilibrium with one killer glance.

The sound of her phone ringing from the depths of her handbag was a welcome distraction. She retrieved the phone and glanced at the caller display before shooting an apologetic glance at Constantin. 'Do you mind if I answer this? It's Carly, probably calling to remind me that we'd arranged a shopping trip this afternoon.'

Her friend's cheerful voice greeted her. 'The photographer from *Rock Style* magazine wants to do the shoot tomorrow instead of midweek. Does that suit you? Okay, I'll let him know,' Carly said when Isobel confirmed she was free the next day. She cut the call and was about to drop her phone into her bag when it rang again. Assuming it was Carly with a second message, she lifted the phone to her ear and her heart jumped when a frighteningly familiar voice spoke.

'Hello, Izzy. It's David, your darling. Remember you wrote "To my darling David" when you gave me your autograph? I know you are in London and I hoped we could have dinner together.'

'How did you get my mobile number?' The instant Isobel blurted out the question she cursed herself. The police had advised her to stay calm and not reveal any emotion or engage in conversation with the man who had been stalking her for the past two months, but hearing David's voice filled her with panic. Her eyes jerked to the window and she scanned the pavement outside. Did he know her exact location in London? Her common sense told her it was unlikely that he had followed her here. But how on earth had he got hold of her mobile-phone number?

Without saying another word she cut the call and then checked the number of the last caller. The number had been withheld. She switched off her phone and dropped it into her handbag as if she feared it were an explosive device.

'What was that about?'

She met Constantin's curious gaze, unaware of the unease reflected in her eyes.

'Nothing.' Her response was automatic. There was no reason to involve Constantin. She would make a note of the call and file it with the other nuisance calls she had received from David as the police had advised her to do. More importantly, she would contact her network provider and change her mobile-phone number.

Constantin frowned. 'Your reaction suggested it was more than *nothing*. When you answered the call, you looked worried.' He placed his hand on Isobel's arm to prevent her from sidling out of the door. 'Do you have a problem with whoever called you?'

'No—it was just someone playing a joke.' She quickly thought up the excuse. Her problem right now was the way her body was reacting to Constantin's nearness. Her heart was racing and she could feel the pulse at the base of her throat beating erratically. She fought a crazy temptation to tell him about David—a fan who had developed an unhealthy obsession with her. The police were aware of the situation and everything was under control, she reassured herself. There was no point in involving her soon-to-be ex-husband.

In a matter of weeks she and Constantin would be divorced and it was likely that she would never see him again. The knowledge felt like a knife-blade through her heart. She pulled her arm free and stumbled into the hall. Her stiletto heels sounded like staccato gunfire on the marble floor as she half ran towards the front door.

'Goodbye, Constantin.' She could not resist one final glance over her shoulder at him. 'I hope one day you'll meet someone who can give you whatever it is you're looking for.'

'The role of Chairman of DSE has historically always passed to the eldest son of the next generation of the family. *It is my birthright, dammit!*'

Constantin paced around his uncle's office at the Rome

headquarters of DSE, his body taut with suppressed fury like a caged tiger enraged by its captivity. His eyes glittered as he stared at Alonso sitting calmly behind his desk. 'If I had been a year older when my father died I would have become Chairman a decade ago, but because I was seventeen, company rules dictated that the chairmanship must go to the next De Severino male who was of age—in this case, *you*, my father's brother. But now you wish to retire, and the chairmanship should revert to me. I intend to combine the role of Chairman with that of CEO, as my father did.'

Alonso cleared his throat. 'It is the belief among many members of the board that the two roles should be separated. An independent board chairman can better protect shareholder interests, leaving the CEO free to concentrate on running the business—which you do extremely well, Constantin.'

'Profits have risen year on year since I became CEO, but many times I have felt that I am working against the board rather than with their backing.' Constantin could barely contain his frustration. 'It is crucial for our continuing success that DSE takes advantage of emerging markets in Asia and South America. The board are slow to embrace change, but we must move fast to keep ahead of our competitors.'

'There is a concern that in your rush to take the company forwards, you have forgotten the standards and moral ethics of DSE that have been the backbone of the company since it was established by your great-grandfather nearly a century ago.'

Constantin slammed his hands down on his uncle's desk. 'I have forgotten nothing. I have lived and breathed DSE since I was a small boy, in the expectation that I would one day be fully responsible for the company. In what way have I forgotten the company's moral ethics?'

Instead of replying, Alonso looked pointedly at a copy of a popular gossip magazine lying on his desk. The front cover carried a photo of his nephew and an Italian glamour model, Lia Gerodi, emerging from a casino. From the amount of naked flesh on display, Miss Gerodi appeared to be experiencing a wardrobe malfunction, Alonso noted cynically.

Constantin shrugged as he glanced at the picture that had been taken a week ago. The only reason he remembered that particular evening was because it had been the night he had returned to Rome from London after his unexpected visit from Isobel. He had been in a foul mood, he recalled. The image of her walking out of the house in Grosvenor Square and climbing into a taxi, without once looking back, had been stuck in his mind. He'd felt churned up inside and, unusually for him, unable to rationalise his thoughts.

Lia had been phoning him for weeks, ever since they had met at a social event the details of which he did not remember. When he'd received a call from her as his jet had landed in Rome he had agreed to have dinner with her purely to take his mind off Isobel. The trip to the casino had been Lia's idea, and he suspected that she had tipped off the paparazzi, knowing that a picture of her with one of Italy's wealthiest businessmen would give her valuable media exposure that might boost her modelling career.

'This is not the image of the company that the board wishes to see advertised around the world,' Alonso said, tapping the photo with his forefinger. 'The public's perception of DSE must be of a company that delivers excellence, reliability and honesty. But how can the public trust that the company believes in those values, when the CEO, despite being married, leads a playboy lifestyle?'

'My private life has no bearing on my ability to run DSE,' Constantin growled. 'Shareholders are only interested in profits, not in my personal affairs.'

'Unfortunately that is not true, especially as you seem to have so many affairs.'

'You know how the press like to exaggerate.' Constantin's jaw clenched. 'If you are seriously considering not appointing me Chairman, who else do you have in mind?'

'My sister's son, Maurio. Since I have no son of my own,' Alonso continued when it became evident that Constantin was too stunned to comment, 'I have taken great interest in your younger cousin. I believe Maurio has many qualities that make him suitable for the role of Chairman, not least the fact that he is a happily married family man who is never likely to be photographed staggering out of a casino, clutching a bottle of Scotch in one hand and a half-naked bimbo in the other.'

'Maurio is spineless. He would be completely out of his depth as Chairman,' Constantin said harshly.

He swung away to stare out of the window while he fought the temptation to shake some sense into his uncle. *He* was the best person to take on the combined role of CEO and Chairman. It was what he had been born to do.

DSE was more than a business; it was his life, his identity. After he had witnessed the deaths of his father and stepmother when he was seventeen, Constantin had focused exclusively on the company as a way of preventing himself from thinking about the shocking tragedy. For ten years he had planned for the day when he took absolute control of DSE, but now there was a real danger that his destiny was going to be snatched away from him.

The hell it was, he thought grimly. DSE was his, and

he was *not* going to lose it. He turned back to his uncle. 'So, if the only problem you and the board have is with my image, I'll change it. I'll become a recluse. I'll live the life of a hermit if that's what it takes for you to choose me as your successor.'

Alonso looked at him steadily. 'I don't expect anything quite so drastic, Constantin. I simply ask that details of your love life are not a matter of media curiosity and titivation. I suggest that you resume your marriage. Prove that you can uphold the personal commitment you made when you married, and you may convince me that I can entrust complete control of DSE to you rather than your cousin.'

Constantin's eyes narrowed. 'That sounds like blackmail.'

His uncle's gaze did not falter. 'I don't care what it sounds like. The responsibility of appointing the next chairman is mine and mine alone, and unless I see you change your lifestyle to reflect the core values of DSE, I cannot be certain you are the right man for the job.'

CHAPTER THREE

IT WAS A PITY, Constantin thought bitterly later that night as he let himself into the house in Grosvenor Square, that the conversation with his uncle had not taken place a week ago, before he had made it clear to Isobel that their marriage was over.

It was past midnight and Whittaker had retired for the night, but the butler had left a decanter of malt whisky on the table in the sitting room with a note informing him that there were sandwiches in the fridge. Constantin had not eaten since lunch, but it had been a hell of a day, with meetings in Milan, Paris and London, and he had no appetite for food. He poured himself a large drink, sank down onto the sofa and picked up the television remote to flick through the channels.

How could Alonso consider handing the chairmanship of DSE to Maurio? His cousin was a pleasant enough young man, but he wouldn't last five minutes in the cutthroat corporate world. Constantin took a long swig of whisky and savoured its subtle warmth at the back of his throat. Nerve, daring and vision were the qualities required to head the billion-pound business that DSE had grown to be since *he* had become CEO. He had great plans for the future development of the company, but if his cousin was made Chairman, certain board members who were set in their ways would undoubtedly try to influence Maurio against him.

He took another gulp of whisky, and it occurred to him that maybe he drank too much. He shrugged. Alcohol worked well as an anaesthetic when he needed to blank out painful memories. If he drank enough, he might be able to snatch a few hours' sleep. Ever since Isobel's visit a week ago, his old nightmares had returned to haunt him and remind him of why he could not risk being with her.

He frowned as he recalled her strange reaction to the phone call she had received as she had been about to walk out of the door. He had not imagined the fearful expression in her eyes, although when he had asked her about the call she had denied anything was wrong. Beneath her air of self-confidence he had seen her vulnerability that had reminded him of the shy young secretary who used to watch him with her big, hazel eyes when she thought he was not aware of her.

He swore, and swallowed the rest of his drink before refilling his glass. He accepted that he bore most of the responsibility for the disintegration of their marriage, but Isobel was not completely blameless. He had lost count of the times he had come home from work to an empty house, and spent the evening alone while she had been singing with her band in pubs and clubs. Isobel had accused him of not understanding how important music was to her, and if he was honest he *had* resented the fact that the Stone Ladies had become an increasingly big part of her life.

When she had left him two years ago, he'd told himself it was best for both of them. Isobel had gone on to establish a hugely successful career. But now *his* career was under threat and the only way he could secure his rightful position as undisputed head of DSE was to persuade her to come back to him, days after he had admitted that the only reason he had married her was because she had been pregnant with his child. The irony of the situation was not lost on him. The expression that he had 'burned his bridges' could not be more apt, Constantin thought sardonically.

The wildlife documentary on the television failed to hold his interest. He flicked over the channel to a popular chat show and his attention was suddenly riveted on the screen.

'The Stone Ladies are arguably the most successful British folk-rock band of the past five years,' the chat-show host said. He went on to list the band's numerous music awards, but Constantin was only half listening as he stared at the image of Isobel that filled his TV screen. She was wearing a black leather minidress and thigh-high boots that drew attention to her endlessly long legs. Her blonde hair spilled over her shoulders and her lovely face was animated as she charmed the chat-show host with her quick wit and impressive self-assurance.

It was hard to believe that she was the same Isobel who had been painfully shy and overawed when he had invited her to spend the weekend with him at his penthouse apartment in Rome, Constantin brooded. He had patiently drawn her out of her shell, but he had still been shocked on their first night together when he had discovered that she was a virgin. His gut clenched as memories flooded his mind. What she had lacked in experience she had more than made up for in her eagerness to please him, he remembered.

On the television, the chat-show host had turned the interview with the band to questions about their personal lives. 'Ben and Carly, you announced your engagement a few months ago, and I believe you are planning your wedding for later this year?'

The couple, who were the drummer and keyboard

player, confirmed that they were planning to marry in the autumn. The interviewer then turned to Isobel and the fourth member of the band, Ryan Fellows. 'And how about you two?' the chat-show host asked coyly. 'You have never confirmed or denied the rumours that you are more than good friends. So, what is the exact nature of your relationship?'

Constantin gritted his teeth as he watched the long-haired guitarist put his arm around Isobel's shoulders. 'It's true that Izzy and I are *very* good friends.' Fellows grinned at Isobel and she smiled back at him. 'I may be making an announcement in the near future,' the guitarist added.

What did the blasted pretty-boy rock star mean by that? Anger boiled Constantin's blood as it occurred to him that the reason Isobel had insisted he could not cite her desertion as a reason for their divorce might be because she did not want to look bad to her fans when she went public about her relationship with Ryan Fellows.

Santa Madre! It was clear she had already got another man lined up to take *his* place. She had insisted that her relationship with Fellows was an innocent friendship, but as Constantin watched Isobel and the guitarist on the TV the closeness between the golden couple was evident for the world to see. Bile rose in his throat. How dared she flaunt her lover in public when she was still married to him? When they had married three years ago, their low-key wedding had gone unnoticed by the press. *But, hell, he felt like a cuckold.*

Constantin reached for the whisky bottle and filled his glass once more, while his mind worked furiously. If Isobel was involved with Ryan Fellows, why had she looked at *him* with a hunger in her eyes that had tempted him to bend her over the arm of the sofa and pull her jeans down so that he could give them both the satisfaction they craved? Could it be that the pretty-boy guitarist did not satisfy her?

His wife was a highly sensual woman, Constantin brooded. *Dio!* The scorching sexual chemistry between him and Isobel had been beyond anything he'd ever experienced with any other woman. When they had first been married they had spent hours indulging in erotic and highly satisfying lovemaking.

Did Isobel miss those wildly passionate sessions? When she had surprised him in the gym the other night, the sexual chemistry between them had been tangible. He had come so close to tumbling her down onto the gym mat and taking her hard and fast—and she would not have stopped him. She had pretended to be outraged, and had denied that she wanted him, but her body language had betrayed her.

Constantin's thoughts turned to his uncle's threat to deny him the chairmanship of DSE. When he had stormed out of Alonso's office it had not entered his mind to comply with the old man's ultimatum to resume his marriage in order to secure the position of Chairman. But as he stared at the TV screen and watched Isobel rest her hand on Ryan Fellows's thigh as they sat close together on the sofa, the burning rage inside him grew cold and congealed into a hard knot of fury.

DSE was his birthright. The company was the only thing that made him feel proud of being a De Severino. What was he otherwise? He was the son of a monster, taunted a voice inside his head. He dared not look too deeply inside himself for fear of what he might discover. He could not risk having a relationship that involved his emotions. DSE was his all-consuming mistress, his raison d'être, and he would do whatever it took to claim what was rightfully his.

By walking out on him two years ago, Isobel had

jeopardised his chance of becoming Chairman of DSE. But if he could persuade her to return to him, his uncle would appoint him Chairman—and once his position as head of the company was unchallengeable he would have no more need of his beautiful, fickle wife.

'Come in.' Isobel turned away from the mirror when she heard a knock on the door of the hotel room that she had been allocated as a dressing room.

'Wow,' Ryan said when he saw her, 'you look stunning.'

'You don't think the dress is over the top?' She gave another doubtful glance in the mirror at the gold sequined evening gown that hugged her body like a second skin and left one shoulder bare.

'The Duke of Beaufort's charity dinner is one of the most prestigious events in London's social calendar, and everything about tonight is going to be over the top. You look perfect for the occasion,' Ryan assured her.

'I can't believe the Stone Ladies have been asked to perform tonight.' She threw Ryan a wry smile. 'Did you ever imagine when we were playing gigs in pubs that we would one day be top billing at a grand party held in a five-star hotel?'

He laughed. 'It's crazy how fast things have happened. Sometimes I'm scared I'll wake up and find I'm back in Derbyshire working behind the bar of the ex-miners' social club.' Ryan hesitated. 'I reckon your dad would be proud of you, Izzy,' he said softly.

Her smile faded. 'I doubt it.'

Isobel recalled the conversation she'd had with her mother when they had stood at her father's graveside on the day of his funeral three months ago. Ann Blake had sobbed quietly, but Isobel had found it impossible to cry for her father, whose dour moods and abrasive temper had

cast a shadow on her childhood so that she had tried to
avoid him as much as possible when she had lived at home.

'Your father was a good man,' her mother had said suddenly. Catching Isobel's look of surprise, she had continued, 'I know he wasn't always easy to live with, especially
when he was in one of his black moods, but he wasn't
always like that. When I married him he was fun to be
with and he had such hopes for us and for the future. But
he changed after he had his accident, and he was no longer the strong, fit man he had been. When the coal mine
closed and he couldn't find work it destroyed his pride,
and losing his dream of making a better life for his family crushed his spirit.'

'It seemed as though he was determined to crush my
spirit and my dreams of a different life,' Isobel had said
fiercely. 'I know Dad often made you unhappy. I used to
hear you crying in the kitchen when you thought I was in
bed. I never understood why you stayed with him.'

'Part of him died with your brother. He never got over
losing Simon—and he needed me. I took my marriage
vows seriously—for better, for worse, for richer, for poorer,
in sickness and in health.' Her mother had looked at Isobel
curiously. 'You made the same vows when you married
Constantin. You've never explained why your marriage
ended. It's not my place to pry into your private life, but I
can't help wondering if you gave up too soon. A year isn't
a long time, and marriage isn't all hearts and flowers. You
have to work at a relationship and make compromises to
hopefully gain a better understanding of each other.'

She *had* tried to understand Constantin, Isobel thought
grimly. But she need not have bothered, because she'd now
had her darkest suspicions confirmed: that he had only
married her because she had conceived his child. She had
never told her mother about Arianna. It would have been

cruel to tell Ann that she had lost a granddaughter as well as a son and husband.

Isobel dragged her thoughts back to the present when she realised that Ryan was speaking. 'I would never have met Emily if I'd stayed in Eckerton village, that's for sure.' He ran a hand through his fair hair, and said awkwardly, 'Izzy, I've done it. I've asked Emily to marry me—and she said yes.'

'Thank heavens for that,' Isobel said in a heartfelt voice as she flung her arms around Ryan's neck. 'You two were made for each other and I know you're going to be very happy together.'

Ryan's expression clouded. 'Emily makes me the happiest man in the world, but I don't deserve to feel like this. I keep thinking about Simon, and how he never had the chance to grow up and fall in love. If only I'd stopped him going into the reservoir that day.'

'Don't.' Isobel pictured her brother's mischievous grin. She could not imagine him as an adult. For her, Simon would always be fourteen, always laughing and fooling around. 'You know what a daredevil Simon was. He wouldn't have listened to you. I know you did everything you could to try and save him, and you have to stop blaming yourself.' She squeezed Ryan's arm. 'You and my brother were best friends. He would be glad that you're going to marry the woman you love.'

Ryan nodded slowly. 'I guess you're right. Thanks, Izzy.' He glanced at the clock. 'Hey, we'd better get moving. We're due on stage in ten minutes. How do you feel?'

'Nervous,' Isobel admitted. 'I always am before a performance, but I'll be fine once I start singing.' She was about to follow Ryan out of the room when her phone rang, and she walked back over to the dressing table where she had left it. Because she was in a hurry, she unthinkingly answered it without checking the identity of the caller, and she tensed when a familiar voice spoke.

'I'll be watching you tonight, Izzy. It is written in the stars that we are destined to be together for ever.'

She cut the call and the phone slid out of her trembling fingers. Was David here at the hotel? Could he be a guest at the charity fund-raising event?

'Come on,' Ryan called from the doorway. He frowned when he saw how pale Isobel had gone. 'Are you okay? You look like you've seen a ghost.' He glanced at her phone as she dropped it into her bag. 'You haven't had any more nuisance calls, have you?'

It wouldn't be fair to share her worries about the stalker with Ryan tonight, when he was clearly ecstatic that his girlfriend had agreed to marry him. There was probably nothing to worry about anyway. She was being silly to let the mysterious David bother her.

She shrugged. 'I told you, I've just got a bit of stage fright, that's all,' she said as they took the lift down to the ground floor of the hotel. 'In a strange way I find it more daunting to perform in front of an audience of five hundred guests who paid a fortune for tickets, than at an arena in front of thousands of fans.'

Keen to take her mind away from the unsettling phone call, she changed the subject. 'Are you and Emily going to announce your engagement tonight?'

'No, I only proposed yesterday, and she's gone to her parents' country estate in Suffolk to break the news to them first.' As they walked backstage to wait until it was time for the band's performance Ryan caught hold of Isobel's hand. 'Thanks for helping me and Emily to keep our relationship out of the media. The speculation that you and I are romantically involved has allowed Emily to stay out of the limelight.'

They were interrupted by one of the sound technicians. 'You're on in two minutes, guys and girls. Do you want to check your mic, Izzy?'

As the host for the evening walked onto the stage to introduce the Stone Ladies, Isobel peeped through a gap in the curtains and felt a sickening sensation in the pit of her stomach. The glare of the footlights meant that it was impossible for her to see the audience clearly, but even if she could make out people's faces she would not recognise David. He had told her in one of his phone calls that they had met after a Stone Ladies concert and she had given him her autograph, but since the band had become famous Isobel had met hundreds of fans and signed her autograph countless times. She assumed David must have asked her to write 'to my darling'—fans often made strange requests—but she had no recollection of him.

Was he out there in the audience? She shivered as she remembered his most recent phone call. What had he meant when he'd said that they were destined to be together for ever? Was it her overactive imagination, or had there been something vaguely threatening in his words?'

The curtains were opening and there were cheers from the audience, but Isobel's feet felt as though they were rooted to the spot. The urge to run from the stage was so strong that she half turned and bumped into Ryan, who was standing behind her.

'Forget everything else and just focus on the music,' he murmured. 'Pretend we're kids again, four friends pretending to be rock stars in Eckerton village hall.'

Ryan's words calmed her and she looked around at Carly and Ben and returned their smiles. During her marriage, she had tried to explain to Constantin that the band had become her family who gave her the love and affection that she hadn't received from her father. After she had lost her baby, it had been her closest friends who had supported her through the darkest days of her life because Constantin had refused to talk about what had happened.

Taking a deep breath, she walked out onto the stage and launched into a song that had recently been a number-one hit in the charts. There was applause from the audience, but Isobel blocked out everything else and sank into the music. Ever since she had been a small child and had picked out simple tunes on her mother's piano, music had been her great love, her joy and her solace when she had needed an outlet for her emotions.

'…Constantin?'

The sound of his name intruded on Constantin's thoughts, and he tore his eyes away from the unedifying spectacle of his wife dancing with her *very* good friend, Ryan Fellows. A nerve flickered in his jaw, but a lifetime of disguising his true emotions came to his rescue and he smiled smoothly at the willowy blonde at his side, who was staring at him accusingly.

'I'm sure you haven't been listening to me!'

Lying was pointless. The woman—Ginny? Jenny? he'd already forgotten her name—had sat next to him during dinner and seemed to think that she had exclusive rights to his attention for the rest of the evening. But ignoring her had been rude. He gave an apologetic shrug of his shoulders. 'Forgive me. I have things on my mind and I'm afraid I am not an attentive companion tonight. But I'm sure there are many other men here who would enjoy meeting you,' he murmured.

The blonde finally took the hint and flounced away. Constantin watched the indignant sway of her bottom clad in tight red satin for all of two seconds, before his eyes were drawn back to the dance floor and Isobel.

Listening to her singing earlier in the evening, he had been struck anew by the liquid quality of her voice, and he had been reminded of a crystal-clear stream tumbling softly over pebbles. He had never understood when she had said that music was part of her. But watching her on the stage tonight, he'd realised that she sang from her heart, from the depths of her soul, and he had felt an inexplicable ache in his chest, a longing for something that might have been, if he had been a different man.

His gaze narrowed on the man who was dancing with Isobel. Constantin presumed that women found the long-haired guitarist attractive. Certainly Fellows and Isobel made a striking couple. Were they already lovers or would she at least have the decency to wait until she was free of her marriage before taking another man to her bed? Violent rage simmered in his gut. The potency of his jealousy terrified him, but he could not control it.

Was this how his father had felt when he had watched his young second wife laughing with her friends? Had Franco De Severino been overcome by murderous rage when he and Lorena had argued on the balcony that fateful day?

Sweat beaded on Constantin's brow. He knew he should not have accepted the invitation to tonight's event once he'd learned that the Stone Ladies would be attending. His brain told him he should get out of there, *fast*, but his feet were already carrying him swiftly across the dance floor in Isobel's direction.

Was David somewhere in the ballroom watching her? Isobel could not dismiss the thought as her mind replayed the stalker's unnerving phone call. During the Stone Ladies' performance she had managed to forget about him, but her tension had returned when she'd left the stage and joined the party guests. She told herself she was overreacting. The stalker had not actually threatened to harm her. But she could not shake off her feeling of unease, and she had stayed close to Ryan all evening.

'Don't look,' he murmured in her ear as he guided her around the dance floor, 'but an extremely dangerous-looking man is heading our way.'

Isobel's heart lurched. 'What do you mean? What man?' Was David going to reveal himself? She gripped Ryan's arm.

'It's Constantin, and I get the distinct impression that he'd like to tear me limb from limb. I thought you said it was all over between the two of you.'

'It is…' The words died on Isobel's lips as she felt a heavy hand on her shoulder and she was spun round to find Constantin's darkly handsome face looming above her. The fear she'd felt when she had believed she was going to be confronted by the man who had been terrorising her with phone calls was replaced by a different kind of tension as Constantin stepped between her and Ryan.

'Excuse me, Fellows,' he drawled in a deceptively soft voice that resonated with menace. 'It's my turn to dance with my wife.'

Ryan looked uncertain. 'Is that okay with you, Izzy?'

It was on the tip of her tongue to say that she would rather walk over hot coals than dance with Constantin, but the determined gleam in her husband's eyes made her swallow her words. She did not want to cause a scene, especially as she knew that members of the press were at the party and would love to report a fracas on the dance floor. Anyway, she had no time to appeal to Ryan for help because Constantin clamped his hands on her waist and whisked her away.

'What the hell are you playing at?' she demanded, but

the asperity in her voice was muffled as he slid his arms around her and drew her towards him so that her face was pressed against his chest. Beneath his crisp white shirt she could see the shadow of his dark chest hairs, and the heat from his body and the spicy scent of his aftershave intoxicated her senses. It had to be at this moment that the upbeat disco music changed to a slow ballad, she thought despairingly.

She tilted her head so that she could look at him. 'Why are you here?'

'I accepted an invitation to support the fund-raising event for a worthwhile charity.' His eyes met hers, and the glitter in his cobalt gaze sent molten heat surging through Isobel's veins. 'I also knew that you would be here,' he admitted. 'Your visit last week made me re-evaluate our situation and I concluded that you were right when you pointed out that there were many good things about our relationship.

She stared at him in confusion. 'So, what are you saying?'

'I'm saying that I've changed my mind about the divorce. I think we should give our marriage another chance.'

Isobel's shock gave way to anger. 'Just like that, you've *changed your mind*? You've got a nerve, Constantin.' It was typical of Constantin not to give an explanation but to expect her to simply accept his decision, and no doubt welcome him back into her life with open arms. 'Last week you were adamant that we should divorce. What happened that brought about this miraculous change of heart?' she asked sarcastically.

As she'd climbed into a taxi and driven away from the house in Grosvenor Square a week ago, she had vowed that her tears were the last she would shed over Constantin, and a clean break was the only sensible thing to do.

Suddenly it was all too much: the romantic music, the way Constantin was holding her close to his body so that she could feel the steady beat of his heart beneath his rib-cage and—she caught her breath as he pressed his hand into the small of her back—the hard ridge of his arousal jabbing into her thigh.

Her brain was sending out an urgent warning that she must step away from him, but desire was unfurling in the pit of her stomach and she was trapped by the sensual heat in his eyes as he bent his head towards her.

'This happened, Isabella,' he whispered against her lips. 'We are both prisoners of the incredible passion that exists between us—that has always existed since the moment we first set eyes on each other. When we met last week it was all we could do not to tear each other's clothes off. You weren't the only one to imagine making love on the gym mat,' he drawled in an amused voice as she opened her mouth to deny the erotic images that had crowded her mind when she had watched him working out.

'I don't want...' she began desperately, but the rest of her words were crushed beneath his mouth.

'Yes, *bella*, you do. And so do I,' Constantin told her firmly, and proceeded to demonstrate his mastery with a kiss that plumbed the depths of her soul as he took with-out mercy and demanded a response that Isobel was un-able to deny him.

CHAPTER FOUR

It HAD BEEN so long since Constantin had held her in his arms and kissed her with mind-blowing passion. The years of heartache fell away and Isobel trembled as he increased the pressure of his lips on hers, evoking a hunger inside her that had lain dormant until he had reawakened her desire with one look from his glittering blue eyes. A tiny part of her mind warned that she must resist the wanton warmth flooding through her body, but as Constantin pulled her even closer so that she could feel the hardness of his arousal press against her pelvis she gave up the fight with herself and succumbed to his sensual demands.

The voices of the party guests, the clink of glasses, faded, and there was only the music and the man who retained the key to her heart. She was barely aware of her feet touching the floor as Constantin swept her around the dance floor. His mouth did not leave hers, but the tenor of his kiss altered and became so sweetly beguiling that tears filled her eyes. She felt as if she had come home after a long journey, and as he deepened the kiss to something that was flagrantly sensual the ache of loneliness in her heart eased.

'Get a room!' Laughter followed the raucous comment, and Isobel was catapulted back to reality. She snatched her mouth from Constantin's and looked around wildly, horrified to find that they were the only couple on the dance floor, and they were being observed by an avid audience. The flash of a camera bulb brought home to her just what a fool she had been.

'The press are going to love this,' she muttered. She shot Constantin a sharp glance and felt infuriated by his amused expression. 'Pictures of us will be in the newspapers tomorrow. It won't take journalists long to discover that we are married, and they'll be curious to know why we've lived apart for the last two years.'

He shrugged. 'Why is that a problem? We'll simply explain that our relationship went through a difficult patch, but now we are back together.'

'But we're not!' Her eyes narrowed suspiciously. 'You set me up, didn't you? You deliberately made a…a public spectacle of us because for some reason you've suddenly decided that we should be reconciled.' She touched her mouth with shaking fingers and cringed when she felt its swollen contours. Why on earth had she allowed Constantin to kiss her, to *ravish* her, in such a public display?

Isobel's words came uncomfortably close to the truth for Constantin. His jaw hardened. 'I didn't hear you object when I kissed you, *cara*.'

Sickening shame swept through her at his soft taunt. Without another word she spun round and marched off the dance floor, but her high heels and long dress hampered her progress and Constantin's long stride easily kept pace with her as she walked out of the ballroom.

'Go away,' she demanded in a fierce undertone as she crossed the lobby. She was desperate to escape the curious glances of the other guests, and as she hurried down the hotel steps she prayed for a taxi to appear.

'My car is over there.' Constantin nodded towards the

sports car parked a little way down the street. 'I'll drive you home.'

'I'd rather wait for a taxi.' She was furious with him, but even more so with herself for allowing him to think she was a pushover. The bitter truth was that she did not dare risk being alone with him, she acknowledged.

The glare of a flashbulb momentarily blinded her, and her heart sank as a reporter whom she recognised from one of the tabloids thrust a microphone at her. 'Izzy, what's the story about you and Constantin De Severino?' The reporter looked curiously at Constantin. 'Have you split with Ryan Fellows, and, if so, what does it mean for the future of the Stone Ladies?'

How was it that a taxi never appeared when you wanted one? she thought, frustrated.

'Do you want to stand here and talk to this jerk, or do you want to go home?' Constantin spoke in her ear.

The arrival of two more reporters decided the matter for her and she quickly followed him over to his car and slid into the passenger seat. Seconds later, the powerful engine roared into life and Constantin accelerated away from the kerb.

'Is your address still the apartment block near Tower Bridge?' When she had left him, Constantin had offered to buy her a place of her own to live, but stubborn Isobel had refused his help and had proudly told him that she was able to pay for a flat with money she had earned from the Stone Ladies' first hit record. She had often accused him of being remote and cold during their marriage, but whenever he *had* tried to build bridges, her prickly independence had come to the fore and she had seemed reluctant to accept anything from him.

Isobel gave a nod of confirmation. She looked over her shoulder as a camera flashbulb shone through the car's rear window. 'See what you've done?' she rounded on him angrily. 'Our so-called relationship is going to feature in all the gossip columns. I'll have to warn Ryan,' she muttered. 'It might make things awkward.'

Constantin frowned. 'You mean it will be awkward when the press report that you are married to me at the same time as you've been carrying on with Fellows? My heart bleeds for you, *cara*,' he said sarcastically.

'I haven't been *carrying on* with Ryan. I've told you a hundred times that he and I are just friends.'

'You have never denied in interviews that the two of you are having an affair.' Constantin's hands tightened on the steering wheel as he recalled how Isobel had been glued to the guitarist's side at the party. 'It's obvious that you have a close relationship with him.'

Isobel's temper boiled over and she threw her hands up in the air in a gesture of angry frustration. '*Yes*, I admit I'm close to him. I love Ryan—but as a brother, not a lover. And he…he has tried to fill the place of the brother I lost.' She could not control the tremor in her voice.

Constantin shot her a puzzled look. 'I didn't know you had a brother. You've never spoken of him before. Your parents made no mention that they had a son when we visited them in Derbyshire.'

Isobel bit her lip as she remembered the one and only occasion that Constantin had met her parents. They hadn't attended the wedding because her father had been too unwell to travel to London. After she and Constantin had returned from their honeymoon, they had driven through the picturesque Peak District, before arriving at the far less attractive village of Eckerton, where rows of ugly terraced miners' cottages stood in the shadow of the abandoned colliery.

Her mother had been overawed by Constantin and kept

up a stream of nervous chatter as she had served tea from her best china. Her father had been his usual, dour self and had barely uttered a word. Looking around the tiny sitting room, with its threadbare carpet and old furniture, Isobel had shuddered to imagine what Constantin had made of her childhood home and her unwelcoming father. The visit had emphasised the huge social divide between her and the enigmatic Italian aristocrat she had married.

'They never speak of Simon. He died in an accident when he was fourteen and my father wouldn't allow my mother or me to mention his name, or even have photos of him on the wall. I suppose it was Dad's way of dealing with the tragedy of losing his son. You dealt with the loss of our baby in the same way, by refusing to talk about Arianna.' Her voice was husky with emotions that she was struggling to suppress.

A nerve flickered in Constantin's jaw, but he ignored her jibe. 'What happened to your brother?'

'It was a scorching hot summer's day and Simon and a group of his friends decided to swim in the reservoir near to where we lived. Actually, it was Ryan who suggested it and he has never forgiven himself. My brother was a daredevil, and while some of the boys went into the water and stayed close to the bank, Simon swam out of his depth. It's thought that he had an attack of cramp. Ryan said that he was fine one minute but then he suddenly started shouting for help. By the time Ryan had swum out to him, Simon had disappeared below the surface. Somehow Ryan managed to grab hold of him and drag him back to the shore. He tried to resuscitate him, but he was unable to save him…and Simon died.'

It was difficult to talk past the lump in her throat. 'Afterwards, Ryan became severely depressed. He felt guilty that Simon had swum in the reservoir. But what happened wasn't Ryan's fault. Simon always pushed the boundaries, and it was typical of him to have swum out of his depth. I didn't blame Ryan. He and my brother were best friends and Simon's death forged a bond between us that will always remain. But friendship is *all* there is between me and Ryan. He is in love with his girlfriend and he and Emily are planning to get married.'

'If that's true, why didn't the pair of you scotch the rumours of an affair?'

She shrugged. 'We told the truth when we said that we are good friends. The press decided that there must be more to our relationship, and we didn't deny the rumours because, while attention was on us, it allowed Ryan's girlfriend to escape the media's interest.' Isobel hesitated. 'I guess it is okay to tell you, as Ryan is going to make a public announcement in the next day or so. Emily's father is a well-known politician and a member of the government. If it had become known that Ryan was dating her, they would have been constantly followed by the paparazzi.'

'So, being a loyal friend, you allowed the speculation about your relationship with Fellows to continue,' Constantin said grimly. 'You did not care if I heard the rumours that my wife was involved with another man. Didn't you think you owed *me,* your husband, your loyalty?'

'Not when hardly a week went by without a picture of you with a different beautiful woman in the newspapers. How dare you accuse me of disloyalty when you paraded the members of your...your *harem* in public?'

Isobel jerked her eyes from him and stared out of the car window, breathing hard. She was not going to admit how hurt she had felt when she'd seen pictures of Constantin with other women. If she was scrupulously honest with herself, she had not denied to the press the rumours of an affair with Ryan because she had hoped that Constantin would realise that she wasn't pining for him.

The simmering tension inside the car stretched her nerves to snapping point, and she felt relieved when he parked outside her apartment building.

'Thanks for the lift.' She glanced at his handsome profile and bit her lip. 'I don't understand why you said you've changed your mind about the divorce. Separating permanently is the only sensible thing to do. Our marriage is well and truly over. The truth is that it would have been better if we had never met,' she said in a low tone.

His head shot round and his blue eyes glittered fiercely. 'You don't mean that.'

If they had never met, she would never have held her tiny baby girl in her arms. Arianna had never lived in the world, but she lived on in Isobel's heart.

'We were good together.' Constantin's husky accent caused her stomach muscles to contract.

'In bed!' She gave a hollow laugh. 'But marriage has to have more than sex for it to work. Trust, for instance. You resented my friendships with the other members of the band. That's clear from the way you were so ready to believe I was having an affair with Ryan. Sometimes I had the feeling that you wished you could lock me away in a tower, away from all other human contact.' Her voice shook. 'And yet you were so remote and cold towards me that you can hardly blame me for wanting to be with my friends.'

An image flashed into Constantin's mind of his father and stepmother, and inside his head he heard Lorena's impassioned cry.

I feel smothered, Franco. You're jealous of my friends, and of any man I happen to glance at. You are even jealous of your own son!

Dio! Had Isobel felt smothered by *him,* just as Lorena had by his father? He had tried to fight his possessive feelings and the dark jealousy that he feared he had inherited from his father, but in doing so he had come across as cold and uncaring.

Isobel got out of the car and Constantin watched her walk towards the front door of the apartment building. She was exquisitely desirable in her gold dress that clung to her slender figure. 'Our marriage is well and truly over,' she had insisted. He frowned as he thought of his uncle's threat to appoint his cousin Maurio as Chairman of DSE.

Nothing was going to stop him from claiming the position that was rightfully his.

Growling a curse, he flung open the car door and strode after his wife.

He caught up with her as she stood on the top step and searched in her bag for her door key. 'Invite me in, Isabella, so that we can talk.'

'We have nothing to talk about.' Isobel located her key in the bottom of her bag and gripped it tightly. Her composure was near to breaking point, and she was desperate to reach her flat before she did something stupid like fling her arms around Constantin and beg him to hold her close and never let her go. Her eyes were drawn to his, and the sensual heat in his gaze made her tremble. 'We're no good for each other,' she whispered.

'Not true, *tesorino.*'

His use of the affectionate term that he had often spoken to her at the beginning of their marriage undermined her defences, and she was unprepared when he slid his arm around her waist and pulled her towards him.

His dark head descended and he claimed her lips, kissing her with a fiery passion that lit a flame inside Isobel. *This* had always been good for both of them, she acknowledged. Sex—white-hot and wickedly erotic! She had been inexperienced when she had met Constantin but he had discovered her secret desires and had used his knowledge mercilessly to take her repeatedly to a sensual nirvana.

She was melting inside. Heat flooded between her thighs and her body was impatient for more, *more* of the exquisite pleasure promised by the bold sweep of Constantin's tongue inside her mouth. She wanted him. She would always want him, she thought despairingly. But he was no good for her.

He traced his lips over her cheek and the slender arch of her neck. 'Invite me in,' he murmured in her ear. 'Let me remind you of how good we are together.'

'*No!*' Determination not to take a path that she knew would lead to heartache gave her the strength to push him away. 'Sex isn't the solution. In our case, it was the problem,' she said shakily. 'We were drawn together by desire, and if we had just had an affair it would probably have burned out as quickly as your affairs with other women. When I fell pregnant you felt obliged to marry me.' She smiled sadly. 'I'll never forget Arianna, but it's time we both moved on with our lives, Constantin.'

That was easy for Isobel to say, he thought grimly. The Stone Ladies were hugely successful, but his career at DSE, his *life* for heaven's sake, was about to go into free-fall unless he could persuade her to come back to him. He didn't doubt that he *could* persuade her back into his bed. He had felt her tremble when he'd kissed her and knew she shared his hunger. If he drew her back into his arms, he was confident that she would offer little resistance. But his conscience stayed him. Her clear hazel eyes reflected her confusion. Undoubtedly she desired him. But for her, it wasn't enough, and Constantin knew he was no more

capable of satisfying her emotional needs now than he had
been two years ago.

As Isobel shut the front door on Constantin and walked
across the lobby to the lift, she assured herself that she was
relieved he had not tried to detain her. She knew she had
been right to turn down having sex with him, but her body
did not agree and the dragging ache in the pit of her stomach was almost as bad as the ache in her heart.

'Evening, Miss Blake,' the concierge greeted her. 'The
parcel that you said you were expecting to be delivered
didn't arrive today.'

'I'll have to phone the courier tomorrow. Goodnight,
Albert.'

As the lift carried her to the fourth floor she focused her
thoughts on the missing parcel, the friend she'd arranged
to meet for lunch the following day, anything but Constantin. Her life was good the way it was. Why alter the status
quo and allow him to turn her world upside down again?

She had no idea why he had suddenly decided that he
didn't want a divorce. There was a time when she would
have immediately given in to him, in the desperate hope
that perhaps he did have feelings for her. She had been
pathetic, Isobel thought grimly. But after she'd had the
miscarriage Constantin had let her down badly by failing to support her. She was no longer in awe of him, and,
although she had a sneaking suspicion that she would always be in love with him, she understood that he was an
ordinary mortal—a complex man, certainly, but he had
his faults just as she did. Unfortunately she simply could
not believe that they would be able to resolve the differences that had driven them apart.

The lift stopped and the doors opened. The front door
of her flat was a couple of hundred yards along the corridor. Isobel glanced down to select the appropriate key

on the key ring she was holding, when something, a sixth sense, warned her that she wasn't alone.

'Who's there...?' She looked over her shoulder down the brightly lit, empty corridor, and cursed her overactive imagination.

'Hello, Izzy.'

She spun round, and her heart cannoned into her ribs as a man stepped out from a shadowed recess and walked towards her. She did not know him, but she had recognised his voice. 'David?'

He was shortish, thinnish—nondescript. For a moment Isobel wondered why she had been so worried about this very ordinary-looking, middle-aged man.

'I knew you must remember me.' He smiled pleasantly. 'You felt the connection between us when we met at a Stone Ladies concert. We were together in a previous world and we will be together again in the next one, my darling.'

The strange expression in his eyes sent a frisson of fear through Isobel, and she sensed that beneath his outwardly benign manner he was a mass of nervous energy and excitement that she found unnerving.

'I bought these for you.' It was only then that she registered he was holding a cardboard box. Something in the man's demeanour told Isobel to remain calm and play along with him. Hoping he did not notice that her hands were shaking, she took the box from him and opened the lid. The sickly-sweet scent of oriental lilies that pervaded the air was so strong she almost gagged.

Feeling that he expected a response from her, she murmured, 'They're lovely.' She stared at the white flowers and repressed a shudder.

'You remind me of a lily, beautiful and pure.' David's voice suddenly changed. 'I thought you were pure, until I watched you kissing another man tonight.'

Isobel swallowed. 'You were there…at the party?'

'Where else would I be but with you, my angel? You belong to *me*, Izzy, and no other man shall try to steal you from me.'

Isobel tensed as the stalker took a step closer. Her key was digging into the palm of her hand and she glanced along the corridor, trying to estimate the distance to her front door, wondering what her chances were of getting past David and making it to the safety of her flat. She did not dare risk it. Although he was not physically imposing, she sensed that he was stronger than he looked. His pale eyes were watching her intently and the manic gleam in his gaze chilled her blood.

'Come away with me.' His voice hardened when she shook her head. 'It is time that you and I left this earthly world.'

The hell it was! Isobel's survival instinct kicked in. She threw the box of lilies at the stalker's face before she spun round and raced down the corridor. Of course the flowers were not a substantial weapon, but her actions had surprised him and given her a vital few seconds' head start. She heard his angry shout, heard his footsteps as he chased after her, but she resisted the temptation to look behind her as she reached the lift, which was thankfully still waiting at the fourth floor. She hit the button to open the doors. Come on, *come on!* she pleaded as they slid apart agonisingly slowly. She heard heavy breathing close to her, and she screamed as a hand grabbed her bare shoulder.

In desperation she rammed her elbow hard into the stalker's stomach. He groaned and released his grip. She fell into the lift and held down the button to close the doors. Only then did she look round and glimpse his crazed expression before the metal doors obliterated him from view.

As the lift descended she tried to marshal her thoughts.

How had David gained entry to the apartment building? The concierge always vetted visitors, and some of her friends had joked that it would be easier to break into the Bank of England than slip past Albert. Reaction was setting in, and she felt sick as the lift arrived at ground level.

'Miss Blake?' The concierge looked up from his desk. 'Is something the matter?'

Isobel did not reply. Through the glass doors of the building she saw Constantin's tall figure illuminated by the street lamp. He was not looking in her direction as he lowered his mobile phone from his ear and walked towards his car. Impelled by an instinct she did not even try to question, she flew across the lobby.

'Constantin—*wait*!'

The sound of Isobel's voice drew Constantin's thoughts from the phone conversation he'd just had with the finance director at the New York office. The East Coast of the USA was five hours behind England, and Jeff Zuckerman had seemed blithely unconcerned that it was midnight in London.

Constantin glanced round and dismissed work issues from his mind when he saw Isobel running towards him. Her blonde hair spilled over her shoulders and he felt a tightening in his groin as he watched the bounce of her firm breasts as she ran.

'Have you changed your mind about inviting me up to your flat, Isabella?' His smile disappeared along with his sense of pleasurable anticipation when he saw the look of terror on her face. *'Santa Madre!'* He caught her as she literally threw herself into his arms and held her tightly as tremors shook her body. 'What the hell…?'

'He was waiting for me outside my flat. He's so weird.' Her words were jumbled and incoherent. 'He wanted me to go with him, and he gave me funeral flowers.'

Constantin cupped her chin and tilted her face to his. '*Who* was waiting for you, *cara*?'

'David…the man who has been stalking me.' Isobel released her breath on a ragged sigh as the fear drained out of her. She felt safe with Constantin. It did not even occur to her that her blind trust in him revealed perhaps too much of her deepest feelings.

'*Stalking you?*' Constantin's eyes glittered fiercely. 'Do you mean to say that your safety has been threatened by this man? For how long has this been going on? Why didn't you tell me? I would have arranged security measures, hired a bodyguard to protect you.'

'I don't need a bodyguard.' The stark terror that had gripped Isobel when David had confronted her outside her flat seemed like an overreaction now, and she felt embarrassed that she had involved Constantin. The determined set of his jaw warned her that he would not let up until she had told him everything.

'I've been getting nuisance calls from a man called David for a few months. I've changed my landline number and mobile-phone number, but somehow he managed to get hold of my new numbers.

'He said we had met at a Stone Ladies concert…but I don't remember meeting him. He phoned me just before I went on stage tonight and said that he would be watching me tonight.' She bit her lip. 'I spent all evening wondering if one of the guests was the stalker. When I stepped out of the lift after you'd brought me home he appeared in the corridor.'

The memory of David's wild-eyed expression sent a shiver through Isobel. 'He said it was time that he and I left this earthly world. I'm not sure what he meant.' She hadn't waited around to find out, she thought, and shivered again.

A nerve flickering in Constantin's jaw was the only

indication of his barely restrained fury. Give him two minutes alone with the guy who got his kicks out of frightening Isobel, and the stalker wouldn't be able to walk, let alone *stalk* a defenceless woman, he thought grimly. The glimmer of tears in Isobel's eyes and the realisation that she was not nearly as calm as she was pretending to be stopped him from rushing up to the fourth floor to look for the intruder.

He pulled his phone from his pocket. 'I'll call the police.'

'I'll do it,' Isobel said shakily. 'I have a direct number to report any incidents with the stalker.'

The terror she had felt when David had accosted her was fading, and she felt angry with herself for not telling the man to get lost. He was probably a harmless overenthusiastic fan, she told herself, although the wild expression in his eyes suggested the possibility that he had mental-health issues.

She remained in the lobby with Albert while Constantin went up to the fourth floor. The concierge was adamant that no one fitting the stalker's description had entered the apartment building, and he was deeply upset when he explained that the CCTV system had developed a fault and was due to be repaired the next day.

The police arrived to take a statement. An officer joined Constantin in searching every floor of the apartment block, but all they found were a few white lily petals. 'The intruder must have somehow accessed the building by the fire escape,' the police officer in charge told Isobel. 'It's a pity for us and lucky for him that the CCTV is down or we would have his face on film.'

Because the stalker had not assaulted her, or made a specific threat to harm her, there was little more that the police could do except to advise Isobel on measures she should take to ensure her personal safety. While she was giving her statement she saw Constantin walk out of the flat. She assumed he felt he had done all that he could to help her, but she wished he had stayed a few minutes longer so that she could have thanked him.

After the police had gone, she purposefully concentrated on the mundane tasks of removing her make-up and washing her face, before exchanging the gold evening gown for her favourite item of nightwear—namely one of Constantin's tee shirts that she had taken with her when she had called time on their marriage. Despite her best efforts not to think about the stalker, the memory of his strangeness lingered in her mind, and although she knew she was being ridiculous she checked inside the wardrobe and the hall cupboard to make sure he had not somehow gained entry to her flat.

There was no question of trying to sleep. She would make a milky drink and watch TV for a while. Walking into the sitting room, she stopped dead and drew a sharp breath.

'How did you get in here?'

CHAPTER FIVE

CONSTANTIN HAD DISCARDED his tuxedo and tie and unfastened the top buttons on his shirt to reveal the bronzed skin of his throat, and a few curling black chest hairs. He was leaning back against the sofa cushions, his long legs stretched out in front of him and his arms crossed behind his head in an attitude of indolent relaxation that was far removed from the stomach-squirming tension that gripped Isobel as she stared at his handsome face.

'I saw you leave and assumed you had gone home.'

'I went to get something from my car and borrowed your door key so that I could let myself back into the flat. You were talking to the police officer, and I guess you didn't notice me go into the kitchen.' He nodded to the cup and saucer on the coffee table. 'I made you a cup of tea.'

Isobel was less interested in the tea than the holdall on the floor by his feet.

'I always keep an overnight bag in the car,' he explained, following her gaze, 'in case I decide to stay away from home for some reason.'

No doubt 'some reason' meant an invitation from a woman to spend the night together. Isobel felt a shaft of pain at the idea of him making love to one of the numerous gorgeous females he had been photographed with in the newspapers during the past two years. Jealousy burned hotly inside her—another unwanted emotion to add to the list of unpleasant experiences tonight, she thought grimly.

The discernible gleam of amusement in his eyes was the last straw. She gave him a tight smile. 'I hope you find somewhere comfortable to stay tonight.'

He laughed softly and patted the cushion. 'I'm sure your sofa is very comfortable. I'll let you know in the morning.'

'There's absolutely no reason for you to stay.' Constantin made her feel more unnerved than David did, albeit in a different way, Isobel thought ruefully. 'I'll put the double lock on the front door, and, unless the stalker is Spiderman, he won't be able to climb through a window on the fourth floor.'

Constantin merely gave her a lazy smile. 'Humour me, hmm, *cara*?'

'This is ridiculous. I don't want you here.' Her tone was unknowingly desperate. He unsettled her way too much for *her* comfort.

He stood up and strolled towards her. Isobel sensed that beneath his laid-back manner he was utterly determined to have his own way. 'If I leave, I will demand the immediate return of my personal property, which you took without my consent.'

'What personal property...?' She stiffened as he took hold of the hem of her tee shirt, *his* tee shirt. The shirt reached to just below her hips, and the light brush of his fingers against her thigh felt as if a flame had burned her flesh. Her breath caught in her throat as he slowly began to raise the hem.

'You really want this old shirt back?' she said in a choked voice.

'I particularly like this shirt.'

If he continued to lift the tee shirt up he would reveal her bare breasts. She gave a little shiver—half excitement and half apprehension—as she imagined him stripping her and cupping her breasts in his hands. She would be a fool to take this route again, but when had she ever behaved sensibly where Constantin was concerned?

Constantin was tempted to whip the shirt over her head and then pull her close, trace his hands over her body to rediscover every delicious dip and curve before taking the same path with his mouth. It was how they had always communicated best, two bodies joined and moving in perfect accord. The suspicious brightness in Isobel's eyes warned him that her emotions were on a knife edge. The stalker had scared her more than she had admitted to him or the police, and what she needed from him now was not passion but compassion.

'Stop fighting me, Isabella,' he said gently. 'You know you won't win. Sit down and drink your tea before it gets cold.'

If she didn't feel like a wrung-out rag she would tell him where to go, Isobel thought. But she must be suffering from delayed shock or something because her legs refused to support her and she sat down abruptly. She wished she had chosen an armchair when Constantin joined her on the sofa, and she sipped her tea, trying to ignore her awareness of him.

'I was looking at your photos,' he remarked, glancing at the montage of photographs on the wall.

'I've kept a pictorial record of every city where the Stone Ladies have performed.' She recognised his ploy to keep her mind off the stalker and went along with it. 'Often we only play at a venue for one night before moving on to the next town but I have a list of places I'd like to go back and visit properly.'

'I've always wondered about the name of the band,' he

mused. 'Why did you call yourselves Stone Ladies when two of the band members are male?'

She smiled, and Constantin was glad to see evidence that some of her tension had eased. 'The name refers to an ancient stone circle on the moors near to the village in Derbyshire where we all grew up. The legend says that a group of ladies from the royal court loved to dance so much that they risked the wrath of the king by dancing on the Sabbath, and as a penalty they were turned to stone.

'Our group, Carly, Ben, Ryan and I, felt a lot of sympathy for the ladies because we had similar difficulties playing our music when we wanted to. None of us were allowed to practise at home.' She sighed. 'My father thought I should be studying, not singing, and Ryan's father expected him to spend all his spare time working on the family farm. Our parents couldn't understand how much our music meant to us. I had countless arguments with my father, who thought music was a waste of time and that I should focus on passing my exams and getting a proper job.'

The bleakness in her voice caught Constantin's attention. 'Your father must be proud of you now that you and the band are so successful?'

'Dad died a few months ago.' Isobel shrugged. 'He wasn't interested in my music or how well the band was doing. I couldn't live up to the expectations he'd had of me.'

'What do you mean?'

'My brother was Dad's favourite. Simon was really clever at school and had planned to go to university and train to be a doctor. My father was so proud of his son and he was devastated when Simon died. I'm afraid I was no substitute. I wasn't interested in academic subjects and Dad ridiculed my dreams of making a living as a musician. I couldn't be the person my father wanted me to be.'

She glanced at Constantin. 'When we married, I couldn't be the person *you* wanted me to be, either,' she said flatly.

He frowned. 'I did not have expectations of you. When we married I thought, *hoped* that you would be happy to fulfil the role of my wife.' His face darkened. 'But it wasn't enough for you.'

'What you wanted was a glamorous hostess who would organise dinner parties and impress your guests with her witty conversation and sublime sense of style,' Isobel said bitterly. 'I failed miserably as a hostess, and the designer clothes I wore were not *my* style, they were what you decided I should wear.'

'I admit there were occasions when your hippy-chick clothes were not suitable. DSE is synonymous with style and superb quality, and I needed my wife to help me to represent those qualities. The tie-dyed, flowers-in-your-hair look was not a good advertisement for the company,' he said sardonically.

'But it was *me*. The hippy look, as you call it, was *my* style. You didn't object to the way I dressed when we first met.'

He had not taken much notice of her clothes because he had been more interested in getting her out of them as quickly as possible, Constantin acknowledged cynically.

'You were determined to mould me into the perfect wife, in the same way that my father had tried to mould me into the perfect daughter,' Isobel rounded on him, her eyes flashing. 'But neither you nor my dad were interested in me as a person. And like my dad, you never showed any interest in my music or encouraged my singing career.'

His mouth tightened. 'When we were first married, you were not hell-bent on pursuing a music career. You've said yourself that we were happy living in London at the time, and you gave the impression that you were content to be a wife and soon-to-be mother to our child.'

His words sliced through Isobel's heart. 'But I didn't get the chance to be a mother.' Her voice was raw. 'It's true that in the early months of our marriage I was absorbed in my pregnancy,' and in *you*, she thought to herself, remembering the man she had married. Constantin had been a charming and attentive husband and she had let herself believe that her happiness would last.

'After we lost Arianna I was left with nothing. For reasons I didn't understand, you had become a remote stranger and I felt that I hardly knew you. All I had was my music. Writing songs and singing with the band were my only comfort in those terrible days when I sometimes wondered if I would go mad with grief.'

She swallowed the lump in her throat. Revisiting the past was always painful, but tonight, when her emotions were ragged after her scare with the stalker, being bombarded with memories was unendurable.

'This conversation is pointless,' she told Constantin as she jerked to her feet. 'We should have had it two years ago, but we didn't and now it's too late. One of the reasons I left was because you refused to talk about the things that mattered, like the miscarriage. You might have been able to forget about our baby but I felt desolate and unsupported by you.'

He leapt up and raked a hand through his hair. 'Perhaps we might have talked more if you had spent more time at home. I lost count of the number of times that I arrived home from work to be told by Whittaker that you were out with your friends.' His blue eyes glittered as cold and hard as sapphires. 'Don't put all the blame on me, Isobel. We couldn't work on the problems with our marriage because you were never there.'

She shook her head. 'It was you who was absent from our relationship. I don't mean in a physical sense, but on an emotional level you had distanced yourself from me. My friends gave me what you seemed incapable of giving—emotional support. You never allowed us the opportunity to *share* our feelings about the loss of our daughter. Even now, whenever I mention Arianna you clam up.'

'What's the point in going over and over it?' Constantin saw Isobel flinch at his raised voice and knew she was startled by his violent outburst, as well she might be, he thought grimly. He *never* lost control.

Only once in his life had he seen his father show emotion—on the day of Constantin's mother's funeral. He had been eight years old, and had managed to get through the church service and watching his mother's coffin being lowered into her grave without crying because he knew it was what was expected of him. 'De Severino men never cry,' his father had told him many times. But later, on his way up to bed, Constantin had heard a noise from his father's study, a sound like a wounded animal in great pain that had chilled his blood.

Peeping round the door, he had been startled to see his father lying curled up on the floor, sobbing uncontrollably. Franco's outpouring of grief had been shocking and terrifying to witness for an impressionable young boy. Constantin had felt sad that his mother had died, but his father's agony had scared him. At the age of eight he had decided that he never wanted to feel such pain. He never wanted to love so intensely that love's dark side, loss, would bring him to his knees.

He dragged his mind from the past and found Isobel staring at him with a bitter expression in her eyes.

She might have guessed that Constantin would not show

even a flicker of response to their daughter's name, Isobel thought angrily.

'You really are made of stone, aren't you? On the surface you are a man who has everything: looks, wealth, power, but you're an empty shell, Constantin. Inside, you are an emotional void and I actually feel sorry for you.'

Her words rankled. What did she know about the emotions he kept buried deep inside him? What did she really know about *him*? But the fact that she did not know him was his fault, taunted a voice inside Constantin's head. He had not dared open up the Pandora's box of his emotions to Isobel for fear of what he might reveal about himself.

He looked at her wearing the baggy tee shirt that disguised her shape, and was infuriated by the realisation that even if she wore a sack that covered her from head to toe he would still want her more than he had ever wanted any other woman. Goaded by the accusation in her eyes, and by the knowledge that he *had* failed her when she'd had the miscarriage, he shot out his hand and caught hold of her wrist.

'I don't need your pity, *mia bella*. There's only one thing I ever needed from you,' he told her, pulling her towards him. 'You keep saying that you wished we had talked more, but the truth is neither of us wanted to waste time talking because we were so damned hungry for each other.'

'Sex would not have solved our problems,' Isobel cried, panic filling her as she tried vainly to break free from him. In truth, his grip on her wrist was not very tight. It was his grip on her heart that prevented her escape.

As she watched his dark head descend she wondered if, when their marriage had been falling apart, sex might have been a solution that would have given them a way to communicate again. But ever since Constantin had suggested that they make love two months after the miscarriage, and she had rejected him, a chasm had opened up between them and he had not approached her again.

At the time she had been angry with him for what she had perceived as his lack of support. But perhaps he had been trying to reach out to her, she thought with hindsight. In bed they had always understood each other perfectly and their desire had been mutually explosive and fulfilling.

While her mind had once again been focused on the past, she had forgotten the danger of her present situation. When had Constantin unclamped his fingers from her wrist and slid his arm around her waist? Her breath rushed from her lungs as he tugged her against him, making her agonisingly aware of every hard muscle and sinew on his whipcord body as he locked his other arm around her. Her eyes flew to his face, but her demand for him to release her died in her throat as his mouth came down on hers and he made demands of his own, his kiss hot and potent and utterly ruthless in its mastery.

He moved one hand down to clasp her bottom, jerking her pelvis into burning contact with the solid ridge of his arousal. She found his dominance shamefully thrilling. Beneath his civilised façade Constantin was all primitive, passionate male. It had been so long since she had felt him inside her. The thought weakened her resolve to resist him and when he slipped his hand beneath the hem of her shirt and stroked his fingers over her stomach and ribcage, she held her breath and silently willed him to move his hand higher and touch her breasts.

He had always had the ability to read her mind, and when he brushed his thumb pad across one swollen nipple she gave a choked cry. He took advantage of her parted lips to push his tongue into her mouth. Isobel's senses were swamped by him. The scent of his cologne was achingly familiar. She remembered the first time he had made love to her; she had been overwhelmed by the responses he had drawn from her untutored body, and afterwards she had pressed her face into his neck and tasted salt on his sweat-sheened skin.

He transferred his hand to her other breast and rolled her nipple between his fingers, causing a shaft of exquisite sensation to shoot through her. With a soft moan she melted against him and tipped her head back as he traced his lips down her throat. Constantin pushed the neck of the too-big tee shirt over her shoulder and trailed kisses along her collarbone.

'*Mio Dio!*' His savage imprecation shattered the sensual mist as he stared at the livid red mark he had uncovered. 'What happened to your shoulder?'

Isobel had noticed the beginnings of the bruise while she had been undressing for bed, but when Constantin had kissed her she had forgotten everything but her need for him. 'He...the stalker caught hold of me as I ran for the lift, but I managed to get away from him.' She shivered as her mind flashed back to those terrifying moments before the lift doors had closed, when she had turned and seen David's face contorted with fury. She had tried to convince herself that he had meant her no harm, but the memory of his wild-eyed expression was stuck in her mind.

Constantin glimpsed the fear in Isobel's hazel eyes and felt a surge of anger at the stalker, but also at himself. *She had run to him for safety.* He choked back a mirthless laugh. The bitter truth was that, far from being safe with him, she was innocently unaware of the danger he posed to her. His—as it turned out—unfounded jealousy of Ryan Fellows was proof that he had inherited a dark side to his nature from his father. The monster that had been inside Franco De Severino also lived within Constantin and the only way to control the beast was to avoid awakening it.

So what the hell was he doing coming on to Isobel?

He stepped away from her and raked an unsteady hand through his hair. 'I'm going to stay here tonight,' he said roughly. She could argue all she liked, but the welt on her shoulder was a stark reminder of the terror she must have felt when the stalker had confronted her outside her flat.

He frowned as he remembered something she had said after the attack. 'What did you mean when you said that the stalker gave you funeral flowers?'

'Oh, the white lilies.' Isobel wondered if she had overreacted when the stalker had presented her with the flowers, and she felt silly that she'd mentioned them to Constantin. 'I don't suppose David meant anything sinister, but I've always hated lilies since my brother's funeral. The church was filled with them. My strongest memory of that awful day was the sickly perfume of lilies.' She shuddered. 'Since then I've always considered it the scent of death.'

'I had no idea you disliked them,' Constantin said slowly. He remembered that he had taken a bouquet of lilies to Isobel in the hospital after she'd had the miscarriage. Of course, giving her flowers had been a totally inadequate gesture when she had lost their baby, but he hadn't known what else to do. He had felt helpless to comfort her in her grief. Standing outside her room listening to her sobbing had ripped his heart to shreds. But from boyhood he had learned from his father to suppress his emotions. He had been unable to respond to Isobel the way she had needed him to, and was incapable of voicing his own devastation at the loss of their baby girl.

When he had found the bouquet of lilies had been stuffed into the rubbish bin he had taken it as a sign that Isobel blamed him for the miscarriage. The trip to Italy had been his idea, but it had been disastrous for so many reasons, he remembered grimly. She had rejected the flowers and it had felt as though she were rejecting him. But now it occurred to him that perhaps she had thrown the lilies away because she'd been unable to cope with the sad memories they evoked of her brother.

He glanced at her pale face and then at his watch, shocked to see that it was two a.m. 'You'd better try and get some sleep. You're safe, and no one can hurt you tonight.'

Isobel stifled a bitter laugh. Was Constantin unaware that his abrupt rejection a few moments ago was a hundred times more painful than the injury the stalker had inflicted on her? His chiselled features revealed no emotion. Clearly he had been unaffected when he had kissed her and maybe had even been amused by her eager response to him.

She flushed, remembering how her body had betrayed her, and an idea crept into her mind that perhaps he had deliberately set out to humiliate her. Suddenly it was all too much. *He* was too much. She did not want him here in her flat, but she knew him well enough to realise that she would be wasting her breath if she asked him to leave. 'You'll find a spare pillow and blanket in the hall cupboard,' she told him, proud that her steady voice did not reveal her inner turmoil.

Without sparing him another glance, she walked down the hall to her bedroom and shut the door, wishing that she could lock it. But the likelihood that Constantin would enter her bedroom was zero, she reminded herself, thinking of how he had pulled back from making love to her. Reaction to the night's events was setting in and she felt bone weary. Her last thought as she lay back on the pillows was that it was too late to recapture the fleeting happiness they had once shared.

* * *

Isobel's sofa was probably very comfortable as a sofa, but as a makeshift bed for a man of six feet four it failed to provide a good night's sleep. But perhaps his restless night could not be entirely blamed on the sofa, Constantin acknowledged fairly as he stood up and ran a hand over the dark stubble covering his jaw. The insistent throb of his arousal had kept him awake and his mind had been active as he had replayed the events of the previous night.

Wearily he slid his hand from his jaw and rubbed the back of his neck. There had been some truth in Isobel's accusation that he hadn't understood how she had sought comfort from her grief in music and song writing. He had been jealous that she had turned to the company of her friends from the band, but his inability to express his own feelings about the loss of their baby meant that he had failed to support her when she had needed him.

He glanced at the photos on the wall of the Stone Ladies performing at various venues around the world. Despite the tensions in their marriage he had not expected her to leave him. Isobel had made a new life for herself, and the pictures seemed to mock him with the message that she did not need him—financially, emotionally or any other way.

But she had needed him last night, Constantin mused. It was significant that when she had escaped from the stalker, she hadn't asked the concierge to call the police, but instead had run straight to *him* for help. When he had driven her home from the party she had been adamant that their marriage was over, but after her terrifying confrontation with the stalker she had rushed into *his* arms, desperate for his protection.

The way she had responded to him when he had kissed her was further proof that she was not immune to him as she would like him to think.

Constantin's jaw hardened. His uncle's threat to hand the role of Chairman of DSE to his cousin Maurio was nothing short of blackmail, but to claim his birthright he knew he had no option but to play Alonso's game. The hard truth was that he needed to show his uncle that he was reconciled with his wife. The incident with the stalker had given him an ideal opportunity to get close to Isobel and persuade her to give their marriage another chance. Only he would know that the reconciliation would be temporary, he thought grimly.

CHAPTER SIX

MEMORIES OF THE previous evening snapped into Isobel's mind the second she opened her eyes. Amazingly, she had slept soundly and not dreamed about the stalker, but now that she was awake she remembered David's strange air of nervy excitement, which had quickly turned to anger when she had refused to go away with him.

She rolled over in bed and squinted against the bright sunshine pouring in through the open curtains, feeling puzzled because she distinctly remembered pulling them shut last night.

'I apologise for waking you.' Constantin's deep voice spoke from the doorway and Isobel's heart performed a somersault as she watched him walk towards the bed. He placed the cup of tea he had made her on the bedside table. It was unfair that even after spending the night sleeping on the sofa he still looked as if he had stepped from the pages of a glossy magazine, she thought wryly as she studied his superbly tailored light grey suit, expensive white shirt and blue tie that matched the vivid blue of his eyes.

She ran a hand through her tousled hair, feeling self-conscious that her face was scrubbed of make-up and flushed with sleep. 'That's okay. It's time I was up anyway.' The clock showed that it was nine-thirty. 'I don't usually sleep in this late.'

He shrugged. 'You had an eventful night.'

The glint in his gaze made Isobel think that he was remembering, as she was, the passion that had flared between them when he had kissed her. He could have taken her to bed last night, she acknowledged, embarrassed to recall how eagerly she had responded to him. Hell, he could have tumbled her down onto the sofa and possessed her fast and hard with no foreplay and she would have let him. But he hadn't taken what she had offered so freely, and that made his next words all the more surprising.

'I have to go to the New York office today. I would cancel, but a problem has arisen which requires my personal attention. I want you to come with me. The stalker is still at large,' he continued, predicting her question *why* before she voiced it. 'The police don't have much to go on to help them find the man, but until they do I don't think you should be alone.'

He sat down on the edge of the bed, and his nearness immediately sent Isobel's pulse-rate soaring. He had obviously taken a shower in her small bathroom, and the distinctive spicy fragrance of his aftershave teased her senses. Her breath became trapped in her throat when he lifted a strand of her hair and coiled it around his finger.

'My concern for your safety is not the only reason I would like you to accompany me to the States,' he murmured. 'How about us starting over, Isabella? Once my business is finished in New York we could spend a few days in the city and get to know each other again.'

His sexy smile was almost Isobel's undoing. Her heart had leapt at his words, and there was a part of her that desperately wanted to agree to his suggestion. But she had noticed that he did not smile with his eyes, and she sensed an air of reserve beneath his charming manner that chilled her. Something about his sudden U-turn over the divorce made her suspicious, and her voice was cool when she answered him.

'Why?'

Constantin was thrown by the question. It occurred to him that this new, more self-assured Isobel was no longer besotted with him as she had been when he had married her. If he was to stand any chance of persuading her to agree to a reconciliation he would have to be more open with her.

'I accept that many of the problems which led to us separating were due to my reluctance to talk about my feelings, and in particular about losing our baby.' He visualised Arianna, so tiny and perfect, so still and lifeless, and his heart clenched. 'As a child, I was not encouraged to show my emotions, and the habit carried through into my adult life,' he said gruffly.

Isobel bit her lip as she recalled her feeling of desolation after the miscarriage. 'Your attitude towards me changed after I lost the baby,' she said huskily. 'I couldn't get close to you, and you never wanted to talk about what had happened. I couldn't understand why. At the beginning of our marriage we were happy. We spent time together, and not only in bed,' she said quickly when his eyes glinted.

She took a steadying breath. 'Losing our baby was devastating. But things had changed—you had changed—*before* I had the miscarriage. In Italy, when we stayed at Casa Celeste, you...you were suddenly not the man I had married.'

Her mind flew to the exquisite villa on the shores of Lake Albano, close to Castel Gandolfo—the Pope's summer residence. Casa Celeste had been the De Severino family's ancestral home for four hundred years, but Constantin preferred to live in a modern penthouse apartment in the centre of Rome, or, when he was in London, the house in Grosvenor Square.

When Isobel had first visited Casa Celeste she had felt overawed by its elegant façade, and its myriad bedrooms and bathrooms and grand reception rooms with their sumptuous frescoed walls and ceilings. She had commented that the house seemed like a museum, and Constantin had explained that his father had been an avid collector of art and antiques.

Studying the portrait of the previous Marchese De Severino, Isobel had seen no warmth in Constantin's father's eyes and she had wondered what kind of parent he had been to his only son. Constantin's tight-lipped expression when she asked about his father made her think that they had not been close. The wood-panelled entrance hall of Casa Celeste was lined with portraits of Constantin's aristocratic ancestors, and Isobel had been struck by the realisation that the child she was carrying was the next generation in the noble lineage of the De Severino family. Looking at the haughty faces of her baby's predecessors, she had felt out of her depth, and she had wondered if Constantin was secretly disappointed that the mother of his heir had been a miner's daughter before he had made her his Marchesa.

'I had the feeling when we stayed at Casa Celeste that you thought our marriage was a mistake. I didn't fit into your sophisticated lifestyle and I wasn't a glamorous socialite like the women you were used to. I…I sensed that you were ashamed of me,' she said huskily.

He looked genuinely surprised. 'That's nonsense.'

'Is it? Then explain why you turned into a stranger on that trip, and why you became cold and distant.'

Constantin frowned. 'Nothing changed. You imagined things.'

'You slept in another bedroom—at the opposite end of the house.'

'I moved into another room because you felt uncomfortable as your pregnancy advanced and you were too hot when we shared a bed.'

Isobel was unconvinced, especially when she remembered how well the villa's air-conditioning system worked. The only reason she'd been able to think of for why Constantin had insisted on separate bedrooms was that he had found the visible signs of her pregnancy unattractive. She had loved her rounded belly, but when she had excitedly placed Constantin's hand on her stomach so that he could feel the faint fluttering as their baby moved he had tensed and quickly stepped away from her.

His reaction had been all the more surprising because a few days before they had gone to Italy he had accompanied her to her second antenatal scan, and his hard features had softened when he had seen the image of their baby girl on the screen. Arianna had been perfectly formed and appeared to be healthy. Her little heart had been beating strongly. There had been no reason to think that her pregnancy would not continue, Isobel thought emotively, no indication of the terrible events that had followed days after she and Constantin had arrived at Casa Celeste.

'You were unsettled at the villa,' she insisted, recalling how he had seemed permanently on edge. They had gone to Italy because he had needed to attend a board meeting at DSE's head office in Rome, but in August Isobel had found the scorching temperature in the city too much, and so they had transferred to Casa Celeste, where it was cooler by the lake. The moment they had walked through the front door she had sensed a change in Constantin, and she had been puzzled by his reluctance to spend time at his childhood home.

On their first night at the villa she had been woken by him crying out in his sleep, but he had dismissed his nightmare as a result of drinking too much red wine and told her he couldn't remember what he had dreamed about. From then on he had slept in a different bedroom, but Isobel knew that his nights had been disturbed.

'You had nightmares. I heard you shouting in your sleep.'

He shrugged. 'I seem to recall that I had a dream the night we arrived. I also remember that the wine I'd drunk that evening hadn't tasted right. I suspect it had gone bad, which probably accounted for my disturbed sleep.'

'No.' Isobel held her ground. 'You had nightmares on other nights.' She shivered. 'Your cries were...ungodly—like an animal in terrible pain. You must have dreamed about something truly horrific.'

Constantin stiffened. 'How could you have heard me? My room was far away from yours and the walls of Casa Celeste are too thick for sound to carry any distance.'

'I...' She flushed, and wished she had not started the thread of conversation, but it was too late to backtrack. 'I was standing outside your bedroom door one night and I heard you shouting. Your words didn't make sense. You kept saying, "He meant to do it, he meant to kill her." I had no idea what you meant and I guessed you were dreaming.'

Constantin knew exactly what his shouts had meant and what his dream had revealed, but he had no intention of giving Isobel an explanation.

'Why did you come to my room?' His curiosity deepened as he watched rosy colour flare along her cheekbones. 'Had you felt unwell, or been concerned about the baby?' His voice became terse as a thought struck him. 'Did you have warning signs that something was wrong with your pregnancy which led to the miscarriage a few days later?'

'No...it was nothing like that.' She sighed. 'If you must know, I went to your room because I...I wanted you to make love to me.'

She glimpsed a flash of some indefinable emotion in his eyes. As his mouth curved into an arrogantly satisfied smile she fought the urge to cover her hot face with her hands. 'Why is that so surprising?' she said defensively. 'Up until that trip to Italy we had enjoyed a passionate love life.'

'Yes, you certainly disproved the theory that pregnancy can have a negative effect on a woman's libido,' he drawled.

Constantin visualised Isobel in the second trimester of her pregnancy. The morning sickness she'd suffered in the early months had disappeared and her skin had glowed, her hair had been glossy and her body had developed lush curves that he had found intensely desirable. When they had first met, their passion for one another had been mind-blowing, and to his pleasure pregnancy had heightened her enjoyment of sex.

Before the trip to Italy they had made love every night, but the return of his nightmares had been a grim reminder that he should never have got involved with her.

'I'm not ashamed to admit that I missed having sex when you decided that we should have separate bedrooms,' Isobel said tautly.

They had only slept apart at the villa for a handful of nights before she'd lost the baby, and life had never been the same again, Constantin remembered. When they had returned to London he had attempted to comfort her, but she had been inconsolable and he had told himself he deserved her rejection.

He glanced at her lovely face and her mass of honey-gold hair tumbling around her shoulders, and felt a tightening in his groin.

'Why *didn't* you come into my room when we were at Casa Celeste and tell me you wanted to make love?'

Isobel shrugged. 'I couldn't.' She did not want to admit that she had been afraid he'd been turned off by her pregnant shape and might have rejected her. 'When I realised you were having a nightmare I wondered if I should wake you, but then you stopped shouting and I thought it best not to disturb you.'

Her voice trembled. 'Two days later I lost the baby, and there was no reason for us to stay together. You told me last week that you had only married me because I was pregnant,' she reminded him. 'That's why I'm surprised by your suggestion that we could start again.'

She watched Constantin's eyes narrow, and sensed he was trying to think of a reason that would convince her to give their marriage another chance. It was lucky she had not expected him to make a declaration that he loved her, she thought drily.

'Anyway, I can't jet off to New York. I've been writing songs for the Stone Ladies' next album and I'll be working with the band in the recording studio this week.'

'Couldn't you put the recording session off until another time?'

His casual tone riled her. 'No, I can't. A lot of other people are involved, sound engineers, studio technicians. We are professional musicians,' she told him curtly. 'My career is as important to me as DSE is to you.'

Constantin struggled to hide the anger in his voice. 'I'm well aware that your career with the Stone Ladies is your top priority, but for heaven's sake, Isobel, the stalker hurt you last night when he tried to grab you. Surely you take the issue of your safety seriously?'

'Of course I do, and I appreciate your concern. But it's unnecessary. I sent a text message to Ryan last night telling him about the stalker, and he invited me to stay with him and Emily for a few days.' She glanced at the clock again. 'As a matter of fact, they'll be here at any minute to collect me. Ryan said he'll ring the doorbell twice so that I know it's him.'

Constantin felt the acid burn of jealousy in his stomach at the thought of pretty-boy Fellows rushing to Isobel's rescue like a proverbial knight in shining armour. The guitarist was engaged to his girlfriend, he reminded himself. In his mind he heard the voice of his father's second wife.

'*You are jealous of any man I happen to glance at, Franco,*' Lorena had cried.

Dio! His jealousy of Isobel's friendships with other people was proof that he was no better than his father, Constantin told himself grimly. De Severino blood ran through his veins, and it was possible that an unpredictable, violent monster lived inside him as it had in his father. The idea sickened him. It was imperative that he persuade Isobel to return to him until he had secured the chairmanship of DSE, but the reason he had deliberately drawn away from her in the first year of their marriage still remained. She was the only woman who had ever incited feelings of jealous possessiveness in him.

He visualised his father stretching a hand towards Lorena as they stood on the balcony. Seconds later she had fallen to her death. Her scream would haunt Constantin for ever.

The sound of two rings on the doorbell dragged his mind from the past. He stared at Isobel and his gut ached with a longing that was more than physical desire. However, his voice gave away nothing of his thoughts. 'The cavalry are here,' he drawled sardonically. He sauntered across the room but paused in the doorway and glanced back at her. 'Promise me you'll take care, *piccola*?'

How could Constantin sound as though he cared about

her when she knew full well that he didn't give a damn? Isobel wondered. She shrugged helplessly. 'I promise.'

'Bene.' His voice was soft, and his smile stole her breath. She closed her eyes while she fought for composure, and when she opened them again he had gone.

'Jezebel!' David's high-pitched voice shook with fury. 'I read in the newspapers that you are married. But you are *mine*, Izzy. You should not have allowed this other man to lay his hands on your body. You have betrayed me, and you must pay, *bitch*…'

Isobel's fingers trembled as she hit the button on her mobile phone to end the call, cutting off the stalker as he issued a string of obscenities. It was the first time that he had actually threatened her, but as yet the police had been unable to trace him and they were powerless to do anything to help, other than to advise her not to answer calls from a withheld number.

It was so unfair, she thought, frustrated. She felt hounded and increasingly worried. Although she had changed her mobile-phone number again, David had somehow got hold of her new number. Her heart had leapt into her throat when the message *number withheld* had flashed on her phone's screen, but out of fearful curiosity she had listened to the stalker's latest hysterical outburst.

The day after the charity fund-raising party, pictures of her and Constantin kissing on the dance floor had been in all the tabloids. The journalists must have done their homework, because the revelation that she was married to the billionaire head of the luxury goods company DSE was prominent in the gossip columns, as was speculation about the state of her current relationship with Constantin. Fortunately the Stone Ladies PR office had dealt with the press interest, but the phone calls from David had started again, and over the past few days his messages had become increasingly menacing.

'Are you sure you'll be all right while Emily and I are in the Caribbean?' Ryan strolled across the patio to where Isobel was sitting in the garden of his house in Chelsea. 'You're welcome to stay here until the police have caught the nutter responsible for the nuisance calls you've been receiving.' He shot a sharp glance at her tense expression. 'Has the stalker phoned you again? Emily won't mind if we postpone our trip.'

'I haven't heard from him,' Isobel lied. 'And I certainly don't want you to postpone your plans. I know you've been looking forward to your holiday, especially since you announced your engagement to Emily in the press. Hopefully you'll avoid the paparazzi while you're in St Lucia.'

Ryan still looked concerned. 'I don't like the idea of you going back to your flat. I'd be happier if you would go and stay with Carly and Ben.'

She shook her head. 'I'd have to tell Carly about the stalker. I don't want to cause her any stress, especially in the first crucial weeks of her pregnancy.'

Isobel had hidden the shaft of pain she'd felt when her friend had revealed that she was expecting a baby. She was truly delighted for Carly and Ben, who had already asked her to be godmother to their first child. The business with the stalker was getting out of hand, she brooded. It was bad enough that her life was disrupted, but she did not want her problems to affect her friends.

Her phone rang and she jumped like a startled deer, which spoiled her pretence that she was unconcerned by the stalker and earned her a close look from Ryan. Her eyes flew to the phone's screen and she let out a shaky breath as she recognised the number, and at the same time her heart-rate accelerated.

'Has the stalker contacted you since I spoke to you yesterday?' Constantin said without preamble, ignoring her query about the weather in New York. 'I assume you have told the police that David has somehow discovered your new number and phoned you several times this week?'

'I reported his calls,' Isobel confirmed.

'Has he rung today?'

She glanced at Ryan, who was standing within earshot of her conversation. She could hardly tell Constantin about the stalker's recent, threatening call when she had denied to Ryan that she had received any more nuisance calls. If she told the truth, she knew Ryan would cancel his holiday with his fiancée.

'He hasn't phoned today,' she said with forced airiness. 'Hopefully David has got bored of his game.'

A snort of disbelief was followed by a tense silence from the other end of the line as Constantin struggled to control his frustration. He felt a strong urge to return to London immediately so that he could shake some sense into Isobel. 'I don't believe the stalker is playing a game,' he said curtly. 'I wish you would allow me to hire a bodyguard to protect you while this man remains a potential threat.'

'You're overreacting. I don't want a bodyguard.'

He gave an exasperated sigh. 'I should have known that you would not accept my help, but in this instance your determination to be independent is foolish.'

Isobel's nerves were on edge following the phone call from the stalker, and her temper flared. 'I'm not six years old,' she reminded Constantin coldly. 'I can take care of myself.' She winced as he swore down the phone. 'Really, there is no need to worry about me. I'm going up to Derbyshire to visit Mum. I think she's lonely now that Dad has gone, and while I'm away from London maybe the stalker will lose interest in me.' Realising that she could spend all day arguing with Constantin, she said quickly, 'I've got to go. I hope your business trip is successful,' she added in a conciliatory tone before ending the call.

The roads in central London were fairly quiet in the middle of the afternoon before the start of the rush hour. As Isobel drove past the front of her apartment building she waved to the new concierge who she had met when Ryan had accompanied her to her flat a couple of days ago to collect her post. The concierge had introduced himself as Bill. Apparently, he was ex-army and had been a champion boxer for his regiment, a statement borne out by his massive build and misshapen nose that looked as if it had been broken on several occasions.

A ramp led down to the underground car park beneath the building. She parked in her bay, slid out of the car and opened the boot to retrieve the bag she had taken with her when she had stayed with Ryan and Emily. The couple were well suited, she mused. It was wonderful to see Ryan so happy after the depression he had suffered following Simon's death.

On the other side of the car park an engine started up. Out of the corner of her eye Isobel saw a white van drive towards her, but she paid it no attention; every other vehicle in London seemed to be a white van. In her mind she planned what clothes to pack for the trip to visit her mother in Derbyshire. She closed the boot of her car and turned to walk towards the lifts, but the van was blocking her path and as the driver jumped out her heart crashed painfully against her ribcage.

'You!'

David did not reply, and his silence unnerved her more than if he had verbally abused her as he had over the phone.

He stared at her with wild eyes and when he did finally speak his tone was coldly menacing.

'You must come with me, Izzy.'

Her eyes darted to the van's open rear door and the length of rope coiled up inside. Constantin's words jerked into her mind. 'I don't believe the stalker is playing a game,' he had said seriously. Fear paralysed her, but as David suddenly lunged towards her and grabbed hold of her arms she reacted instinctively and kicked him in the shin. He yelped, but tightened his grip, his breath coming in panting rasps.

'You will be mine for all eternity. Death will unite us for ever.'

Let me go! She struggled frantically as he tried to force her into the back of the van. He was surprisingly strong and Isobel found she was no match for him. If only she could alert someone's attention, but there was no one in the car park and her desperate scream echoed around the underground vault.

The stalker's fingers were biting into her arms and her thin jacket offered scant protection. She renewed her efforts to escape, but he possessed a manic strength and pushed her so violently that she crumpled half inside the van. She felt sick with terror. If he managed to get her inside the van and restrained her with the rope before driving away she dreaded to imagine what he intended to do with her.

Fired by desperation, she fought like a wildcat, kicking out at him so that he swore and released her arms. David renewed his attack, but the adrenalin coursing through Isobel meant that she barely felt the blows he dealt her. Distantly she became aware of the sound of pounding footsteps, a harsh male voice shouting. Suddenly the blows from the stalker ceased and Bill the concierge's bulky figure appeared.

'Get your hands off the lady!'

With a roar of fury, David threw her into the van. Her head struck the edge of the door with such force that she felt agonising pain shoot through her skull before blackness descended.

CHAPTER SEVEN

CHAPTER SEVEN

TWENTY-FOUR HOURS after she had been attacked by the stalker, the doctor at the hospital where Isobel had been taken by ambulance explained that, following an episode of concussion, it was common to experience a moderate to severe headache.

'You were admitted overnight as a precaution. If your vision becomes blurred, or you start vomiting, you must return to hospital, but you were only unconscious for a few minutes and there should not be any lasting damage.'

Isobel nodded and winced as the slight movement hurt like mad. She wondered if the doctor would consider the pneumatic drill vibrating inside her skull was merely a moderate headache. All things considered, she knew she had got off lightly. The bruises on her arms, ribs and temple would fade and she had been assured by the medical staff that the nauseous sensation and the feeling that she wanted to burst into tears were side-effects of shock.

'I can't believe such an awful thing happened,' Carly said for probably the tenth time. 'Thank heavens the new concierge at the apartment building saw you being attacked on CCTV and rushed to your rescue. You should have told me about the stalker, Izzy.'

'I didn't want to worry you.' She gave her best friend a rueful glance. The band's keyboard player looked visibly upset, and Isobel added guilt to the list of emotions churning inside her. Ben and Carly had rushed to the hospital as soon as they had heard what had happened. The Stone Ladies' manager, Mike Jones, as well as various other friends, had also visited and expressed shock and sympathy. Ryan had phoned when he had heard about the attack, but thankfully she had managed to dissuade him from cutting short his holiday to come home. Isobel was grateful for everyone's concern, but she longed to be alone and have some peace and quiet.

She closed her eyes, but the sound of a familiar gravelly voice made her jerk them open again and her stomach dipped as she looked towards the door and met Constantin's brilliant blue gaze. For several simmering seconds it was as if they were the only two people in the universe, connected by a mystical force that defied description.

'Dio! Isabella.' There was a curious nuance in his tone, and Isobel was shocked by his haggard appearance. His skin was grey beneath his tan and his jacket was badly creased as if he had slept in his clothes.

'You're in New York.' She grimaced at the inanity of her statement, and told herself it was the shock of the attack, not the shock of seeing Constantin, that had scrambled her brain.

'I flew back the moment I received Carly's call.'

Isobel shot her friend a reproachful look. 'There was no need...' she began, but Constantin stalled her.

'There was every need,' he said grimly. 'I am your husband and as such your next of kin.' He did not add that when he had learned Isobel had been attacked by the stalker he could have sworn that his heart stopped beating for what had felt like a lifetime.

He came into the room and immediately dominated the small space. Isobel swallowed as he leaned over the bed and gently, so gently, traced a finger over the swelling above her left eye. A muscled flickered in his jaw.

'Thank goodness Bill got to you before you were seriously harmed.'

Her eyes widened. 'How do you know the name of the concierge at my apartment building?'

'Bill Judd is a private protection officer. You refused to allow me to hire a bodyguard to look after you so I did the next best thing and appointed Bill to watch your flat in case the stalker returned.' Constantin ignored her swift intake of breath. 'I did not know you had learned to drive while we've been separated, and Bill wasn't expecting you to park in the car park. Fortunately he kept a close eye on all the CCTV screens and was able to reach you before the stalker forced you into his van. But he was not quick enough to prevent you from being injured.'

Once again, Isobel heard a strange catch in his voice, as if he was struggling to contain his emotions. But she must have imagined it, she decided, because the one thing she knew about her enigmatic husband was that he was never troubled by strong emotions.

'Do you happen to have your passport with you?'

She gave him a puzzled look. 'It's in my handbag. I always carry it with me.'

'Good, that means it won't be necessary to stop off at your flat on the way to the airport.'

'Hold on a minute.' She lifted her head from where she had been resting it against the pillows and felt as though a red-hot poker had been thrust into her skull. 'Why do I need my passport?'

'My jet is being refuelled ready to fly us to Rome.' His eyes glittered fiercely as she opened her mouth to protest. 'Don't even think of arguing, *cara*. The stalker escaped capture. He demonstrated when he attacked you that he is disturbed and dangerous.'

Carly made a distressed sound. 'You mean he might try and hurt Izzy again?'

'H…how did he get away,' Isobel asked shakily. 'Before I was knocked out I saw the concierge…bodyguard grab hold of him.'

Constantin hesitated, reluctant to frighten Isobel more than she had already been, but he could not hide the truth from her. 'The stalker was carrying a knife. He stabbed Bill in the hand and managed to drive away. The police were immediately alerted and they found the hired van abandoned a few streets from your apartment building, but unfortunately they have been unable to locate the man yet.

'His name is David Archibald, by the way. It was possible to identify him from the CCTV film. He was employed as caretaker at the offices of the Stone Ladies' management company. He must have had access to personal files and computer records after the staff had gone home in the evening, and that's how he was able to discover your phone number and address.' Constantin sought and held Isobel's gaze. 'The man has a history of psychotic behaviour and the police believe he poses a threat to your safety.'

'Izzy, you have to go away with Constantin until the police catch this man,' Carly said fiercely. Her face was white and strained beneath her bright red curls, and the sight of a tear sliding down her cheek made Isobel hurt inside. She and Carly had been friends since nursery school and were as close as sisters.

'Don't worry, I'll take care of her,' Constantin assured Carly. His gentle tone surprised Isobel. In the past he had seemed to resent her close bond with the other members of the band.

After extracting a promise from Isobel that she would

accept Constantin's help, Ben and Carly left. 'There's no reason for me to go to Italy with you,' she told him as soon as they were alone. 'I realise it would be sensible not to return to my flat until the police find the stalker, but why can't I stay at the house in Grosvenor Square?'

'Whittaker has taken an extended period of leave to visit his niece in New Zealand. I need to be at DSE's head office to oversee a new project, and I want you in Rome with me so I can keep you safe.'

Isobel grimaced. 'You are not responsible for me. I need to be in London to work.'

'I checked with your manager. You've finished recording songs for the new album, and the Stone Ladies' next concert is not until September. In this instance I *am* responsible for you, Isabella.' Constantin's jaw clenched. 'I blame myself for the attack. The stalker only started acting aggressively after pictures of us kissing at the fund-raising party were published in the newspapers. That, together with the revelation in the press that you are my wife, was probably enough to have tipped the mentally disturbed man over the edge.'

He leaned over the bed and cupped her chin. 'I will never forgive myself for putting you in danger,' he said in a husky voice that sent a quiver of sensation down Isobel's spine. 'If I have to, I'll carry you out of here and put you on my plane.'

Constantin's eyes glittered as he studied her stark pallor and the vivid purple bruise on her brow. He'd read her medical notes and knew she had suffered bruising to her arms and torso as well as concussion caused by a blow to her head. It could have been worse. He shuddered to think what might have happened if the stalker had succeeded in kidnapping her. He had decided against telling Isobel that

David was a schizophrenic with a history of violent behaviour. 'Don't fight me, *tesorino*,' he murmured.

She ached all over and felt as if she had fought several rounds with a prize boxer. She did not have the physical or mental strength for a battle of wills with Constantin, especially when his face was so close to hers that she could count his silky black eyelashes. It was impossible to ignore the electric awareness simmering between them, impossible to prevent the slight tremble of her mouth as emotions threatened to overwhelm her.

Tears filled her eyes and she felt his warm breath whisper across her skin as he made a muffled sound in his throat before he claimed her lips in an achingly sensual kiss that touched her soul. After the terror she had experienced when the stalker had attacked her, the sense of safety and security she felt in Constantin's arms weakened her resistance and she simply opened her mouth beneath the gentle pressure of his and gave herself up to the pleasure of his kiss.

The memory of the passion that had flared between them, as well as the underlying tenderness in Constantin's kiss, stayed with Isobel as they drove to the airport and boarded his private jet. She had taken some strong painkillers for her headache and once the plane had taken off she leaned back in her seat and closed her eyes. Moments later, she opened them again when Constantin unfastened her seat belt and lifted her into his arms.

She peered at him groggily as the painkillers took effect. 'What are you doing?'

'Taking you to bed,' he told her as he carried her to the rear of the plane and into the bedroom, which was fitted with a large double bed. Other memories pushed into Isobel's mind, of the occasions when he had made love to her for the duration of the journey between London and

Rome. Despite her pounding headache she still managed to sound defiant.

'The hell you are! I agreed to go to Rome with you, but that's all.' She glared at him as he deposited her on the bed, but her treacherous heart leapt when he kicked off his shoes and stretched out next to her. 'I am not going to provide you with inflight entertainment.' She sat upright and groaned as pain shot through her head.

'Relax,' Constantin drawled, and pushed her gently back down onto the pillows. 'I haven't slept in thirty-six hours. When I received a phone call from Carly to tell me what had happened to you, I was…extremely concerned.' He could not begin to describe his mixture of fear for her well-being, and fury with her attacker, not to mention anger with himself that he might have triggered the stalker's aggression by kissing Isobel in public. 'I'm beat. When I make love to you I intend to be wide awake and fully energised.'

Isobel frowned as the meaning of his words penetrated the sleepy haze fogging her mind. 'Don't you mean *if*, not, *when*?'

He raised a lazy eyebrow. 'We both know that I could have hot and very satisfying sex with you any time I choose, *mia bella*,' he drawled. 'But I'm content to wait until you are ready to accept that I'm the only man who can blow your mind.'

Temper gave her the energy to snatch up a pillow and thump him with it. 'Your ego is *enormous*!'

His rich laughter echoed around the bedroom as he tugged the pillow out of her hand and pulled her down so that her head rested on his chest. He curled his arms around her, trapping her against her strong body. 'It's not the only enormous thing about me,' he whispered wickedly.

Despite herself, Isobel's lips twitched. In the early days

of their marriage Constantin had often teased her and made her laugh. They had laughed together, had fun together. What had happened to them? she wondered. Everything had started to go wrong when they had visited his ancestral home Casa Celeste and her charming, laughing husband had turned into a cold stranger.

Constantin's Roman home was a stunning penthouse apartment in the heart of the city overlooking the Piazza Navona and its famous fountains. From the outside the property was a magnificent historical building, which had been exquisitely restored by a famous Italian architect. Inside, however, the décor was ultra-modern, with huge open-plan rooms lined with glass walls that offered spectacular views across Rome.

Isobel had first visited the apartment when Constantin had invited her to spend a weekend with him. Boarding his private jet for the flight to Italy, she had noticed the glamorous stewardess glance at her cheap clothes and she had felt self-conscious that she was a lowly office assistant and her billionaire boss was in a different league. When they had arrived at the penthouse she had been overwhelmed by the luxurious surroundings and even more overwhelmed by Constantin. He had been utterly charming as he had dispelled her shyness as quickly as he had dispensed with her clothes, and, soon after, her virginity.

Now, as she walked through the apartment, Isobel felt a sense of sadness for the innocent girl of three years ago who had been swept off her feet and fallen irrevocably in love with her Italian lover. How naïve she had been to believe that Constantin had returned her feelings. The ugly truth was that she had been just another notch on his bedpost until he had discovered that she was carrying his heir. Her pregnancy had prompted him to marry her, but she'd never been comfortable with her title of Marchesa De Severino. She had felt like an imposter among his aristocratic friends, and after she had lost their baby she had felt like a fraud.

She assured herself that she was relieved when Constantin showed her to one of the guest bedrooms rather than the master suite. His taunt on the plane that he could take her to bed whenever he chose was not something she wanted to put to the test.

'I kept the clothes you left behind two years ago,' he said, opening a wardrobe to reveal a rail full of elegant designer outfits that she had worn on the occasions when she had accompanied him to glamorous social events.

At least she would not have to immediately go shopping, Isobel thought. All she'd brought with her from England was the bag containing a few items of clothes and makeup that she'd taken to Ryan's and she'd had with her when the stalker had attacked her.

Her eyes were drawn to the vase of yellow roses on the dressing table. Following her gaze, Constantin explained, 'I asked the housekeeper to put yellow roses in your room because I know they are your favourite flowers.'

Isobel recalled that when they had returned from their honeymoon he had filled the house in London with yellow roses and her foolish heart had leapt as she'd taken the gesture as a sign that he cared for her.

'You remembered,' she whispered, feeling a sudden rush of tears to her eyes. Needing time to regain her composure, she leaned forwards to inhale the roses' heady perfume. 'They're beautiful. Thank you.'

He grimaced. 'Perhaps I should not have told you of my involvement, knowing how you dislike accepting anything from me. No doubt you'll consign the roses to the rubbish bin.'

She was startled by the bitterness in his voice. 'What do you mean?'

'You left every single gift that I'd given you behind when you abandoned our marriage, including the diamond necklace I gave you for a birthday present.'

She pictured the exquisite pear-drop diamond pendant that he had fastened around her neck on the evening of her birthday, when they had been about to host a dinner party for some of Constantin's business associates. Isobel would have preferred to celebrate her birthday quietly, maybe dinner at a country pub, but he had insisted on holding a lavish dinner in her honour.

'Only the finest quality diamonds will do for my wife,' Constantin had told her as she'd stared in the mirror at the glittering necklace that had felt cold and hard against her skin. His words had made her feel cold inside as she'd wondered if he had given her the necklace to make a statement of his wealth.

'The necklace must have cost thousands of pounds. I didn't feel comfortable wearing something so valuable.'

'Why don't you be honest, and say you didn't want the necklace or the other items of jewellery and the clothes I bought you because, although you were happy to accept birthday presents from your friends, you hated accepting anything from me?' Constantin growled. 'You accused me of being distant, but when I tried to bridge the gap between us you pushed me away.'

'I didn't want presents, I wanted…' Isobel broke off, frustrated that she could not make him understand that she hadn't been interested in material things. What she had longed for was for him to share himself with her, to open up his thoughts and emotions that he kept locked away. 'I wanted you to take an interest in me as a person,' she muttered. 'I wanted our marriage to be an equal partnership, but you seemed to think that if you gave me expensive presents I should be content, and not want anything else such as to see my friends or pursue my music career.' Her resentment and unhappiness had increased until the only answer had been for her to leave him.

'Everything had to be your way, Constantin,' she accused him bitterly. 'My hopes and dreams didn't count. You reminded me of my father. My mother was a wonderful pianist, and years ago she had the chance to play professionally with an orchestra, but Dad persuaded her that she wasn't good enough. He said she should carry on working as a piano teacher and not give up her job for a silly dream.'

'In our case, there was no need for you to work,' Constantin said curtly. 'I provided you with a good lifestyle.'

Isobel sucked in a breath, trying to control her temper. 'That statement shows just how little you understood me. I didn't want to be provided for. It was, *is,* important for me to work and provide for myself, to feel independent...'

'Your desire for independence did nothing to help our marriage.'

'Our marriage was beyond help. After we lost our baby there was nothing to hold us together.'

Her throat suddenly ached. 'Constantin...' She swung round to face him and thought she glimpsed hurt in his eyes, but his lashes swept down and hid his emotions. 'I admit I felt uncomfortable when you gave me expensive gifts. I felt like a...a charity case, like Cinderella. I was the penniless secretary, who landed herself a billionaire husband,' she reminded him. She bit her lip.

'When we announced our engagement, your PA, Julie, made a snide remark in front of many people in the office that I was a gold-digger and I must have deliberately engineered falling pregnant with your baby so that you would marry me.'

'Why did you care what my PA said? You knew as well as I did that it was my fault you conceived,' he said curtly. 'You had told me on the weekend we spent together here that you were not on the pill. Contraception was my responsibility, but I wasn't as careful as I should have been.'

Isobel felt her face grow warm as she recalled the occasion Constantin had made love to her in the shower. Their scorching desire had been as uncontrollable as a wildfire, and she had only remembered that he hadn't used protection that one time when she had stared at the blue line on the pregnancy test and felt sick with worry at the prospect of telling her father that she was going to be a single mother.

'Why did it matter what anyone else thought about our relationship?' he demanded.

'Julie was right when she guessed that you only married me because I was expecting your baby. When she said those things in the office, I felt humiliated,' Isobel said in a low voice. 'For most of my childhood my father was out of work. It wasn't his fault. He was injured in an accident in the coal mine, but the pit was closed down and he didn't receive the compensation he was owed. There was a shortage of jobs where we lived, and Dad's injuries limited the type of work he could do, so the family survived on his unemployment benefit. Mum earned a small income from teaching piano lessons, but I know my parents struggled to make ends meet.'

She sighed. 'Kids at school can be cruel. I wasn't the only one who was taunted for being a scrounger. That was the name the pupils from better-off families called those of us whose families depended on social welfare payments. I felt ashamed that my family lived on handouts, and when

I left school I vowed that I would always work and be independent. I guess it was a pride thing, but I was determined never to accept anything from anyone.'

'Surely that did not include gifts from your husband?' Constantin said harshly. 'I enjoyed buying you things. It gave me pleasure to see you dressed in beautiful clothes, and I chose pieces of jewellery that I thought would suit you and because I hoped they would give you pleasure. But instead you acted as if I had insulted you.'

'I didn't want you to think I had married you for your money.' She glanced at him and saw incomprehension in his eyes. 'I didn't belong in your world,' she said huskily.

'You might have believed that, but I certainly didn't.' Constantin frowned, trying to absorb what Isobel had told him about herself. She had clearly been deeply affected by her childhood and her family's financial situation, but he had been unaware that she felt sensitive of other people's opinion that she had married him because he was wealthy. Of the many women he had met who deserved the label gold-digger, Isobel was definitely not one of them.

'How is your headache?' he asked abruptly.

'Completely gone. The couple of hours that I slept on the plane worked wonders.'

'If you feel up to it, we'll go out for dinner.' He strode across the room and glanced back at her from the doorway. It was early evening, and the sun sinking below the horizon emitted golden rays that streamed through the window and gilded her slender frame. 'I never thought you married me for financial gain, Isabella,' he said gruffly. He hesitated. 'And, contrary to what I told you when you came to see me in London a few weeks ago, I did not marry you only because you were carrying my child.'

Isobel was stunned into silence by Constantin's enigmatic statement, and as she watched him walk out of the room she wondered if she dared to believe him.

CHAPTER EIGHT

'TRATTORIA PEPE!' ISOBEL smiled as she recognised the charming trattoria tucked in a corner of a small piazza, which was rarely discovered by tourists. Constantin had shown her many of Rome's hidden gems when they had lived together, and the trattoria had been their favourite place to eat traditional, expertly prepared Roman food. 'You brought me here the first time I visited Rome.'

'Pepe's signature dish of *porchetta* served with herbs, olives and mozzarella is still the best dish you'll find in all of Rome, in my opinion,' Constantin said as he ushered her inside the tiny restaurant.

They were welcomed by Pepe himself, and the trattoria's owner greeted Isobel like a long-lost relative, kissing her on both cheeks as he spoke to her mainly in Italian, with the odd English word thrown in.

'*Sono lieto di incontrarvi di nuovo.* I am happy to meet you again,' she replied, when Pepe finally paused to draw a breath. The conversation continued for several minutes before the trattoria's patron and head chef hurried back to his kitchen.

A young, good-looking waiter came to take their order and flirted outrageously with Isobel, until he saw the warning gleam in Constantin's eyes and beat a hasty retreat.

'I'm impressed by your fluency in Italian,' he told Isobel drily when they were alone.

She shrugged. 'It seemed a shame not to continue the lessons that I'd started when we were together.' When she had married Constantin, she had been keen to learn his language, aware that he wanted to bring their child up to speak Italian. But there had not been a baby, she thought painfully, and soon she would no longer be his wife.

The waiter returned with their first course and gave Isobel a lingering look, before a terse word from Constantin sent him scurrying away.

She frowned. 'Why were you rude to the waiter? He was just being friendly.'

'If he had been any *friendlier,* he would have made love to you on the table.' Constantin's jaw hardened as he struggled to control the hot rush of possessiveness that had swept through him when the waiter had smiled at Isobel. He had felt a burning desire to rearrange the waiter's handsome features with his fist. 'We might get served quicker if you refrain from flirting with the restaurant staff,' he growled.

'I wasn't flirting with the waiter.' Isobel's temper simmered. 'You're being ridiculous.'

Constantin took a long sip of wine. 'It's not surprising that you command attention from other men. You are very beautiful.' He leaned back in his chair and subjected her to a slow appraisal, noting the glossy sheen of her long blonde hair and the sensual shape of her mouth. 'But it's not only your looks that make you noticeable. It's something more than that. You were beautiful when I met you three years ago but you were painfully shy. You blushed every time I spoke to you,' he said softly, 'whereas now you have an air of self-confidence that most men would find undeniably attractive.'

Did he include himself with most men? Isobel wondered. 'I have grown more confident.' She gave him a wry smile. 'It was something of a necessity to overcome my shyness when the band became successful and I had to sing in front of huge audiences.' She chased a prawn around her plate with her fork, remembering the first time Constantin had brought her to the trattoria she had been so nervous that she had clumsily knocked over her glass of wine.

'When I first met you, I was a nobody, just an ordinary office assistant who dreamed of making it as a singer but never really believed it would happen. When I fell pregnant, my hopes and plans for the future were centred on being a mother to our baby and nothing else seemed as important.' A shadow of pain crossed her expressive face. 'But after we lost Arianna, I felt…irrelevant. I wasn't a mother and I sensed from the widening gap between us that I didn't live up to your expectations of a good wife.'

She shook her head when he looked as though he was going to argue. 'We both know that our marriage wasn't working. I guess we dealt with our grief about the baby in different ways. I wanted to talk about Arianna but you withdrew into yourself, and I had no idea what you were thinking…or feeling.'

'So you turned to your friends who you had known since you were a child,' Constantin said heavily. In his heart, he knew he had not been able to give her the support she had needed from him. He had shied away from acknowledging the pain of losing their baby. It had been easier to lock his emotions away and ignore them—just as he had done as a young boy when his mother had died—but in doing that he had also ignored Isobel's need for them to grieve together for Arianna.

'I poured my feelings into the songs I wrote, and found some small comfort playing the piano and creating music.

When I'd moved to London from Derbyshire with the rest of the band, we played gigs in pubs, but I stopped performing after I married you. I hadn't thought about the band becoming successful when we started performing again, it was just something to take my mind off the miscarriage. But to my amazement the Stone Ladies were spotted by a record producer and everything quickly escalated.'

She leaned across the table and trapped Constantin's gaze. 'When the Stone Ladies were offered a record contract it was a chance for all of us in the band to have the music career that we had longed for since we were teenagers. My father had told me I was a fool to chase a dream, but the dream was coming true. I had an opportunity to be someone in my own right, not a daughter, or a wife, but *me,* a girl from nowhere who was suddenly a serious musician earning more money that I'd ever imagined.'

Constantin frowned. 'You were married to a billionaire and did not need to earn money.'

'Yes, I did,' Isobel said fiercely. 'It was important to me to make my own way in the world. On our wedding day, at the reception, I overheard a comment from one of the guests that I had landed myself a meal ticket for life.'

The memory of that excruciating moment still made Isobel shudder. The catty remark had been made by Contessa Ghislaine Montenocci, a member of the Italian nobility who looked down her thin, aristocratic nose at anyone who did not have a title. 'I felt embarrassed, like I'd felt when the kids at school called my family scroungers because my father claimed unemployment benefit.

'Being a professional singer gave me a sense of pride.' Her voice became husky. 'I wanted to make my father proud of me, although I'm not sure he ever was. I...I also hoped that you might be more interested in me if I had a successful career,' she admitted. 'The women we met at social events, the wives of your friends, were all sophisticated and well educated,' she explained when he looked surprised. 'I felt I couldn't compete with them.'

'I never wanted you to compete with them,' Constantin said tersely. 'I was happy with you the way you were.'

'If that was true, why did you become so cold towards me? The truth is that you didn't feel proud of me as your wife, and no amount of designer dresses or expensive jewellery could turn me into a glamorous *marchesa*.'

Isobel stared at Constantin's chiselled features and felt frustrated that she could not make him understand. 'You told me once that your appointment as CEO of De Severino Eccellenza, and your success in driving the company forwards and making it one of Italy's highest earning businesses, was your greatest achievement.' She sighed. 'Being part of a successful band is *my* greatest achievement. But my career was one of the things that drove us apart.'

A nerve jumped in his jaw. 'We weren't driven apart. *You* walked out.'

Isobel tore her eyes from the angry gleam in his and looked down at her half-eaten dinner. Suddenly she had lost her appetite, and it seemed that Constantin was no longer hungry because he called the waiter over and requested the bill.

They walked back to the penthouse in silence, both of them lost in their private thoughts. Isobel's statement that her singing career had given her a sense of self-worth had touched a chord in Constantin. DSE's increased profits, and the fact that the company had become a globally recognised brand name since he had taken over as CEO, were the two things in his life that he felt proud of.

The trauma of witnessing his father and stepmother's fatal accident, and the terrible suspicion that Franco might have been responsible for the tragedy, haunted Constantin.

Since that dreadful day, he had avoided relationships that demanded his emotional involvement and instead focused his energy and passion on the company.

But his uncle Alonso was threatening to award the chairmanship of DSE to his gutless cousin Maurio.

It would make all his hard work over the past decade a waste of time, Constantin thought savagely. The company would not last five minutes with Maurio in charge. When he had asked Isobel to give their marriage another chance his sole aim had been to convince his uncle to appoint him Chairman. He glanced at her walking beside him, and his jaw tensed as he noted the admiring looks she attracted from every red-blooded male they passed. Somewhere along the line his priorities had changed, he acknowledged.

Isobel looked up at the full moon suspended like a huge silver disc in an indigo sky. The night air was warm and the bars and street cafés were busy. It was the first time in months that she had walked down a street without glancing over her shoulder and wondering if the stalker was watching her. The police still hadn't caught David, but she felt able to relax while she was in Rome with Constantin.

Although she did not feel very relaxed as he curved his arm around her waist when they walked past a group of young men. The close contact with his body sent molten heat surging through her veins, and memories of happier times they had shared tugged on her heart. When they had stayed in Rome soon after they were married he had taken her to dinner at Pepe's, and on the way home he had paused at every street corner to kiss her. By the time they had reached the apartment they'd been so hot for one another that they had only made it as far as the nearest sofa, she remembered.

Her face grew warm as she visualised him stripping

her naked and pushing her back against the cushions, slipping his hand between her thighs to find her wet and ready for him. She had *always* been ready for him, she thought ruefully.

'Would you like a nightcap?' he enquired as they entered the penthouse.

'No, thanks. I think I'll go straight to bed.' Isobel could not meet his gaze when her mind was full of images of him making love to her. 'Hopefully we'll hear from the British police tomorrow that they have caught the stalker. I'll be able to go home, and once the divorce is finalised we will be free of each other.'

Constantin's eyes narrowed. 'Is that really what you wish for, Isabella?'

'Yes.' Emotion choked her voice. Dinner at Pepe's had been a poignant reminder of everything she had lost, everything that might have been. 'I admit I had wondered if perhaps there was a chance we could get back together, but our conversation tonight proved that our differences are too great.'

She did not trust herself to continue and turned away from him before he saw the tears she was trying to hold back. 'It's like you said, Constantin. There's no point dwelling on the past. We need to move forwards, in our case, *on separate paths.*'

Constantin stood in front of the sliding glass doors in his bedroom, which led outside to a balcony that ran the length of penthouse and overlooked the piazza. Not that he ever ventured onto the balcony, but the view across the city even through the pane of glass was spectacular. Tonight, however, as he nursed a crystal tumbler of single malt, he barely registered Rome's famous historical skyline. Instead his thoughts were focused on his wife, who was occupying the guest room next door to his suite.

It was happening again. He had spent less than twenty-four hours in her company and already his resolve to keep his distance from her was under threat. He swallowed a mouthful of whisky and seriously contemplated drinking the entire bottle in the hope that it would dull the ache in his gut.

It was her smile that did it, he brooded. When Isobel smiled her whole face lit up—like when she'd recognised Pepe's Trattoria, and when she'd noticed the yellow roses in her room. She was the only woman he knew who would prefer to be given roses than diamonds.

He frowned as he recalled her telling him that her father had been out of work for much of her childhood and the family had been dependent on social welfare. Finally he understood why she was so fiercely independent. She had said that her career with the Stone Ladies had given her a sense of pride, but he had believed that she had left him because she was in love with the band's guitarist Ryan Fellows.

Jealousy was a poisonous emotion, he thought grimly. It festered in your soul like a vile worm. It was a shameful secret that he was determined to keep hidden from Isobel. For her safety he *must* control the green-eyed monster that he was convinced he had inherited from his father. *Dio*, tonight at the restaurant he had wanted to *kill* the young waiter who had flirted with her.

Was that how his father had felt when his beautiful young wife had smiled at other men?

Constantin pictured his stepmother's laughing face. He saw her tossing her hair and leaning forwards so that her breasts almost fell out of her tiny bikini top. *Be an angel and put sun cream on my back, Con, sweetie.*

He had gone home to Casa Celeste for the school holidays and had spent all summer having erotic fantasies about his stepmother. His father had noticed him following Lorena around like a lovesick puppy and there had been a huge row. He had never seen Franco as angry as he had been that day. Later, he had heard his father and Lorena arguing on the balcony.

Santa Madonna! Would the images in his mind ever fade? He finished his drink, but as he was about to turn away from the window a movement outside caught his attention. Isobel had stepped onto the balcony, and Constantin was transfixed as the breeze moulded her long white silk nightgown against her slender body. In the moonlight she was ethereal and so very lovely that the ache inside him intensified.

For her sake he had to ignore the hot throb of desire that skewered his insides, he reminded himself. But despite his good intentions he could not stop looking at her. She had her back to him and his eyes lingered on the twin curves of her bottom beneath her silky gown. As he watched she leaned further forwards over the balcony railing.

A vision from the past flashed into his mind. His stepmother leaning over the balcony rail; falling, falling… Lorena's scream echoed inside his head.

'Get away from there!' The calm of the velvet night air was shattered by Constantin's loud shout. Startled, Isobel looked round, and gave a cry of fright when he clamped his hands around her waist like a vice and lifted her off her feet, bundling her through the sliding glass doors into his bedroom.

'What are you *doing*?'

'What am *I* doing? *Mio Dio*, what were *you* doing leaning over the railing like that?' He swore savagely and raked his hair back from his brow with a hand that was actually shaking, Isobel noticed. He was grey beneath his tan, and the expression in his eyes was like none she had ever seen before. For a few seconds she saw stark terror in his eyes before he swung away from her, poured whisky from the bottle into a glass and gulped it down.

'I was trying to get a better view of the fountains. Constantin...I was quite safe. The balcony rail is too high for me to have fallen over.'

He slowly turned back to her, and she was relieved to see he had regained some colour in his face. To her surprise, he looked almost embarrassed by his strange behaviour.

'I guess I overreacted,' he muttered. 'It's just that I hate heights.'

Her eyebrows rose. 'You hate heights, yet you live in a penthouse with a balcony.' She compressed her lips in an unsuccessful attempt to disguise their betraying quiver.

'It's not funny,' he snapped.

'Oh, come on, Constantin, it is a bit,' Isobel giggled. Her shock when he had grabbed hold of her and hauled her in off the balcony—coming so soon after the shock of being attacked by the stalker—had left her feeling slightly crazy. 'You must have one of the best views of Rome but you're too scared to enjoy it.' She gave a peal of laughter. 'It's the most human reaction you've ever shown.'

Constantin closed his eyes and tried to block out the memories that swirled like black storm clouds in his brain. It was no good. He could not prevent the film reel in his mind from playing.

He was seventeen and spending the summer at Casa Celeste. He saw his father and Franco's young, pretty second wife standing on the balcony at the top of the tower. He heard his father's harsh voice and Lorena's high-pitched tones. Standing below in the courtyard, Constantin had realised they were arguing again. For years afterwards he had been unable to remember who had moved first— his father, or Lorena. His heart had crashed with fear as he saw Lorena topple over the balcony railing and fall through the air. He would never forget the sound of her scream. Moments later he had watched his father fall after Lorena. Everything seemed to happen in slow motion but it must have only been seconds before he heard two thuds. Thankfully he had closed his eyes at the moment of impact. For years he had blanked out the details of what he had witnessed—until his nightmares had revealed exactly what had taken place on the balcony.

He jerked his eyes open and saw Isobel staring at him. She had teased him for being scared of heights, but she had no idea of the stark terror that had seized him when he had seen her lean over the balcony.

'Surely not, *cara*,' he said grittily. 'I have never failed to react like a normal human male when I'm with you.'

Isobel belatedly realised that he was furious with her for teasing him. Remembering the strained look on his face when he had rushed onto the balcony, she acknowledged that her amusement had been misplaced.

'I'm sorry,' she muttered. But her apology was also too late. The glitter in Constantin's eyes warned her that she had pushed him beyond his limit. But while her brain urged her to run from his room, her limbs refused to obey. The atmosphere between them trembled with tension that built, second by simmering second, until it was an explosive force.

He swore as he caught hold of her and dragged her towards him. 'It will be my pleasure to demonstrate that I have all the normal human reactions, *mia bella*,' he told her harshly. Without giving her a chance to reply, he brought his mouth down on hers and kissed her with savage possession.

Constantin slid his hands down and clasped Isobel's bottom in a statement of bold intent. She felt the heat of his touch brand her through her thin nightgown and she gasped as he dragged her hard against him, forcing her pelvis into contact with the solid length of his arousal. He gave her no opportunity to voice her objection as he plundered her mouth and stole his pleasure, thrusting his tongue between her lips and exploring her with a flagrant eroticism that turned her bones to liquid.

The fire had been building all evening. Long before that, she conceded, remembering the electricity that had sizzled between them when she had watched him working out in the gym at his London home. Their hunger for each other had always been a driving force in their relationship, and however much her common sense told her to stop the madness her body recognised its master and was a willing slave to the delicious sensations he was creating with his hands and mouth.

He trailed his lips down her throat, each kiss sending a little shockwave through her that made every nerve-ending tingle. She arched her neck and gave herself up to hedonistic pleasure that intensified when he drew the straps of her gown over her shoulders and peeled the sheer silk away from her breasts.

She knew she should stop him, but the realisation that she was playing into his hands was driven from her mind when he cupped her breasts in his palms and kneaded them gently. It felt so good, but good became unbelievably wonderful as he flicked his thumb pads across her nipples, sending starbursts of sensation from her breasts down to her pelvis. The ache there grew to a desperate need that made her press her hips to his so that the hard bulge beneath his trousers rubbed against the hidden sweet spot at the heart of her femininity.

He growled something against her mouth and with one fluid motion yanked her nightgown over her hips and it slithered to the floor, leaving her naked to his glittering gaze. She made a little murmur of embarrassment as he slid his hand between her legs and gave her a mocking smile when he parted her and discovered the moist heat of her arousal.

'It appears that your human reactions work well too, *tesorino*.'

She closed her eyes to block out his cynical expression. 'Constantin—*don't*!' Taunting her about her weakness for him was bad enough, but his casual use of the endearment that she had once hoped meant that he cared for her was heartbreaking.

He caught hold of her chin and tilted her head up. 'Tears, Isabella?' An expression of pain flitted across his hard-boned face. She looked fragile and achingly vulnerable, the bruises on her arms a grim reminder of her narrow escape from the mentally disturbed stalker who had become obsessed with her. 'Do you honestly believe I would hurt you?'

Isobel recalled his stark expression when he had leaned over her hospital bed. *I will never forgive myself for putting you in danger*, he'd told her with a roughness in his tone that she had never heard before.

She shook her head. 'I know you were trying to protect me when you saw me on the balcony.' She met his gaze, her clear hazel eyes containing a breathtaking honesty. 'I know I'm safe with you.'

Santa Madre! He did not want to go there. He did not want to think of the past and all its secrets. What he wanted, needed, was to lose himself in the sweet seduction of Isobel's body. To kiss her and have her kiss him back, to caress her silken skin and feel her gentle hands on his body as she stroked his own aching body and brought him to the edge of ecstasy. He would take her with him on that tumultuous ride for they shared a passion that he had never experienced as intensely with any other woman.

Isobel gave a broken sigh as Constantin claimed her mouth once more, but this time his passion was tempered by a beguiling tenderness that shattered her soul. He was *everything*. The love of her life. The two years they had been apart had been unendingly lonely. She had thousands of fans around the world and sang in front of vast audiences, but every night she had slept alone and her heart had ached for one man.

He traced his lips over the fragile line of her collarbone and made a muffled sound almost as if he were in pain as he kissed each black bruise on her arms. A shiver of pleasure feathered down Isobel's spine as he moved lower to caress her breasts, painting moist circles around each aureole before he suckled her nipples in turn while she closed her eyes and gave herself totally to his sensual magic.

Reality faded, and was replaced with a new reality where only she and Constantin existed. She felt the mattress dip when he laid her on the bed. She watched him strip, and her heart beat faster as she studied every olive-skinned, muscle-packed inch of his body. He was a work of art, but unlike Bernini's incredible sculptures on the Fountain of the Four Rivers down in the *piazza*, his skin was warm beneath her fingertips and the wiry black hairs that covered his chest and arrowed over his flat stomach and thighs were faintly abrasive against her palms.

The jutting length of his arousal was further proof, as if she needed it, that hot red blood ran through his veins. She had forgotten just how powerfully he was built and her hesitation much have shown in her eyes because he smiled crookedly as he stretched out next to her and drew her into his arms.

'Are you having second thoughts, *tesorino*?' he murmured.

And third and fourth thoughts, if he but knew it. She gave him a shaky smile. 'Two years is a long time…and I'm out of practice.'

His eyes darkened. 'There has been no one else?'

She would not lie to him. 'No.'

'Not for me, either.'

Now she was shocked. 'You mean you haven't…in *two* years?'

'We were living apart but you were, *are*, my wife.'

No wonder he was so hugely aroused, whispered a little voice in her head. Her husband was a highly sexed male and frustration must have had him climbing the walls.

He had the uncanny knack of being able to read her mind. 'Believe it,' he said drily.

Their eyes met, and the sultry promise in his focused her mind on what he was doing with his hands as he trailed a path of fire down to the cluster of golden curls at the apex of her thighs. Despite the passing of time he had total recall of how to please her, knew the exact moment when she needed him to slide one finger into her, then two, and move them in a relentless dance until she gave a husky cry of delight and desperation.

He loved that she was so unguarded in her response to him. Aware that he was about to explode, Constantin felt his iron control shatter, and with a groan he pulled her beneath him, slid his hands beneath her bottom and drove into her with a powerful thrust that brought a gasp from her.

'*Dio*, did I hurt you?' Remorse thickened his voice, but

as he made to withdraw she wrapped her long legs around his hips.

'No. It just feels so good.' Her shy smile reminded him of the first time he had made love to her, when her guileless enjoyment had made him come much faster than he had intended.

He focused entirely on giving her pleasure as he began to move, slowly at first, with strong, measured strokes that heightened their mutual excitement. She quickly learned his rhythm, lifting her hips to meet each powerful thrust. Their bodies moved in perfect accord, riding a sensual roller coaster that gathered speed—faster, faster, hurtling them towards the highest peak and hovering there for timeless moments before they crashed and burned in the climatic explosion of their simultaneous release.

A long time afterwards, Constantin rolled onto his back and immediately curled his arm around her and cradled her against his chest. The steady thud of his heartbeat beneath her ear soothed the knot of apprehension in Isobel's stomach. They needed to talk, and she was no longer sure what she hoped the outcome of the conversation would be. Had making love to her meant something to him, or was it simply to slake his sexual frustration?

'Constantin…?'

'Sleep now, *tesorino*,' he murmured. Was it her imagination, or did she sense that he was reluctant to break the languorous haze? The drift of his fingertips along her spine was hypnotic and she closed her mind to everything but the pleasure of simply being with him in the private world they had created.

Isobel had no concept of how long she'd slept, when something, a sound, woke her. Surfacing from the fog of sleep, she realised that she had heard a voice shouting. Her memory returned.

She'd had sex with Constantin last night.

Why did things never seem such a good idea the next morning?

Pale grey light slivered through the blinds, and she saw on the clock that it was four a.m. Constantin was sitting up in bed, breathing hard, as if he had run a marathon. She put her hand on his shoulder and he jumped as if he had been shot.

'*Dio!* Isobel—' he took a gulp of air '—I didn't realise you were awake.'

'I heard a noise.' Her brow wrinkled as a memory pushed up from her subconscious. 'Why were you shouting?'

'I knocked over the damned water jug. I'm sorry, *cara*, I didn't realise I'd cursed so loudly.'

She looked at him doubtfully, not quite believing his explanation. 'I thought I heard you say, "He meant to kill her," or…or something like that.' She had a vague recollection of hearing those curious words some time in the past. 'Do you still suffer from nightmares like you did two years ago at Casa Celeste?' She wished it were light enough for her to be able to see his face clearly. She looked over at his bedside table and felt even more puzzled when she made out the water jug standing upright.

'I think *you* must have been dreaming.' His breathing had slowed to a normal rate and he sounded amused.

Isobel frowned. 'I'm sure I wasn't.' It was becoming harder to think when he was nuzzling her neck. She tried to push him away but her hand somehow crept up to his shoulder as he trailed soft kisses down her throat and the slopes of her breasts. Her nipples were ultra-sensitive from his earlier caresses, and she caught her breath as he anointed each tender pink tip with his tongue.

'Constantin…' She fought the swift rush of desire that swept through her, trying to focus on the reason why he had called out. One of them had been dreaming, and she was certain it wasn't her. But his hand was between her legs, and a little moan escaped her as he unerringly found her clitoris and with skilful fingers took her swiftly to a place where only exquisite sensation existed. When he bent his dark head and replaced his fingers with his mouth, she instinctively arched her hips and quivered like a slender bow under intolerable tension before she experienced the sweet ecstasy of release. But hazily, in the back of her mind, was the thought that he had deliberately set out to distract her.

As the cool grey of pre-dawn turned to iridescent shades of pink and palest gold Constantin watched the hands on the clock move unhurriedly towards six a.m. From outside the window he could hear the pigeons cooing, the faint rumble of traffic that would grow louder as the Eternal City woke to a new day.

There was no chance he could fall back to sleep now, thank goodness. But his nightmare had been so vivid that he broke out in a cold sweat as he recalled the details. He had dreamed of two figures standing on a balcony. Not the balcony of the tower at Casa Celeste, but here at the penthouse. And the figures were not his father and Lorena, but *him* and Isobel.

She was tossing her hair, laughing as she teased him that she preferred the handsome waiter at the restaurant to him. *Basta!* Her taunts filled him with rage. *Violent rage— seething up inside him like boiling lava inside a volcano.* He reached out his hand…and then she was falling, falling.

Mio Dio! It was just a dream, Constantin told himself.

It did not mean anything. He turned his head and stared at
Isobel's face on the pillow beside him. She was so beautiful. His gut clenched. He shouldn't have brought her to
Rome. He had wanted to protect her while the stalker was
still at large, but perhaps his dream was a warning that she
was in as much danger from *him*.

CHAPTER NINE

ISOBEL MOVED AWAY from a group of noisy tourists outside the Church of Sant'Agnese in Agone and held her phone closer to her ear. 'I'm sorry, I didn't catch that.'

'I said, do you remember that we've been invited to the Bonuccis' party tonight, to celebrate the opening of their new hotel?'

Constantin's sexy voice made her toes curl, and she took a steadying breath before replying. 'I haven't forgotten,' she said drily. She had been in Rome for a week, and tonight's party would be the fifth social event that she and Constantin had attended. They barely spent any time alone, she reflected. He worked all day and returned home late, just in time to shower and change before they went out for the evening. It was always past midnight before they arrived back at the penthouse and Constantin invariably seemed to have a reason not to come straight to bed until she had fallen asleep.

It would be easy to think that he was trying to avoid her. That was what the insecure Isobel from two years ago would have believed, she acknowledged ruefully. But she was older, and hopefully wiser, and instead of leaping to conclusions she reminded herself that Constantin was the CEO of one of Italy's most prominent businesses and socialising and networking were part of his job.

'You should receive a delivery today.' Over the phone line she heard him hesitate. 'I bought you a dress to wear tonight.'

'It's already been delivered, and it's beautiful, thank you.'

'You don't mind?'

She sensed his surprise. In the past she had always been uptight when he'd bought her presents, and although she had politely thanked him her words had been stilted. It was little wonder that he'd felt rebuffed by her, Isobel brooded.

'I'm glad you like it,' Constantin told her. 'I saw the dress on display in a shop window and immediately knew it would suit you.'

'If you're home in time, I'll model it exclusively for you,' she murmured.

There was a pregnant pause. 'I'm sorry, *cara,* I have a late meeting scheduled. Can you be ready to leave for the party at seven-thirty?'

'Con…' Discovering that he had cut the call, she dropped her phone into her bag and started walking back to the apartment. Her brow wrinkled. Something was going on that she did not understand. The few times that they'd had sex it had been amazing for both of them. Constantin could not have faked his groans of pleasure as he'd come inside her.

Nor was it conceivable that he had become bored of her already. He was always up and dressed when she woke in the mornings, but she'd seen the way he looked at her with a feral gleam in his eyes and she knew he wanted to join her back in bed. So why didn't he? Was he under pressure at work, or was something else bothering him?

She sighed as she let herself into the penthouse. Maybe, like her, he was wondering where their relationship was going. By silent, mutual agreement they hadn't discussed the state of their marriage, but Constantin had not refuted reports in the Italian media that they were reconciled, and there had been several photos of them together in the newspapers.

He arrived home at ten past seven and walked into the bedroom to find her in her underwear as she was getting changed for the party. To Isobel's astonishment dull colour flared on his cheekbones as he studied her black lace thong and matching push-up bra, before he muttered something incomprehensible and shot into the bathroom like a one-hundred-metre sprinter.

Enough was enough, Isobel decided. When her virile, stallion of a husband started acting like a shy virgin, it was time to demand some answers.

Constantin stiffened when he felt two slender arms wrap around his waist. Isobel had stepped behind him in the shower cubicle but the noise of the spray had muffled her arrival, and now he was in trouble. Stiff was an apt description of a certain part of his anatomy, he thought derisively. He did not need to glance down to know that he was massively aroused, and her throaty murmur of approval made a bad situation even worse.

All week, he had tried to keep his distance from her. His nightmare had scared the hell out of him. Isobel was the only woman who stirred blood-boiling jealousy in his gut. Look how he had reacted to the waiter! The guy had only smiled at her but Constantin had wanted to rip his head off.

He did not want to feel the possessive, manic jealousy that had gripped his father. He did not want to *feel* any emotions. Somehow he had to get whatever it was he felt for Isobel under control, but every time he made love to her he felt himself slipping deeper beneath her sensual spell. The solution, he'd concluded, was to resist the temptation of her gorgeous body. But her hands were creating havoc and ruining his good intentions.

He couldn't restrain a groan as she skimmed her fingers over his stomach and thighs and along the length of his arousal. 'Isa…bella,' he said through gritted teeth, 'we don't have time before the party.' He made a last-ditch attempt to stop her roving hands.

She slipped round in front of him and kissed his lips. 'It doesn't start until eight o'clock. You must have misread the invitation.' She wrapped her fingers around him and gave him a smile of pure witchery. 'Anyway I have a feeling this won't take long.'

Constantin sucked in a harsh breath as she dropped to her knees and replaced her hands with her mouth. *Madonna*, how could he fight his gut-aching desire for her when she was running her tongue lightly over the sensitive tip? It was all he could do not to spill his seed into her mouth. Only a man with ice running through his veins could resist his beautiful, generous, *bold* Isobel. But Constantin's blood was on fire. Giving a muffled curse, he lifted her into his arms and as she hooked her legs around his waist he entered her with a deep thrust that drove them both close to the edge.

It was urgent and intense, and it couldn't last. After a week of sexual frustration, the excitement of their primitive coupling was electrifying. Isobel dug her fingernails into Constantin's bunched shoulders, anchoring herself to him as he cupped her bottom and pumped into her with hard, fast strokes until she sobbed his name over and over. Her man, her master, she belonged to him and he claimed her utterly, bringing her to a shattering orgasm that sent shudders of indescribable pleasure through her body. His climax was no less spectacular, and at the exquisite moment of release he threw his head back and let out a savage groan before burying his face against her throat while their hearts thundered in unison.

Afterwards Isobel had to rush to get ready for the party. Luckily she had gained a light golden tan from a week in the Italian sunshine and needed nothing more than a coat of mascara to define her eyelashes and a slick of rose-coloured gloss on her lips.

'You look stunning,' Constantin commented quietly when she joined him in the lounge. She had already taken his breath away once this evening, but the sight of her in the floor-length scarlet silk gown held in place with narrow diamanté shoulder straps evoked a curious tightness in his chest.

'It's a beautiful dress.' She did a little twirl in front of the mirror and threw him an impish smile. 'I have a present for you.'

He gave her an intent look as she handed him a black leather box with the distinctive DSE logo embossed on the lid. The platinum wrist watch nestled on a velvet cushion was the most prestigious and expensive watch in the DSE range, and it happened to be his personal favourite.

'You told me that your watch had developed a fault and needed to be repaired. I thought you might like this one to replace the old one.'

'I don't know what to say.' Constantin was aware of a curious scratchiness in his throat. He knew exactly how much the watch was worth in financial terms, but even more touching was the fact that Isobel had chosen this particular model from the collection for him. He smiled. 'This is the first present I've been given since I was eight years old.'

'Apart from Christmas and birthday presents, I suppose you mean.'

'My father didn't believe in celebrating holidays or

personal milestones after my mother died.' His voice became reflective. '*Madre* gave me a model of a sports car for my eighth birthday. Her cancer was untreatable by then and she died a few weeks later.'

Isobel was struck by the lack of emotion in his voice. She was reminded of when she'd had the miscarriage and he had been so matter-of-fact. 'It must have been a terribly sad time for you and your father when your mother died,' she said softly.

For a fleeting moment an indefinable expression crossed his face, but he shrugged and said levelly, 'Life goes on.' He slid the watch onto his wrist. 'Thank you. This is the best present I've ever received.'

Considering that the only other present Constantin had been given was a toy car when he was eight, his enthusiasm for the watch she had bought him was not surprising, Isobel mused later that evening.

She glanced around the packed ballroom of the five-star hotel that had been refurbished by the fabulously wealthy Bonucci family. The décor was opulent and unashamedly luxurious and the guests at the opening party included many of the social elite not just from Rome but across Europe. It was the sort of event that she had dreaded when she had first married Constantin. She had felt awkward and out of place among his sophisticated friends and had convinced herself that they regarded her as a cheap gold-digger.

Despite the fact that she now had a successful career and had 'made it' some of those old, insecure feelings returned as Constantin escorted her around the ballroom and introduced her to the other guests. Their exquisite manners when they greeted her did not disguise the speculative glances they gave her as Constantin slipped his arm around her waist. Isobel told herself she was imagining the coolness she sensed from one or two of the guests, but when Constantin murmured in her ear that he had spotted a business associate he wanted to speak to, she had to fight the temptation to cling to his arm as she had done in the past.

She reminded herself that she had attended countless parties and functions in the past two years and could hold her own in any social situation. She did not need Constantin as a prop. But the sight of a familiar figure making a beeline for her across the ballroom made her heart sink.

'Isobel! I must admit that I did not expect to see *you* here tonight.' Ghislaine Montenocci had recently married, and pictures of her fabulous wedding to a French duke had filled the pages of a well-known celebrity magazine. 'My husband, Duc Alphonse de Cavarre, is over there,' she lost no time in telling Isobel, waving her hand towards a sandy-haired man who looked a good twenty years older than his new wife. Isobel wondered if the social-climbing Ghislaine had been attracted to her husband's title.

'I heard rumours that you and Constantin had reconciled, but I didn't believe it. You must be *so* relieved that he has taken you back.'

Ghislaine's name had changed with her marriage, but unfortunately her personality hadn't, Isobel mused, recalling the other woman's nasty comment that when she had married Constantin she had secured a meal ticket for life.

The insecure Isobel of three years ago had been overawed by Ghislaine, but now she smiled coolly. 'Why relieved?' she queried.

'Well, I would have thought that, having managed to marry a billionaire, you wouldn't want to lose him,' Ghislaine said cattily.

'As a matter of fact, Constantin supported my decision to establish my singing career during the past two years.' It was laughably far from the truth, but Isobel refused to be beaten by Ghislaine. 'I think it is so important for women to have aspirations and a *purpose* in life, rather than simply being a wife, don't you agree?' Isobel guessed that Ghislaine had never done a day's work in her life, and, although it was not in her nature to be unkind, she could not help feeling a little sense of victory when the other woman flushed. 'A strong marriage is one where both partners are able to fulfil their dreams. I admit that I am proud of my career success.'

'So you should be.' Constantin's deep voice behind her made Isobel jump, and her heart did that annoying leap that it always did when he slid his arm around her waist and gave her a sexy smile before he spoke to Ghislaine.

'Isobel and her band the Stone Ladies are amazing, aren't they? I am incredibly proud of my talented wife.'

Ghislaine muttered something about needing to join her husband and moved away. Isobel frowned at Constantin. 'There was no need for you to pretend that you are proud of me. I can fight my own battles,' she said drily.

Something in his bright blue eyes caused her breath to become trapped in her throat.

'I wasn't pretending. I *am* proud of you, Isabella. You weren't born into wealth and privilege like I was, or like Ghislaine. Everything you have achieved has been through your talent, hard work and determination.'

Isobel swallowed the lump that had formed in her throat. 'But you resented the time I spent performing with the band. You blamed my career for driving us apart.'

Constantin grimaced. 'I didn't understand how important music and singing were to you. I believed you preferred to spend time with your friends than with me, and deep down I knew I could not blame you,' he admitted roughly. He met her gaze, and Isobel saw regret in his eyes. 'I had my reasons for drawing away from you, and I see now that you thought I was rejecting you.' He glanced around the crowded ballroom. 'This is not the place to discuss our relationship, *cara*,' he said ruefully. 'I'll go and get us a drink.'

Isobel watched him stride across the room to the bar and had the strangest feeling that he felt tense at the prospect of a discussion about their relationship that was long overdue. She had been stunned to hear him say he was proud of her career. His admiration meant a lot, she acknowledged. For so long she had lived in the shadow of her clever brother, and her failure to match Simon's academic achievements or fulfil her father's expectations had made her feel useless and unworthy of the rich, handsome, successful man she had married. Now she felt she was Constantin's equal, but was it too late for them to turn their marriage around and be lifelong partners?

She studied him as he stopped on his way to the bar to chat to someone. They had lost their child, and he was under no obligation to remain married to her, so why had he told her that he had changed his mind and wanted to give their marriage another chance, unless—her heart thudded against her ribs—could it be that he felt something for her?

'Your husband is a handsome devil. I remember he was a good-looking boy, but then it's hardly surprising when his mother was one of the most photographed models of her era.'

Isobel turned towards the woman who had come to stand next to her. She had met Diane Rivolli when Constantin had introduced them at a dinner party two nights ago, and she remembered he had said that Diane lived outside Rome, near to Casa Celeste on the shores of Lake Albano.

'Did you know Constantin's mother?'

'I knew Susie when she was Susie Hoffman. We belonged to the same modelling agency in New York but Susie was gorgeous and she got far more bookings than any of the other girls.' Diane shrugged. 'In fact I met my husband when Susie invited me to stay at Casa Celeste after she'd married Franco De Severino. I think she was lonely, shut away in that huge house that's more like a museum than a home. As for her husband...'

Diane paused, and Isobel's curiosity grew. 'What about Constantin's father?'

'Franco was a cold fish. I gained the impression that the only thing he cared about was Susie. But he loved her *too* much, if that makes sense?' Seeing Isobel's puzzled expression, Diane tried to explain. 'Franco was obsessed with Susie. He disliked her having friends, and although my husband and I only lived a short distance away we were hardly ever invited to Casa Celeste. On the few occasions when we were invited, Franco was always on edge. He hated other men looking at his wife. I even think he was jealous of his own son,' Diane said meditatively. 'Susie doted on Constantin, but even when he was a baby Franco seemed to resent her spending time with her son. I caught him looking at Constantin once with such a strange expression on his face, as if he hated the child.'

Isobel was fascinated to hear about Constantin's family. She had often wondered why he was reluctant to talk about his childhood. 'Franco must have been devastated when Susie died.'

'You would think so, but if he was upset he didn't show it. At her funeral he stood in the church like a cold statue without a flicker of emotion on his face.' Diane shook her head. 'I found it even stranger that Constantin never cried for his mother. He stood stiffly at Susie's graveside like a miniature image of his father and didn't shed a tear. I didn't see him again for years because Franco packed him off to boarding school. Constantin must have been about sixteen when Franco married his second wife.'

'I had no idea that Constantin had a stepmother.' Isobel frowned at this new revelation. 'He's never mentioned her.'

'Maybe that's because he was in love with Lorena.' Diane paused again, allowing her startling suggestion to register with Isobel.

'Constantin was in love with his stepmother?'

The other woman shrugged. 'Why not? Lorena was much younger than Franco. She was probably only in her early twenties, very attractive—and she knew it! It was pretty obvious that she had married Franco for his money. She enjoyed socialising and she often invited me and my husband to pool parties, although it was clear that Franco hated having visitors.

'I suppose you couldn't blame Lorena for wanting to have fun with Constantin when she was stuck with a dour older husband. She turned the boy's head, flirting with him and paying him attention.' Diane frowned. 'There was something quite cruel about the way Lorena deliberately encouraged Constantin's crush on her, and the way she played father and son off against each other. Franco was jealous of his second wife in the same way he had been with Susie. He was furious if another man so much as looked at her, and Constantin's puppy-dog devotion to Lorena created a lot of friction between father and son.

'I don't know what would have happened if the situation had continued,' Diane went on, 'but then Franco and Lorena died in that terrible accident. Poor Constantin, not only did he witness what happened, but the leadership of DSE was thrown into chaos.

'Constantin should have automatically become joint Chairman and CEO when his father died, but, because he wasn't eighteen, his father's brother, Alonso, assumed control of the company. Constantin worked his way up to CEO, and it's no secret that he wants complete control of DSE.'

Diane took a sip of champagne before continuing. 'It's my belief that Constantin would go to any lengths to claim the chairmanship of DSE that he thinks is his birthright.'

Isobel's head was reeling from everything Diane had said, and she only vaguely registered the bit about Constantin wanting to be Chairman of DSE. Why hadn't he told her that his father and stepmother had died in an accident when he had been a young man? The tragedy must have had a fundamental impact on Constantin, especially if he had been in love with Lorena. Could it explain his strange behaviour when he had taken her to Casa Celeste? she wondered. Had he become cold and remote with her because he was *still* in love with his stepmother?

'What actually happened to Constantin's father and stepmother?'

Diane gave her a strange look. 'You mean he hasn't told you?' She seemed suddenly flustered when she caught sight of him walking across the ballroom towards them. 'I've probably said too much. Why don't you ask Constantin what took place at the top of the tower at Casa Celeste?'

CHAPTER TEN

'THE HOUSE IS shut up and unstaffed apart from a caretaker and gardener because I rarely go there. I don't understand why you want to visit Casa Celeste.'

'I've told you why. I want to visit Arianna's grave.' Isobel held Constantin's gaze and refused to be intimidated by the impatient expression etched on his taut features. 'I don't need staff. I'm perfectly capable of making up a bed and cooking meals.'

He frowned at her across the breakfast bar where they had been enjoying a leisurely Saturday morning breakfast until she had stated her wish to make the twenty-kilometre journey south of the city to Lake Albano. 'I don't see the point...'

'Your lack of understanding says a lot,' she interrupted him, struggling to hide the hurt in her voice. 'You've obviously been able to forget about our daughter, but I haven't, nor do I want to forget her. I would like to spend some time at the chapel where she's buried.'

Last night, when they had arrived home from the party, she had tried to talk about the past and in particular the things Diane Rivolli had said about Constantin's father and stepmother being involved in a terrible accident at Casa Celeste. But Constantin had refused to be drawn into a discussion, and had distracted her by sweeping her into his arms and whispering in her ear exactly what he was going to do to her once he had removed her dress and the tantalising wisps of her black lace underwear that he had pictured in his mind all evening.

Resistance would be futile, he had warned her. But Isobel had had no intention of resisting him, and by the time he had kissed her senseless before trailing his lips down her body to bestow a wickedly intimate caress that had resulted in her shuddering orgasm, she had forgotten that she had wanted to talk to him. When they had made love last night she had felt closer to him than she had ever felt, and, waking in his arms this morning, she had been filled with optimism that they had a future together. But her request to visit Casa Celeste had created a distinct chill in the atmosphere.

'It's never a good idea to revisit the past,' he said harshly.

'That's your way of dealing with things, isn't it? You pretend they never happened and refuse to talk about them. Are you going to keep running away for ever, Constantin?' Isobel said bitterly. She looked away from him. 'I've come to terms with the miscarriage, but our baby will always have a special place in my heart. I'm going to Casa Celeste, with or without you.'

Constantin's jaw clenched. He did not know how to handle this confident Isobel who wasn't afraid to argue with him. She had changed immeasurably in the two years they had been apart, although her sensuality and generosity when they made love still set her apart from any of his previous lovers, he brooded, feeling his body stir as he remembered the erotic session in the shower that had made them late for the Bonuccis' party.

'I can't spend time away from the office right now,' he said curtly. 'I don't want you to go to the house on your own while the stalker is still a threat to your safety. For all we know, he could have discovered that you are in Rome.'

'The police in England have arrested David and he is receiving psychiatric care. They phoned with the news yesterday and I meant to tell you when you came home from work, but...' she blushed as X-rated images of them in the shower flooded her mind '...we were distracted.'

'Hmm...*distracted* is one way to describe what we were doing,' Constantin murmured. He walked round the breakfast bar and lifted her off the bar stool, holding her so that her pelvis was in burning contact with his. 'Why don't we go back to bed and distract each other some more, *mia bella*?'

It was hard to think straight when his lips were trailing a sensual path along her collarbone. Isobel felt a familiar melting sensation in the pit of her stomach as he began to unbutton her shirt. She definitely should have worn a bra, she mused, stifling a moan when he rubbed his thumb pads across her nipples and they instantly hardened. All week, when he had rushed off to work each morning, she had longed for him to stay home and make slow leisurely love to her, but now she fought the temptation of his roaming hands and mouth. She recognised his diversionary tactics and refused to be sidetracked from her determination to go to Casa Celeste.

She had told him the truth when she'd said she wanted to visit their baby's grave. But she also sensed that there were secrets at the De Severino's ancestral home that she needed to uncover if she was to have a chance of understanding her enigmatic husband.

'I know what game you're playing, Constantin,' she told him. She slid out of his arms and refastened her shirt, wincing as the cotton brushed across the sensitive peaks of her breasts. 'It won't work. Either you come with me

to Casa Celeste, or I'll go there on my own before I catch
the next flight back to England.'

Constantin gave her a frustrated look. 'That sounds like
blackmail.' He remembered making the same accusation
to his uncle not so long ago.

The stubborn set of Isobel's jaw infuriated him. She
used to be so amenable! 'I'm tempted to put you over my
knee,' he growled, and had the satisfaction of seeing her
eyes widen and her cheeks suffuse with colour. 'But if
I did, I guarantee we wouldn't leave the bedroom for a
week.'

Constantin suddenly decided that he had to make several
urgent business calls, and he spent all afternoon in his
study, meaning that they did not set out for Casa Celeste
until early evening. He was uncommunicative during the
journey to Lake Albano, and when the car turned through
the gates of the De Severino estate onto a long driveway
lined with poplar trees he tightened his hands on the steering wheel so that his knuckles whitened.

Diane Rivolli's suggestion that Isobel should ask him
about the accident that had resulted in the deaths of his
father and stepmother was not as simple as it seemed, she
brooded as she glanced at him. His grim expression did
not encourage her to probe into his past, but she was convinced that they could not have a future together unless
she could find the key that would unlock his emotions.

Her thoughts were diverted as they drew up in front
of the house. The first time Isobel had visited Casa Celeste she had been awed by the grandeur of the four-
storey building with its tall windows, elegant columns, and
a tall tower topped with a spire that gave the house the look
of a fairy-tale castle. Inside was no less magnificent. The
frescoes on the walls and ceilings were adorned with gold

leaf, and the white marble floors created an ambiance of welcome coolness to visitors entering the house from the heat of the Italian sun.

Diane had been right when she'd said that Casa Celeste was more like a museum than a home, Isobel acknowledged as she walked past a row of portraits of Constantin's ancestors. It was something she had thought herself when she had stayed there in the past. The dust sheets draped over the furniture added to the impression that this was a house of ghosts.

She shivered. It had been in this house that she had suffered a miscarriage. Shortly after dinner one evening she had been violently sick. The doctor Constantin called out had initially thought she had food poisoning, but the stomach cramps had worsened, and when she had started to bleed she had been rushed into hospital, but nothing could be done to save the baby.

It's never a good idea to revisit the past, Constantin had warned her before they had left Rome. She wondered what memories filled his mind when he came to Casa Celeste. Blinking back her tears, she walked outside to the courtyard at the back of the house and found him sitting on a low wall surrounding an ornamental fountain.

'Why didn't you tell me that your father and his second wife died here at Casa Celeste?'

He stiffened and shot her a searching look. 'I suppose Diane was gossiping,' he said tersely. 'No doubt she filled your head with lurid tales.'

'Diane didn't tell me anything, except that they had been killed in an accident which you witnessed.' The cold gleam in Constantin's eyes warned Isobel that he wanted her to drop the subject, but her determination to resolve the issues that she was sure had come between them during their marriage made her press him for an answer. 'What actually happened?'

A nerve flickered in his jaw. 'Are you sure you want to know? Be careful, Isobel. Some secrets are best left hidden.'

She did not know how to respond, and after a few moments he shrugged and glanced up at the tall tower attached to the main house. His voice was devoid of emotion when he spoke.

'My father and stepmother fell to their deaths from the balcony up there at the top of the tower.' He kicked the hard cobblestoned courtyard. 'They were both killed instantly, which was some small mercy, I suppose.'

She gave a horrified gasp. 'You saw it happen?'

'Yes. It wasn't pretty, as I'm sure you can imagine.' His tone was so matter-of-fact that he could have been discussing something as mundane as the weather.

Isobel was lost for words, shocked not just by the details of the fatal accident but by Constantin's lack of sentiment. 'What a terrible thing to have witnessed. You must have had nightmares afterwards...' Her voice faltered as she remembered how she had heard him shouting out during the night when they had stayed at Casa Celeste. No wonder his cries had been so blood-curdling if his dreams had relived the horror of seeing his father and stepmother plunge to their deaths.

'You should have told me.' She felt hurt that he had not confided in her about the traumatic event in his life that must have affected him—and quite possibly *still* affected him, she mused, remembering what she had heard about Constantin's relationship with his father's second wife. 'At least I would have understood why you dislike coming here.' She bit her lip. 'Diane said that you were in love with Lorena.'

His reaction was explosive. He jumped to his feet and slashed his hand through the air. '*Mio Dio!* That woman should have her tongue cut out. Diane Rivolli was never party to my thoughts. She knows *nothing*, and she has no right to make slanderous accusations about me.'

He had paled beneath his tan, and the hand he raked through his hair shook, Isobel noticed. It was the first time she had ever seen him so worked up. Gone was his air of cool detachment. His jaw was rigid and his eyes glittered with anger. 'I warned you that the past is best left dead and buried,' he said savagely.

'Constantin...' She stared after him as he strode out of a gate in the courtyard wall that led to dense woodland surrounding the house, which was home to wild boar. He had once told her that *cinghiale* could weigh up to four hundred pounds and the males had fearsome tusks. But a wild boar was probably not as dangerous as Constantin's mood was right now, Isobel thought ruefully. His violent reaction when she had mentioned his father's young wife pointed to him having been in love with Lorena.

She suddenly wished she had heeded his advice and stayed away from Casa Celeste. There was a strange atmosphere in the courtyard where Franco and Lorena had died. The sun sinking below the horizon was blood-red, and cast long shadows on the house. Despite the warm evening air Isobel shivered as goosebumps prickled her skin, and, giving a low cry, she ran back inside. But there was no comfort to be found in the coldly elegant rooms. Casa Celeste was an impressive house, but she wondered if it had ever felt like a home to Constantin.

She unloaded the car and carried the food they had brought with them into the kitchen, where she put together a salad, forced herself to eat a small dinner, and put the rest in the fridge for Constantin, if and when he returned later. He still had not come back when she made up the bed in the master bedroom, before choosing one of the guest bedrooms for herself. She avoided the bedroom where she had stayed on her last disastrous visit two years ago.

Constantin's revelation about the tragedy that he had witnessed at Casa Celeste went some way to explaining why he disliked the house, but there were so many things about him that she still did not understand. Her marriage was as full of secrets as it had always been and she was no closer to discovering what, if anything, Constantin felt for her.

She must have slept deeply, because she did not hear him enter her bedroom much later that night, and she was unaware that he stood by the bed for a long time, a grave, almost tortured expression on his face as he watched her sleeping.

When Isobel opened her eyes, bright sunlight filled the room and she immediately saw Constantin sitting in an armchair next to the window.

'You look terrible,' she told him bluntly, raking her eyes over his haggard face and the black stubble covering his jaw. 'Have you slept at all?'

Instead of answering her question, he said harshly, 'Let's go back to Rome. There is evil here in this house.'

She nodded slowly. 'I can understand why you think that. But our daughter is here. I'm not leaving until I've visited Arianna's grave.'

The tiny private chapel where for centuries the members of the De Severino family had been baptised and buried was a little way off from the house. Isobel followed a path that wound through the estate, passing olive groves and vine-yards before she caught sight of the ancient stone build-ing. When she had last been there, on the day of Arianna's funeral, the chapel grounds had been overgrown and sunlight had struggled to filter through the trees. She remembered how she had felt hollow with grief and utterly alone. Constantin had been with her, but she had been chilled by his lack of emotion as they had said goodbye to their baby.

The gloomy surroundings had augmented her misery on that day two and a half years ago. But as she pushed open the gate and walked towards Arianna's headstone she was shocked to see that dozens of rose bushes had been planted around the grave, and a bench had been placed nearby beneath the delicate fronds of a young weeping willow. The tall oak trees had been cut back allowing sunshine to bathe this corner of the graveyard in a golden halo of light.

Isobel stopped in her tracks and stared. She caught sight of an elderly gardener pruning a hedge and walked over to him.

'The roses are beautiful. It must have taken a lot of work to plant so many.'

His lined face creased into a smile. 'Not for me. *Il Marchese* planted them for his *bambina*. He comes often. Not to the house. He sits there.' The old man nodded to the bench. 'There is peace here.'

Isobel understood. The only sound was birdsong and the whisper of the breeze gently stirring the willow tree. The gardener moved away, leaving her alone to admire the roses that were just coming into bloom. All the bushes had pink buds, she realised. Pink for a girl. In the hushed stillness of the garden she thought she heard tinkling laughter. Her vision was blurred with tears and for a moment she was sure she glimpsed a little figure running along the path.

'Arianna!'

She whirled round, but no one was there. The ache in

her throat became unbearable and she sank down onto the bench and allowed her tears to fall.

'I knew it was a mistake to come.' Constantin's voice, deep as an ocean, sounded close by. Isobel had been unaware that he had followed her from the house. 'I knew you would find it too painful,' he said thickly. He sat down on the bench and pulled her into his arms, but said nothing more, simply held her and stroked her hair while she wept.

At last she lifted her head and scrubbed her wet face with the back of her hand. 'I'm not only crying for Arianna. I'm sad because I didn't know how much losing her hurt you.'

She waved her hand at the rose garden. 'You created this beautiful place in memory of our baby, but I had no idea that you cared. You were so distant, so...contained and unemotional. I needed you,' she told him in a choked voice. 'I wish we could have grieved together. I was angry because I believed you didn't feel the pain I felt. I even thought that you hadn't wanted our baby. Why couldn't you have told me that you were sad too?'

'I couldn't,' he said heavily. 'I can't explain.'

'Please try, because I want to understand,' she whispered.

Something flared in his eyes, but he turned his head away from her tear-streaked face and said nothing.

'Diane said that you didn't cry at your mother's funeral. I don't understand. You were eight years old and I know you loved her. You keep the model sports car she gave you for your birthday locked in a glass cabinet.'

'My father told me I mustn't cry,' Constantin said harshly. 'He said that crying was a sign of weakness and De Severino men are not weak.'

'So that's why your father didn't show any emotion

when he stood at your mother's grave. Diane said...' Her voice faltered when he frowned.

'Diane obviously said a damn sight too much.'

His mouth twisted. As Constantin had walked through the grounds of the chapel and heard Isobel weeping he'd felt a pain beneath his breastbone, as if his heart had splintered. His first instinct had been to leave her to grieve alone as he had done when she'd had the miscarriage. But something had made him turn back to her. *Are you going to keep running away for ever?* she had asked him.

Dio! She had made him take a long, hard look at himself, and he had felt ashamed. Since he was a boy, he had believed that emotions were a sign of weakness. But who was the coward—brave, strong Isobel who was honest about her feelings? Or him, a grown man too scared to allow himself to feel the emotional highs and lows that were part of life?

'Diane did not see what I saw.'

Isobel stared at him, shocked by the rawness in his voice. 'What did you see?'

He shook his head and hunched forwards, his shoulders bowed. 'I saw my father crying.'

Constantin was eight years old again, standing outside his father's study listening to the terrible moans coming from behind the closed door. He'd been scared that a *cinghiale* had got into the house and was goring his father with its sharp tusks. His heart had thudded beneath his ribs as he'd slowly pushed open the door.

'On the night my mother was buried I heard strange noises from my father's study,' he told Isobel. 'I went in and saw him rolling on the floor as though he was in agony.' Constantin let out a ragged breath. 'Franco was crying in a way I'd never seen anyone cry before. I was just a child...and I was frightened. My father had told me that only weak men cried. He looked up and saw me and he was angry, shouting at me to go away. I ran to the door, but he called to me. "Now you know how cruel love is, how it brings a man to utter despair and misery."'

Constantin could hear his father's voice. He glanced at Isobel and saw a mixture of shock and sympathy in her hazel eyes that tugged on something deep inside him.

'The next day, my father was his usual, cold self. Neither of us ever spoke about what had happened, but I sensed he was ashamed that I had witnessed his breakdown. He sent me away to school and I saw very little of him when I was growing up. But the memory of him sobbing, and the realisation that love had reduced my proud father to a broken man, stayed in my mind. I was frightened by the destructive power of love, and how it could make a man weak. At eight years old I learned to keep my emotions locked inside me.'

'But you did care about our baby,' Isobel said softly. 'You couldn't cry for Arianna, but you planted this garden for her.'

She stood up and walked among the rose bushes, leaning down to inhale the delicate perfume of the unfurling petals. Her heart ached. She felt unbearably moved by Constantin's admission that he could not show his emotions, but Arianna's garden was proof that he had shared her devastation at the loss of their daughter.

Constantin broke off a rosebud from a bush and handed it to her before he swept her up in his arms.

'What are you doing?' Her breath left her body in a shaky sigh. The temptation to rest her aching head on his shoulder was too strong to resist.

'What I should have done two years ago. I'm going to take care of you, *tesorino*,' he said softly. 'I'm going to run you a bath, and I'm going to cook dinner for you—'

he looked into her eyes, and Isobel's heart leapt at the sensual promise in his gaze '—and then I am going to make love to you.'

'You can't carry me all the way back to the house,' she murmured. But he did, and when he entered the cool marble hallway of Casa Celeste he continued up the stairs to the master bedroom and into the en suite bathroom, where he filled the sunken bath with water and added a handful of rose-scented crystals.

His hands were gentle as he unbuttoned her shirt and placed it on the chair before he removed her skirt and underwear. She gathered her hair up and pinned it on top of her head, exposing her slender neck.

'You're beautiful,' he said roughly. 'I knew the moment I saw you that I was in trouble.' He turned to walk out of the bathroom, but she touched his arm.

'After I lost the baby I felt angry when you suggested we make love because I thought it was proof that you didn't care.'

He shook his head. 'I didn't know how else to reach out to you. Bed was the one place where we understood each other's needs perfectly, and I wanted to show you what I couldn't say with words. I knew I had failed you. I knew you wanted more support from me...' his voice became husky '...but the truth is that hearing you crying was something I couldn't deal with. When you pushed me away, I told myself it was no more than I deserved. I decided to wait until you gave some sign that you wanted me.'

Isobel glanced ruefully at her swollen nipples. Her breasts felt heavy and the sweet ache between her legs could only be assuaged by Constantin. 'In case you've missed the signs my body is sending you, I want you,' she said softly.

His chest lifted as he drew a jerky breath. She looked

heartbreakingly fragile and emotionally spent. 'You need food, rest...'

She stepped towards him and reached up to brush her mouth lightly across his. 'I need you.'

Luckily it was a big bath. He helped her step into the water and slid in behind her. She leaned back against his chest and sank deep into a world of pleasure, where nothing existed but the drift of his hands on her body as he caressed her breasts, cupping them and feeling their weight, before he moved lower.

'Mind where you put that bar of soap,' she murmured and heard his husky chuckle in her ear as he dropped the soap and used his fingers in an intimate exploration that made her catch her breath. 'Constantin...' Her voice was urgent as she felt her pleasure build. Liquid heat pooled between her thighs and she tried to turn towards him.

'This is for you, *tesorino*.' He held her firmly in place and used his fingers to wicked effect while his other hand stole up to her breasts to tease each rose-tipped point in turn until her breathing quickened. He felt the sudden tension in her muscles, and he held her there, poised on the brink for a few seconds before sliding his fingers deeply into her to capture the frantic pulse of her orgasm.

Afterwards he dried her with a soft towel and smoothed fragrant oil over every centimetre of her skin, paying such careful attention to certain areas of her body that Isobel ached to take him inside her. Somehow they made it into the bedroom, and he placed her on the edge of the bed and stood between her legs, spreading her wide and sliding his hands beneath her bottom to angle her for his complete possession.

Their eyes met, held, and time stood still. There was no teasing gleam in his bright blue gaze now, just a stark need that touched Isobel's heart and made her think of the young boy who had stood beside his mother's grave and forced his lips not to tremble and his tears not to fall.

There were still many unanswered questions, but he had been right when he'd said that when they made love they understood each other perfectly.

There was no need for words. Their bodies moved in total accord and she arched beneath him to meet each powerful thrust as he drove her higher and higher. She sensed he was holding back, and his infinite care brought tears to her eyes. Tenderness was a new element to his desire and she loved him all the more for it, but what she needed right now was his hunger, his primitive need to claim her as his own.

There was no need for words. She told him in her evocative kiss that shook him with its innate sensuality exactly what she wanted from him. Passion, raw and honest and demanding a response she gave him with a willingness that rocked him to the depths of his soul as they climaxed simultaneously and tumbled together in a glorious freefall.

A long time later, hunger of a different kind prompted Constantin to head downstairs to the kitchen to prepare the dinner he had promised Isobel. They had picked up steaks and salad on the drive to the house, and the cellar offered a wide selection of vintage wines. He chose a fifteen-year-old Barolo, collected glasses and cutlery and set a table outside on the terrace overlooking an informal flower garden.

The mingled scents of jasmine and night-scented stocks greeted Isobel as she sat down opposite Constantin. Her heart fluttered madly like a trapped bird beneath her ribcage as she stared at the jewellery case he placed in front of her. The yellow diamond solitaire he had given her when he had asked her to marry him, the day after she had told him she was expecting his baby, lay next to the plain gold wedding band she had pulled from her finger before she had rushed out of the house in Grosvenor Square two years ago.

She lifted her eyes to his, silently questioning him.

'I would like you to wear your rings again, Isabella,' he said levelly.

He did not embellish the statement with flowery phrases, or say that he loved her, but she had not expected him to. Maybe he would never be able to share his feelings in words, but hadn't he shown her when he had made love to her with tender passion that he believed they shared something special?

But was it enough? She bit her lip. 'My career…?'

'Will, I'm confident, continue to go from strength to strength. I listened to the Stone Ladies' latest album while I was making dinner, and there is no doubt that all the members of the band are talented musicians, but you especially, *cara*. You have an exceptional voice.'

He was blown away by her talent, Constantin thought to himself. Isobel had a gift for singing and song writing, but when they had been together he'd been jealous of the time she spent with the other band members and he had not been supportive or understood why having a career was so important to her.

He picked up her wedding ring and felt her hand tremble as he slid the gold band onto her third finger. Her diamond engagement ring caught a moonbeam and sparkled with fiery brilliance that reflected the fire in her eyes.

'Food,' he said huskily, uncovering the serving plates where he had piled the grilled steaks. 'Something tells me I'm going to need plenty of protein for strength and stamina tonight.'

'Believe it,' she told him sweetly. 'You have two years to make up for.'

The sultry gleam in his eyes heightened Isobel's anticipation, as did his murmured, 'I will endeavour to give you complete satisfaction, *tesorino*.'

CHAPTER ELEVEN

THE SEQUENCE OF events was familiar. The sound of raised voices at the top of the tower. He looked up and saw his father and stepmother. Lorena was falling, screaming—and then her screams stopped. There was so much blood. It was on his hands as he knelt beside her, rolled her over and saw that it wasn't Lorena, but Isobel, lying lifeless on the ground. And now he was standing on the balcony at the top of the tower, stretching his hands towards Isobel. There was blood on his hands.

No! *Mio Dio*, no!

Constantin jerked upright, panting, his breath coming in short, sharp bursts like a marathon runner pushing himself towards the finishing post. He ran a trembling hand across his brow and turned his head slowly, almost scared of what he might see on the pillow beside him. The pale gold of dawn's first light drifted through the half-open curtains and played in Isobel's hair. Her face, flushed rose-pink in sleep, was serene and so lovely that his stomach muscles clenched. There was no blood, and she wasn't lying in a crumpled heap at the base of the tower. He had been dreaming.

Taking care not to wake her, he slid out of bed and walked across to the window. The bedroom overlooked the courtyard. The bloodstains that had covered the cobbles beneath the tower had long since been washed away, but the images in his head, *Dio!* He would never forget what he had witnessed when he had been seventeen, Constantin thought grimly. He would never forget watching his father stretch a hand towards Lorena seconds before she had fallen. His nightmare, like all his other nightmares, was a warning. What if he was truly his father's son? What if he had inherited the monstrous jealousy that had turned Franco into a murderer?

He looked back at Isobel, sleeping peacefully and unaware of the danger she was in. But he knew. He had known from the first night that they had become lovers and he'd had his first nightmare that he should never have got involved with her.

He stood by the window for a long time, lost in his dark thoughts that the sun, rising high in the sky, could not lighten. Isobel stirred but fell back to sleep. Her exhaustion wasn't surprising after they had spent all night pleasuring each other. Constantin closed his eyes and pictured her slender body poised above him as she had lowered herself onto him; her sweet smile as she had taken him deep inside her and their two bodies had become one.

The sound of a car driving into the courtyard below pulled him back to the present. His uncle was early for their meeting. He paused on his way out of the room to look at Isobel. His resolve hardened. The time had come for him to take control of his future.

Isobel stretched languorously and felt a pleasurable ache in certain muscles. Her entire body tingled, especially her breasts and between her legs where Constantin had devoted his lavish attention. Her face grew warm as she recalled vividly the many and varied ways he had made love to her the previous night. She turned her head towards the empty pillow beside her and wished she had woken in his arms. But the clock told her that the morning was nearly afternoon and he had obviously decided that she needed to sleep in after their energetic night.

The diamond on her finger glinted as it caught a sunbeam, and she could not hold back a smile of pure happiness. Last night Constantin had returned her engagement and wedding rings to their rightful place, and today was full of hope and promise for the future.

She heard his voice from the study when she went downstairs, and guessed he was speaking on the phone. Deciding not to disturb him, she continued into the kitchen in search of a caffeine fix. The percolator was bubbling. Her eyes flew to the man seated at the table, sipping a cup of coffee. She recognised him as Constantin's uncle, Alonso, whom she had met briefly when he had been a guest at their wedding.

He stood up as she entered the kitchen and proffered his hand. 'Isobel, I am delighted to find you here at Casa Celeste with your husband.' Alonso spoke in a thick Italian accent.

His words sent a little jolt of surprise through her until she realised that he was looking at her wedding and engagement rings on her finger.

'I'm glad to be here with Constantin,' she murmured as she poured herself a cup of coffee and sat down at the table.

'So, all is well with you and Constantin and you are reconciled. That is good news. The board of DSE are pleased that he has put an end to his playboy image and the newspapers now portray him as a respectable married man. It's amazing what a little coercion can do.'

Isobel set her coffee cup carefully back in its saucer. 'Coercion?' she said faintly. 'I'm not sure I understand.'

'But yes, I prompted my nephew, I…how do you say in English? I gave him a little push to encourage him to resume his marriage.' The elderly man smiled at her. 'I think I do you the favour, hmm? I told Constantin that I would appoint him as Chairman of the company only if he mended his wild ways and returned to his wife.'

'When…' she swallowed, trying to stem the nausea that swept through her '…when did you tell Constantin this?'

He shrugged. 'I know the exact date. It was the fifteenth of this month, my seventieth birthday. I told him that I wanted to retire and I was considering making his cousin Maurio Chairman unless Constantin could convince me that he was ready to commit to DSE by honouring his commitment to his marriage.'

The *sixteenth* of June had been the date of the fundraising party in London where the Stone Ladies had performed, and later Constantin had kissed her very publicly on the dance floor.

Functioning on autopilot, Isobel drank the rest of her coffee, grimacing as she swallowed the bitter grounds at the bottom of the cup. Constantin had told her that he'd changed his mind and wanted to give their marriage another chance the evening *after* he had been given an ultimatum by his uncle to return to his marriage or lose the chairmanship of DSE.

She had been such a fool! She felt as if the spark of life itself had drained out of her, and her coffee cup slid out of her numb fingers and clattered onto the saucer.

'I can't believe it,' she whispered.

Alonso chuckled, blithely unaware of the bombshell he had dropped. '*Sì*, for me also it is hard to believe I am seventy. I am looking forward to spending more time on the golf course now that Constantin is to be Chairman.'

He looked concerned when he noticed how pale she had gone. 'Are you ill?'

Isobel scraped her chair on the tiled floor as she staggered to her feet. 'I feel a little...*nauseato.*'

'Ah.' Alonso nodded. '*Un bambino,* perhaps?'

Sweet heaven! Her heart missed a beat. Fate would surely not play such a cruel trick as to give her a child now, when she had proof of Constantin's duplicity, she tried to reassure herself as she hurried out of the kitchen. But thudding inside her head was the knowledge that she had left her contraceptive pills behind at her flat in London when Constantin had driven her straight from the hospital to the airport and they had boarded his jet to fly to Rome. When they'd had sex she had completely forgotten that she was not protected.

She was halfway across the hall, marching towards the study, when the door opened and he emerged. *'Tesorino.'* His smiled faded when he saw the grim purpose in her expression.

'Don't *tesorino* me!' she snapped, but her eyes absorbed his male beauty; the sculpted angles of his face, and his powerful body clothed in sun-bleached jeans that clung to his hips and a cream cotton shirt open at the throat to reveal a fuzz of black chest hairs. She would love him until she died and the knowledge fuelled her anger.

'I want the truth.'

He raised an eyebrow, but beneath his nonchalance she sensed that he was as tense and watchful as a jungle cat stalking prey.

'I have never lied to you, Isabella.'

'Did you ask me to give our marriage another chance so that your uncle would appoint you Chairman of DSE instead of your cousin?'

Isobel's question echoed around the marble hall, and

it seemed to Constantin that the air trembled as it waited for him to reply. He watched dust motes dance in a shaft of sunlight streaming through a window, while his mind relived the nightmare he'd had about her. The sun touched Isobel's hair and bathed her in a halo of golden light, and as he stared at her lovely face he suddenly knew what he must do.

He shrugged. '*Mea culpa.* I assume you have spoken to Alonso, so it would be pointless for me to deny it.'

The world rocked beneath Isobel's feet but through sheer force of will she remained standing. She wanted to hurt him as she was hurting, and her hand shot out to connect with his cheek, leaving a scarlet imprint of her fingers on his skin. He flinched, and she felt sick with shame. She abhorred physical violence and she hated herself for her betraying loss of control.

'You bastard,' she choked. 'I suppose you returned my rings last night knowing that Alonso was coming to Casa Celeste today.'

In her mind she heard Diane Rivolli at the Bonuccis' party. *Constantin would go to any lengths to claim the chairmanship of DSE that he thinks is his birthright.*

She tugged her engagement ring and wedding band off her finger and hurled them at him one at a time.

'*You keep them,*' she said hoarsely. Her throat felt as if she had swallowed glass. 'I don't want them. Maybe in the future you'll fool another woman into thinking that you do actually have a heart rather than a lump of stone in your chest, and you can give them to her. But sooner or later she'll discover that there's nothing but an empty, emotionless void where your heart should be.'

The rings bounced off his chest and flew up into the air. The yellow diamond glinted in the sunlight before the two rings fell back to the ground and skidded across the marble floor. Isobel did not see where they landed. She spun away from Constantin and flew across the hall. His car keys were on the table and she snatched them up on her way out of the front door.

'*Isobel!* For Christ's sake be careful,' he shouted after her, sharp urgency in his voice. 'You're not used to driving such a powerful car.'

It was typical that he was more concerned about his car than her, she thought bitterly as she thrust the key into the ignition. The engine roared into life, and when she touched the accelerator pedal the car shot forwards so fast that the tyres spun and sent up sprays of gravel. Tears choked her. Her marriage had been a farce from the start, and now it was over for good.

The sports car was a strong-willed beast that needed to be firmly controlled and as Isobel negotiated the sharp bends along the narrow road leading from Casa Celeste she focused on staying alive. But with every mile that she drove away from Constantin the pain inside her intensified until she could barely breathe and she could no longer hold back her tears.

After a narrow shave with a cart being pulled along the road by a donkey, she turned off into a small village and parked in the central square that was deserted in the middle of the day when the sun was at its hottest and the villagers retreated to their houses.

She cried until her chest hurt. She had been such a fool. When Constantin had told her a few days ago that he had not only married her because she had been pregnant, she had actually believed him. Anger burned in her gut. She wanted to rip his heart out as he had ripped out hers. She wanted him to suffer as she was suffering, but he never would because he was made of stone.

He had deliberately and cold-heartedly used her to gain the chairmanship of DSE. He had seduced her and made love to her, he'd even gone to the length of asking her to wear her wedding ring again—*but it had all been lies*!

She stuffed her fist into her mouth to hold back her cry of pain. She would never, ever forgive him for his cruel deception. Why hadn't she gone ahead with the divorce when he had first asked her, instead of clinging to the stupid hope that he might actually care for her? Memories of her father's lack of interest opened up an old wound. She hadn't been good enough, clever enough—simply not enough for her father, who had loved her brother but not her. It was bitterly ironic that Constantin, the only man she had fallen in love with, had never loved her either.

Wearily, Isobel dug out a tissue from her handbag and wiped her eyes. What had she expected from Constantin? He had told her that he found it difficult to show his emotions, but the truth was that he only cared about one thing and that was DSE. He was driven, ambitious and utterly ruthless.

She took a ragged breath, and was about to turn the ignition key to restart the car when she pictured in her mind the rose garden he had created in memory of their baby. He had chosen pink rosebuds for Arianna, and he had dug the garden himself, laboured long and hard to make a place of beauty and peace where he could sit and remember a little girl who had never lived but had a special place in his heart.

Those were not the actions of a ruthless man, Isobel conceded. She bit her lip, remembering how he had taken care of her after she had been attacked by the stalker. He had been determined to protect her, and had even hired a bodyguard, even though she had told him not to.

But it had been in his interest to protect her, she reminded herself. He had needed to show his uncle that he had reconciled his marriage, and she had just been a pawn in his ambition to take control of DSE…hadn't she?

It was too hot inside the car for her to think straight. She climbed out of the vehicle and locked it. The luxurious sports car was very noticeable in the village square, and a group of small boys were staring at it with wide-eyed fascination. Perhaps all boys loved sports cars, Isobel thought as she walked over to the shade of an oak tree. She remembered the model car that Constantin's mother had given him for his eighth birthday and which he kept locked in a cabinet as if it were as priceless as the crown jewels.

He had loved his mother, but his father had forbidden him to cry at her funeral. Isobel groaned. How could she have expected Constantin to show his emotions when he had been brought up to hide his feelings? He had not cried at Arianna's funeral, but perhaps he cried alone when he sat in the rose garden he had made for her.

She stopped pacing up and down, and hugged her arms around her body, trying to hold her own emotions in check as her treacherous mind recalled his tenderness when he had carried her upstairs to the bedroom last night. His hands had shook as he'd undressed before sweeping her into his arms and kissing her with such beguiling sweetness and breathtaking sensuality that tears had filled her eyes.

Constantin's actions had not been those of a man without a heart, or of a man who did not care.

She would be the biggest fool on the planet if she went back to Casa Celeste, Isobel told herself. The sensible thing to do would be to continue her journey back to Rome and catch the next available flight to London to begin divorce proceedings. Constantin did not deserve another chance. He did not deserve her love.

But she could not dismiss the image in her mind of a little boy standing dry-eyed at his mother's grave. She could not forget the aching sweetness of Constantin's kiss. *She deserved to know the truth of why he had married her.* He owed her that much. Suddenly she was running back to the car, determined to uncover the secrets that she was sure he still hid from her.

CHAPTER TWELVE

THE HOUSE APPEARED to be deserted. Isobel's footsteps echoed hollowly on the marble floor as she walked into the hall. It crossed her mind that Constantin might have asked his uncle for a lift back to Rome, but in that case why was the front door unlocked? There was no sign of him downstairs, and she had just reached the first-floor landing when she heard a noise that froze her blood. The moan of pain had come from the master bedroom. She hurried along the passage and opened the door, and reeled with shock at the sight that met her.

Constantin was sitting on the bed, hunched over, his face buried in his hands, and he was crying—great, tearing sobs that shook his body. Only once before had Isobel seen a man cry so broken-heartedly. Her father had howled like an animal in terrible pain when they had dragged her brother's body from the reservoir. She hadn't known how to comfort her father, and deep down she had wondered if he'd wished that it had been her instead of Simon who had drowned.

When she had married Constantin her insecurity had not helped their relationship, she acknowledged. She had believed she wasn't good enough for him, as she hadn't been good enough for her father. She had never questioned why Constantin hadn't shown any emotion when they had buried Arianna because she had been too wrapped up in her own feelings to care about his, she thought guiltily.

'Oh, my darling, what's wrong?' she whispered, dropping down onto her knees in front of him.

He jerked his head out of his hands and stared at her through red-rimmed eyes. 'Isobel?' He seemed to realise he was not imagining her, and his expression became even more ravaged. 'Why are you here?' He ran his hands through his hair. 'You have to go,' he told her harshly. 'You have to go away from me…and never come back.'

She touched his wet cheek that she had slapped before she had run out of Casa Celeste. 'Why do you want me to leave you?'

'Because…' He gave a ragged groan. 'Because I'm afraid I could hurt you.'

'The only way you could hurt me is if you send me away,' she said with raw honesty. 'When you asked me to wear your ring again yesterday I hoped it was because you wanted our marriage to work. Hearing that you had been forced into a reconciliation by your uncle in order to be appointed Chairman of DSE made me think that you… you didn't care about my feelings. But that's not true, is it?'

She wished he would say something instead of allowing her to blunder on and no doubt make a fool of herself. A memory flashed into her mind of the look of worry and strain on his face when he had rushed back from New York to be with her at the hospital after the stalker had attacked her. 'I think you do care a little,' she said huskily.

Instead of replying, he got to his feet and strode into the en-suite bathroom, emerging moments later rubbing a towel over his face. He seemed more in control of himself, but his chest heaved as if it hurt him to breathe.

'There are things you don't know,' he said abruptly. 'A secret that I have kept since I was seventeen.'

'If our marriage is to stand a chance, we can't have secrets from each other.'

A nerve jumped in Constantin's jaw. 'If I tell you this secret I guarantee you will leave and you'll wish you had never heard the name of De Severino.'

For a moment Isobel felt afraid of what he might reveal in this house of ghosts. Whatever it was clearly haunted Constantin, and he had borne the burden of his secret alone for all of his adult life.

'I think we both have to take that risk,' she said quietly.

He was silent for a few moments—and then, heavily, 'So be it.' He walked over to the window that overlooked the courtyard and stood with his back to her.

'I'm convinced that my father murdered his second wife.'

Shock sent a shiver down Isobel's spine. 'But…I thought Franco loved Lorena.'

'He did love her. He was obsessed with her and he could not bear any other man to look at her.'

'Including you?' Once again, Diane Rivolli's words came into Isobel's mind. *There was something quite cruel about the way Lorena deliberately encouraged Constantin's crush on her, and the way she played father and son off against each other.*

Constantin sighed. 'I was seventeen when my father married again. I returned to Casa Celeste from an all-boys boarding school to find I had a stepmother who was only a few years older than me.

'Lorena's idea of dressing for dinner was to wear a sarong over her bikini,' he said with heavy irony. 'She would flirt with anything in trousers. For a hormone-fuelled, sexually inexperienced teenager she was the ultimate male fantasy.'

'Your father can't have liked you taking an interest in his wife.'

'He hated me spending time with her. There were many rows between me and my father, and my father and Lorena.' He fell silent again, before forcing himself to go on. 'On the day it happened...I had walked into the courtyard and I heard voices from the top of the tower. My father and Lorena were fighting as usual. She was taunting him that he was too old and she told him that she desired *me* more than him.' Constantin grimaced. 'Stupid youth that I was, I actually felt flattered.

'My father was furious. He was shouting at Lorena, and the next minute I saw her topple over the balcony rail, followed seconds later by Franco.'

'I can't imagine how terrible it must have been for you to watch, helplessly,' Isobel murmured.

'I was the only witness,' Constantin said flatly. 'At the inquest I gave evidence that I had seen Lorena fall, and my father had reached out to try and save her but he leaned out too far and also fell. A verdict of accidental death was recorded for both of them.'

'Surely your father was a hero who died attempting to save his wife?'

'That was what everyone believed. I assured myself the events had happened as I had stated. But I'd blocked out much of what happened because I couldn't bear to remember.' Gruesome images flashed into Constantin's mind and he could not repress a shudder. 'There was always something at the back of my mind, something wrong about what I had seen, but I didn't know what bothered me—until the nightmares started.'

He turned his head and glanced at Isobel. 'It was the weekend that I took you to Rome and we became lovers. You were unlike any woman I'd met before, beautiful, innocent, and, as I discovered when I took you to bed, incredibly sensual.' He gave a self-derisive snort. 'I shouldn't have been so pleased that I was your first lover but I felt like a king.'

Isobel swallowed. 'If that's true, why did you dump me the minute we got back to London? You said it had been a fun weekend but that you were not looking for a relationship, and the next thing I heard you had left the London office and disappeared back to Rome.'

Constantin looked away from her hurt expression. 'While we were in Rome I had a horrific nightmare about what had happened to my father and Lorena at Casa Celeste. I saw them standing on the balcony at the top of the tower. At the inquest I'd stated that I had seen Lorena fall and my father reach for her. But in my dream I saw my father reach towards Lorena *before* she fell.

'It was the missing piece of the puzzle that had troubled me for so long. My nightmare showed me what my conscious mind had blocked out. My father hadn't tried to save Lorena. He had *pushed* her from the top of the tower in a fit of jealous rage before he jumped to his death after her.'

'That's awful!' Isobel's words were an instinctive response to Constantin's shocking revelation. 'It seems unbelievable.'

'I wish it was,' he said grimly. 'Unfortunately it's true. My nightmares always show the same sequence of events. My father was responsible for my stepmother's death.'

Isobel's brow creased in a puzzled frown. 'If it *is* true, I appreciate that your father did a terrible thing. But why did your nightmares only start when you met me? Do I look like Lorena, and remind you of her?' Was that why Constantin had been attracted to her when she had been his office assistant? she wondered.

'No, you look nothing like her.'

'Then why was I the catalyst that made you remember what had happened?'

He did not reply, but Isobel could sense the fierce tension emanating from him. 'I believe the nightmares are a warning from my subconscious,' he finally muttered.

Her confusion grew. 'A warning about what?'

'That I might have inherited the manic jealousy which turned my father into a murderer.'

She tried to make sense of his words. 'You're afraid that you might fall in love with someone in the obsessive way that your father loved Lorena?'

Constantin gave a harsh groan. 'Not someone. *You*, Isabella, I love you. And it's for that reason that I am going to divorce you.'

Isobel's heart swooped and dipped as if she were riding a roller coaster. 'You love me?' she said faintly. 'But you admitted earlier that you asked me to come back to you because your uncle had said he would only appoint you as Chairman of DSE if you reconciled your marriage.'

'I had to make you leave because it's the only way I can ensure your safety. You are better off without me in your life. I hadn't anticipated that you would come back,' he said grimly.

He raked his hair back from his brow with an unsteady hand. 'I realised when we became lovers in Rome three years ago that I was in trouble. You got to me in a way no other woman ever had. The nightmare terrified me because I wondered if I could have a jealous streak like my father, so, I backed off and ended our affair.

'When you told me you were pregnant it seemed that fate had played a hand. I told myself it was my duty to marry you, but secretly I was glad of the excuse to continue our relationship.'

'We were happy in those first months of our marriage,'

Isobel remembered. 'But everything changed when we came here, to Casa Celeste.'

'The nightmares started again, but they were worse, because I dreamed that it was you and I at the top of the tower, and I pushed you from the balcony in a jealous rage. I'd never felt possessive of any woman but you,' Constantin said rawly. 'I thought that if I stopped myself from loving you, then you would be safe from my jealousy. But after you had the miscarriage I didn't know how to help you. I couldn't blame you for turning to your friends from the band for support, but I hated the fact that you wanted to be with them rather than me.

'Jealousy is the worst kind of poison. It seeps into your blood and eats away at your soul. When you left me to go on tour with the Stone Ladies it was almost a relief to know that you were no longer in danger from me. You had a new life, a successful career, and I assumed that you and Ryan Fellows were lovers.'

Constantin paused, aware that he had to be totally honest with Isobel. 'I was furious with my uncle for issuing an ultimatum to go back to my marriage. I'd seen you and Fellows on a TV chat show hinting that you were in a relationship. When I kissed you at the party in London I'd intended to persuade you to come back to me purely so that Alonso would make me Chairman.'

Isobel bit her lip. 'So it was all fake? Your kindness, the yellow roses you bought for me?' His tender passion that had given her hope for their marriage, she thought, her heart aching.

'When you were attacked by the stalker, my *only* thought was to protect you. I brought you to Rome and immediately fell under your spell again. But the evening we had dinner at Pepe's forced me to accept that I was still a threat to you.'

'We had a lovely evening,' she said, puzzled. 'I felt safe from the stalker for the first time in months. *You* made me feel safe.'

'The waiter at the restaurant smiled at you and I wanted to rip his head off.' Constantin's jaw clenched. 'I hate other men looking at you.'

'Well, I hate women looking at you. When I saw pictures in the newspapers of you with beautiful women I felt sick with jealousy. It's a normal human emotion,' Isobel said gently.

'My father killed his own wife out of jealousy. You can't tell me that was normal behaviour.' Constantin shook his head. 'I've turned down the role of Chairman of DSE and resigned from my position as CEO. I asked my uncle to meet me here this morning to give him the news, but you spoke to him first, before I'd had a chance to tell him my plans.'

'What are your plans? DSE is more important to you than anything else and I can't believe you've resigned.'

'I have no idea what I'm going to do,' he said listlessly. 'I had thought that if I left the company and Casa Celeste, cut myself off from everything connected to my father, you and I could start a new life together. But last night I had another nightmare, and I realised that I can't hide from my past and I can't change the fact that I am Franco De Severino's son. I inherited my father's jealous streak, and I never want to find out what it might make me capable of.'

He stared at Isobel's beautiful face and visualised his stepmother's broken body at the base of the tower. 'Don't you see, Isabella? I can't risk loving you,' he said harshly. '*For God's sake*, and, more importantly, for *your* sake, leave me and go and get on with your life.'

For a long time after Constantin had heard the bedroom door close behind Isobel, he stood and stared unseeingly down at the courtyard. *It was over.* She now knew that she had married the son of a murderer. She understood that De Severino blood was bad blood, and, unsurprisingly, she had gone.

Raw emotion clogged his throat. If there was a hell, it could not be worse than the place he was in right now. His single consolation was the knowledge that he had done everything he could to protect Isobel. Telling her about his father had made him feel unclean, and, growling a savage imprecation, he stripped out of his clothes and stepped into the shower.

The powerful spray cleansed his body but nothing could wash the darkness from his soul. Memories of Isobel filled his mind; her smile, her honey-gold hair spilling across the pillows, her lips parting beneath his. *Dio,* she had gone, and his life had no purpose. He tilted his head and let the spray run down his face, because that way he could kid himself that they were not tears streaming from his eyes.

The steam from the hot water and the noise of the powerful spray blinded and deafened him, and he was unaware that he was no longer alone until a hand touched his shoulder.

'*Santa Madre!* You nearly gave me a heart attack.' He took the towel Isobel handed him and roughly dried himself, before hitching it around his waist. It was only a hand towel and barely covered his thighs. He saw her eyes flick down his body and felt an inevitable tightening in his loins. 'Why are you still here?' If she did not leave he was afraid he might never let her go. 'If you're worried about driving my car, I'll call a taxi for you.'

'I'm not going anywhere,' Isobel told him calmly. 'I went to the courtyard and looked up at the tower. I'm not sure that you could have seen clearly what took place on the balcony all those years ago.

'You witnessed a terribly traumatic event when you were seventeen,' she said gently. 'I think you felt guilty that you'd had a crush on your stepmother and you heard your father arguing with Lorena about you. Maybe you even felt that Franco had a right to be angry with his flirtatious wife. When you saw Lorena fall you believed that your father might have pushed her in a jealous rage, but you don't really know that he did.'

'My nightmares always show the same thing.' He closed his eyes briefly, haunted by images that sickened him. 'Sometimes in my dreams I see *you* falling from the tower,' he muttered. 'I wake up with my heart pounding with fear because I could not bear for something so terrible to happen to you as happened to Lorena.'

Isobel's heart contracted as she watched his eyes darken with pain. How could she ever have thought that he was emotionless and cold? 'You were deeply traumatised by what you witnessed that day. But, Constantin, even if you *did* see your father push Lorena, it doesn't mean that you have inherited murderous tendencies. You are not Franco, you're you, and from what I've heard about your father you are very different from him.

'We are each of us in charge of our own destinies,' she said fiercely. 'You should be proud of the man you are, and all you have achieved at DSE, as I am proud of you.'

He let out a ragged breath. 'So, are you a psychologist now?'

'No, I'm your wife who loves you with all her heart.' Isobel held his gaze. 'I found this on your desk.' She held up the new divorce petition his lawyer had sent him stating that they had lived apart for two years, and tore it up.

'I am going to remain your wife until death us do part, as we both promised.'

For timeless seconds he said nothing, and fear curdled in her stomach that she had misunderstood him earlier, that he hadn't meant it when he'd said he loved her. But then he moved and hauled her against his big chest.

'Dammit, Isobel, I can't fight you when you don't play fair.'

'Why do you want to fight me?' she said softly.

He took a shuddering breath. 'Because I'm scared of loving you,' he admitted in a low tone that revealed the intensity of his emotions. 'Because I'm scared I'll lose you.'

She thought of the little boy who had been forbidden to cry at his mother's funeral, the man who had been dry-eyed when they had buried their baby daughter but who had created a rose garden in Arianna's memory.

'You won't lose me,' she told him fiercely. 'I will love you for ever.' She cupped his face in her hands and sought his mouth, kissing him with all the love inside her, with her heart and soul, willing him to take the risk and find the happiness she knew belonged to them.

'*Ti amo, Isabella.*' His voice shook. 'I swear I will keep you safe, and I will never hurt you.'

'Then you must promise that you will always love me.'

'Let me show you.' He swept her up into his arms and carried her into the bedroom where he made love to her with such tender passion that she could not hold back her tears. 'Don't cry, *tesorino*,' he said huskily, 'or you'll make me cry too.'

She saw the brightness in his blue eyes, his vulnerability that he no longer tried to hide from her, and her heart overspilled with love for him.

'There will be times when we will smile and laugh, but there'll be other times when we'll cry, because that is the way of life. But we will laugh and cry together. And always we will love each other,' she vowed.

Constantin smiled. 'Always, my love.'

EPILOGUE

Eighteen months later.

THE AUDIENCE AT Wembley Arena were calling for the Stone Ladies to return to the stage. *One more song*, they chanted, but the band had already played three encores and there were groans from the crowd as the lights came on, signalling that the concert was over.

Backstage it was manic as usual. The sound crew were already busy dismantling equipment, the band's manager, Mike Jones, was giving a live TV interview. Someone from the PR team grabbed Isobel and asked her to sign autographs for fans who had backstage passes. She paused to chat to the fans for a couple of minutes before she squeezed through the crowd.

Ryan caught up with her. 'Izzy, do you and Constantin want to come and have a drink with me and Emily?'

'I think we'll go straight home tonight. But the two of you will come to dinner next week with Carly and Ben, won't you? Constantin wants to show you his new car. Honestly, the two of you are like kids when it comes to fast cars,' she said drily.

Ryan grinned. 'We're looking forward to it.'

He disappeared into his dressing room, and Isobel reached the place she wanted to be. 'It's lucky you're taller than everyone else,' she told her husband as he curved his arms around her waist and drew her close. 'It makes you easy to spot in a crowd.'

He dropped a light kiss on her mouth and when she parted her lips he deepened the caress and it became a sensual prelude to the passion that would soon follow. 'It was another fantastic concert, but you must be exhausted after performing on four consecutive nights. It's time I took you and our son home, *tesorino*.'

Isobel felt her insides melt as she looked at the four-month-old baby boy who was tucked securely into the crook of Constantin's arm and was fast asleep. 'How was Theo while I was on stage? Did he settle okay after his feed?'

'He slept through the entire concert.' Constantin laughed. 'The fans obviously love your music but I'm afraid your son isn't impressed that his mother is a rock star.'

She laughed. 'Wait till he's old enough to learn to play the drums.'

'I'm already planning on having the nursery sound-proofed.'

Whittaker was waiting outside to drive them back to Grosvenor Square. Once Theo had been strapped into his baby seat Constantin climbed into the back of the car and Isobel rested her head on his shoulder.

'Home sounds nice,' she said sleepily.

'It won't be long before our new home is finished. I spoke to the architect today, and he says we will be able to move into the villa before Christmas.'

'Theo will spend his first Christmas at Casa Rosa. I can't wait.'

Constantin smiled to himself as he thought of the surprise he had in store for Isobel. She had no idea that he had commissioned a recording studio to be built adjoining the new house. She had understood why he hadn't wanted to live at Casa Celeste, and the four-hundred-year-old house was now a museum managed by a group of historians who were restoring the huge art collection acquired by past generations of the De Severino family.

Casa Rosa was a modern villa, which had been built close to the chapel where their daughter was buried. Constantin had been closely involved with the construction of the home he had helped to design for his wife and son and the children they hoped to have in the future. Although he had withdrawn his resignation from DSE, he had chosen to share the roles of Chairman and CEO with his cousin Maurio, which gave him time to travel to concerts with Isobel and take care of Theo while she was performing.

She lifted her head from his shoulder. 'What are you smiling about?'

'I was just thinking that life is pretty damned perfect.' He stared into her clear hazel eyes and knew that her look of love was reflected in his own gaze. 'I never knew I could be this happy, *mio amore*.'

Isobel looked at her baby son who had arrived in the world without fuss and had helped to heal the ache in her heart. When Theo was old enough they would tell him about his older sister and take him to play in Arianna's rose garden.

She turned back to her husband and caught her breath when she saw the raw emotion revealed in his bright blue eyes. There were no secrets between them now, just a love that would last a lifetime.

'I love you,' she said simply. They were only three little words, but they meant the world.

* * * * *

MILLS & BOON

MODERN

Power and Passion

Prepare to be swept off your feet by
sophisticated, sexy and seductive heroes, in
some of the world's most glamourous and
romantic locations, where power and
passion collide.

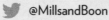

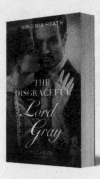

MILLS & BOON

THE HEART OF ROMANCE

A ROMANCE FOR EVERY READER

MODERN

Prepare to be swept off your feet by sophisticated, sexy and seductive heroes, in some of the world's most glamourous and romantic locations, where power and passion collide.

HISTORICAL

Escape with historical heroes from time gone by. Whether your passion is for wicked Regency Rakes, muscled Vikings or rugged Highlanders, awaken the romance of the past.

MEDICAL

Set your pulse racing with dedicated, delectable doctors in the high-pressure world of medicine, where emotions run high and passion, comfort and love are the best medicine.

True Love

Celebrate true love with tender stories of heartfelt romance, from the rush of falling in love to the joy a new baby can bring, and a focus on the emotional heart of a relationship.

Desire

Indulge in secrets and scandal, intense drama and plenty of sizzling hot action with powerful and passionate heroes who have it all: wealth, status, good looks…everything but the right woman.

HEROES

Experience all the excitement of a gripping thriller, with an intense romance at its heart. Resourceful, true-to-life women and strong, fearless men face danger and desire - a killer combination!

To see which titles are coming soon, please visit

millsandboon.co.uk/nextmonth